Flamingo Moon

Carolyn Holm

Mockingbird Press

FLAMINGO MOON

Published by Mockingbird Press
July 2013

ISBN: 978-0-9648066-1-0

Flamingo Moon

Prologue

MAYBE I WAS doomed right from the start, born with LOSER already written on my little baby forehead, thanks to Vivian, who clearly wasn't cut out for motherhood. My mom was so busy screwing up her own life that she didn't have time to look out for mine. But I can't blame her for everything. I'm the one who took that beginning and went on to make an epic mess of my life. Though God knows it could have been worse: if Vivian had raised me on her own I'd have been snatched up by Child Protective Services. It's a good thing she had help.

Rose helped her. Rose in her dumpy little El Cerrito bar and motel on San Pablo Avenue, tucked between A-1 Smog Testers and the Korean burrito shop. For years Rose tended the bar at The Last Stop while keeping an eye on the door to the Welcome Back Motel. When a traveler came into the tiny motel foyer, she just stepped through the door that connected the motel to the back of the bar, and there she was, at the motel's front desk. It was typical of Rose to lay things out so that she could take as few steps as possible; she weighed something like three hundred pounds and the only exercise she ever got was to climb the stairs to her little apartment over the Last Stop. Huffing and puffing and leaning on the railing.

That's where she assembled herself a family. Rose, as Vivian liked to say when she got eloquent after a few beers, was a plus-sized woman with a heart so big she had room to spare for two pregnant losers who wandered into the Last Stop. Vivian being one of those two losers. The way she told it, she had been going through a rough patch anyway, but when she found herself pregnant with me, she fell apart. She went on a two-week Smirnoff bender, got fired from her job as a payroll clerk at Clorox, and could no longer afford to pay her rent. Rose put her up in a room at the Welcome Back

Motel—gave it to her for free—and that's where we lived for the first four years of my life.

According to Vivian's story, Bobbie was the other pregnant loser who walked into the bar. But Bobbie wasn't a loser. It's true that she was pregnant with Franny and had lost her job as an exotic dancer, but when she told the story herself she always liked to say that just as she was looking to reinvent herself, she found a brand-new life at the Last Stop. I guess while she was hanging out there she and Rose must have fallen in love, because Bobbie moved in with Rose in her apartment over the bar, and she's been there ever since.

As a result, when Franny and I came into the world we were surrounded by something already resembling a family. I'm using the term loosely. It's not like we were actually related to each other. And strictly speaking, we didn't all live together all the time. But as irregular as things were, we always had Rose there trying to make our lives as normal as possible. She was the sun and the rest of us were the planets, going about our business around her and turning to her for light. Of course by the time Franny and I were old enough to be in school we knew this setup wasn't conventional, so we told everyone we were cousins.

In this lovely family story there is one thing missing. I'll point it out in case you haven't already noticed. There is no sign of anything like a father here. Not a man in sight. Just Vivian's friend Dieter, who dated her years ago and has been hanging around ever since. The token man in our lives. Franny has an actual dad she visits sometimes, but all I ever had was Dieter. A sweet man, but a stand-in just the same.

Dieter was born in Germany, but he came here as a little kid when his mother married an American. She died when he was a teenager, and he didn't get along with his stepdad, so he didn't have much in the way of family. I guess that's one reason he continued to hang around us. We had become his family. That and the fact that he still had a soft spot for my mom. So as it turned out, through the years he was the only guy who stuck around while the rest of my mom's boyfriends came and went. Fortunately Dieter came to his senses and stopped dating her years ago or he'd have been long gone by now as well.

Sometimes I wonder how different my life would be if I had grown up in a normal family. Would I be listening today to a chorus of *Honey Barkin, for the love of God, how could you end up in such a mess?* That's what they're all asking, and because I don't have an answer for them I'm taking a long hard look at my life. Kind of like Hansel and Gretel hoping to stumble their way home by following a trail of crumbs, I'm trying to follow my path back to the beginning. And maybe the beginning was my hot rush to get out of there. To be with Danny.

Chapter 1

THE FIRST TIME I ever saw Danny Gonzales was in November of our senior year. He had just transferred to our high school, and showed up at the beginning of Spanish class because he needed a signature or something from the teacher. After a few words with Mr. Pascal he stood there in front of the class, his hands on his hips, turning to grin at us, completely at ease, while Mr. Pascal read whatever it was Danny gave him and then bent down to his desk to sign it. You know the expression "tall, dark, and handsome"? That was Danny. Well, okay, except that he wasn't tall. In fact, he was on the short side. But he was definitely handsome, and beautifully dark. His hair and eyes were almost black, and his skin was smooth and golden brown. He was slender and graceful, and supremely confident. By the time Mr. Pascal finished that paperwork, I had noticed all this and more, so you can imagine how I felt when Mr. Pascal nodded toward an empty seat and Danny sauntered over and dropped into it.

That was the beginning of my watching phase.   All through class I would watch him. I was sitting behind him, in the next row, so I was able to stare at him without his being aware of it. Sometimes he looked like he was asleep. I don't know if he really was, because I couldn't see his eyes from where I sat. What I could see was how his hair curled a little on the nape of his neck, and how his elbows were rough and grayish compared with the rich brown of the skin on his arms. I could see that he had a scar on his thumb, just a little nick, but white and shaped like a *V*.

I began to see him everywhere and I couldn't help but notice that he was hanging out a lot with a girl in our class named Brianna. Now, I'm not saying I was sitting around mooning over Danny. But I was keeping an eye on him. For the longest time I had to watch him from a distance because he was with that Brianna girl. Now school had actually become interesting. So much so that I was disappointed when suddenly it was Thanksgiving break. I thought I was going to go crazy because I didn't have him to watch. And then the day after Thanksgiving when Franny and I went to a movie, there he was behind the candy counter. So we saw a couple more movies over the weekend, and when I came in with Franny and my friends, he slipped me a box of Junior Mints no charge when his boss wasn't looking, because he knew that was my favorite movie candy.

Then school started again, and suddenly Brianna was out of the picture. On Friday night when I went to the movies with my friends, he came out from behind the counter as we were leaving and said to me, "I'm off. Wanna hang out?" I just turned to the others and said "Bye, bye," and we were out of there. We went to his house. His mom was out on a date and his sister was at a sleepover, so no one was home. Finally I had Danny to myself. We made out on his living room couch, and I felt like I was on fire. I wondered if it was like this for my mom with her boyfriends, and that was an odd thing to think about.

I asked him about Brianna, and he said they weren't going out anymore, but he wouldn't say more than that, no matter which way I brought the subject up. But I didn't really care. I was the winner. I felt like I'd won the lottery of love. We started going to his house after school to goof around. His mom, Erin, was usually around then because she was a nurse and went to work at five-thirty in the morning so she could be back when her kids got home from school. So it was a little awkward, as Erin would try to be nice and offer me something to eat or drink, and ask me how school was, and I tried to be polite and think of an answer that was different from the day before. Danny and I ducked away as soon as we could and headed for the living room to watch TV. We could hear her walking around the house, doing the laundry, answering the phone, yelling at the dog to stop barking, clanking pots and pans together in the kitchen. We were waiting for her to go pick up his sister at school and do her various errands. Thank God for all those things that needed doing. Getting groceries. Going to the cleaners. Going to the library to return books. Dropping his sister at her Girl Scout meetings. We were so grateful for all these mundane tasks. Because the moment Erin walked out the door we were on each other.

Danny knew all there was to know about sex. When he was eleven he had found a book in his dad's bookcase that was an honest-to-goodness sex how-to manual. Naturally he read that thing cover to cover. More than once. I mean he had been studying it for years, so by the time I came along he practically had a PhD in sex. Of course he showed me the book.

Sex was something I already knew a bit about. In High School a group of us would hang out after school together. It was like a club. And although my friend Madison was popular—she was not as pretty as I was, but she had a lot of confidence, and she was funny, so that went a long way—I was the queen. I was pretty much the hottest girl in school, so all the boys were attracted to me, and they all wanted me to like them. They wanted to be chosen. Because from where we hung out at the end of the field, behind the storage building, there was always the possibility that I would go under the bleachers with one of them to make out.

I didn't go under the bleachers with just anybody, and I didn't go all the way, either. It always started with kissing and a fair amount of touching, but if I particularly liked the boy, I went a step further. It was a great moment, and it gave me such a feeling of power. I would sit up, arch my back as I peeled off my shirt, and then, ta-dah, unhook my bra. I was wearing a D cup by then, so this was a big moment. And the reaction was the same every time. As my breasts bounced free, a worshipful expression came over the boy's face; he almost swooned with gratitude and lust. I would let him bury his face in my chest, and to kiss and touch my breasts, which I really liked, but I never let any of them pull my panties down.

It was okay to rub me through the panties, but no reaching inside. I was not a slut. The boys were happy with my rules, because they really liked my breasts. In fact, they got so excited by them that they would pretty much do anything for me.

Bobbie told me that when boys get a hard-on it drains all the blood from their brains. I don't know if that's true, but when I'm with a guy and I feel that thing getting bigger and bigger, I have to wonder what it's like for him. Can he think about anything at all with all that going on down there? Probably not.

I loved touching Danny. His skin was so smooth and dark, and his stomach so flat, with a soft line of hair pointing to his navel, which I loved to kiss, like I loved to kiss his thumb with its little white nick, and all the other landmarks as I traveled over his body. His hair was as soft and silky as a baby's, and I ran my fingers through it whenever his face was buried in my breasts. His dark eyes were heavy-lidded and sleepy-looking when he was with me, and they would close as I took his penis in my hand, to feel it grow magically even harder.

It wasn't long before we had progressed to feverishly pulling our clothes off the minute his mother walked out the door, getting right to it, all breathless and sweaty, rubbing each other all over and working up to where even our pores were throbbing. But we were afraid I'd get pregnant if he came inside me, so we pretty much did everything but that. Then when we heard Erin's car pull into the driveway we had to frantically pull our clothes back on, laughing and snorting, sitting up to pretend we were watching the TV we had left on. I'm amazed Erin never noticed that my hair was a mess, and my lips were puffy and my chin was red from all the rubbing that went on.

One day I couldn't stand it any longer. It was time for birth control pills. I went to my mom when I knew she had already had a couple of beers and was feeling particularly mellow, and told her that the school counselor had recommended birth control pills for my skin. I did have the occasional zit, and she bought it. She made me an appointment at the clinic and that's all there was to it. I was covered. That's when Danny and I really got into it, big-time. We were all over each other, sucking and licking and rubbing, and then I could finally take him inside me, and we would explode with the spasms and spurts of orgasm.

Birth control made me think of my phantom dad. Did he and my mom use birth control? I had to wonder if I had been planned, like they had thought they were going to stay together forever, or if I was just an accident. Knowing my mom it was probably an accident. But she would never tell me. When I asked, she just said, "You are lucky to have a happy home. It wouldn't be if he and I had stayed together." That's all. End of story.

I'm not sure about that happy home part. By the time I was in High School her so-called happy home was driving me crazy.

It was around this time that Danny sort of moved things to the next level. It was always when he had a few drinks in him. He would tell everyone in the room that I was his angel, and that I was the perfect woman, the best thing that ever happened to him. This was sweet, although it was a little embarrassing when he laid it on really thick. Then he would announce that we were going to get married. The first time he did this I wondered if it was the booze talking, and I asked him the next day if he meant it. He got all evasive and said he didn't remember saying it, but he quickly added, "Not that I don't think it's a good idea." But we agreed that maybe it was a little early to be talking about that. I mean, we were still in high school. What was he thinking? Secretly, though, it made me feel good.

This went on for months, with Danny bringing marriage up every time he had anything to drink. His friend Ryan would say, "Hey, dude, why get married?" and Danny would say, "Look at her. She's gorgeous, dude, she's a fucking angel. And that angel is going to be my wife. Mine, all mine." And

Ryan and Matthew would say, "That's awesome," and then they would talk about football.

When he did this in front of my family it created a sensation. We were all at Rose's for dinner. After a couple of beers Danny started in. "Honey is my sweet angel," he rhapsodized, "and I'm going to marry her and take care of her forever." Rose said, "Son, you need to slow down on that beer there. Here, have a cup of coffee." Vivian was just as hammered as Danny was, and feeling sentimental, she began to weep, whining, "My little baby is all grown up." Meanwhile Bobbie chirped, "Can I help you plan the wedding?" And Franny just rolled her eyes, muttering, "Prince Charming rides again." You could always count on Franny for sarcasm. She liked to remind us that she wasn't going to miss the family freak show when she went away to college.

Of course Dieter weighed in too with his doubts. "Honey, you are both just kids. Don't rush into anything. Grow up, have a good time, don't settle down until you're older." I tried to tell him that it wasn't my idea, that this was the beer talking, but Dieter wouldn't stop worrying. So now there was all the more for them to interfere with. Me, I didn't care if we got married or not. I just wanted to get out of the house, and I liked hearing Danny talk like that about me.

When we graduated Rose threw us a big party. We didn't get fancy Tiffany bracelets like some of the other girls, but the three moms got together to give us each a set of suitcases with little wheels: one big suitcase, one small one, and a matching tote bag. My set was powder blue with white welting, and Franny's was red. Bobbie picked them out and Rose paid for them, and Vivian got a free ride. Typical. Dieter gave us each an iPod speaker. Bobbie's friends—who Vivian dubbed The FOBs, for Friends of Bobbie—all got together and gave Franny a beautiful red satin quilt for her college dorm room. Notice there were no Friends of Vivian to get together on a nice gift for me. Franny also got a gift from her dad Barry—a watch with a tan leather band. Again, no dad to give me a watch. Vivian just said, "Oh, get over it" when I brought this up.

I guess I shouldn't complain, especially since the graduation as a whole went so well and for once Vivian didn't make a spectacle of herself. This was just the sort of occasion that she was likely to screw up. But she got through the ceremony without doing anything wildly inappropriate. Strictly speaking she wasn't exactly sober, but with Rose on one side and Dieter on the other, she wasn't allowed to do anything embarrassing.

The problem with graduation was that it marked the end of the first stage of our lives. Though the ending wasn't the problem. The problem was the question it raised. Because graduation raised the question: *what next*? College in the fall was not in my plans. I had no plans. I once thought I wanted to be a veterinarian because I loved Bobbie's dog Muppet, but when I was in high school Rose pointed out that to be one I would have to improve my math grades. I began to see that maybe I wasn't cut out for that career, and by the time I graduated I pretty much had no idea what I was going to do with myself. With one exception: I planned to get out on my own. Other than that I was flexible.

More and more of my time was spent at Danny's now. I didn't have Franny to hang with because she was spending all her time with her boyfriend, Colin the Weasel. That wasn't his real name, that's just what I called him to make Franny crazy. His real name was Colin Weaser. He was a good student just like Franny. They both got into fancy colleges. Excuse me, Universities. Franny to the University of California at Davis, and Colin to the University of Southern California in Los Angeles. The two of them were obsessed with their plans: for college in the fall, for careers in four years, for raging success after that. Whenever I was with them I had to hear this crap. Just listening to them I figured I may as well kill myself now because frankly I was never going to be their kind of success.

"So what are you going to do?" Franny asked me more than once. She was so cocksure because she had a freakin' plan. I couldn't see why I should have to follow right in her footsteps. College sounded like a lot of work. My preference was to get out in the real world. I figured I'd get a job, then get a place of my own, and I'd be out of that house forever. But everyone wanted to know exactly how I was planning to do that. Especially Rose. She thought my plan should include school. She kept talking about classes at the community college, and pointing out that Madison was going to go there. Only my mom stood up for me. "Honey is going to do fine," she'd say. "Not everyone has to be a college hot shot." Then I'd slip out of the room while she and Rose got into it about how low expectations just lead to mediocre results (Rose) and how no one should force a child be something she wasn't cut out to be (Vivian). They had this argument at least once a week. Over and over Vivian said, "College isn't for everyone" and "You don't learn everything from books." She had gone to college, but as she liked to point out, it hadn't done much for her. She had a job doing payroll and accounting for some architects but she didn't need college for that. And there were plenty of times in her life when she wasn't doing much of anything. So much for college, as far as I was concerned. Bobbie tried to stay clear of these discussions, but inevitably she would say something vague, like "Honey just needs some direction," that usually got the argument rolling again.

Even Dieter weighed in to ask me about my plan. One day he came by after he'd stopped in at the bar, and I was sitting on the back porch, in the evening sun, brushing bright pink nail polish on my toes. Dieter always smelled good, with just a little whiff of nutmeg that maybe came from his aftershave, and when he sat down beside me I could smell that, plus his breath, which was a little beery now. "Hey, babe," he said.

"Hey," I answered, concentrating on my toes. If you didn't brush carefully in three strokes—left side, right side, then one down the middle—the nail would look sloppy.

"So," he said, "now you've graduated. Do you know what you want to do?"

So now he was joining the crowd. I was beginning to appreciate the days when all their focus had been on Franny and her full-court press for college. "I guess I'll get a job."

He was quiet for a while. Then he said "What kind of job?" and now I was getting exasperated.

"I don't know. I'll have to see what's out there."

Dieter just sighed. I could tell he wanted to be helpful but he didn't know what to say. But the way I saw it, if he wanted to be helpful, he should tell me what to do. That would be helpful.

Danny had decided not to go to college right away. He had been accepted to the University of California at Santa Cruz, but he figured he'd defer it for a year. So right after graduation he got himself a second job, working afternoons in a pet-supply store, which was perfect for him because he loved animals. His next project was to move out of his mom's house and into a place of his own here in El Cerrito. I guess she was fine with that, because it was her cousin Martin who became Danny's new landlord. Martin was an old guy with a gray ponytail and one gold earring who went around buying decrepit houses that were practically falling down. Then he flipped them. His word. Cracked me up. It made houses sound like pancakes. He worked on them and fixed them up and the idea was he'd make a killing on them when they were sold. I don't think Martin ever made a killing on anything in his life, but he got by, and he liked messing around with wood and drywall, so it was probably as good a way as any to make a living. He had picked up a pathetic little dump on Liberty Street that needed a lot of fixing and agreed to give Danny a sweet deal on the rent if he gave him a hand with the work. As Dieter pointed out, Martin was able to have access to the place to work on it at the same time that he was renting it out, so it was a pretty good deal for everyone. The only downside to it, from Danny's perspective, was that Danny wanted a dog and Martin had a no-dog policy, which he said was nonnegotiable.

The house was tiny, and it needed just about everything you could think of. The floors and walls were dirty and stained. The kitchen and bathroom tile was chipped and the grout was black with age. And someone had written about fifty phone numbers in smudgy pencil right on the wall next to the phone. When you picked up the phone there was no dial tone. No one uses landlines any more, so who knows how long ago those numbers were scribbled on the wall. They made the kitchen look even dirtier. But the place was sunny and bright, and there was still some furniture left behind by the previous tenants, so Danny and I were pretty excited by it all.

For the move Dieter let us use his truck, and I helped Danny move his stuff to the house. There wasn't much. He had a black trash bag full of clothes and shoes, and a basketball. He had an old TV that his dad, Ray, had picked up at a garage sale. And he had another trash bag full of sheets and towels that his mom gave him. She also gave him a frying pan and a can opener, and she made some wisecrack about how that's all he needed to prepare his meals. We looked around the kitchen and realized he needed a lot more. Like a sponge to wipe the filthy counter, and soap, and paper towels, and plates and forks, all those things that you use every day without even thinking about it. So we went to Target and had a blast rolling a cart down the aisles, picking things out. Ray had given Danny some money to buy what he needed, but when Danny pulled the shopping cart over and began to add it all up, we were shocked to realize that we didn't have enough to even cover part of it. So we began to pull things out. First the coffeemaker; he could buy coffee on the way to work. Then the garbage can; he could always use a paper bag for garbage. Pretty soon we had pulled out most of the contents of the cart. In the end all we bought there were some paper towels and two sponges, toilet paper and a basketball hoop. Then we drove over to the St. Vincent de Paul Thrift Shop to get dishes and silverware and another pan.

When we brought everything back to the house and put the things away, I began to scrub the counters and the filthy refrigerator, while Danny attached the basketball hoop to the front of the garage using tools that Martin kept on the back porch. It felt so cozy, the two of us there setting up the house, as if we were married. Unfortunately Danny had told his friends Ryan and Matthew that they could stay there for a few days if they brought groceries, so eventually they showed up, plunked a couple of bags down on the counter, and headed straight outside to try out the basketball hoop. I took everything out of the bags. There was cereal, milk, hot dogs, beer, chips, the works. They had thought of everything. And I was like the mom in the kitchen, putting it away. It made me feel important. I know this sounds dumb, but it made me feel grown-up.

Rose had become more and more annoying to be around. Just watching her slowly fold the laundry put me on edge. I knew that any minute she would launch into a lecture. She would pick up a pillowcase, snap it in the air, fold it in half against her enormous belly, and then freeze there and look at me. "Torie," she'd start, and then I knew she'd be off and running, droning on about how important it was to have a plan.

Rose was the only person who called me Torie, which was short for my real name, Victoria. One day when I was an infant my mom slapped her forehead and said, "Victoria! Jeez, what was I thinking! What kind of chemical imbalance made me name a baby after my mom?" Rose suggested she shorten the name to Vickie, but Vivian said she hated that name. Then Rose suggested Torie. Vivian said she had never heard of anyone called Torie, but she'd think about it, but I don't think she actually gave it any consideration. Since she was already in the habit of calling me Honey, she just slipped into using it more and more like a name, and it wasn't long before everyone was calling me Honey. Everyone except Rose, who persisted in calling me Torie, because, as she liked to point out, for Honey to be an appropriate name for me I'd have to be a cocker spaniel. Finally though, when I got to be about three years old, I began to correct her, and she finally caved and called me Honey like everyone else did. But in High School she started with Torie again.

"Torie, sweetheart, you just graduated from high school and you don't even have a plan." I knew what her next sentence would be. It would be Franny. "Frances is going to college. She's working hard to ensure a good future." Fabulous Frances. Didn't Rose know that Franny didn't intend to come back home, ever, even for vacations? She didn't want any part of our crazy family.

I didn't either. I had pretty much had it with all of them. Rose, Bobbie, Dieter, and most of all my mom. And all the drama that went along with her boyfriends. I just wanted it all to go away. Vivian's latest boyfriend was some guy named Kevin who thought he was Brad Pitt. When he looked in the mirror he probably couldn't see the little bald spot on the back of his head. Kevin was an architect, and his claim to fame was some house he had designed, all glass and steel and bare surfaces, that was written up in *Better Homes and Gardens* magazine, and of course we were all supposed to ooh and ahh over that. But that was past history, and lately things had become a little sketchy for him and he needed a place to live, so for the moment he was housesitting for a San Francisco client who had been incarcerated for embezzlement. Those were Kevin's words: "incarcerated for embezzlement." He couldn't just say the jerk was in jail for stealing from his boss. So Kevin was house-sitting for the guy until he got out on parole, and Vivian was spending more of her time over there with him. Kind of like me at Danny's, only the house in San Francisco was a lot more glamorous. But Danny didn't have a bald spot.

Vivian wasn't all that happy about hauling her ass over to San Francisco all the time for this Kevin, but he made it clear he didn't care much for her family so he usually refused to come over to her place. She constantly bitched and moaned about that and we all had to listen to her. You'd think from all her whining that she'd look at this as a deal-breaker, but instead she just complained and went along with it, and then, about half the time, in some twisted kind of passive aggressive payback, she'd refuse to stay overnight there. Like I said, it was a lot of drama.

When I was a little kid most of Vivian's boyfriends tried to be nice to me in order to impress her. Some of them brought me treats thinking that was a good way to rack up points with her. It was usually something like a Kit Kat bar, or a bag of M&M's. But once in a while it was more substantial, like a small plush dog, or a Hello Kitty notebook. Some of the boyfriends gave things to Franny too, because she was at our place so often. And I have to say a couple of them really went out of their way to be nice to us.

One was the chubby bald guy who would take us in his truck to get ice cream. I always wanted to touch his smooth, tanned head, but I never did. I was sorry when he and my mom split up. There was the one that Bobbie dubbed the Cowboy, a wiry guy who wore jeans no matter what the occasion and talked with a drawl. He brought Franny and me along with them when they went out for pizza. He thought he was a comedian, but we didn't think he was all that funny.

Then there was Yoga Dan. Bobbie had been taking yoga for a while, and she kept urging Vivian to come with her. "You'd like it, it's relaxing," she kept saying, and finally Vivian agreed to give it a shot during a time when she had sworn off drinking and was making a big show of starting healthy activities. "It was hilarious," she said later. "There's this thing called downward dog, where the whole class is bent over with their butts in the air, and jeez, someone farted. I nearly choked trying not to laugh out loud." Still, she kept going back, and pretty soon it was apparent that her tremendous interest in yoga was because of Yoga Dan. He was lean and buff, and he treated Vivian nicely, but he didn't have much rapport with kids, and we got tired of his enthusiasm for things we weren't remotely interested in. He tried to get us all to go vegetarian, which Bobbie was all for trying, but Rose said no way. On the other hand, he talked Vivian into getting a nicotine patch, which was good, but she was still sneaking cigarettes when he wasn't around. Eventually Vivian went back to drinking again, and of course Yoga Dan didn't like that one bit, and they fought about it. He was a very serious person, and if you're having a relationship with Vivian while she's drinking, you don't want to be too serious.

Before I was born there had been a wacko boyfriend. Franny and I loved to ask Bobbie about him. Right after my mom split up with him he murdered his ex-wife. Seriously. A murderer. How many people actually date a murderer? Bobbie said it was a good thing Vivian split up with him, or who knows, she might have been the one who got bopped on the head. We loved this story, it was so lurid, but Rose said we shouldn't talk about it. And Vivian clammed up completely whenever anyone brought it up, and got surly when we pestered her for details. I can't blame her. She probably felt embarrassed that she had gone out with such a loser. No one wants to be reminded of their bad choices, and Lord knows Vivian probably had a shitload of stuff she didn't want to be reminded of.

It was around this time that Vivian decided she needed to be a better mom. When she wasn't at Kevin's, she began to hover over me. When she got home and found me still awake she would come into my room, the ice clinking in her glass, slide my stuff to one side and plop down on my bed. She'd kick off her shoes and pull up her feet to sit cross-legged, and then she'd light a cigarette. She wanted to get chummy. She wanted to know how I felt about things: about Danny, about her and her boyfriends, about all my so-called plans for the future. Basically she was looking for heart to heart talks. When she was really hammered, she'd get maudlin about us, saying that she had failed me, and that she was going to make it up to me. Other times she went on and on about how we were so close we were like sisters. It got so I turned out the light when I heard her noisy car come rattling up the street, so that she would think I was asleep and wouldn't come in to talk.

I didn't know what I wanted to do with myself, but I did know two things. I needed to get out of there. And I didn't want to turn out like Vivian.

Big Jeff, the other bartender at the Last Stop, told Bobbie that Vivian was coming in after the lunch rush for an afternoon bump. You could tell that she was drinking more because she was crabby and looked puffy and tired. And she was starting to talk to herself. About me, right in front of me, when I was in the same room. "Honey had better get it together," she would mumble, shaking her head. Where did she think I was? In the next county?

One night Danny was over for dinner, and she had a big heat on, and went on and on about something she had heard someone say, that life is a temporary condition. This really made a big impression on her, like it was something really cool and philosophical. Maybe it was, but after about the fortieth telling that cool philosophical quality kind of loses its luster. There was no shutting her up when she got going like this. Most of what she said that night made no sense whatsoever. I was sorry Danny had to see this side of her.

Meanwhile Dieter's girlfriend moved to Florida to take care of her mother, who had Alzheimer's, so he began hanging around like a lost dog. He had taken to showing up after his evening beer at the Last Stop, just in time to join us for dinner. It became so regular that he started bringing something, usually a take-out salad from the deli, to contribute to the meal. I loved Dieter, but he was bringing the mood way down at dinner.

And if I ever forgot that I was in a real loony bin, all I had to do was think of the day I saw Bobbie in her bedroom with an electric hair straightener in one hand, pretending it was a mike, while she did her dance moves, singing to the mirror and to her dog Muppet, who lay on her bed and watched.

Forty-two years old and she was singing into a hair appliance for a dog. All I could think was I really needed to get away.

So moving in with Danny seemed like a no-brainer. I was at his place most of the time anyway, and Danny was fine with the idea. One afternoon I packed all my clothes and things into my two powder blue suitcases and matching tote bag, and put everything else into a cardboard box. Danny had a car by that time, and we loaded it with all my stuff and hauled it over to his house. He wasn't using his closet because he didn't like to be bothered with hanging things on hangers. In fact he had never unpacked his clothes from the black plastic trash bag. So I had the whole closet for my things.

I looked at him stretched out on the bed, watching me put clothes on hangers, his shirt unbuttoned, his flip-flops kicked off. I couldn't believe how lucky I was. I was living with a guy who was hot enough to be in an underwear ad. Really, he was. And he was mine. Mine to touch, to smell, to feel wrapped around me, to watch as he went about the house unaware that I was watching him. I wondered why I hadn't moved in before this.

That night we broke the news of my move to Vivian, but she was getting ready to go out with Kevin, and I could tell she wasn't focused, and when I told her I had moved in with Danny, she didn't really react. Then after a few minutes she said, "Well, okay. So what kind of job are you going to get?"

Everyone kept coming back to that. I told her I was looking for one. That wasn't strictly true, because I hadn't started looking, but I intended to, which I figured was the same thing. But I was a little disappointed that she didn't seem to care that I was moving out.

Rose had more to say, of course. She went on and on, basically about how unprepared I was for life, and actually asked me if I was really ready to be out on my own. Which made it perfectly clear to me that she didn't understand one thing about me. I was completely ready to be on my own. Finally Bobbie pointed out, "She's eighteen. She's an adult now." Which I really appreciated. And then they backed off. I was surprised that Rose gave up so easily, because it wasn't like her. Later I overheard them talking in the next room, Rose's loud voice announcing her opinions and Bobbie's soft voice answering, and then Rose practically shouted, "That's why it won't last. When she gets this out of her system, hopefully she'll get serious about her life." There's a vote of confidence for you. But it turned out she was right, of course.

In the beginning it was wonderful. We couldn't keep our hands off each other. I would wake up early in the morning while Danny was still asleep and look at him lying there, so beautiful and unguarded, his eyes closed, his mouth open. He usually had a hard-on. We would lie close together, my leg draped over his, and looking at his pale eyelids I would wonder what he was seeing in his dreams. I would try to imagine what it would be like to see the world through his eyes, and I wished that I could step into his brain. But all I could do was imagine. Then he would wake up and we would put our arms around each other, before he'd jump up and go pee—he always needed to pee as soon as he woke up—and then he'd come back and we'd get it on. I loved the taste of him. His skin, his lips, his saliva. It's funny how a person won't share a toothbrush but will put their tongue in someone else's mouth. Danny was puzzled when I said that once, because there was no way that he would ever share his toothbrush, and he didn't think that was odd at all.

We slept late, because he didn't have to go to work at Pet Station until one o'clock.   We would have breakfast and horse around some, and then he'd shower and go to work. I'd clean up the house, spend some time on Facebook, read magazines, do my nails, and generally try to stay out of Martin's way while he did his sawing and hammering. But Martin was gone by late afternoon so we had the house to ourselves again by the time Danny got home. I would slowly undress him, and he would undress me, and then we'd fuck and then we'd lie there and talk and laugh. He managed to sneak the sex book out of his dad's house, and we went through it page by page together. Sometimes the instructions were downright funny, and we would stop horsing around and laugh our heads off. In fact we laughed a lot when we were fucking. I don't know if that's normal, but it was fun. Once Danny got out Martin's tape measure and we measured his boner. We thought that was hilarious.

In the evening Danny went to work at the movie theater, or we hung out with our friends. Ryan and Matthew could be counted on to show up at our house with beer and snacks. Then they'd go outside to play basketball with Danny until it got dark and sometimes even after it got dark, because then the motion-detection light switched on. Martin had installed this for security, but it was perfect for playing at night.   I would watch TV inside, listening to the *thump thump wonk* of the ball hitting the pavement and the backboard, and marvel at how much energy those boys had. Then they would come in and have a beer.

Basically sitting around and drinking beer was the main entertainment. Though I wasn't much of a drinker myself.   In high school I went to all the parties where everyone danced a lot, made out a lot, and drank the beer that various older brothers got for us. Franny was able to have a beer or two and not make herself sick or do anything embarrassing, but right off the bat I found that drinking made me puke, and I don't know about you, but if there was one thing in the world I did not want to do, it was puke. I could never be bulimic, even if I were as big as Rose. I never understood how girls could do that. After that first time, I decided I just didn't need to drink so much to have a good time. I think my attitude might also have had something to do with Vivian.   I mean, just the thought of Vivian wobbling across the room, looking pathetic, was a huge incentive to stay sober.   So I'd have a beer now and then, but I stopped there. I didn't need to get a buzz on to have a good time.

One night Danny went off and stayed out late without me. He never called or anything, just rolled in at about 2:30am with some lame excuse. He said that he had gone over to Ryan's brother's house after work, and they'd had a few beers, and he'd lost track of the time. I didn't know what to say to that, so I kept my mouth shut. When I don't know what to say I generally just wait until I do. But it bothered me that he never even thought about me. He dropped onto the bed and immediately fell sound asleep, and I lay there looking at him, his face pale in the moonlight coming through the window. His lashes were dark against his face, and his mouth was slackly open, and it was all I could do to keep from running my hand over his cheek. The next morning he nuzzled me awake and he was his sweet self again and I just let it slide.

A couple of weeks later it happened again, and again a week after that, and then it was becoming a regular thing. The next day he'd ask me what time he got home, and I'd tell him, and he'd apologize really sweetly, and for a while we'd be back to normal. If you could call that normal. Because it bothered me more and more, and finally I stopped being the sweet sad mouse and challenged him when he rolled in late.

"You couldn't just call?" I asked him as he stood before me, unsteady on his feet, trying to disentangle his arm from his jacket. "How hard is that?"

"Who are you, my fucking mother?" he replied, freeing himself and dropping the jacket on the floor.

That's the kind of smartass answer that stopped me cold. How can a girl stand up to the mother retort? I figured the best thing was to ignore it and move on. So I did. "Do you figure I'm sitting at home, waiting up for you?"

"Don't do me any favors," he said sarcastically, "waiting up for me."

"Good," I said, "I don't. I always find something else to do." I figured that would remind him that I could have a life without him. Not that I did. Not much, anyway. When he didn't show up at home I would go over to Madison's house and hang out there with some other kids I knew from High School.

"You're just looking for an excuse to go hook up with some asshole," he said, glaring at me. I was completely unprepared for an answer like that. I left the room while he hollered, "Tears aren't going to get you anywhere, you know."

These fights started to become part of our routine. Sometimes I figured it would be better to bring it up the next day when he was sober, but then he would get irritable, telling me I was trying to control him, that I was smothering him, that I was tying him down. He had a million ways of saying that I was wrong. Things went on like this for weeks, alternating between good times and bad and then back to good again. There were mornings when we lay together in the sunny little bedroom, stroking each other and smiling and whispering, and mornings when we fought about his showing up at two in the morning after I had spent all evening trying not to think about him, and hating myself for wondering where he was.

What kind of loser came home to an empty house and sat around wishing her douchebag boyfriend would come home? Me I guess. But finally one night I resolved that this was the night that things would be different. I may have been a loser before, but now I would act like someone who wasn't a loser. Like Franny. What would Franny do? This would be my new motto: What Would Franny Do. WWFD.

One thing you can count on about Franny is that she'll stand up to people. She stood up to Mr. Carney, our fifth-grade teacher, when he took away her paper because she was talking during a test. When he snatched it away she was so astonished she sat there for a minute, watching him return to the front of the room. Then she walked right up to where he had turned to write some stuff on the board and she said very slowly and deliberately, "Mr. Carney, that isn't fair. I was telling Carter to stop looking at my paper. If you want to take someone's paper away, it should be his."

Mr. Carney turned around and looked at her standing there, her chest stuck out and her hands behind her back. From where I sat I could see that her fingers were all twisted together. He took off his glasses and said, "Well then, Frances, maybe you should have ignored Carter."

She stood there a moment and then said, cool as a cucumber, "Okay, that's what you want, next time I'll ignore him and he can copy off my paper all he wants." And then she pirouetted around and walked very stiffly back to her seat.

She sat down, her back so straight it looked unnatural, with her hands folded on the desk like an old-fashioned picture, looking straight ahead, ignoring Mr. Carney as he came down the row to her.   Probably no one else could see this, but I figured she was trying not to cry, because Franny was a real test taker.   She loved to show what she knew, and she studied for these things like they were important, which I always thought was interesting, because I have to say I could never really see the point.   Anyway, I knew what she was doing in her head: She was making a list. That's what she did when she wanted to focus really hard and not show she was upset. She probably still does it. She taught this to me, and I did it sometimes myself. You'd say to yourself, list the towns along San Pablo Avenue: Oakland, Emeryville, Berkeley, Albany, El Cerrito, Richmond, San Pablo, El Sobrante, Pinole, Hercules . . . trying to keep them all in order in your head and not miss a single one. And while you were doing that no one realized that inside you were trying not to cry.

Mr. Carney came slouching down the aisle, and put the test back on the desk in front of her, saying, "Maybe next time you'll be more careful, Frances," then went back to the front of the room. We talked about that later, and I asked what on earth that was supposed to mean. Careful about what? And Franny said it didn't mean anything, it was just all he could think of saying rather than say "I was wrong and you were right, Frances."

Maybe Franny worried too much about right and wrong, and about what she was going to do in life. But no one but me knew this: when she was doing a lot of worrying she chewed the inside of her cheek until it was a raw sore inside. She made me promise not to tell, so I didn't, but I always wished she could find another way to be worried. Still, for all the worrying she did inside, on the outside Franny was all about standing up for herself. So when I asked WWFD, I knew the answer.   Franny wouldn't sit around waiting for her loser boyfriend to show up. She'd go out and look for that dipwad. So I did.

I walked down to the Last Stop to see if I could borrow my mom's car. Outside on the sidewalk it was cool, dark and quiet, so when I opened the door and stepped inside, I was stunned for a moment by the deafening noise and damp warm air. There was music playing but all I could make out was an insistent base line. Dieter was sitting near the door hanging with Rose, while Bobbie worked the other end of the bar. I couldn't see Vivian anywhere, and Rose said she was off somewhere, probably at her boyfriend's in San Francisco. So her car would be with her. Just my luck.

"Take the truck, Honey," Dieter shouted over the din, fishing the keys from his pocket. "I can get a ride from one of these folks." He gestured the length of the bar in the mirror, filled with faces, mouths open, animated with sound and gesture. As he handed me the keys he added, "Take it slow until you're used to the clutch." Dieter had taught both Franny and me how to drive stick shift, but I still stalled it on a regular basis.

So there I was at 11:00pm, out on the dark streets in Dieter's truck, chewing on a hangnail and struggling with the stick shift, trying to think what Franny would do if she were searching for Danny. I seriously doubted Franny would have put up with him this long to begin with, but never mind, I'd still use her as an inspiration. WWFD.

Franny would be methodical. So would I. First I drove slowly by each of his friend's houses, looking for his beat up old car out front. Nothing. What next? Food. I drove by MacDonald's, Nation's Hamburgers, and Al's Burgers. No sign of Danny's car. I drove by the movie theater. Nothing. And finally, at 12:30, I couldn't think of anywhere else to look, so I just drove up and down random streets looking at cars parked in the dark shadows under the trees. What would Franny do now? I couldn't think of anything else she would do, so I drove home. I could return Dieter's truck the next day.

What would Franny do next? Probably get a good night's sleep and yell at Danny in the morning. Point out that staying out all night was disrespectful, and didn't even make sense coming from the guy who told everyone he wanted us to get married.

I walked around the house in the dark, from room to room, looking out of each window. From the front room there was enough light from the streetlight to see the driveway, but the back yard was inky black. My finger was bleeding where I had been chewing on it, but my teeth wouldn't leave that hangnail alone. I went back into the kitchen, turned on the light, and opened the refrigerator. I wasn't really hungry, I just needed something to do.   Apples, milk, peanut butter, mayonnaise, mustard, catsup, a package of hotdogs, some little cartons of vanilla yogurt, half of a loaf of bread, and some beer. I took out a piece of bread and a can of beer, opened the can and sat down at the table. I tore the bread into bite-sized pieces and ate them one by one as I drank the beer. The bread was stale.

My laptop was on the table. I pulled it over to me and opened it up to see if there was anything going on. There wasn't much. From where I was sitting I had a good view of the phone and all the phone numbers scribbled next to it. Who writes on the wall?   What kind of loser keeps their contact list in pencil on a kitchen wall? I turned out the light and sat in the dark.

The motion detector light suddenly flashed on outside. I was so sure it was Danny that I scurried to the bedroom and sprang into bed to fake sleep. I wasn't going to let him find me wide-awake at three-thirty in the morning, pacing around the house in the dark, freaking out over him. I hadn't heard his car pull into the driveway, but I figured maybe he got a ride, which would be a good idea because by now he had to be seriously hammered. I lay without moving, listening for him, but all I could hear was my noisy breathing into the sheet pulled halfway over my face. Breathing in. Breathing out. (Was there something wrong with me to make it so noisy there under the sheet?) I held my breath to listen for Danny. Nothing. It was like the night had sucked the life out of the house. Finally I threw off the sheet and sat up. Silence. I got up and shuffled into the front room where I peered out the window.   The motion light was still on and a skunk was waddling down the driveway. It figures.

I finally went back to bed at six-thirty, and that's when I heard his car. He rolled in, said, "Hey," like it was nothing, and fell into bed. He slept until two-thirty. When he woke up, I lay down on the bed beside him, and suddenly he said, "Remember how you kept asking what happened between me and Brianna, and I never told you?"

Clearly this conversation was not going to end well. The only person who can possibly benefit from a conversation that begins with an ex would be the speaker. And possibly the ex. Actually, *probably* the ex. "Uh-huh," I murmured, not making eye contact. He hitched himself up on his elbow, facing me. I focused on his arm, with its blue-green veins showing on the underside of his wrist, like rivers on a map.

"It was because she was trying to own me." There was a long silence. I was beginning to feel sick in the pit of my stomach, but I wasn't going to say anything until I knew where this was going. Finally he said, "She acted like we were married or something. It was just too much." That sick feeling was getting stronger. But still I didn't say anything. I wasn't going to help him out. He was going to have to do this on his own.

"Now it's happening with us." There it was. He said it. And he was waiting for a response. But I couldn't think of a thing to say. After all, it wasn't me who kept saying we were going to get married. But it seemed pointless to bring that up now. I didn't know what to bring up. I was full of feelings that didn't have sentences attached to them. I could see our mornings lying in the sun, waking up to each other. I could feel how his skin felt against mine, and how it tasted to kiss. And I could remember cracking up over the tape measure. I could picture us out dancing at a party, drenched with sweat and both of us singing along with the music. And all of these pictures had my love in them, but none of them had a paragraph that I could recite like a magic charm to win Danny back. Not while he was freaking out about being hemmed in.

Of course, taking off without me all those nights made more sense now. That's what he was doing. Freaking out. And now, looking back, I can see that he didn't have a magic charm either, a paragraph to recite to me to say he wasn't ready for what we had become. That we shouldn't have moved so fast. That I shouldn't have moved in. Here he was trying to say something now, and I didn't have a single thing to say in answer.

Since then I've come to understand that when I moved in with him all I was thinking about was getting the hell out of my mom's crowded apartment and away from the family freak show. And not just because my mom was being a pain in the ass. Because they all were, with their laser focus on me, constantly on my case. Franny was out on her own, even if it was just in college, which I wouldn't have done if you'd paid me, but still, she was away, and I wanted some of that freedom. So I had been confident that living with Danny would be the best move ever. I just hadn't thought it through.

"It's just too much for me, Honey," Danny went on earnestly. "And in a year I'm going to college. And, well, I don't know. I don't know how to say this. I just think it would be weird for us to be living together when that time comes."

I knew he was trying to do the right thing, but I couldn't think of any words that were not sad and pathetic. And the one thing I was clear about was that I did not want to appear sad and pathetic. WWFD? Franny wouldn't sit around looking sad and pathetic either. Franny would stand up tall and walk out of there. She'd be all *Ciao baby, you'll live to regret this.* So I sat up, got dressed, and started to pack. Danny sat there watching me, a stricken look on his face. By the time I had all my things stacked by the front door he was up and dressed and following me around saying, "Don't go. Not yet. Stay here. Let's talk." But I knew that he had been telling me for weeks now that this was a mistake, telling me with his absence. There was no point in further conversation, so I just kept shaking my head, no, no, no. Finally he put his arms around me, and we kissed, and I almost let it change my mind because I still felt everything the same way, even when my mind knew it was over. It was a sizzling last kiss, and when it was over we just looked at each other, our eyes locked, tenderness radiating out of us and filling the whole room, but I broke that spell. "I'm leaving now." I was really glad I had Dieter's truck so I could just walk right out of there and drive home. It would have been lame to have to ask for a ride.

Danny helped me put my stuff in the truck, and we said goodbye there on the sidewalk, and then I turned abruptly, got in the truck and managed to drive it away without stalling, leaving him to watch me go.

Of course, everyone at home wanted to know what was going on. Vivian acted really sweet and sympathetic, and I could tell she was dying to know what happened, but whenever she asked I just said, "No, we didn't have a big fight. It's no big deal. We just split up." Rose, though, was not going to let this get by her.

"What happened, sweetheart?" she asked.

"Nothing."

"Don't tell me nothing. Did something bad happen between you? Did Danny do something hurtful?" and that just irritated me. Of course he didn't. Danny wasn't like that.

Franny was the only one I confided in, until she said, "Don't split up with him, Honey. Just scale it back." I didn't think I could tell her that she had been my inspiration to walk out. Later I heard that Brianna was back in the picture, though Danny did call me from time to time. He thought we should go out again, but I said no way. I may have been stupid once, but I wasn't going to be stupid twice.

Chapter 2

WHAT TIME IS IT?   I can't see the clock.   Someone has moved it to make room for a vase of sticks, and I have to wonder why someone would put sticks in a vase.   They weren't there before.   What time was it then? Who knows?

There is nothing to anchor me to time.   Nothing, there is nothing.   I don't know if it's day or night.   The noises are the same either way.   From somewhere behind me a monotonous CLICK, PING *repeats over and over.   And continuous voices that I can't make out, a wordless murmur like musical notes forming flat queries and urgent responses.   Day or night there is always the TV on in the next room and mysterious announcements over a PA system.   And always, always there is the eerie shush of the massager, breathing like an animal, curled around my legs.   I open my eyes and Rose is here.   I close them just for a moment, open them again, and she's gone.   Dieter shows up with the newspaper, but it's too difficult to read.   I can't concentrate on all that gray and black.   I tell him to bring some magazines, for crying out loud.   Meanwhile I still have no idea what time it is.*

Chapter 3

I HAVE TO SAY coming back to the family wasn't much of an improvement.

Mom was going through one of her times of financial difficulty, as she put it. Translated, that means she had been laid off and was way behind in her rent, so Rose and Bobbie had invited her to move into Franny's old room. It was strange to walk in and see Franny's room full of Vivian's things. And now my things as well. Franny's bed was a double, so I had a place to sleep, but it meant sharing the bed with my mom. Rose said that when Franny came home she could sleep on the living room sofa.

It was close quarters. We're talking here about a sorry little apartment crammed with four adults and a small dog at the top of a narrow staircase running up from the back of the bar. Perfect for Vivian because bars have always played a big part in her life. She started coming by the Last Stop a gazillion years ago when she had a boyfriend who was a semi-regular there. So at first she came in with him, and she just got to hanging out there more and more, even after the boyfriend became history, until pretty soon she was one of the regulars, trolling for attention and dates, and she and Bobbie and Rose became thick as thieves, as Rose liked to say. Then I came along, and Vivian was having some problems adjusting to motherhood, and in all the confusion apparently she mislaid the boyfriend who had gotten her pregnant.

By this time it should be clear to you that Vivian has had some issues relating to alcohol. That's an understatement. She's always been a total lush, and as a result from time to time her life would spin completely out of control. When I was a baby this had been one of those times. Being an infant, I wasn't in on the details, but I've since heard all about it. We lived in Rose's motel for years, moving from room to room, depending on which was vacant, or more to the point, depending on which needed something fixed, because Rose couldn't rent a room to a paying guest if it had something broken in it. There were times when Rose even gave Vivian a job cleaning the motel rooms, when Vivian had what she called an employment emergency, which happened now and then because, as Rose liked to point out, Vivian's life tended to be disorganized. This never lasted too long, because Vivian was a terrible cleaner. She was slow, she left the cleaning supplies behind here and there in the room, and she was sloppy about dusting and vacuuming. Rose had to continually nag her, and Vivian would whine and complain, until finally she'd find a new job so she could quit the cleaning charade.

But other than the cleaning, living in the motel worked out pretty well, because my mom could go to work, and Rose would take care of me. She was already taking care of Franny, so the two of us were raised together. Things didn't change much when mom and I finally moved out of the motel and into a little house just down the street. We went back and forth so much between Rose's apartment and our house that they didn't feel like separate places. Each night Bobbie and Big Jeff worked the bar while Franny and I were upstairs in the apartment with Rose. My mom was around, but for her *around* could mean anything from hanging in the bar to partying with one of her boyfriends, so it was Rose who made sure we ate a proper dinner, did our homework, and took a bath.

The bar was nothing to write home about, but it always had a cozy feel to it. As long as you didn't turn on the bright lights, because then it looked downright dingy. But those are only turned on for cleaning. The one nice thing about the place was the old wooden bar itself, running almost the length of the room. Dark and glossy, Rose said it was real mahogany.

Behind it the wall was made up of dark wooden shelves lined with bottles, surrounding a large mirror. On the opposite wall there was a crowd of small red laminate tables, and at the front of the room, near the door, two maroon sofas faced each other over a low coffee table. Out the back door there was a tiny patio covered with a fiberglass roof, and a prehistoric orange vinyl sofa. That was for the smokers.

Like every bar the Last Stop had its regulars. The FOB's for instance, the Friends of Bobbie, who came by when Bobbie was working the bar to schmooze and get the FOB benefit of a long pour. Vivian's boyfriends tended to be regulars too. So was Dieter, and a bunch of folks who came by after work. But a couple of regulars were real standouts. One was Coyote Girl. Sometime way back the regulars started calling her that, and she thought it was cool, like some sort of Indian name or something. Franny and I didn't really know her personally, but we heard all about her. She looked okay from a distance, but up close was another story. Her long dirty blond hair was stringy, and her face, with its yellowish skin etched with lines, looked pretty beat up. Rose called her a sleepwalker, going through life without goals, without plans, without thinking about what she wanted to make of herself. Instead she pretty much hung out with losers every night and got up the next day to do it all over again. Anyway, that's what Rose told us. What she didn't mention, but we knew because we were good at eavesdropping, was that Coyote Girl was giving guys blow jobs in the bathroom and would go home with any guy who was too hammered to care about how skanky she was. She never suspected that behind her back everyone knew that she got the name Coyote Girl out of sheer disrespect. Rose says coyotes are animals that trot along after other predators, eating their leftovers. But no one ever repeated that to Coyote Girl's face.

The other standout was the Troll. She was called that to her face by everyone in the bar, but she didn't take offense because she gave herself the name. Go figure. She was short and heavyset. She worked dispatch for a trucking company so she sat all day at work, and she sat all evening in the Last

Stop, and with all that sitting over the years her butt just got bigger and bigger. It's a wonder that little barstool could hold her up. She always wore the same thing, a fleece vest, jeans and cowboy boots, and a Raiders cap on her head. She had a huge chain connected to her wallet and carried a big bunch of keys on her belt. Her eyebrows and ears were pierced, and her arms were covered with tattoos of snakes and lizards. I was terrified of her when I was very little, but I soon learned that for all the alarming wildlife on her arms, she wasn't the least bit fierce. Her face, round as the moon and pink with broken capillaries, was kindly. Rose had a soft spot for the Troll, maybe because she was so big herself.

All these regulars were immortalized in snapshots taken by Rose over the years, and framed and hung on the walls of the Last Stop. Most of these photos fell into one general category: People Sitting at the Bar. There were people sitting and smiling, sitting and glaring, sitting and holding hands, sitting with arms flung over shoulders, sitting with glasses raised, and far too many with folks who didn't know how lame it is to hold up "horn" fingers behind someone else's head. Then there was a subcategory of photos with people sitting on the sofas, some with everyone lined up neatly, some with people piled on in a drunken melee, and one with everyone on their knees with their butts facing the camera. Ha ha. There were sports pictures, mostly of the girls' soccer team sponsored by the bar, and one of a softball game that no one can remember. There were several pictures with a Christmas theme—one with Dieter wearing a Santa hat and two involving anonymous Santas sitting at the bar. There was one picture with a bride in her wedding dress, surrounded by smiling girlfriends and several smiling men holding up their drinks in a toast. And because every bar needs a celebrity picture, there was a snapshot of Rose with Linda Ronstadt, who came in one evening to see if she could get change for a twenty. Rose was thrilled because she loved her, and she offered her a free drink, but Ronstadt said she didn't drink, and just had a glass of water instead. I've heard the story a thousand times. Bobbie had to explain to us who Linda Ronstadt was.

Next door to the bar was Rose's motel. Nowadays the Welcome Back Motel is considered fun and quirky, and it was written up in a *Sunset Magazine* article about offbeat California hotels, but when I was growing up, it was just a dump. It was when I was about three and my mom and I were living there that Rose decided it was time to upgrade the place. Bobbie had some ideas, and Dieter, who was hanging around the bar those days, decided this would be a good investment. It was Bobbie's brilliant concept that each room would be decorated differently. She and Rose and Dieter went to thrift shops and salvage yards for interesting pieces of furniture and painted them bright colors. There was a Red Room, a Zebra Room (yes, black-and-white stripes everywhere—imagine trying to sleep in that), and a Victorian Room, which my mom always sarcastically called the Frou Frou Room.

My favorite room was the Flamingo Room. It got its start one day when Rose and Bobbie came home with a rattan sofa in the back of Dieter's truck. It was tropical and exotic looking, with green leaves and huge pink hibiscus flowers on the cushions. Dieter and Bobbie wrestled it off the truck, and as soon as it was in place, Franny and I hopped onto it and watched Bobbie measure the window and floor dimensions, making notes on a pad of paper. Sometime after that Bobbie began her mural. On one wall she painted a huge palm tree that went from floor to ceiling, with a big glowing moon and a pink flamingo standing on one leg in front of the moon. She painted the other walls the same soft pink as the flamingo, and painted the bed and tables apple green with gold trim, and when the sun came in the window in the late afternoon, the whole room glowed golden and pink. When we lived in that room the last thing I saw every night was that flamingo in the moonlight, and my mom and I would make a wish on the moon. Ever since, when something reminds me of that moon glow, the memory makes me smile.

Right after I moved back from Danny's, Vivian and Kevin-With-the-Bald-Spot broke up, so my mom was around much of the time, just my luck, and had made a firm resolution to spend more time with me. Fortunately that turned out to be much less ominous than it sounds, because most of what we did together was cook dinner and watch TV. It could have been worse. She could have wanted to tag along when I went out with my friends. That would have made me completely homicidal. Instead, I was mostly just irritated.

We were all in each other's faces, getting on each other's nerves. Vivian moped around, coughing and complaining, instead of looking for work. In that little bedroom she and I were engaged in a constant territorial battle over the precious little space we had for our clothes and things. Vivian had taken over Franny's closet, so I had to keep my clothes in my suitcases, and my shoes and everything else I owned in a couple of cardboard boxes.

It wasn't much better in the rest of the apartment. You never felt like you were alone; there was always the murmur of someone talking in the next room. Vivian made her presence known with some sort of cough, an annoying pathetic sound that seemed suspiciously like a bid for attention. Someone was always eating the last of the Cheerios, or forgetting to wrap up the bread so it dried out, or leaving the clothes in the washing machine so that by the time the next person found them they were musty with mildew. Usually the ones making all these mistakes were me and Mom, so we had to skulk around trying to remember to do everything right. Meanwhile Rose was on my mom's case about her cigarette butts on the back porch, so Vivian was irritated about that.

Around this time Bobbie got a new puppy to replace her old dog Muppet. Muppet was a fluffy little white dog who had been part of the family for as long as I could remember, but by the time Franny and I were in high school she was getting old and beginning to fall apart. Then one afternoon Bobbie came home and found her curled up on the bed, dead.

She was pretty upset about it because she considered Muppet to be one of her kids, which Franny wasn't too crazy about, but we knew it was just because Bobbie loved that dog so much. I think this was the first time I saw an adult really cry. Not just weeping at a sad movie. Or Vivian's beery tears when she was hammered and convinced the world was a Terrible Place. But real honest-to-goodness sobbing. I was the only one around at the time, so I tried to comfort her but I had no idea how to go about it. I sat on the bed next to her and put my arms around her shoulders, which felt really thin, something I'd never noticed before, and Bobbie sat there hunched over and crying into her hands. Finally she stopped and her nose was running so I got up and got the box of tissues and she blew her nose and said, her voice thick and hoarse, "We have to do something with her." I volunteered to go down to the bar to get a cardboard box, and Bobbie appreciated that. While I was there I told Rose what happened, and she asked one of the regulars to watch the till, and she heaved herself up the stairs to comfort Bobbie.

So like I said, after a while Bobbie got Bitsy, another fluffy white poodle mix. Bitsy was cute enough to be in a dog food commercial, but she was a real pain in the ass. She chewed everything in sight—chair legs, books, watchbands, anything she could get her teeth on. One weekend Franny came home from college for a day to go to a party, and Bitsy chewed up one of the white Coach flats she had planned to wear. Franny went crazy. It wasn't so much that she paid a lot for the shoes, because she didn't, she got them on eBay. But they were so stylish, so perfect. Franny loved those shoes. So when she walked into her room and found a lone Coach flat mauled in the middle of the floor, with the entire back end chewed off, she went berserk. She tore into the kitchen screaming, "That *pinche* poodle ate my shoe!"

Rose said, "Whoa, what did you just say?"

And Franny screamed again "Bitsy completely destroyed my shoe!"

But Rose wouldn't let go. "Did I hear you say the *pinche puta*?"

"No!" Franny howled, "For chrissake, I said the *pinche* poodle."

It was hard to keep a straight face through all of this. If I laughed, Rose would turn on me too. But to call that miserable mutt a *pinche puta*, a fucking whore, was even funnier than *pinche* poodle.

"The WHAT poodle?"

"Okay," said Franny, suddenly more subdued. "I didn't know you knew that much Spanish."

"I know everything," said Rose icily. Danny had taught me and Franny some useful bad words in Spanish. Who knew Rose knew them too?

So Bitsy became yet another stress point in that apartment. She was one of my mom's favorite things to rant about when propelled by a few too many beers. "Bitsy." She'd roll her eyes. "Bitsy is pathetic. Bitsy isn't anything like Muppet was. Now, Muppet. *Muppet.*" She'd stop, distracted. "What the hell kind of name is that?" She didn't really expect an answer, and after a pause she would get back on track. "Muppet. Now, there was a dog. Muppet was one of the world's great dogs. A great dog. What's Bitsy? Not a great dog. A Not Great Dog. More like a noisy little rag. With teeth." She laughed as she emptied the bottle into her glass. "A little bitchy rag with teeth."

Sometimes Bobbie would fall for this and get involved. "No she's not," she'd say sadly. "She's a sweet little dog."

"Little," said my mom, "but not sweet. No, not sweet. Jeez, Bobbie, you should just put her to sleep."

That's about when Bobbie would leave the room. The next day Vivian wouldn't remember the conversation, but she would apologize over and over until Bobbie was mollified. She did this kind of thing all the time. I never knew what would set her off, or which direction she'd go with me. On one hand, she could launch into a maudlin monologue about how sweet I was. "Honey, you're a good kid. A real good kid. Your heart is in the right place." Even though I knew she was tanked, I lapped it up. But she could just as well start ragging me with all the usual stuff—what was I doing with my life? Did I know how hard it was to bring up a child, blah blah blah—and the next day she wouldn't remember a thing. So she had no idea how offensive she had been.   I tried to keep in mind that this was just the beer talking. But still, she was my mother.

I had to get away from her, get away from that voice. Once I tried taking a bath, thinking she would leave me alone when I was in the tub, but she followed me in there, and sat on the toilet, talking nonstop. Sometimes I left the apartment and went over to Madison's house, but I didn't like to do that too often because Madison's mom was so concerned about me that she wouldn't leave me alone either. My best bet was to convince Mom to go downstairs to the bar.

There was no place to escape, not even in sleep. I missed being able to sleep late whenever I chose like I did at Danny's. Now when I slept late in the morning I got all kinds of grief from Rose. She would sigh and say, "Torie, sweetheart, you need to get a job." I was still under a lot of scrutiny about the job thing. I kept saying I wasn't a child anymore, but they didn't seem to hear me, and they all kept saying you need a plan, you need a plan, you need a plan. Vivian would make suggestions. "Starbucks always needs people," she'd say one day. The next day it was "Honey, what about Jamba Juice? They always have young people working there."   Bobbie suggested that I go talk to one of the FOBs who was a dog groomer, and had mentioned that she needed help.

"Terrific," I said. I had heard enough from Danny about bathing dogs, something that he had to do a lot of when he worked at the Pet Station. "That's what I need, a job where I can shampoo dogs who have rolled in something nasty. And work with psycho dogs like Bitsy."

Bobbie was hurt. "Bitsy isn't psycho," she said sadly.

Poor Bobbie, she had to take so much grief about that mutt. I did feel guilty sometimes for making cracks like that, but who could resist?   We all did it.   When Franny called home she'd ask me, "How is the *pinche* poodle?" and the two of us would crack up. Unfortunately, though, when she called home Franny didn't stop at the *pinche* poodle remark. No, she jumped right on the train with everyone else. "Honey, you've got to get out of there. Do something, anything, to get out of there." She suggested cosmetology school. "You could learn to do facials." That didn't sound so bad. But I didn't know where to start.

Meanwhile, Dieter was coming over a lot. His girlfriend was still in Florida, and it didn't look like she was ever coming back. Vivian was generally hammered or hung-over, and her annoying cough was getting noticeably worse. Bobbie was back to singing to herself in the mirror and had started weeping whenever there was anything remotely sad on the news. I think she was missing Franny. And I was still missing Danny. I missed his skin, his navel with the soft path of hair leading from it, and his beautiful brown eyes. Then I'd think about what a shithead he was and I'd stop sniveling for a while. Our whole household was in loser overdrive.

Franny didn't come home for Thanksgiving because she got invited to go to Mexico with one of her rich friends. That girl had a family who always spent their holidays somewhere exotic and let their daughter invite a friend to come along. How the hell did Franny get so lucky? Meanwhile we all missed her. We didn't usually make a big deal about Thanksgiving, but Rose roasted a turkey and Dieter bought a pumpkin pie, and we sat around eating the dinner feeling like there was an enormous black hole where Franny should be sitting. It pretty much sucked the life out of the room.

So it was a real relief when she did come home for Christmas. She said she had considered staying at Davis over the holiday as a sort of statement about her independence, but then she realized that the university was going to empty out and all her friends would be home with their families, so she might as well do the same. And, she finally admitted, she really missed all of us.

It was hard to find a time when we could hang together, just the two of us, in that tiny crowded apartment. But when Vivian went out we had the bedroom to ourselves, and we could finally have a real conversation. Which felt strange considering this was originally Franny's old room.   But Franny was philosophical about that and we flopped down on the bed just like old times.   One thing that Franny and I talked a lot about was sex.

"Remember," she said, "when we were little and we suddenly understood how sex worked?"

I remembered. "Yeah, the Joke."

We were in third grade, and we had some vague ideas about what a guy did with his penis, but the real Aha moment came when a fifth-grader told us the Joke, which went something like this: A guy and a girl are making out in the backseat of his car. He says, *Can I put my finger in your belly button?* And she says, *okay.* And then there is a pause. And then she says, *That's not my belly button,* and he says, *That's not my finger.* Then the fifth-grader explained it, in case we didn't get it. Franny and I just said *Oh*, with our eyebrows way up. It seems funny now that this was such a big moment for the two of us. But we were just little kids then.

Franny came to sex a bit later than I did. She was still pretty much a virgin when she graduated from high school, and now, looking back on it, this was probably because she was dating the Weasel. She saw on Facebook that he's come out now. "Did you ever suspect he was gay?" she asked me when we talked about it. No, I'd never really thought about it. Sometimes people surprise you.

She had finally gotten laid at Davis, after a Halloween party, and lately she was seeing some boy in Animal Science. Now that she had discovered sex she was horny all the time. And of course I was missing Danny. We sat around and reminisced about how great it was to be with someone you can just jump into the sack with, no hang-ups, no hassles, just get it on. Franny called it joyous fucking. She was impressed when I told her that Danny and I made love at least once a day. She said I was a bonobo, which is apparently a kind of chimpanzee that has sex all the time, at the drop of a hat, with anybody and everybody. At first I was insulted, but she told me that bonobos were practically a utopian community. They all got along, and shared with each other, and the females were in charge. For bonobos sex was just another way to feel good. There's a lot to be said for that. We considered how it would be if she and I were bonobos, an interesting thought until it occurred to us that it would mean spending the Christmas vacation rubbing each other's genitals as an expression of friendship. That was too weird so we dropped that line of thought and just went back to appreciating bonobos for their healthy happy appetites.

We marveled at how sex worked, how the body just took over, so that one moment you could be admiring a guy because he had nice muscled arms and a cute way that his hair hung into his eyes, and then next thing you knew, you had no idea where you left off and he began, and his skin and hair, sweat and saliva, his tongue and his penis, were all part of a highly charged swirl of sight, taste, and smell. Franny said at this point you probably wouldn't even see things like pimples, dirty fingernails, yellow toenails, or greasy hair, and that might be true. Because all of a sudden you would find yourself totally focused on very specific parts of the body. For girls, it's the little girl in a boat, as Bobbie once called the clitoris. For guys it's that demanding pecker. And for both it's all about orifices. I mean, normally the last thing on your mind is one of the body's openings, unless you are doing something with it. Like going to the bathroom. Or eating, and even then you're thinking about the food, not your mouth. The mouth, the asshole, the vagina, they are nothing but openings, that's all. Openings. But during sex they are suddenly all you can think of. It is odd when you think how exciting it is to put one person's part in another person's opening. Whether it's a tongue, a finger, a penis, they are all welcome in the opening.

"Funny, though," said Franny, "there's nothing sexy about sticking anything in the ears and nostrils." Though we agreed that this could very well be sexy to someone else. You never know.

I was so glad to have her home. There was no one else I could talk to like this. I missed her when she headed back to school after Christmas. Everything went back to the way it was before she came home. Rose said we were drowning in claustrophobic hostility. Those were her actual words. She made that remark one day when I was barely speaking to anyone, Bobbie was offended by something Vivian said, and Vivian was offended by the world in general. So it was a real relief when Dieter saved the day, one day in January.

Chapter 4

SOMEONE FINALLY MOVED the damn sticks, and now I can see the clock. 6:02. Does that mean six in the morning or six in the evening? Or maybe it's not six at all. After all, it's just a clock. It could be set it for anything. I could reset it for 12:00 and say it's noon. Or midnight. My choice. Or I could go by the time in another time zone. But apparently it's six here. Morning, I think. So the nurse should be coming in soon. Or maybe not.

Dieter came by, but I think I fell asleep and he was gone when I woke. He brushed my hair and told me something about the new issue of Vogue. *I think Bobbie told him to bring it over but he forgot. I'm not sure what I was supposed to do with that information. Dieter is so sweet he makes the rest of us look bad, but he doesn't mean to be annoying. Meanwhile he keeps talking to me about Honey. On and on about Honey. He's been calling her, to try to get her to come home. I tell him to leave the girl alone. It's not like I'm going anywhere. And I'm not so sure I want her to see me like this.*

He says she's only thinking of herself. So what else should she be thinking about? She's young. That's when it's natural to think about yourself. It's when you get old and you're still self-centered that the points start adding up against you. My father was self-centered, but that was according to my mom, and she may have been an unreliable source. She said he wanted to be considered a generous man, but he always thought of himself first, so even when he did something for someone else, it was just to make him look good. He thought of himself in a thousand ways that cut her deeply, so she divorced him. But maybe he wasn't so self-centered after all. Maybe it was just something between the two of them.

Anyway, he pretty much washed his hands of the whole thing. He took off without looking back. He didn't have much to say to children, so he didn't have much to say to me, and he didn't come around. She said he didn't know what to do with a kid. He wasn't all that far away, just over in San Francisco, but the bay might as well have been an ocean separating us. Then he was killed in a plane crash. Not a big airline crash, just a little private plane piloted by his new girlfriend's brother. A group of friends flying to Las Vegas together; instead they flew into a mountain. It barely made the third page of the paper. There were no survivors, just a cold list of names. My mom was shaken by this, but please, she's the one who banished him.

She was too hard on him. Narcissistic she called him. All men, she liked to say, are narcissistic. I always thought that word meant someone who looks in the mirror all the time, but Rose says well, that too sometimes, but it can refer to someone who thinks they are the center of the universe. But when you stop to think about it, who isn't the center of their own universe? Rose says I'm narcissistic. She lays that on me when I leave cupboards open, when I don't pick up my stuff. She says a normal person would be horrified to leave a mess for someone else to clean up. She says that as if it were some kind of intentional plan on my part. I've got news for you, Rose, sometimes it's just sloppiness.

Rose thinks too much.

When I can I'm going to get my own place again. It will be much better for our friendship. Dieter should move in with Rose and Bobbie. Dieter and Rose get along great. The two of them can close cupboard doors and do the dishes together all day long.

Chapter 5

DIETER FOUND ME A JOB. Even better, it sounded like the easiest job in the world. All I would have to do was walk around a San Francisco convention hall wearing shorts and carrying a sign that read:

TASTEE OIL
TASTEE PROFITS

The convention was the Gourmet Importers' winter trade show, and Tastee was an olive oil company from China. Vivian asked Dieter since when did China make olive oil, and he said don't be ignorant, they make everything. I asked him how it was he had connections with the gourmet show, being as he owns a hardware store and not a restaurant or something, and he acted all hurt.   Apparently he's proud of his housewares section and he goes to this show every year to look for new products.   How would I know that?   But I apologized anyway. It was nice of Dieter to help me find a job.

I had to get up at the crack of dawn, so Rose woke me or I would have overslept. Dieter came by to pick me up, and together we drove to San Francisco. The hall was enormous, and filled with people setting things up, looking stressed-out, and getting in each other's way. At the Tastee booth there were four Chinese men. Three of them were very formally dressed in black suits, but the fourth was more casual, in khaki pants and a green polo shirt. It turns out he was the only one who spoke English. His name was Wilson, and he looked relieved to see me. He took me by the arm and led me to a stack of cartons with a picnic basket on top. The basket was filled with straw and there were some olive oil bottles placed carefully inside, turned so that the Tastee label was facing out. The whole thing looked phony cute. He handed me the sign that said *TASTEE OIL TASTEE PROFITS*, and gave me my instructions. Dieter patted me on the back and slipped away.

My job was to stand next to the basket but not to block it, and to smile at everyone who came by, and most important, I was to gesture to the booth where the other three were setting up a little table with a red checked tablecloth. "Samples," Wilson explained. "Remember, smile pretty, don't block the basket, and send them over for samples." He gestured to the three men in suits who were hovering behind the table, laying out bowls of oil. Then he returned to another stack of cartons topped with a cutting board and a big paper grocery bag of baguettes, where he had been cutting the bread into tiny slices. Meanwhile, the aisles were clearing of hand trucks and frantic people, and then all three guys in suits looked at their watches at the same time, looked at each other, and then looked at me. I guessed that things were ready to roll.

After about ten minutes we got our first attendees, and I smiled and gestured like I was supposed to, but they strolled right by. Who would want to dip some bread in Chinese oil first thing in the morning? But I kept trying. I smiled until my cheeks hurt, and I gestured with the sign, with my arms, with my eyes, even with a flirty kick of my foot, and now and then someone would change course and come into Wilson's orbit, where he could steer them to the table and start his pitch while the three suits stood beaming.

My face ached from all that smiling, my legs were killing me from standing in high heels all morning, and I was starving when Dieter finally came by and told Wilson he was taking me to lunch. We went to a sandwich shop next to the hall, and Dieter seemed as glad as I was to sit down. He groaned as he plunked down a tote bag bursting with brochures and freebie junk, and he pulled out some of the crap that he'd picked up. There were key chains, notepads, magnets, and a coffee mug. "How're you holding up?" he asked me. I just sat there slumped, trying to think of how I could tell him that this was the worst job in the universe, when he interrupted my thoughts to say, "I know it's not much fun, but just remember, it won't last long." What could I say then? He already knew it was a shitty job.

The afternoon was just more of the same, a lot of lame old people doddering past the booth lugging tote bags full of loot. But all of a sudden it got a little more interesting, when a man showed up at Cremona Imports, the booth next door, and began to order everyone around. He was an older guy, but good-looking in a kind of scrappy, wiry way, with expressive dark eyes and that sexy needs-a-shave look, and I noticed his clothes were stylish and he wore a leather jacket. It was clear from the way he strutted around that he was the boss, and even though his people had been working hard at the booth all day, I guess he needed to show off by telling them what to do. And somehow I had the feeling he might be showing off because of me. Sure enough, he wandered over, and coming very close he said almost in a whisper to me, "Tastee? Are these clowns serious?" I didn't know what to say. His voice was low and suggestive, and I suddenly felt all wobbly. Yes, wobbly. The moment I met him I could feel something. And by something I mean something sexual, like an electric charge, which totally amazed me, because this guy was old.

"What kind of lousy jerk-off olive oil comes from China?" he said.

I didn't have an answer for that and just giggled nervously. Then Wilson saw him and came scuttling over.

"May I help you?" he said awkwardly.

"I'm just meeting your lovely assistant," the man said smoothly to Wilson.

"Well, she needs to work," said Wilson, getting snippy.

"I don't want to interfere with her work," said the man, and then he turned back to me and whispered, his voice low and sexy, "Babe, you and me will talk later. I'll see you at five o'clock." I nodded, astonished, and watched him swagger back into his booth.

At five o'clock, after Wilson had paid me for the day and I was cramming the cash into my purse, the guy came back over. He took me by the elbow and steered me over to his booth. "I hope you don't mind waiting a moment," he said. He was so polite, treating me like a real lady. "I have to wrap things up here." Just then Dieter came walking up, looking a little surprised to find me in the Cremona booth instead of the Tastee booth.

"This is my ride," I said to the man, realizing that I didn't even know his name.

"Oh, I'll give you a ride home this evening" he said smoothly, and he stepped forward to Dieter with his hand out. "I'm Eddie Bertoli," he said, shaking Dieter's hand. Dieter's eyebrows were a couple of question marks by this time, but he shook Eddie's hand and mumbled something about it being up to me.

I said, "Hey, Dieter, thanks, I'll see you in the morning!" And he just stood there. I could tell he was trying to work out what he should do. But it's not like he was my father or anything. And I figured at eighteen, I was an adult. "I'll be okay," I said. He still looked worried, but finally he turned and left me with Eddie.

At the back table at a little restaurant in North Beach I found out a lot more about Eddie. I heard about his business, which was importing stuff from Italy, including really good olive oil, not like the crap that Tastee was bottling. (His words, not mine. I really didn't care.) I found out that he lived in Los Angeles. And that he had just bought a place that looked like an Italian villa, only it was sort of a fixer-upper. And it had a swimming pool. How cool was that?

This was the first time I'd ever been with a man who was older and sophisticated and smart and rich. Eddie was thirty-nine. A man. What a difference compared to the boys my own age that I'd known up until then. I was eighteen, but I would be nineteen in only five months. I was flattered that he didn't seem to think the age difference was such a big deal. Clearly he was completely turned on by me. It was like I had spent my whole life making myself beautiful for this moment, for capturing Eddie Bertoli. Of course, now, looking back, I can see that this was not the high point in my life that I thought it was at the time. But sitting there in that darkened restaurant, I was pretty excited by the way things were going.

I told him I had to work the next day, and he asked me what Wilson was paying me. I told him, and he scoffed at it. "I'll pay you twice that," he said. "Come work for me."

"When?" I asked, thrilled.

"Tomorrow," he said expansively.

"I can't do that," I said, thinking about what Dieter would say. There was only one more day of the show, and I was pretty sure Dieter wouldn't be happy about me jumping ship, leaving the Tastee people high and dry for their second day. "It wouldn't be fair to the Tastee people. I think they're counting on my being there."

Eddie stared at me for a moment, and then he said solemnly, "Honey, you are an upstanding young woman. I admire you for it."

I almost swooned. No one had ever noticed my being upstanding before. One thing led to another, and we ended up at his hotel room that night, and by the time we got there we could hardly keep our hands off each other. Too bad he lived in Los Angeles. I really wished he could be my boyfriend. He dropped me off at the apartment, and after I stepped inside I listened through the door to the sound of his footsteps as he walked back to his car. I heard the car door open, then close, then the engine started and it drove away. I listened for a long time, imagining I could still hear the car as it drove down the street. I listened until all I could hear was silence.

After the trade show I was offered a permanent job with Tastee Imports. Wilson had a dusty little third-floor office on Folsom Street, and I took the BART train to San Francisco and back every day, which made me feel grown-up and important. But the best thing about my job was that it wasn't home.

Wilson wasn't bad once you got to know him. He was trying to juggle every aspect of this little business, typing orders, writing letters, arguing with his warehouse people, even making little displays like that lame picnic-basket arrangement he had at the booth. As for the three suits, they vanished after the show. I think they went back to China, but I was never too clear about that. Once in a while I got someone on the phone who was impossible to understand, and I figured it was probably one of them. I'd just buzz Wilson and say, "It's for you." Fortunately the phone didn't ring all that much. I was there to look nice and make it appear that Wilson's office was a thriving enterprise. There was a steady stream of people who came to see him—the guys from the bank, the insurance agent, and Wilson's pals from U.S. Customs—and they all flirted with me. So did the postman and the delivery guys from UPS and Federal Express who came in every day and stopped to chat. I kept a magazine in my desk drawer to read when nothing else was going on. Overall, as jobs go, it was tolerable.

Eddie called me there every day. "Hi, babe," he'd say in his low, sexy growl, guaranteed to make me melt, and then he'd ramble on about how hot he thought I was. He told me I was a pink-and-gold confection. I didn't even know what a *confection* was. It's candy. He said that I was like a piece of candy. And he told me that he loved that my eyes had flecks of gold in them. Everyone else had always described my eyes as hazel green; Eddie saw flecks of gold. He loved my hair, and said it was honey-colored to match my name. He went on and on about how soft, how luscious, how irresistible I was. No one had ever talked about me like that. Even better, every few weeks he'd show up and surprise me, walking into Tastee Imports at closing time, and we'd go out for dinner and then to his hotel. This went on for months, and all I was getting at home was grief.

Naturally the moms and Dieter were all concerned about Eddie. They were like Muppet the time she smelled a mouse behind the stove. Their ears perked right up and they began circling around trying to pick up the scent. Of course Dieter had told them that Eddie was, and I quote, pushing forty, and that freaked them out. They all went into Protective Mode, reading all kinds of sinister things into his intentions. "Yeah," I told them, "he's going to carry me away and make me his sex slave." They didn't think that was funny.

Vivian tried to ask me about him, but I wouldn't give her the satisfaction of a heart-to-heart conversation about my love life. She soon gave that up and just rolled her eyes every time he was mentioned. To tell the truth, I was surprised when Vivian backed off. But she hadn't been herself for a while. She'd been dragging around, listless, tired, coughing, and complaining to anyone who would listen. I knew she wasn't feeling so hot when she asked Bobbie about vitamins. Bobbie knew all about vitamins. Every morning she tossed back an entire handful of them. And for years she'd been urging Vivian to take B vitamins to offset the damage of her drinking. So all of a sudden now Vivian wanted to know about vitamins. I could see Rose was worried about her, and I was too. It didn't seem like a good sign that she was suddenly interested in doing something healthy. So I guess that's why Vivian didn't have the energy to go after Eddie.

Bobbie took a different approach. When the others got on my case, she would say, "Oh, leave her alone, she's over eighteen," but later, in private, she asked me, "Just how old is this guy?" She tried to give me indirect advice by launching into a conversation about being too available.

"Vivian makes that mistake," Bobbie confided. "Vivian makes herself too available because she's worried about losing. But if a guy is taking you for granted, you should do just the opposite. You should become less available."

"Okay," I said, keeping everything expressionless. I wasn't going to get too emotionally involved in this conversation. She was trying to bring me in by talking about Vivian, but I was too smart for her. I wasn't going to bite.

"Becoming less available does two things. For one thing, it gives you time to step back and reevaluate things. You know, ask yourself is this the one?" She looked at me brightly. I just stared back at her.

"And the second thing?" I finally asked. Okay, I probably should have waited and made her say it without my asking.

"The second thing is that becoming less available turns you into catnip. Irresistible." So that was Bobbie's advice.

Rose just said, "Why doesn't this guy have a girlfriend in L.A.?"

I ignored everyone's comments. Eddie was a whole new experience for me, and I was hungry for new experiences. I was used to being with boys like Danny; Eddie was something altogether different. He was grown-up. He wasn't off playing air guitar or basketball. He was eager to be with me. He owned a suit. In fact he owned more than one suit, and he talked to business associates on his BlackBerry. He didn't talk about football or cars, or some lame minimum-wage job. He talked about Cremona Imports, or about his new house.

He talked a lot about his new house. It was his dream house, his Italian villa. Honestly, that's what he called it. His Italian villa. A classic Italian house to go with his Italian heritage. He described it so well that I could clearly picture it. Pink stucco, with a curving staircase, and a palm tree. And it had a swimming pool. It was pure Hollywood. When the work was completed, he'd have the house of his dreams. It sounded so romantic.

Then one day, during one of our usual phone conversations, Eddie just dropped it like a gift in my lap. He said, "Come to L.A." For a moment I was too surprised to say anything. Then I worried that if I said something, it might be the wrong thing. I mean, maybe he just meant I should visit him. Or move there to be near him. But on the other hand, maybe he really meant what I hoped he meant, that he wanted me to come live with him. I held my breath. "Come to L.A.," he repeated. "Quit your job. Move in here, babe. With me."

It's not surprising that I didn't need a moment's consideration to walk away from answering the phones at Tastee Imports. But I have to wonder now, looking back on things, that I made the decision between two heartbeats to move something like four hundred miles to Los Angeles, regardless of the fact that I didn't know anyone in L.A. except Eddie, and I knew precious little about him when it came to that. But at the time the thought was so intoxicating that my heart pounded in my head, and I could hardly hear myself tell Eddie of course I'd move there. Just as soon as I could. All I knew was that it sounded perfect. It was like something straight out of a movie.

Apparently some people have a smart little voice in their head that gives them good advice. Rose was all the time saying, "Listen to that little voice in your head. When it says something smells fishy, you'd better listen." But I didn't seem to have that smart little voice in my head. I just had the dumb voice that said, *Wow, I can't believe this is happening to me! It's like I'm in a movie!* So I quit Tastee. To hear Wilson, you'd think that no one had ever quit a job before, but I told him he probably would be happier with someone who could type, and after that he just sulked.

Now, as excited as I was, I wasn't foolish enough to think that everyone else would find this wildly romantic. I knew for certain that Rose wouldn't. Rose always rolled her eyes at anything romantic. She just didn't believe in it. And if Franny had been home, she probably would have had something sharp to say, though I wouldn't have listened to her, because I was too excited. But I was not prepared for Vivian's reaction. She went crazy. "What are you doing? Have you thought this through? How well do you know this guy?" Blah blah blah. All this was pretty funny, coming from the queen of the serial boyfriends. The woman whose entire life was a monument to Not Thinking Things Through. So I ignored her, and she decided she'd better bring in reinforcements. Her first reinforcement backfired, because it was Bobbie, who listened to Vivian's wild-eyed account and then told me earnestly that only I could know if this was the right decision for me. Thank you, Bobbie. At least someone thought I was an adult. But then Vivian got big-time reinforcement when Rose got home and told me sadly that I had holes in my head. Then Dieter came by for dinner, and naturally he chimed in.

Please.   You'd think I was joining a religious cult or moving to Uganda, instead of moving to a Hollywood villa with a swimming pool and a grown-up boyfriend.

Chapter 6

DIETER IS HERE. He did my nails.   Then he sorted through my magazines, ordering me not to move, to leave my hands flat on the blanket, fingers splayed out, while the polish dried. He held up each magazine to me.   Are you through with this? he'd ask.   Don't toss it, I told him.   I will look at it later, but it's too hard to read now and I never seem to get to it.   For some reason I can't read.   I think it's the morphine they're giving me that makes it impossible to read.   The words refuse to connect.   Just. One. Word. After. Another. Unrelated. Non-sequential.   Inconsequential.   Even the pictures are hard to make sense of.   There's a story in each one, but it is eluding me.   Dieter said okay and he stacked the magazines, making the pile neat, all facing the same way, all the corners lining up.

He brought me a cupcake from the little bakery he likes.   I say thank you, but I will give it to the nurse when he leaves.   He tells me he sent Honey a box of goodies.   What he likes to call a care package.   A bag of chocolate chip cookies, a pound of good coffee, and a black T-shirt from the cupcake shop.   It says SWEET *across the front in big pink letters.   He thought she'd get a kick out of it.   He's always trying so hard to be some kind of a dad to her.   Honey will love it, of course.   She will be thrilled to get something from Dieter.   I think she secretly believes he is her dad.   She refuses to consider anything else.   Honey is always strangely positive.   She's a very upbeat person.   I think this is because she lives in a constant state of denial.   She has since she was a little girl. She never sees the world the way it really is.*

When I first got pregnant I suggested to Dieter one night that maybe this baby was his.   I'd had a little too much to drink; otherwise I don't think I would have said that. Because he was too eager for it to be so. He latched right onto it. I suppose there's an outside chance that he could be Honey's dad, but that's a way outside chance. It's much more likely he isn't. I'm sure it was AJ. But that loser is out of the question. So it's just as well that Dieter thinks there is that possibility. And meanwhile AJ will never know.

Honey makes a big issue out of this. She doesn't realize that she has it pretty good. The best of both worlds. She has all the good of a dad in Dieter, and none of the bad of that toxic loser AJ. And she doesn't have to be around Dieter and his goodness all the time. I hate to say it, but all that goodness gets old.

It got old when he and I were dating. That was so long ago and so much has happened since then that thinking about it is like thinking about another person's life. Dating is a tricky thing. It starts out well enough, even euphoric, but the euphoria never lasts. Pretty soon there are expectations, expectations that you'll be there when you say you will, that you'll feel everything you need to feel, that you'll say the right thing at the right time. And the next thing you know he's hurt and reproachful, and all you can do is stand there with your hands at your sides while he asks all the questions. It doesn't help much to think of the good answers later.

Chapter 7

EDDIE PICKED ME UP at the airport. It was thrilling to get off the plane, walk down the corridor, come out to face a wall of expectant people, and to see my very own boyfriend standing there among them. Eddie took my bag in one hand and cupped my elbow with the other, and we walked together through the crowds of people to pick up my suitcases in the baggage claim.

What a difference from a couple of hours before, when I was dropped at the airport. Rose couldn't come because she had to cover at the Last Stop, so she said goodbye when I got into the car. But the other three came with me. Vivian was all high drama, with tears and hugs. Dieter and Bobbie were quiet and sweet, and they each gave me a big hug. Bobbie slipped me a CD she made for me of her favorite playlist, and Dieter gave me a couple of twenties in case I needed cash. Then I waved to them all and went through security. When I turned around for a last look, they were still there, watching me, Bobbie and Dieter on either side of Vivian, with their arms around her. The three stooges. It was going to be good to start a new life.

While Eddie stood off to the side talking on his cell phone, I kept an eye on the baggage carousel, watching for my bags. I was so proud to claim them. It was a nice feeling to use them as they were intended, not just as storage for my clothes. I was feeling very sophisticated as we wheeled them outside into the white-hot sun.

Los Angeles. I was finally in Los Angeles. Even the name sounded foreign and romantic. And it looked unlike anything I'd ever known. You'd never mistake it for El Cerrito or Berkeley or San Francisco. Even the light looked different in Los Angeles, the sky not so much blue as glowing white, and everything a little hazy, like a bleached-out old color photograph.

Eddie had a black Mercedes-Benz. It was the first time I'd ever been in a car that luxurious. Inside it was all upholstered in soft black leather, and the wooden dashboard was so glossy that it looked like plastic. When the door closed with a muted *thunk*, even the air was hushed, except for a musical tone, soft but insistent, that gently reminded us to fasten our seat belts. It was a long way from Vivian's old Honda, with its rattles and its rust hole on the trunk.

That first drive is just a blur now, because it was all so new to me. We drove on the freeway, and it was thrilling to realize how enormous this city was. Los Angeles seemed to spread out forever. But the best thing was my first sighting of a row of palm trees. That completely said *Los Angeles* to me. And there were rows of them everywhere, entire streets lined with tall, slender palm trees. Yes, I know, there are palm trees in Northern California. Franny made a big point of telling me that later, but like I explained to her, it's not the same. Not like the stately rows along the streets in L.A. I wanted Eddie to get off the freeway and drive along one of them, but he said it wasn't a very good neighborhood. Los Angeles is so exotic that even the poor neighborhoods get rows of palm trees.

Finally we got off the freeway, and I was amazed to see that there was a lake right in front of us, with beautiful water geysers shooting straight up from the middle. Eddie said this was Echo Lake. When I thought of Los Angeles I had never pictured it having a lake. But it does. Then we drove past the lake and up into the hills.

Now, I should stop here and explain that I had been hearing nothing but the villa this and the villa that, so I really had some big expectations. From the way Eddie had been talking about it I was picturing a big Hollywood house with a huge gorgeous pool and there would be palm trees and flowers everywhere. But first of all, this wasn't Hollywood. It wasn't even the seedy part of Hollywood. It was near Hollywood. There is a difference. This was a part of Los Angeles called

Silver Lake. And to give Silver Lake its due, in itself it is a nice enough place. Yes, there are palm trees. And there are some attractive houses, and there are flowers, and on that first day, my first day in L.A., the Jacaranda trees were decked out in their purple display. But Hollywood it wasn't.

And that was just the location. The villa itself was a pretty big disappointment all on its own. Eddie wasn't kidding when he called it a fixer-upper. It was a big house of cracked and faded pink stucco, with broken green shutters hanging every which way. It sat up above the street, surrounded by a jumble of weeds, pale blue blooming Plumbago, and some scrawny yellow-flowering succulents. It did have its own palm tree though. We stepped carefully up the broken path way and Eddie set down my suitcases, fumbled in his pocket, and pulled out a big jangly bunch of keys. He peered at them, fanning them out on his palm, until finally he found the right one, fit it into the lock, and opened the door with a flourish. We stepped into a large foyer with a ceiling that soared high above us. The golden light of late afternoon was streaming through tall windows and onto a stairway that curved up to the second floor. Everywhere there were sawhorses, tools, boxes of nails, stacks of wood and drywall board. There was a ladder, a generator, and thick orange extension cords snaking around the floor, dusty with sawdust. I wondered how Eddie lived in all this mess. There was no furniture, and no curtains for privacy, just all this construction. I had grown up watching Rose and Bobbie remodel the Welcome Home Motel, so I knew perfectly well how unlivable this mess really was.

Eddie led me through the kitchen, though you'd never guess that's what it was. It was just another bare room with gray walls and white tape on the seams. Cartons were stacked at one end. "The cabinets," said Eddie, waving in their general direction. I couldn't exactly admire them because they were all boxed up, so I didn't say anything. He led me out the back door and onto the patio, an expanse of cracked and uneven pavement next to a small swimming pool. So much for the big Hollywood pool. Not only was it pathetically small, it was dry as a bone. Instead of cool blue water, it held dead leaves, beer and soda cans, a filthy gray sneaker, and a flattened cardboard box. Eddie didn't even notice that I had stopped in my tracks as I exhaled in disappointment looking at that empty pool. He continued over to the garage, opened a side door, and turned to look at me expectantly. I couldn't think of anything to say, so I just walked on over to him and we went up the stairs to find ourselves in a hot, airless studio apartment over the garage. Eddie unlatched a window, grunting as he pushed it open. The fresh breeze felt wonderful. The room had a double bed, a table and two chairs, a TV, and an armchair, and along one wall there was a kitchenette, with a green laminate counter. There was a door ajar that led to a tiny bathroom with a shower. There was no bathtub; there would be no long hot bubble baths in this apartment. "This," Eddie said gesturing expansively with his arm, "is my temporary apartment."

I couldn't think of a word to say. He turned away from me and opened the refrigerator, took out a bottle of wine, found a corkscrew in a drawer, and uncorked the bottle. He opened a cupboard that looked almost empty and took out a couple of wineglasses that he held by the crossed stems in the same hand that held the neck of the bottle. "We'll have a housewarming party," he said with a smile, waggling his eyebrows. He ushered me back down the stairs to the patio by the pool, where there was a green metal table and chairs.

And there we sat while the sun went down, sipping wine. Gradually I began to feel better about things. I could see that one day the villa would be finished and beautiful, and it would eventually have a real pool filled with actual water. The wine made us feel light-headed, and of course we started getting all tingly over each other. Eventually we made it back upstairs, and by this time we couldn't keep our hands off each other so we fell right into it. We made love and then we lolled around on the bed, and then we got up and made some sandwiches, and then we made love again. It was strange but useful having everything in one room. The bed, the food, all right there. Perfect for when all you wanted was sex and food.

That first weekend went by quickly. I felt almost weak with all the lovemaking and the excitement of desiring each other so much. I wasn't even hungry and could have done without the pizza for dinner Saturday and Mexican takeout for lunch on Sunday. Then on Monday Eddie had to go to work. The night before he told me that he was counting on me to hold down the fort. That's what he actually said. Hold down the fort. No one my age would ever say hold down the fort. Eddie cracked me up. Anyway, he said he would let the workmen into the house first thing in the morning, but I needed to lock up after them when they left at four, and to stick my head in and look around at their work a couple of times during the day to make sure they weren't stealing the light fixtures or something. So it began to dawn on me that I was a real partner here, and that felt good.

After Eddie left the next morning, I went back to sleep until the banging of hammers and the whine of the saw in the villa became impossible to ignore. For a moment I was back in that little house of Danny's with Martin banging on the walls of the next room. Then I woke up completely, to hot and sweaty sheets and the bright sunshine of a Southern California morning. It was going to be a very warm day. I rolled out of bed, made some coffee, and brought it down to sit by the empty pool. I kicked off my flip-flops and spread my toes in the sun. Maybe I would be able to talk Eddie into filling that pool sooner rather than later. I had already asked him about that but he insisted it would have to wait until the house was finished because it was too hard to keep out the construction debris and he didn't want to be constantly fishing shit out of the pool. Maybe if I told him I'd do the fishing. I moved my chair to the other side of the patio, where it was shaded from the sun. There was a lull in the hammering, and I could hear a mockingbird in a nearby tree, singing its complicated song.

After my initial disappointment in the place, I was growing philosophical about it. In fact, the more I thought about it, the more I could see that things were pretty good, even though I was living in a stuffy little apartment instead of a Hollywood villa. It sure beat living in Rose's apartment, crammed in there with Vivian and Rose and Bobbie. And it was exciting to be in Los Angeles. L.A. I was already calling it L.A., like a native. And being here with Eddie made me feel sophisticated and appreciated. He treated me like I was some kind of goddess.

Chapter 8

*THE VIETNAMESE NURSE is back.   She told me her name,
but I couldn't make sense of it, a series of syllables, short and
abrupt, that sounded odd to my ear, so it slipped from my
memory as soon as she said it, and now it's gone on too long
and I'm embarrassed to ask her again.   She was here for days,
and then she was inexplicably gone.   She looks in my eyes and
gives me a smile as she sits me up.   A cheerful whirlwind of
activity, her hands never stop moving, shaking the water
pitcher to see if it's empty, picking up the untouched food tray,
setting aside the unopened yogurt so that I can eat it later
(though I tell her I won't), straightening the bedding,
freshening my world with her hands and her smile.   She
explains that the mysterious sticks in the vase are plum twigs,
just starting to blossom out with spring flowers.   She brings
the vase closer to me so I can admire the buds.   Most are tight
and pink and glossy, but some have burst open into pink-and-
white flowers, like popcorn from a kernel.   She says that
Bobbie brought them in.*

*She is much more cheerful than the hefty blond nurse.
That one, built like a wall of bricks, has the arms of a wrestler,
and she frowns while she works.   She's so serious I want to
say to her, Unwind darlin', you only live once.   But maybe
she can't help it.   Some people have eyebrows that they have
plucked into a perpetual frown.*

*At night there is a boy nurse with red hair.   My first
boyfriend was a redheaded kid, a senior in high school when I
was a sophomore.   He was crazy about his car, an old hippie
VW bus that used to belong to his uncle.   It was orange with a
peace sign crudely painted in green on the side.   Jimmy, that
was his name, painted over the orange and the peace sign so*

that the bus was all tan and green and black camouflage. The hippie uncle freaked out about that. He strongly objected to the military connotation. But there wasn't much he could do. He had given the thing to Jimmy—it wasn't his anymore. Everyone has trouble with letting go.

We got it on in the back of the bus, where Jimmy had taken out the backseats and spread an old sleeping bag. My mom hated Jimmy. He didn't come over and kiss her ass saying yes ma'am and may I please speak to your daughter ma'am. He just honked his horn for me out front, and that made her crazy. She told me I couldn't see him anymore, so I went out the window at night and met him at the corner by the gas station. When she found out she slapped me, and then when I sassed back she got out her wooden yardstick, it had WOLFE HARDWARE *printed on it, and whacked me with that on the back of my legs. I hate to think what she would have done if she had known I was screwing him in the back of that dirty bus.*

I was crazy about Jimmy. He was all sinew and bone, not a bit of fat on him, and he stood tall and ramrod straight. By contrast I felt soft and small next to him, like a little animal that he could pick up and cuddle. I told him that once and he laughed at me, but after that he called me his wild little animal. Then he graduated and joined the navy and went to San Diego. And that was the end of it. We wrote once or twice, but somehow without seeing him it was hard to maintain all those feelings. I couldn't keep an image of him in my head. I kept forgetting what he looked like, and I had to look at his picture, the one from school with his graduation cap perched precariously on his head, to try to recapture him. That picture got more and more difficult to penetrate, and finally I couldn't find him in it anymore.

But that happens. Even with AJ. After all these years and after all that drama, I can hardly picture him. But for some reason I can still remember his smell. The laundry-clean white cotton T-shirt scent and the toasty smell of his skin underneath. Funny how one man's smell is delicious and another just seems a little off. And it's not about sweat either.

Sweat is just another layer. It's something underneath, and it is either right or not. I've been thinking about AJ a lot.   I guess that's because I've got too much time here.   What else am I going to do?   The memories of those days are tainted by a kind of vague anxiety, but I keep coming back to him.

We had a lot in common.   Both the black sheep of our families.   He said to me, So you think you're the only one with a Nazi parent?   His dad wouldn't allow dancing—it was against their religion.   Fun was the work of the devil.   AJ beat his way out of there as soon as he was old enough to leave, and never looked back.

Chapter 9

THAT FIRST DAY after Eddie left I realized I had no idea what to do with myself. I went back upstairs and showered and dressed, and then went on Facebook to see what everyone was doing. Not much. I called Franny, but her phone was turned off. She was probably in class. I pictured her wearing her glasses and sitting with other students in one of those steeply pitched auditorium classrooms, everyone with their eyes on a teacher on the podium below. She would be taking notes on a yellow pad. And her turned-off phone would be in her purse at her feet.

It was odd to think of her so far away and disconnected from me. First she went off to college, and then I went off to LA, and now I missed her more than ever. She was a distant voice on the phone and unfamiliar pictures on Facebook, where once we had been like sisters, raised together, sharing everything. We even used to sleep together. Not all the time, but when my mom went out I stayed over with them and Rose put me to bed with Franny. Franny complained about this, but I would wake up in the morning to find myself curled up in her arms, my back to her chest, spooning. Maybe we were able to be close because we were so different.

Though Franny liked to remind me that she was older than I was, it wasn't by much, and at school we were in the same grade, and usually in the same classroom. We walked home from school together, and every day she would come up with suggestions for what to do that afternoon. She was always full of ideas. Once in a while she'd ask me what I wanted to do, just to appear democratic, but then she'd talk me into her idea, which was okay because her ideas were usually interesting. She'd start messing around in the kitchen, and Rose would

say, "Girls, what are you up to? Do you have a plan?"
because to Rose plans were important, and Franny always had
an answer. She'd say something like "we're going to play
grocery store," and we would set up the kitchen table so that it
was our shop counter, and put all kinds of stuff from the
pantry on it, and then we'd beg Rose to come in and "buy"
something from us. Rose grumbled a lot about that, but she
usually went along with it.

Franny had lots of games like that. A fair number of them
involved dressing up and pretending things. One of our
favorites was to be doctors in a hospital. Bobbie's little dog
Muppet would let us dress her up, and we'd pretend she was
our patient. Sometimes we'd spend an afternoon grooming
Muppet and putting ribbons in her hair. Once we even tried to
put nail polish on her toenails, but she struggled because she
didn't like her feet to be touched, so we got pink nail polish on
the bathroom rug and Rose made us clean the entire
bathroom—the tile, the grout, the walls, the toilet,
everything—as a punishment for being certifiably stupid. Her
words. We also tried to teach Muppet various tricks, like
jumping through a hoop or dancing in a circle on her hind
legs. The only thing Muppet refused to do was play dead,
because she was too interested in what we were doing to lay
still.

Some days we'd be walking home and Franny would say
"today we'll do makeup." We'd slip into my mom's room and
sample her cosmetics. Little did I know then how useful that
would be later in life. We'd experiment, trying different
combinations of eye shadow and eyeliner, and putting on lots
of mascara. Or we'd go to Bobbie and she'd let us try on her
lipsticks, one after another, and we'd wipe them off with
Kleenex so that pretty soon the bathroom counter was covered
with bloody-looking tissues. Sometimes Bobbie joined us.
Once she bought us each a set of false eyelashes and showed
us how to trim them to fit, then carefully apply a thin line of
glue, and put them in place. By the time we were old enough
to wear makeup in public we were pretty good at it. Rose
didn't allow us to wear makeup to school, but she didn't

always see me before I left, so I have to say I usually got away with it.   Franny had to go out the door under Rose's eagle eye, but Rose shouldn't have worried, because even though Franny put it on when she got to school, she didn't wear very much.   Franny didn't have a very high opinion of girls who wore a lot of makeup. She said they looked slutty, though she always followed that by saying immediately that I was an exception, that because I was so pretty makeup couldn't make a difference. It's funny that everyone thought I was so pretty and no one talked about her at all, because now that we're grown up I think it's become the opposite. She always looks elegant, with tasteful makeup, and her hair is glossy and sleek and never a bit out of place. When she goes to work she wears heels, a white shirt, and a blazer.   Look at me, in my jeans skirt and a tank top and my hair that never stays in its ponytail. But she's interning in a big public relations office and people expect her to look like that, and if I tried to look like that, they'd probably just laugh.

Franny used to say that I was slovenly. For the longest time I thought that was a compliment. *Slovenly* sounds a little like *lovely*, don't you think? Anyway, when I finally found out it was not at all complimentary my feelings were hurt, but she said not to take it personally, it was just a statement of fact.   When Franny said things like that I usually couldn't come up with an answer. She liked to point out that I forgot to brush my teeth and that I frequently had pillow hair, and that when I was younger, if Rose didn't brush my hair every night it ended up in one huge knot. Which actually happened once, when I was seven. Rose went to Bakersfield to be with her sister when she was dying of breast cancer, and no one brushed my hair for a week. Finally my mom realized that we had a situation. That's what she called it, a situation. By this time she couldn't get a comb through the tangle, and when she tried I was yelling for her to stop, so she got angry and said forget it, be a mess if you want. Well, that was upsetting, because I didn't want to be a mess, and so finally we came to an agreement. She rented a movie about a pig who talked, and we watched it together as I sat on her lap and she very slowly, very gently brushed my hair, coaxing it out of its tangle. The movie was almost over by the time she finished, but when it was finally all brushed through, she said I was beautiful like a princess, and she announced, "We're going to keep it like this." From that day on until well into high school either she or Rose braided my hair every single night before I went to bed, in one long braid down the back, so that I wouldn't get tangled bed hair. There were two nice things about that. One was it made my hair beautifully curly when I took the braid out in the morning. And the other was that it made me feel loved.

Sitting by the dirty empty pool I spread my hands out in front of me and examined them. A manicure. That would pass the time. I got out my nail polish remover and began to clean up my nails. If Franny were with me she would point out that I needed to stop biting them. Someday I would try.

While the polish dried I tried to call Madison, and she answered, but she told me she was at work, so she wasn't supposed to be answering her phone. She asked me to send her a text. So I sent one: *Im bord.* Then I decided to go for a walk. But going for a walk meant more work than I had anticipated, because Silver Lake seemed to be nothing but hills. I was soon out of breath, and the heat made me sweat like a pig. I trudged back home and showered again. Now it was afternoon. I wished I knew someone I could call. Someone to talk to, to do things with. I went down to look at what Eddie's workmen were doing. They all smiled and said *hola* and went back to work. I watched for a few minutes, and then I went back upstairs and watched TV. Pretty soon it would be four, I would lock up after the workmen, and *Oprah* would be on.

It was a huge relief when Eddie got home later that evening, although the first thing he wanted to do was walk through the villa to see what the workmen had done that day. Then we went out for dinner. It wasn't until we got back again that we really had some time to hold each other, and I could tell him how much I missed him.

This went on for days.   Each day was just like the one before it, except each day seemed longer than the one before. Finally on Thursday, when I was sitting on the front steps of the villa, a girl about my age came out of the house next door and walked over to a car parked right in front of the steps where I was sitting. I was thrilled to think someone my age might actually live next door.

"Hi, you live there?" I asked.

"Nope, I'm the housecleaner," she said.

"Oh," I answered, disappointed. "I was hoping you did because I'm new here, I don't know a soul, and I'm bored out of my skull."

Well, that was as good a conversational opening as any. The girl's name was Sandy, and I liked her smile. She sat down on the steps with me and pulled out a cigarette, and pretty soon we were like old friends.   But then she was gone, because she was meeting someone for drinks, and there I was, alone again.   But now at least I knew one person in Los Angeles, one person other than Eddie.

That night Eddie told me he had to leave the next morning to be gone for a week. He explained that he needed to be on the road a lot for his import company, and that I should expect him to be gone for a week at a time, because he traveled all over the western states selling his Italian olive oil and his balsamic vinegar and his packages of dried pastas, his boxes of panettone, and all the other stuff he imported from Italy. Terrific. Now I not only had time to kill during the days but the nights as well. I needed to figure out how to get hold of Sandy. I was annoyed with myself because I hadn't thought to ask her for her phone number. I didn't even know her last name.

I went for a walk every day. There wasn't much else to do. I'd usually start out by heading down to Sunset Boulevard. I could turn one way and follow Sunset into the nearby neighborhood of Echo Park, shabby but colorful, full of artists and Mexican immigrants, or turn the other way toward chic Los Feliz. Either way, there was always something to look at on Sunset. There were countless restaurants. You could find pretty much anything here, from vegan to sushi to kabob, and most places had outdoor seating along the sidewalk and water bowls for the diners' dogs. There were hipster bars, gay bars, and a few of the old-style bars that reminded me of the Last Stop. There were vintage shops with racks of clothes on the sidewalk, a huge hair salon that looked like an art gallery, lots of interesting graffiti, and a little hookah place with old men sitting out front, their white mustaches bright against skin as brown as walnuts. I'd stop and watch a yoga class through big plate-glass windows that lined the sidewalk and think of Bobbie doing her downward dog. I'd stop and lean on the railing that overlooked Silver Lake Boulevard, idly watching the cars passing below. And I'd usually end up at one of the Mexican stands for tacos and some watermelon, sitting on a nearby retaining wall to eat and watch the people passing by. You couldn't be bored here.

After I'd had my fill of Sunset Boulevard, I'd walk back up the hilly streets to Silver Lake reservoir. I'd walk to the dog park and watch people throw tennis balls for their dogs. And sometimes I'd just walk around the neighborhoods. I think I covered every street in Silver Lake and Echo Park. And all this walking got me in great shape. After a few weeks I could walk all over the hills and never get out of breath.

Mostly I would look at everyone's front yards. Some houses had nice gardens, all planned and groomed. Others had nothing but weeds and overgrown bushes. There was one with statues of deer in the front yard, and lots of white gravel. Another was mostly cactus. I also met the people who went with these front yards. There was a lady that I saw regularly watering her garden. Her name was Gail and she always wanted to talk, mostly about property values. She knew what every house on her block should cost. I thought it was an odd way to look at a block of houses. I looked at a house and saw a red front door and deer statues. She looked at it and saw Six Hundred and Fifty Grand.

There was another lady I saw once in a while, a very old lady who walked slowly with a cane when she came down to get her mail. Her mailbox was a little blue wooden house perched on a pole with a wooden cutout of a bird on top, and it was probably nice when it was new, but now it looked like it was going to fall apart any minute. Just like her house, which wasn't in much better shape. Martin would have pounced on it. It was a real fixer-upper, something he could have sunk his teeth into. The lady's name was Mrs. Hansen. Except at my Catholic high school, where the brothers insisted we call all the teachers by their last names, most people introduce themselves by their first names, even when they're old. But this old lady introduced herself as Mrs. Hansen. Sometimes I picked up her newspaper or her mail and brought it up to her front porch. She loved that. Then she'd invite me in, but I always said I had somewhere to go. She said she used to work in wardrobe for Warner Brothers, and before that for MGM, but she didn't do that anymore. She didn't do much of anything, I imagine, because she moved so very slowly. Like a snail. Taking all day just to get somewhere. Sometimes when I was walking by I could see into her front room through her open front door, and though it was dark through the screen door, I could just make her out slowly pushing an aluminum walker, with little wheels that squeaked as she slowly shuffled by. *Squeak SQUEAK. Squeak SQUEAK. Squeak SQUEAK.* If it were me, that squeak would drive me nuts.

Before he went away, Eddie left a hundred bucks on the dresser for anything I needed. It was when I decided to go out for groceries that it dawned on me that without a car to haul the stuff back home I would have a hard time of it. But I did have Eddie's money, so I called a taxi. I felt almost rich riding back home in a musty cab vibrating with Bollywood music, behind the turbaned Sikh driver. After that I always used a taxi for grocery shopping.

Mostly though when I wasn't walking I was lounging next to the empty pool and reading magazines. There was an old bird feeder hanging from a pole on the patio by the pool, so one day I bought some birdseed for it, and it was immediately hit on by some tiny brown birds. It was just like old times when Franny was in her Scientist Phase.

The Scientist Phase began some time during sixth grade. I think it got its start when Franny discovered an interesting book in the school library. It showed the human body with acetate overlays, and she checked this book out several times. The best part was the page that started with the skeleton, and then you turned an acetate page and suddenly there were some of the organs in place. Then you turned over another acetate page and there were more organs in place. Next came the muscles, and finally the skin. Since this was a book for kids, the man in the picture was wearing a green bathing suit, sort of a Speedo. We were disappointed the first time we looked at it, because we were hoping to see a penis. But Franny loved the book anyway.

Science experiments brought out the best in Franny. They were right up her alley. In the seventh grade she entered the school's science fair with an experiment to test mouthwash, to see which brand was most effective. It involved little petri dishes, swabbing the insides of our mouths, and several kinds of mouthwash. I always thought the point of mouthwash was to cover up the nasty smell of bad breath, but apparently it's all about killing germs. Because, as Franny pointed out, germs are what cause the bad smell. Who knew? Of course, the whole family was riveted by this experiment. You'd think Franny was discovering the cure for cancer. They all checked her petri dishes every day and exclaimed over the results, and Rose made a big point of buying Listerine after that because it was the winner. Then Vivian told Franny that she saw on *Oprah* that germs were actually good for us. Rose said that may be, but rinse with mouthwash anyway.

The science phase was probably more fun for Franny than it was for me. In our biggest project we set up bird feeders and observed birds. Franny had read about the Chimp Lady,

Jane somebody who studied chimpanzees. This person spent every day for years watching chimps in their natural environment, and Franny wanted us to do the same with our finches and doves and hummingbirds, taking notes about them on a clipboard. Well, Franny took notes. I was supposed to be drawing the birds we saw. There were a lot of chickadees and house finches, but I preferred to draw flamingos. And when I got bored with that I'd move on to hairstyles and shoes. To my mind the bird feeders were just plain boring after a while, and I finally revolted. Franny moved on to cooking, which when you think about it, wasn't all that different from science experiments.

She was big on cooking all through middle school. Rose said we could have the run of the kitchen as long as we cleaned things up. Our notion of cleanup was sloppy by any standards, but as long as we made a half-hearted stab at it, Rose was mollified, even though she grumbled the whole time she cleaned after us. We began with brownies, then chocolate chip cookies, and then we moved on to cakes, with moderately satisfactory results, though our cakes tended to be lopsided and not tall and fluffy like the ones you see pictured on cake-mix boxes. Then we tackled what Franny called real food. We made macaroni and cheese, and tuna casserole. Tacos. Roast chicken and mashed potatoes. Once we made a huge pot of chili. Rose loved this phase because we were making dinner, and she was glad to turn that job over to someone else.

Then Franny decided she should worry about gaining weight. She said she didn't like the way her stomach stuck out, and she worried that she was going to get big like Rose, and I had to remind her that she wasn't related to Rose. Not that way, anyway. I told her she looked normal, and then we both took off our clothes and stood there next to each other in the mirror in our underpants, comparing our bodies. We did this from time to time. It had started some years before when I began to get breasts, and Franny was curious to see them. My rounding buds were a big source of interest and a new body awareness, two growing shapes to wear proudly in front. They took some getting used to, but were a kind of status symbol, setting me apart from the other little girls, who had flat sexless nipples on their skinny chests. My breasts had also become tender and uncomfortable, and I complained that it hurt when I ran in PE. No one would guess looking at the soft mounds that jiggling them would be so painful. So Franny was curious, and we looked at each other from time to time, and finally, to her relief, her breasts began to emerge.

So she worried about gaining weight, and we stood side by side in our underwear in front of the mirror. My stomach was soft and rounded, and compared to me and my curves she looked sturdy and sleek. I don't know how that translated to overweight in her mind, but she decided then and there that her cooking experiments would switch to salads. Maybe she thought that a diet sounded more grown-up. Of course, if anyone needed to diet, it was Rose, who had become as big as a house, to quote Bobbie, but dieting wasn't part of Rose's program, if you know what I mean. Still, she went along with it, saying that salads would be good for all of us.

Meanwhile my breasts were getting bigger and bigger, and even Rose commented on that. "What are you feeding her?" she said dryly to Vivian when she didn't realize that I was within earshot. I was the only girl I knew in middle school who wore a D-cup bra.

Franny probably would have been able to identify the little brown birds in my feeder by the pool. I just called them finches. They would perch in a nearby lemon tree and take turns dashing to the feeder to pull out a sunflower seed and fly back to the tree to hull it. Once I was standing near the feeder when one of the finches flew boldly to it. I could see its round bright eye, black and shining, as it looked at me. Then it took a seed and flew to the lemon tree. It was so busy, so bustling, so sure of itself. I wondered how it knew what to do. Did mother birds show their babies how to dine at a feeder? To take the seed quickly and fly immediately back to the safety of the lemon tree? Or did they somehow simply know to do this?

Watching the birds left me with a sad, empty feeling. I missed Franny and Madison. If I were home, we could go to Telegraph Avenue in Berkeley and check out the hippie street vendors, or walk around the university pretending we were students there. Or take the BART train to San Francisco and go to Chinatown and find cute flip-flops from Korea and have dim sum for lunch. Or we could go shopping downtown. Not necessarily to buy anything, but to try lots of things on. I was even missing Danny and Ryan and Matthew. I kept thinking nostalgically of Danny's dumpy little house in El Cerrito. Even with Martin around too much of the time working on the house, and with Ryan and Matthew there playing basketball at all hours, even with Danny's disappearing act, it still seemed good in retrospect. I sort of forgot all the bad stuff, and kept thinking about how the sun poured in through the bedroom window, and how good it felt to wake up to Danny, and how much fun we had. Now I was beginning to wonder if I had made a bad decision to walk away. After all, he was just being honest with me. And he was right. We shouldn't have tried to live together. It was dumb to make that kind of commitment. But we could have continued to see each other. Maybe I had made a really foolish mistake to let him go. I just couldn't shake my memories of some of the fun times we had together, the laughter, the sex, and the dancing.

Eddie wasn't the sort of person who went out dancing. He was too old. I told this to Franny when we talked on the phone, and she said, "That's the price you pay when you get yourself a silverback." Just the sort of thing Franny would say. She explained that a silverback is a gorilla, a mature male gorilla. "Eddie's not a gorilla," I told her, but she didn't pay any attention. She called him my silverback all the time after that. But just because he didn't dance didn't mean we didn't have fun. Eddie and I went out to dinner to nice places, and we had great conversations when we lay on the bed together after sex. He would tell me things about himself. He told me once that he had a bad temper, but I couldn't imagine that. I had never seen any sign of it. It's strange to get to know someone who refers to things in his life that you have no clue about. Eddie had years and years of life before I came along, so I had a huge amount of things to learn about him. I wished I knew all about everything, so I could be the Knowing Partner, nodding and knowing all about the bad temper, but at least I had the warm feeling that comes from being confided in. He said he expected that I would see his temper one day. That was a way of saying that the relationship would last. That we would be together with enough time and enough intimacy for me to see that temper.

Finally it was Thursday again. I sat waiting for Sandy on the steps right in front of her car. This time she didn't have to go meet someone for drinks, and I didn't have Eddie coming home that night, so she invited me to come over to her house. Though, as she explained, strictly speaking it wasn't her house. And strictly speaking the house had only just been built and it wasn't quite finished inside. But it was in the Hollywood Hills and it was gorgeous. No one was supposed to be living there, but she knew the guy who was building it, and he said she could stay there. She got it rent-free, and in exchange he had someone there to keep an eye on it. That was what you call a sweet deal.

I had to lock up the villa at four, so we hung out by the empty pool, and then I waved goodbye to the workmen, locked up, and we got into her car. She had some errands to do, but I was fine with that. It was more entertaining than anything I had done all week. First we dropped off clothes at the cleaners for the guy next door. She told me that the people she worked for paid her to do this for them. Amazing.

Then we stopped at some guy's house because she had left her jacket there the night before. His name was Kyle. We sat around in Kyle's living room for a while, smoking a joint and talking about Sandy's boyfriend, Marcos, who was a DJ. Kyle had worked with Marcos for a while, and you could tell he wished he still worked with him and shared some of his success. Kyle looked like a real loser. Marcos had been in New York for a while now, and Sandy missed him, so between the two of them, the mood of the room pretty much took a nosedive. After we exhausted that subject, there wasn't much else to talk about, so we talked about nothing much for a while, and then we were getting hungry and he was going out, so we left and went to the grocery store to pick up something we could make for dinner. We got two rib-eye steaks, a bag of frozen French fries, a bag of salad greens, and a huge bag of M&M's. The candy was an impulse buy, from a bin next to the cashier. Obviously we were still stoned. Our last stop was a liquor store, where Sandy bought a six-pack of beer and a bottle of merlot. By the time we got to the house it was pitch-dark.

You could tell it was a beautiful house, even in the dark. It wasn't a wreck like Eddie's villa. It was modern, all straight lines and big windows, and overlooked the city. When Sandy unlocked the door we could smell the new-house smell of fresh paint. We stepped into the pitch-black foyer, where we could see across the room and out a window to a view of the city sprawled below, sparkling with lights. It was magical. I walked in the dark toward the window while Sandy groped around for the light.

"Where's the damn switch?" she muttered.

Suddenly I found myself stepping blindly into nothing— the floor had disappeared in the dark, and I dropped into the void, landing on a soft carpet. It wasn't a long drop, maybe five feet, but still, it was a stunning surprise. The light came on.

"Where'd you go?" Sandy asked slowly, clearly spooked.

Now I could see that I was sprawled on the floor of the living room, which was on a lower level than the foyer. There were stairs down to the living room, but I had stepped right off the edge of the foyer, out into thin air. Sandy came to the edge and stared down at me. Then we began to laugh. We were both still a little stoned, so that made it even funnier. She came down the stairs doubled over laughing and sat down on the floor beside me while we howled. We almost peed in our pants. Finally we pulled ourselves together. "Jeez," I said, "there should be a fucking railing there." "No kidding," Sandy said. And we started laughing all over again.

Now that I had Sandy to pal around with, things were a little better. It was strange, the way my life divided in two. There was my time spent with Eddie on the one hand, and my time without him on the other. When he wasn't around I was mostly bored, except when I was with Sandy. She introduced me to some of her friends, and she got me a false ID so I could get into the bars and clubs with them. My new ID was a Texas driver's license with a picture of a strawberry blonde who might have looked a little like me if you didn't look too closely. I was tempted to tell Eddie about my Texas self, but something held me back. I figured I'd better stick to using it only when I went out with Sandy and her friends. For one thing, I wasn't sure how Eddie would react. For another, I had the feeling that the fancy restaurants that Eddie liked were not at all like the clubs and bars that will overlook just about anything if you are young and pretty and stylish. I was afraid that they would look a little too closely at the license and then take it away from me. So I never told Eddie about it, and this became one more way that we were beginning to live in two different worlds.

When I went out with Sandy and her friends we did a lot more than just go to bars and clubs. Once we went to a gallery opening, where we ate crackers and stared at huge canvases smeared with gobs of black paint. We went out for little three-inch *carne asada* tacos from a tiny take-out place in Echo Park. We ate sushi downtown, where food looked like jewelry and didn't taste anything like you would expect from raw fish. We sat on someone's patio overlooking the city, gazing at the grid of lights spreading out in the dark below, breathing in the fragrance of star jasmine. We went shopping at two in the morning for ice cream and chocolate sauce. We went skinny-dipping in someone's parents' pool up in Sherman Oaks while the parents were at a medical conference in Atlanta. We braved the choked traffic of the Coast Highway down to

Laguna Beach and walked on the hard, wet sand, our feet lapped by silver waves. And sometimes we simply hung out at the house that Sandy was house-sitting. Just about anything we did was better than me sitting at home alone and watching TV.

Chapter 10

ROSE SAID that if you lined up my boyfriends from end to end, they would reach from here to heartache. Now, doesn't that just sound like Rose? Typical.   She should write songs. Wise Rose, that's what she is in her movie.   And strong as the Rock of Gibraltar.   But she's human like the rest of us.   I don't know what she would do if Bobbie walked out, but I'll bet she'd do something stupid.   Everyone does.   There is no smart way to handle that kind of catastrophe.   It's normal to flail around and do things you'll regret later as it all comes crashing down.

It's a wonder a person picks herself up and moves on.   But we do.   We all do.   And we always hope that the next guy will be love.   And if not love, then at least some good times.   And it's nice to think about them, those men who made me feel desired, at least for a while.   To think about those days when I wasn't broken, when I could still look down at my lithe body and glow in my skin.

I can see some of them so clearly.   Stephen, his long legs in faded jeans bridging the sofa to the coffee table.   I can see him lean forward, all slow-moving, lanky angularity, concave in the chest, scooping up a handful of chips.   And I remember Dan, silky-skinned Dan, who meant well in spite of trying to make me over into a tea-drinking vegetarian.   I remember Evan with his coffee-brown eyes, long lashes, and crooked penis.   Smithy, his grinning eyes looking up at me as I held on to his tousled hair.   And the guy from the bait shop with the scratchy beard and dirty jokes.   I don't know why I can't remember his name.   Maybe it will come back to me.   It seems wrong to forget their names.

Malcolm and his brother Charlie, both broad-shouldered with a dusting of freckles across their backs. Alvin with his monkish ways, living in that tiny room with just a mattress and stacks of books. And Marvin, kindly Marvin, with his pale blue eyes and his pale blond pubic hair. Back then he was muscular and handsome in a chiseled, movie-star way, but now he's got a pot belly and his face is red. And Elliot, who showed up at my door looking for the girl who lived there before me, and stayed for dinner and then breakfast, and who came back again and again, until he was around long enough for the inevitable disappointment. Because sooner or later that's how it ends. Even with Dieter, who loved me. I loved him too, but his expectations were just way too high. It's better the way things are now.

Dieter never left. I don't know if he stays for me or for Honey. I think Honey did the math and figured out that it's possible he's her dad. She asked once if that's why Dieter sticks around. So what is that supposed to mean—that Dieter wouldn't stick around just for me? It figures. Anyway, I don't know how she got that in her head. I haven't encouraged it. I don't tell her anything about those days, but she continues to think she's going to ferret the truth out of me. Sometimes I think maybe she should know the truth. But then I'd have to tell the whole story, and the day I tell her the whole story is the day I lose her. And besides, what's she going to do with a felon for a daddy? But she wants the dramatic revelation. Drumroll please. Maybe I'll leave that for a deathbed revelation. Or maybe not. Too much drama.

Chapter 11

IT'S FUNNY how much time I spent waiting for Eddie to show up. It made me realize that I was sitting around waiting for Eddie to come home just like I sat around waiting for Danny. Makes you wonder. While I waited, I felt as though my life had been put on pause, while everywhere else in the world things were going on as usual. It was an eerie feeling that things were continuing without my being part of them. At home Vivian and Rose and Bobbie were all living in that little apartment getting on each other's nerves. I could picture them so clearly. Vivian sitting at the kitchen table swirling the ice in her drink, bitching about someone or something. Bobbie on the floor doing ab crunches with her headphones on, listening to her Deepak Chopra tapes. Rose wiping down the bar, or doing the accounts and complaining about the distributor. And Dieter hovering around in the background as usual. And somewhere Franny was studying, wearing her sweats and her glasses, with her hair pinned up out of the way. All these things I could picture. But I had no idea whatsoever what Eddie might be doing. Something vague about olive oils.

When he did finally show up, usually after about a week away, the first thing he wanted to do was see what the workmen had done to his house. He never seemed very happy about what they had accomplished, and it would put him in a grumpy mood for a while. Finally he'd get that out of his system, and then he'd be his sweet old self with me.

And he was sweet. For our six-month anniversary, six months since we had met at the trade show, he showed up with an anniversary gift, a pink satin-and-lace boudoir pillow with HONEY embroidered on it in gold thread. What a romantic. But that's what Eddie was like. He made me feel loved. He would hold my hand at dinner, across the table, and he'd turn my hand so he could see my fingernails, stumpy because I couldn't stop chewing them and chipping the polish.   He would lift my hand saying, "Babe, why do this to yourself?" and kiss my fingers.

Once he found me looking at myself in the mirror, standing there in my underwear, assessing myself and unhappy with my soft round tummy, dimpled by my belly button. I turned to the side and back to the front, wondering if I could persuade myself to diet. I hate to diet. I guess I just love food too much. I'd be a lousy model. They have to be anorexic, it's practically part of their job description. But when I looked at that round tummy, I wondered out loud if I should go on a diet. Eddie had a fit. "You don't need to diet, Honey! You're gorgeous! You're luscious, that's what you are. Luscious!" He pulled me to the bed beside him and he kissed my belly. "The world has gotten completely messed up about womanly beauty. Everyone seems to think that a girl has to be skinny, a stick, all angles and bones. But that's not beauty. You are lusciously beautiful."

So, like I said, he was sweet and all, but still there was a lot I didn't know about the guy.   So it was a real shock one day when he suddenly slipped out a reference to his daughters.

"Daughters?"   I   asked,   incredulous.   "You   have daughters?"

He nodded slowly, standing there, stricken, his toothbrush held up in one hand because he had been brushing his teeth when this bombshell went off.

"You're married?" I asked, dumbfounded.

"Was," he said weakly.

"You were married," I said. Eddie nodded silently.   So, what happened, he just forgot to tell me? I stood there, gaping at him. A middle-aged man frozen in place, with toothpaste on his chin.

"Babe," he started.

"What's wrong with you?" I interrupted.

"I know, it's all wrong, I should have told you. Don't be mad at me, babe."

"Jeez, Eddie, I live with you.   Doesn't that mean anything?"

"Baby, you're right. I made a big mistake."

"So where are they?"

"Who?"

"Your daughters!"

"Honey, don't worry about them."

"So you're divorced?"

"Yes," he said eagerly, "and I thought if I mentioned the kids, you'd think I was too old for you."

I stood there looking at him, his eyes pleading, his toothbrush still tightly gripped in his hand. Then I grabbed my purse, wheeled around, and walked out.   I could hear Eddie whine, "But babe . . ." as the door slammed.

It felt good to walk out the door. It felt assertive. I did it with Danny, and now I was doing it with Eddie.   And I did it certain that this was what Franny would do too. If they were going to hurt me, then I was simply going to walk away. It was the only power I had. I stormed down the front steps of the villa and onto the sidewalk. Then I had to decide what I was going to do next. I had nowhere to go. What was I going to do, hop on a plane and go back home to Vivian and Rose and Bobbie?   I started walking down the street.   It was unfortunate that I didn't have a car. A car would have taken me somewhere far from Eddie in no time. Instead I had to walk. So walk I did. I didn't like the way I was feeling, and I needed to walk it off.

I walked for a long time, ending up at a little café on Sunset Boulevard.   I ordered a latte and sat down by the window to sip it slowly and think. Eddie should have told me he had a family.   It was not a big deal that he had one somewhere, but to keep it from me was weird. Still, it was an interesting revelation that he was insecure enough to hide it from me.   I was seeing a whole new side of him. A more vulnerable side.   He didn't tell me because he was worried about losing me. He was actually worried about losing me.

I finished the coffee and contemplated what I would do next. I had about twenty-six dollars on me. Not enough to do anything. Not enough to go off on my own. Clearly, if I were going to be on my own, I would need to find a job right away. Meanwhile I supposed I could call Sandy and see what she was doing. But tell her what? That I had just walked out on Eddie and had no place to go? That sounded so lame. Also I wished I had thought to grab my jacket on my way out the door. It was a cool fall day, and I was getting cold without it. I sighed, got up, bused my coffee cup, and headed back to the villa. When I got there Eddie wasn't around. By the time he came in that night we were both ready to make up.

He told me a little about his ex-wife. He said that they were too young when they got married, and that they had grown apart. We talked about his girls, and I could see he was crazy about them. I tried to picture him with them, but it was difficult because I'd never seen them. All I knew about them were their ages, four and six. I asked him to show me a picture, but he never got around to it. I figured one day he'd introduce me to them. After that he never talked about his ex-wife, but now I knew he spoke to her. Now I knew that this is what he was doing when he would go outside and talk on his cell phone. Once I asked him why he still called her, and he pointed out that he had no choice but to talk with her, because they had a responsibility to the two little girls. I told him he could talk to her while I was in the room, that I wouldn't make a sound, but he insisted that it was private. I tried to imagine how Franny would handle this situation. I wasn't sure what Franny would do about the ex-wife, but I had no doubt that she would be supportive of Eddie's efforts to be a good dad, so those two little girls could grow up in as normal a family as possible.

When we were kids Franny and I were on the receiving end of a lot of hassle about our unusual family. There were a few snarky questions about Franny having two moms, though in my opinion she blew that out of proportion. This was the San Francisco Bay Area, after all, and where we lived in the East Bay it was practically ground zero for lesbians, so any grief she got over that was just kids looking for a way to give her a hard time. By the time we were in middle school, which is the hardest age to be different, most of the kids knew Rose, because she was the one who brought the birthday cupcakes to school. And if you knew Rose, you liked her, because while she was tough she was kind, and she always showed kids respect. Meanwhile, it went without saying that everyone loved Bobbie. It actually got to the point where most of the kids would turn on anyone dumb enough to make remarks about Franny's two moms.

A little more serious was the shit Franny had to take now and then about Bobbie's dancing days. Bobbie hadn't been a dancer since before Franny was born, but every once in a while someone would bring it up. "I hear your mom is a stripper." "No," Franny would answer coldly. "She's a bartender." The first time she came home and reported this to the family, Rose said, "After all this time how does anyone know about that?" and Bobbie said, "Probably his dickhead dad was a regular in the audience." So Franny ended up feeling superior to the kid who'd brought it up but not too anxious to hear any more about it, and relieved when it died away.

But the thing we were most sensitive about was the dad question. That never really went away. At least Franny actually had a dad, even though he wasn't around very much. His name was Barry, he was a plumbing contractor, and he lived with his wife just outside of Santa Rosa. When we were kids Franny went there to visit sometimes, and Barry usually invited me to come along too, because it took him off the hook for entertaining her. His wife, Joan, was a nice lady, and she was used to kids because she had a daughter named Kim, who was about ten years older than we were. Kim's dad wasn't Barry. It was a little complicated and we got tired of explaining it. Joan was a hospice nurse, and she was as sweet and sincere as you'd expect from someone who spent her time making things easier for dying people, but she was a little boring. But that was okay, because it wasn't like we had to live with her.

So like I said, for Franny the dad thing wasn't too big a deal. But for me the question "Where's your dad?" was something to dread.   I felt like I should have a reason for not having one.   Everyone in the world had a dad.   What was wrong with my mom that she didn't know where mine was? How can you overlook something like that?   Bobbie once told us that Saint Anthony was the patron saint of lost things, and when I was little I always pictured him finding my dad for me. Then I got older and I knew it didn't work like that.   When people asked me about him I'd duck my head down in embarrassment and answer, "Dunno."   Then I went through a phase where I invented stories to explain his absence. Like, he died in a car accident. Or he worked in the CIA. Or he lived in Hollywood. Once I started working with the Hollywood angle, I pretty much settled in and elaborated on it. I had never been there, but it had a lot of appeal to me. So I came up with things like he was a movie stunt man and lived in Hollywood. Or he was a celebrity photographer with a huge house in Hollywood. Or he had a fancy restaurant in Hollywood. That sort of thing.

By the time I was in high school, I stopped with the stories. When they'd ask, I'd shrug my shoulders and say, really casually, "He's a missing person."   Most people were too startled by that to say anything further.

Another thing I didn't have was a grandmother.   Franny had two grandmothers, Barry's mom, who was cute and tiny with gray curly hair, and Bobbie's mom, who was a little strange.   She was tall and angular, and no matter the occasion, always wore the same outfit: jeans, a white shirt, and a straw cowboy hat. She was so tanned, her face looked like leather. She lived in Gardnerville, Nevada, and sometimes she drove down to visit, but not very often because she couldn't leave her dogs.   She bred German shepherds, and it seemed like there was always one of them ready to whelp or something. *Whelp*, there's a word. It's not my word, it was hers. It means "have puppies". Anyway, I guess that's where Bobbie got her love for animals, though I think it's interesting that when she got a dog she chose something that was about as opposite of a German shepherd as a dog can be. A little ball of white fluff.

Compare that with a big police dog, and it's enough to raise your eyebrows.

Rose's mom had died a long time before, otherwise I guess Franny would have had three grandmothers. That would probably be a record. Still, she was lucky to have two. I only had one, Vivian's mom, Victoria, and she died when I was three years old, so I barely remember her. There are just two faint memories that I recall that include her. One was a time when she put a Band Aid on my arm after the cat scratched me and told me it wasn't bad enough for me to be crying about it. The other was a time when I was sitting in the backseat of my mom's car, watching my mom and Victoria up on the porch arguing loudly. My mom came stomping down to the car, slid in, and dramatically slammed the door. She rammed the key into the ignition. And then the car wouldn't start. She tried a couple of times to get it to turn over, and then she leaned forward and laid her forehead on the steering wheel. I don't remember what happened after that. And I never asked her.

Rose said they fought a lot. My mom called Victoria a Nazi, but Rose said she was just strict and old-fashioned. I didn't remember her well enough to judge for myself. Still, she was the only grandmother I knew anything about. Sometimes when she'd been drinking my mom would get started on that subject, going on and on about her mom's funeral. She'd say she was sitting there looking at the coffin when she really got it that her mother was in that box. And that all the arguments were cut short by that box. And that there was nothing she could do about it. She would get really weepy at this point, and start saying that her childhood was in the box too, and that she would always regret that they never resolved things before Victoria died. I heard this so many times I would just leave the room when she started the windup.

All this family drama has been like background music to my life. It was always there. And it got us noticed. Over the years it always seemed that Franny and I had a lot of explaining to do. I don't know why people cared, but they did. People were curious, all fired up to find out what the relationship was between me and Franny, or Bobbie and Rose, or Bobbie and Vivian, or Vivian and Rose, or any of us with Barry, or my Mystery Dad, and how Dieter figured into the picture. But Rose always said there was no point trying to define things, no point in explanations. Things were what they were. "Easy for her to say," said Franny. "She isn't in school."

When Eddie was home I got to see a lot of him because he did much of his work there from the apartment. First thing in the morning he would get up and make coffee. He was a nut about his coffee, which was way too strong for my taste. Then he had his bowl of Grape-Nuts, which he had every morning because it made him poop. Honest to God, I'm not making this up. After he had his coffee and Grape-Nuts he would disappear into the bathroom for what seemed like hours while he had his daily poop and read the newspaper. What is it about men and spending half an hour on the toilet reading? I don't know any women who do that. Then I'd hear the toilet flush and the shower would start, and I could hear him snuffling and snorting in the shower, trying to clear out his sinuses. Eddie had allergies. I guess it's because he was old. I don't know anyone my age with sinuses that had to be blasted out every morning. Then I'd hear his electric toothbrush running on and on, because he was a fanatic about his teeth. I watched him one time as he stood in front of the mirror, looking at his teeth. Then he stuck out his tongue and looked at it. It looked like a soft pink sea animal. He brushed his tongue so he wouldn't have bad breath. He used a special brightener on his teeth, and he was always flossing. He went every three months to have his teeth cleaned by his dental hygienist Kimberly, and he followed her instructions like it was a religion. You'd think that would give him perfect teeth. But he kept complaining to me about a pain in one of them, and finally he complained to Kimberly, and she had the dentist look at it, and it turned out he needed a root canal. I don't know what a root canal is, but I've noticed that when people want to joke about something being simply awful they say it's like having a root canal.   So I made a point of being sympathetic when he called me from the dentist, until he told me he had to go to Fresno for a few days.   So much for sympathy.   If he could travel, he didn't need my sympathy. Anyway, I guess worrying about teeth is another old-guy thing.

Me and my silverback.

Franny still called him that.   She wanted to know if I was having bonobo sex with my silverback.   Actually I had asked her first, about the guy she was seeing, some blond dude she met when they got stuck in an elevator together.

"So is it bonobo sex?" I asked her.

"No," she said almost sadly.   "It's okay, but it's not like that.   It's more like thank you sex.   Like he's really nice, and he likes me a lot, and he cooks things for me and drops off little Tupperwares with mac & cheese on my doorstep, and he fixed my computer when it was running really slow, and I like going places with him, and he's nice-enough-looking.   But no, it's not bonobo sex."

I told her that it wasn't bonobo sex with me and Eddie, either.   "Maybe it's thank-you sex.   Maybe it's something else. Maybe you don't have bonobo sex when you're forty years old."

"Honey," she said, "don't you ever ask yourself what you're doing with someone who represents a whole different generation?"   I didn't have a good answer for that.

Franny had a good answer for everything.   She told me she was going to do a study of all the different kinds of sex.   Trust her to take sex and make a science of it.   I asked her, "What are you planning to be, a sexologist or something?"   She was continually changing her major, and the last I heard it had been public policy or something.

"No, but I'm thinking about changing my major to anthropology."   Franny started to list all kinds of sex. "There's thank-you sex.   And mirror sex, when people are really in love with themselves.   And there's pity sex, groupie sex, fuck-you sex, fuck-someone-else sex, fucked-up sex, and of course, low self-esteem sex for when you don't know how to say no." By this time she was cracking me up. I told her there was one more, make-me-young-again sex. I think that's what Eddie was having. He worried about not being young anymore. He worried about his teeth and his love handles and his abs and about getting gray hair. And really he shouldn't have worried about all that because I liked him anyway.

He would finally emerge from the bathroom, all cleaned up and put together just as fresh and young as possible, and he would sit down to his cell phone and laptop. While I slept late he would wheel and deal. I got pretty good at tuning out his voice, which became a dull growly droning noise in the background. It was the same sort of background sound as when he went outside to call his ex-wife on his cell phone. I'd sleep through it all until he would wake me up so we could finish out the morning in a lazy, sexy sort of way.

When I first moved in we were spending all our time in bed. The bed was never made because we were always rolling around on it. The comforter would end up in a pile on the floor at the end of the bed, and the sheet had a way of winding up into a rope and draping over the edge. But after about a month I started making the bed when I got up in the morning, because I didn't like to look at a mess. When you live in a studio apartment you have to make an extra effort to be neat, because you can't just close your door on an unmade bed. So I'd make it when I got up, and maybe that's a measure of where a relationship is. Whether or not the bed gets made.

We usually went out somewhere for brunch, and then he'd go to his office for the rest of the afternoon while I was left on my own to go for a walk or sit by the empty pool in the sun. In the evening we'd decide what to do for dinner. Sometimes Eddie made dinner. He had a few Italian dishes that he knew how to make. We'd go to the store together to get the ingredients and come back and he'd go through his CDs and put on Andrea Bocelli, a blind singer that he liked. He preferred to have music while he cooked. Eddie was a romantic. And he believed that anything Italian was romantic.

Italy was like the Holy Grail to him. I was astonished to find out that he went once a week to an evening class to learn to speak Italian. He practiced every day, and he was always nagging me to help him. He had made lists of words on index cards, and I was supposed to quiz him. *Chicken* I'd say, reading from the card titled "Animals." And he was supposed to answer, "*Pollastro*." I asked him how often he'd need to talk about a chicken in Italy, and he was offended. I thought it made more sense for him to learn the words for things that we actually lived with. I would walk around our room and point to things. Ceiling (*soffitto*), door (*porta*), bed *(letto)*, and shoe (*scarpa*). Sometimes he knew the word, sometimes he had to look it up in his dictionary. When he had to look it up, he put the new word on a card. All his index cards were organized by subject. In addition to Animals there were cards titled Room, Clothes, Food, Numbers, and Shopping. And there was one labeled Honey, and on that card he had written words like kiss (*bacio*) and breast (*mammilla*). I asked him if he knew the word for "fuck" and he said it wasn't in his Italian-English dictionary.

Another word he couldn't find in his Italian-English dictionary was the word for "teeth". Like I said before, he had a thing about his teeth. I told him he didn't have a very good dictionary if it didn't include teeth, because they're pretty basic if you asked me. Finally it occurred to me to look up the word *tooth*, and I found it, *dente*, and proudly showed it to him. It just shows that sometimes it's all in how you approach something.

One night, when Eddie was away, I heard creaking noises. It creeped me out so much that I called him, but as usual his phone was turned off. I called Sandy, but her phone was turned off too. Then I called Franny, and she wasn't answering, so finally I called the bar and got Bobbie. Bobbie told me that the sound was just the building's wood frame adjusting to a temperature change. It was November, she pointed out, and even though the days were mild, the nights were getting cooler. I hadn't realized that Bobbie was such a scientist. I guess that's where Franny got it. Then Bobbie asked me if I had called Vivian lately. No, I told her, I hadn't called in a while.

"Is Mom okay?" I asked.

"Not really," Bobbie said.

So I figured I'd better call her, and when I did, Dieter answered. "What are you doing answering Vivian's phone?" I asked him. He said he answered it because Vivian was in the bathroom. They were getting rather cozy, I thought. He told me that Vivian had been going to the doctor because she was having trouble with the cough, and he wanted me to come home to visit. Now they're going to lay the guilt on me, I thought. Vivian should just quit smoking. And I should never have called. All this aggravation because the house creaked.

Still, I was beginning to worry about Vivian, so when Rose called a few weeks later, asking me if I was coming home for Christmas, I actually listened. She said Vivian was sick and I needed to come home because she wouldn't tell anyone what was wrong with her, and everyone thought that maybe she would tell me. As soon as I told Rose I was coming home, I felt overcome by a warm flood of emotion. I didn't realize how much I wanted to see everyone again. I thought Eddie would be upset, but he was great about it, and right away bought me a plane ticket so I could fly home for a ten-day visit. For Christmas gifts I bought scarves and earrings, and a tie for Dieter, things that were small and easy to pack in my suitcase. The night before I left, Eddie and I went out for a special dinner, and we exchanged our Christmas gifts. Eddie gave me a peach-colored cashmere sweater, and I gave him a CD of Andrea Bocelli singing Puccini arias. Eddie had told me how much he liked Puccini, who was Italian, so I was excited when I found this CD. It was like getting two Italians for the price of one. He said over and over that this was one of the most thoughtful gifts anyone had ever given him, and he hugged me to him, and I buried my face in his crisply starched shirt. The next morning I flew home.

Chapter 12

ALFRED JEROME HARRISON.   Alfred Jerome—God what a name.   No wonder he went by AJ.   The first time I saw him was when he came into Rose's bar with that skanky little blond girl Caity.   Short for Caitlin.   I knew who she was—she was one of the regulars.   Caity was tanked up and looking for a fight, and I guess AJ said something she didn't like, and she took a swing at him with her purse.   He jumped back, and her purse missed him and whacked right into me as I sat there at the bar.   It took me by surprise.   You don't expect a red patent leather purse to come out of nowhere, slam into your shoulder, and send your glass flying, spilling everything.

"Now look what you made me do" she said to him with a scowl before she turned to me and said, "Sorry, Viviana.   It was an accident.   You okay?"

As he stood behind her he looked over her bleached head to me and smiled.   And while she was in the ladies' room pulling herself together, he came over to buy me another drink, apologize for her, and ask me for my phone number. He was tall and muscular.   You could tell he worked out, and I was impressed.   Later I found out he went a gym in Emeryville where he got in with a fake membership card.   It figures.   Now I know that was typical of him, he was such a hustler.   He two-timed the world.   He hustled me.   But I didn't know this when I met him.   Mostly at the time I was wondering what he was doing with a loser like Caity.

Caity Coyote.   Coyote Girl.   Someone once called her that and the name stuck.   She's still around.   And she still has a way of looking for a fight.   But I don't care.   I guess she did me a favor.   But no one calls me Viviana.   She's a freak.

When AJ finally called I couldn't go out with him because I already had plans with someone else.   Someone named Ronald. Or Donald? Arnold? I think it was Ronald. We were going to go to the racetrack. I'd never been to the races, and I thought it sounded thrilling, but it turned out to be a disappointment because I lost all my money betting on the wrong horses with fancy names and he drank too much and got nasty. On the way home he called me a cunt and I told him to pull over. Cunt. *Some say it's just a word, it doesn't mean anything, but if that is the case, why is it always said with such venom? Some things you just don't say to someone else.* Bimbo. *That's another one.*

I got out of his truck, walked down to the Quik Stop, and called a taxi. I didn't go out with that Ronald again. He just wasn't all that great, not good enough to make it worth putting up with his crap.   And I was really pissed off because I realized I should have gone out with AJ instead.

Chapter 13

DIETER PICKED ME UP at the airport. He told me that
Mom was a wreck, and that she'd been to a doctor, but he
didn't have any details. It sounded like he was beating around
the bush. I suspected that she had told him what was going
on, because he had been hanging with her a lot lately, and he
seemed to be in on whatever it is, but he wasn't going to tell
me anything if she wouldn't. Then he said I should be calling
her more often. I pointed out that she could call me too. He
got really huffy and said that Vivian was sick, so it was up to
me. I explained that there had never been much I could do for
her. I don't think Dieter realized this. She was always busy
screwing up her life, and I mostly had to stay out of her way.

Everyone showed up when we got back to the apartment.
Rose gave me a hug that nearly crushed my ribs, and Bobbie
was so glad to see me she started bouncing around pretending
to box with me. Rose explained that Bobbie was taking
boxing lessons. Boxing? How does she even think of these
things? Franny was there too. I hadn't seen her since the
previous Christmas. But the strangest thing was seeing
Vivian. She had lost weight, and her skin was like old paper.
She was coughing more than ever. For the next week I tried to
imagine what was wrong with her. Did you cough if you had
lung cancer? I didn't know. But she wasn't telling anyone
what was going on. She just waved away all questions. Rose
told me she had been doing this for a while now.

Christmas itself was low-key. Vivian got exhausted easily,
so we didn't make much of the holiday. Franny and I got a
little three-foot tree, and Bobbie strung the lights on it, but we
never got around to decorating it. We just stuck some
Christmas cards into the branches. The cards were mostly

from businesses, not people: the bank, the beer distributor, the insurance guy. Still they were pretty. But on Christmas morning we took the tree out to the back steps because it was taking up too much room on the corner table. So much for the holiday spirit.

It was good to see Franny. I had a lot to talk about. I told her about Eddie and the daughters who had suddenly materialized. And about how frustrating it was that he kept taking off for days at a time, and that when he was home with me we only did what he wanted to do. There I was in L.A. where there were all those clubs with great DJs, and all Eddie wanted to do was go to a quiet restaurant for a steak. Franny said that it sounded like it was all about him, and I was just a pretty thing on his arm. She said I needed to be in control of my own movie. "If he thinks the movie is all about him, then you have to take charge and make the movie about the two of you together." I wasn't sure what all this movie talk was about, and besides, it sounded like a lot of work. "On the other hand," she said, "I don't know what you expected with a silverback."

Meanwhile everyone wanted to know what I was doing, and why I didn't call more often, and if I was finally working. Nag nag nag. And then toward the end of the visit I made the mistake of mentioning in front of the family that I only saw Eddie on alternating weeks. As soon as the words left my mouth I could see that I was going to regret it. I saw Bobbie and Rose exchange looks, and then both of them zeroed in on me, while Vivian did a slow uptake and turned around to look at me as well. "What do you mean, alternating weeks?" asked Rose. I explained that he took business trips. "Business trips," said Rose. That's all she said, just "business trips." But it was enough to throw a shadow over everything. Somehow she made business trips sound ominous. Then Bobbie wanted to know about Eddie's family. Thanks, Franny, for keeping your mouth shut. Well, I didn't know very much about his family, but I wasn't going to let them know that. I told her about his two little girls, Emma and Allison, and about his ex-wife who he talked to every day.

Bobbie said gently, "So how do you know he's actually divorced?" and now I was starting to get really uncomfortable, because at the back of my mind I had been kind of wondering about a few things myself. Specifically, I had begun to be bothered by something odd in our living arrangement. Eddie didn't have enough clothes in our apartment to make sense, and I was beginning to wonder if he was living somewhere else as well. I actually asked him about that once, and he got annoyed, but then he explained that he kept a lot of clothes at the Cremona Imports office. Which I guess would be handy, though it seemed strange to me.

So between the questions I had about Eddie, and the less than stellar time I was having hanging with my family, I decided I had had enough of this visit. Instead of flying back on January second, I'd surprise Eddie by coming home early so we could celebrate New Years' Eve together. Bobbie helped me change my plane ticket, and book a shuttle for me to get from the airport to the villa.

Before I left I stopped to thank her and say goodbye. She was touching up the wall mural in the Flamingo Room, and it was strange to see this room again because it was not as nice as I remembered it. Maybe I had idealized it because my memories of it were from when I was a little kid and didn't know better. Now I looked at it and I could see the room was all scuffed up and the colors were kind of tacky. I didn't say anything though, because Bobbie was proud of her huge wall mural of the flamingo standing in front of the moon. I told her maybe someday she would paint a big mural like that for me. She liked that. She was dying to see the villa. They all thought I live in a fancy place. Little did they know I actually lived in a dumpy one-room apartment.

When I returned to Los Angeles, my plan to surprise Eddie kind of fizzled out because he was away on one of his trips, selling his olive oil and noodles. I opened up the closet and took a look at his clothes. There were a few shirts, a pair of jeans, some khaki pants, and one suit. Not much, now that I

was thinking about it. Not much for a man who loved clothes.
I looked around the room and it dawned on me that while
there were a couple of pictures of me with my family, there
were no pictures of Eddie's. None. No photos of Emma and
Allison. No photos of Eddie with his family. No pictures of
his mom, or from when he was young. I didn't expect to see
any pictures of the ex-wife, but I was surprised that such a
sentimental guy wouldn't have pictures of everyone else. He
certainly talked about them.   He talked about Emma and
Allison, and I had even helped him buy a birthday gift for
Emma. I had no idea what a four-year-old would like. We
ended up getting her a toy cooking set, with little pink and
purple dishes and tiny pots and pans. He told me Emma loved
it.   Her sister Allison was almost six, and she was really
interested in animals.   When her birthday came along in
February he was planning to give her a set of plush woodland
animals that he saw in a catalog. Eddie also talked about his
mother, who had an apartment in an assisted-living complex in
Irvine. He talked about taking the girls to see their Nonna,
and how his mother complained that the girls were too loud.
So with all this talk it was strange that there were no
photographs.

   I would have liked to have seen pictures of Eddie when he
was young. Seeing a picture of someone when they are a kid
is like looking through a window into the real person way
deep inside. When I saw Dieter's picture of himself as a
skinny little blond kid in Germany, his front tooth missing and
his pretty, laughing blond mother standing at his side with her
hand on his shoulder, I felt I suddenly knew him better. Rose,
too. She has a picture of herself, a little girl on a swing. She
wasn't three hundred pounds then. In fact she looked fairly
normal, though maybe a little chubby, with dimpled knees.
She sat staring seriously at the camera. Her older sister was
sitting on the next swing, leaning over to hold her fingers up
making horns behind Rose's head. Rose loved that picture
because her sister died a few years ago from breast cancer.
Without it I think I would have had a hard time picturing Rose
as a little kid. I haven't seen Bobbie's pictures, but I've never

had any problem whatsoever picturing her as a kid. Somehow that was easy, though it was hard to picture her with her mom, the control-freak dog breeder.   On the other hand, even though I've seen photos of Vivian when she was little, I still can't really picture her as a kid.   When I try, I just see an eight-year-old with a cigarette.

Eddie showed up the day before New Year's Eve, astonished to find me back earlier than we originally planned.   I was ready with some questions. I wasn't going to beat around the bush.   Actually I would have asked in a more roundabout way, if I could have thought of one, but I couldn't. So I just came right out and asked him if he was truly divorced, and was his family the place where he went when he was not with me. As soon as the words were out of my mouth I knew that this was a huge mistake, because at that instant I could see as clearly as if it were on a billboard that the answer would be no and yes. And that's exactly what it was. No, he wasn't really divorced yet. And yes, that was where he was staying when I thought he was out on business trips. First this guy forgot to mention that he had a family, and then he forgot to mention that he was still married. This wasn't a good sign.

"But Honey," he said, "we are getting a divorce. Annie and I haven't gotten along in years. I'm just sticking around for the kids." Finally she had a name. Annie. He told me that he knew he should have come clean right from the start, but we were having such a good time that he just couldn't bring himself to jinx it.

"So if you are separated," I asked him, "why are you staying there a week at a time?"

He looked at me really seriously. "Honey, I owe it to my girls. I owe it to them to be a good dad. I need to be there for them while they are growing up." Well, there was not much I could say against that. Obviously I wished I'd had a dad who was there for me like that. I was hardly going to put my foot down and keep him from his little girls. I just thought he should have told me.

I asked him if Annie knew about me, and he said, still looking deadly serious, that he hadn't informed her about me because he didn't want to jeopardize the custody situation. If the judge thought he was catting around, maybe Eddie wouldn't get to see the girls as much.   Again, there was not much I could say against that, though it hurt to be put in the catting-around category.

After all this, it was hardly news when he informed me that we couldn't spend New Year's together.   All in all, he sounded pretty remorseful.   All he could talk about was how he was going to make it up to me.   He decided that the way to do that was to take us on a romantic trip to Mexico.   When I looked into his warm brown eyes brimming with love, I melted.   I could see how sorry he was about the mess he had made of everything.   And I knew this would work out in the long run.   I just had to work a little harder at it.   I wouldn't give up and move on.   I didn't want to be like my mom and her boyfriends.   And I was dying to go to Mexico.

Chapter 14

WAS OUR FIRST DATE the time we went to the baseball game? The A's were playing, but I can't remember who they played. No, that was later. I already knew him by then. On that first date we drove somewhere. Yes, to the coast. It was a cool gray day. Everything was gray—the clouds, the cliffs, and the surf below. We got out of the car and he took a dirty green-plaid blanket out of the trunk. At the trailhead an empty beer bottle stood on a rock, like a marker. We should put a note in it and fling it into the ocean, he said. He picked it up and hurled it into the air, and it tumbled in an elegant arc from the cliff into the waves below, with something of us inside it. That bottle is probably there still, buried in the sand at the bottom of the Pacific Ocean. It rests there. It's not the crazy bottle that flies through my nightmares.

The path to the beach was steep, lined with ice plant. The magenta flowers and bruised fleshy foliage were trampled and smashed wet where the plants strayed onto the path. Pebbles rolled and my sandals slipped and he held my arm. The wind blew my hair up and into my face, where it stuck to my lipstick. He brushed it back from my face. Later he got a grain of sand in his eye. That wind was like an angry animal.

There was no one on the beach, and we found a little overhang, almost like a shallow cave under the cliff, and we lay down there on the blanket on the cold sand, and one thing led to another. His hand in my jeans, mine in his. We unbuttoned our pants and slid them down our thighs but stopped there. The wind was too cold to undress. Then he was inside me and we were lost in the heat of that other universe, and then when we came back to earth we saw someone approaching, a middle-aged woman with her aging

Labrador retriever plodding along on a leash. We just pulled a jacket over AJ's white goose-bumped rump and lay there quietly until she was past, and then we burst out snorting with laughter.

Chapter 15

EDDIE DIDN'T WASTE any time. We would go to Ixtapa in
a week. As we pored through a glossy guidebook there was a
chilly winter rain pelting the patio outside. "You'll love it,"
Eddie kept saying, as we looked at the pictures of tanned and
toned sunbathers on a white beach, at cheerful models
shopping for colorful rugs, and at a beautifully coiffed couple
staring into each other's glistening eyes at a table set for two.
Then we realized I needed a passport. Naturally I didn't have
one, because I had never stepped outside of California. The
farthest south I'd been was to Laguna Beach, and that's just
Orange County. Fortunately Eddie knew all about passports,
and he knew about a service on-line where we could get one
practically overnight. Like he said, it just took money. First
we went to a shop on Sunset Boulevard where we got a set of
two little pictures of me standing on a box. The picture was
only of my face, but standing on a box is what I mainly
remember. Then Eddie took me to the Federal Building on
Wilshire where they looked at my driver's license and birth
certificate and agreed that I was really me. Three days later,
just in time, the passport arrived by Federal Express. It had an
official looking navy blue cover, and inside, next to my
smiling picture, was a summary of my life: a birth date and a
passport number, and the fact that I was a female born in
California.

"Please remain in your seats until the plane comes to a
complete stop." In spite of that announcement the plane was
still moving when everyone began to stand up. From inside
that big metal cocoon, cool and artificially lit, bland and

cramped, we could hear the rumble of equipment outside, and then they opened the airplane doors. We were to walk down the stairs onto the tarmac, just like in film footage from olden times, and as we stepped out of the plane into the brilliant sunshine and a sweltering blast of humid air, the world was transformed. Ixtapa's airport wasn't much to look at, but already it was more beautiful than the travel book pictures, because where the pictures stopped at ink on paper, Ixtapa was warm and breezy and fragrant.

In the terminal we walked across smooth cool stone floors, to stand in lines where I got my passport stamped with its very first stamp. Then the crowd fanned out, some to pick up their suitcases, some to greet friends, and some to find taxis. Eddie spoke a little Spanish, and he got a taxi to take us to the hotel. The taxi was even more beat up than Vivian's Honda, and it rattled and groaned as the driver zigzagged through traffic. The cars we were passing were driving just as erratically as we were, and as I clung to the side handle I couldn't help but wonder how often these people got into accidents. But I was soon distracted from worrying about crashing cars. The passing scenery was too interesting.

The billboards were all in Spanish. I don't know why that surprised me. Of course they would be in Spanish. But this was the first thing that made it all real to me. We drove through neighborhoods of dirty white pocked concrete buildings draped with wires and antennas, topped with satellite dishes, and fronted with broken sidewalks. Many of the shops were open to the street with their wares spilling out, hanging in the doorways and stacked up outside. Kids were everywhere, riding bikes, playing with soccer balls, sitting on the sidewalks. But then we turned off of the main road onto the neatly landscaped entrance road to the hotel, and the contrast was startling. All of a sudden everything was new and clean and planted with bright flowers.

We pulled up to the front of the hotel. It had no doors, no walls—the lobby was completely open to the outside, and you could look through to the brilliant sunlight on the other side, to the pool, the poolside bar, and the white beach beyond, all the way to the silvery blue line of water that was the Pacific Ocean. The grounds were lushly planted, with banana trees and green grass and borders of bright yellow and orange hibiscus. There was music playing somewhere. I felt like I was in a movie.

We went up to our room and I stood there looking at the view while Eddie tipped the porter. Then, the moment the smiling porter stepped into the hall and the door clicked shut, we tumbled into bed, laughing. An ocean breeze fanned us from the open window, and from the hotel patio below there was the distant sound of romantic Latin music. I loved Mexico.

Then Eddie said he had some business to attend to. "Business!" I said. "This is a vacation!" But no, he said he always had business to do, and he needed to go down to the lobby where the hotel had their fancy executive suite, with computers and fax machines for their guests, but he'd be back soon. "Don't go away," he growled seductively, and then he turned and slipped out the door.

I walked around the room, inspecting everything. There was shampoo in tiny bottles and soaps and hand cream, stacks of towels, and bottled water. There was a hair dryer, an iron and an ironing board, and a plastic bag for laundry. This was nicer than our apartment. When I pointed that out to Eddie when he returned, he was offended. The apartment was just a temporary arrangement, he said in a testy voice. I let it drop, and we went downstairs to explore the place.

The pool was enormous, surrounded by lawns and lounge chairs and waiters carrying drinks. Along one side of the pool was the bar, and you could even swim up to it and get a drink without leaving the water, because along the pool's edge it had a row of little concrete stools that looked like underwater mushrooms. We carried our margaritas to the lounge chairs lining the beach and sat there watching the waves roll in, the ever-present music from the bar like a sound track in our movie.

Indian girls, dark, short, and muscular, with unsmiling faces and long black braids, walked up and down the beach with strings of beads looped over their brown arms, approaching tourists and silently offering their wares for sale. One girl had two younger kids tagging along with her, each carrying an armload of brightly painted ceramics. Eddie haggled with the girl over a ceramic cat that was covered head to toe with zigzags and stripes and dots and swirls of color. Then we walked around the shops in Ixtapa, and Eddie bought us two souvenir coffee mugs, gaudy in turquoise, yellow, orange and pink, with jaunty red cactus lettering: IXTAPA.

That night for dinner we went to the fancy restaurant on the top floor of the hotel. Eddie ordered ceviche for an appetizer, and we had margaritas, and huge steaks. There was a dance floor and Eddie taught me the rumba. What could be more romantic? We had a drink in the bar afterward, and sat at a tiny table with a candle in a red glass candleholder. The flame flickered in the gentle breeze from the French doors that were flung wide open to the warm Mexican night. In that flickering light Eddie's eyes looked sunken and his brows craggy, but when he smiled his eyes crinkled with affection.

The next morning we slept late, had a leisurely breakfast, and went swimming in the gently swelling waves of the ocean. Then we took a taxi into Zihuatanejo, a nearby fishing village, where we walked from shop to shop, admiring everything—the bright colors, the smiling shop people, the cheerful music playing in the restaurants. We got back to the hotel in the afternoon and made love, and then we went out for dinner and a late-night walk down the beach. It was idyllic. Eddie had to go downstairs periodically to check his e-mail and communicate with his office, but I was fine with that. I sat on the balcony and waited for him, enjoying the cool breeze. Finally my life was taking shape. I liked being a grown-up.

The next morning Eddie woke me up to say that there had been a catastrophe at work. Catastrophe was the word he used when things weren't going well. I'd learned not to get all worked up when he said that, because it was something he always solved sooner or later. But on our vacation? Still, he looked serious, and said he might be tied up for most of the day, so I'd better plan on entertaining myself.

I spent the morning walking up and down the beach, then lying beside the pool. I had lunch by myself in the poolside café and then sat in the breezy lobby watching people come and go. I don't have to tell you how boring this was becoming. I needed magazines, and not all in Spanish like the ones we saw the day before in Zihuatanejo.

I figured the front desk could tell me where to find magazines in English. As I approached the desk I was suddenly slammed off my feet by a large roller suitcase swinging behind a very large man who appeared to be in a hurry to beat me to Reception. Reaching the counter he slapped down a piece of paper and said, "Checking in" in a loud voice. Then he turned to me and pushed his baseball cap back from his red, sweaty face. "Sorry. Didn't see you there," he said, and then turned back to the receptionist.

A woman who had just finished checking in witnessed all this with a shocked expression on her face, and then she swooped over to help me to my feet. "Are you okay?" she asked gently. I nodded and looked down at my tote bag lying there on its side, everything in it spilled out in the middle of the hotel lobby—my sunscreen, hairbrush, dark glasses, lip glosses, wallet, flip-flops and sweater. I felt strangely exposed seeing it scattered there helter-skelter. All I could think of was thank God I didn't have any tampons or underwear in the bag. The woman, shaking her head and muttering about rude tourists, knelt down beside me to help me retrieve my things. Two small children with her stared at us as we crammed everything back into my bag. The whole incident was totally embarrassing. I wasn't having a good day.

Eddie wasn't in the room when I went up, but while I was in the shower he came in. He looked terrible. I asked him what was going on at Cremona Imports to make him look like that, and he said he couldn't talk about it, but the problems were catastrophic. I told him about my hit-and-run encounter at the front desk, and Eddie immediately felt sorry that he was being so grumpy, and he held me and told me that he loved me. That night we had a quick dinner and went back to our room, and then he had to go back downstairs for a while to get onto his e-mail because he was expecting to hear from Milan. "I'm sorry, babe," he said. "You know, with the time difference, I need to do this now. Just go to sleep and I'll be back before you know it." The next morning I woke up earlier than usual, but he wasn't around. I figured I would head on down for breakfast by myself.

And that's when everything fell into place. Because there he was. Walking across the lobby toward the elevators with a woman and two young girls. And not with just any woman, but with the nice woman who had helped me cram all my stuff back into my tote bag the day before. The four of them were walking together and talking together like a family. I was standing there, frozen, staring in astonishment, when Eddie saw me out of the corner of his eye. He did a double take and then stared at me wild-eyed while he kept walking with his hand on the small of the woman's back. He turned to look back over his shoulder at me, mouthing something that I couldn't make out. He ushered the three of them into an elevator, pressed a button, and then jumped out, waving to them as the elevator doors closed. He strode over quickly, saying, "I know what you're thinking." That was good, because frankly I didn't know what I was thinking. I was glad someone knew.

"Annie found out about the trip, and she thought it was for her. So I had to bring her and the girls."

I just stared at him, incredulous.

"Oh, babe," he said, "she saw the travel book and the hotel confirmation. What could I do? She thought I was planning it for them."

I couldn't think of a thing to say in response. I couldn't even think of what Franny would do.

"I have to let her think it's for them for now, because I can't hurt the kids." I let the silence sit there. "Babe," he said, "I don't want to jeopardize the custody settlement. So I had to let her come too."

"You had to," I said.

"I had to. She doesn't know anything about you. I don't want anything to mess things up until the divorce is final."

"Don't you think it's about time to tell her about me?" I asked.

"I will when the divorce is final." He took me by the elbow and started toward the elevator.

I pulled away. "She's the one who helped me when that douchebag ran over me with his suitcase."

"You're kidding. That was Annie?" He had stopped in his tracks, astonished.

I probably shouldn't have brought that up. I could tell he was going to let it become a distraction and I needed to bring him back to the real issue. It was time to be assertive. In my firmest voice I said, "Eddie. I think you need to tell her about me. Now."

"Okay, okay," he said. He looked really harried. "But give me some time. Please go along with things while I work this out. I can't believe this is happening. Oh, my God, I can't believe that you all met each other. That you're all here. Right now. All of you. At the same time." His eyes were bugging out while he tried to process everything. For a moment I wondered if he could burst a blood vessel in his head. Was that what caused a stroke?

"Honey, I'll make it up to you."

So much for our romantic trip to Mexico. For the next two days Eddie danced between me in one room and Annie and the girls in another, all the time saying that he had no feelings for her anymore, but that he had to stay with her so that the girls wouldn't know what was going on. He said that Annie wanted a divorce as much as he did, but that they were trying to act like a family for now to make it easier for the kids.

Which meant that for those two days he spent most of his time with them, and I only saw him while Annie took the girls to the pool or the beach.

What would Franny do? She wouldn't have been here with Eddie in the first place. So I was on my own. As a result I watched a lot of Mexican TV. Evenings were the worst. That's when I felt loneliest. That first night I sat in my hotel room and watched old *Baywatch* episodes in Spanish, and a variety show that featured a lot of women with huge toothy smiles, meaty thighs, and bulging breasts. I saw an ad with a thrilled voiceover in rapid Spanish for a knife that cuts anything and everything, just like it's been doing in English on American TV for years. I watched a quiz show where a fat guy chattered on and on into his handheld microphone, all in Spanish, while a gorgeous girl standing next to him smiled and nodded. Finally he handed her the mike and she said something, looking into the camera while he looked away with a *look at her, isn't she marvelous* expression on his face, and the audience clapped. Then I got tired of everything being in Spanish, so I turned to CNN and watched that for a while. There was a freak winter snowstorm somewhere where there shouldn't have been, and some guy in Germany was arrested for something. There was a bomb somewhere in the Middle East and people standing around afterward looking at the blackened skeleton of a car. This was all too depressing so I went back to the Spanish-language stations and found a sitcom that didn't make any sense to me but it was something to watch. And it was better than sitting around thinking too much. Whenever I thought about things, it just made me sad and depressed. Eddie said, "Honey, I'll make it up to you," but I really wasn't too sure about where this was going. I figured I'd better just sit this out, watch a lot of TV, and see what developed.

The second night I walked around the hotel for a while and then I went back up to my room. I sat out on the balcony, looking down at the pool below, turquoise and glowing with lights. There were little candles on the tables, flickering with golden candlelight. The murmur of voices, the clinking of silverware, and the tinkling of a piano rose to my balcony, making me feel even lonelier. I went back downstairs again.

In the bar I found a table by the window, and ordered a piña colada, which had become my new favorite because it was delicious like a milk shake. The next thing I knew a pudgy guy with a comb-over came along and sat opposite me.

"You waiting for someone?" he asked.

"Yes," I lied. He left, and when I finished my drink I got up and went out, heading for the beach. There were clouds gathering and a wind had come up, whipping my skirt against my legs and blowing my hair into my face. The air was heavy with moisture. I turned away from the wind and saw two people lying on the sand together. They were kissing. I turned away and slipped off my sandals to walk along the water's edge. I was beginning to feel even sorrier for myself. The water was strangely warm, but the air was cool now and I was wishing I had brought a sweater with me. Then it began to rain, so I went back up to my room, where I took a bath and watched more incomprehensible TV late into the night. It's just as well that I couldn't understand what I was watching; it gave me a lot of time to think about things. And all I could think about was that Annie was such a nice person. She was lovely, and generous, and she had helped me. Things just weren't very clear.

The next morning was gorgeous, all sunshine and blue skies. It seemed like the sort of morning that would herald a brand-new start. Cheered up, I went down to breakfast, to the sunny little café by the pool. Just as I was just sitting down, something caught my eye that made me stand up again. There they were, Eddie and Annie, walking across the lobby to the formal dining room on the other side, with their two little girls darting around them like baby quail. Eddie and Annie were holding hands. *Holding hands.* Eddie said something to Annie and their shoulders touched and their heads leaned together as she answered. Annie turned and called to the baby quail, gathering them to her as the four of them entered the dining room.

Those two people were not talking about divorce.

I just stood there staring across the lobby. Then I came to, looked around, pushed my chair back under the table, and walked out of the café. I felt like a robot.

"No breakfast, señorita?" asked the lady at the entrance.

"No, thank you," I whispered. I walked across the lobby like I was in a dream and got onto the elevator. Instead of going to the third floor, to my room, I pressed the fifth-floor button. I knew their room number because I had seen it written on the little room key folder among Eddie's things. They were in Room 527.

The maid's cart was blocking the hallway in front of Eddie and Annie's room, and the door was open. I could see two big beds with the covers thrown back. There was a pile of towels on the floor in front of the bathroom door. I stepped inside. The maid was bent over the bathtub with her back to me. I stood there for a moment wondering whether or not I should say anything to her. She was humming to herself as she scrubbed the tub. On the counter there were two toiletries bags, a masculine black leather bag, and a bulging red floral case, with a matching cosmetic bag on top. Lipsticks, mascara, a brush, a razor and shaving cream, two deodorants, and a bottle of lotion were scattered randomly over the counter, and in a drinking glass there were four brightly colored toothbrushes, two large and two small ones. The two adult toothbrushes seemed to be getting along fairly well together.

I stepped quietly into the bedroom. Children's clothes were scattered over the room, and Eddie's jacket lay sprawled on a chair by the window. Beneath it there was a woman's cardigan sweater. There was a table at the window, covered with papers and brochures and a hair dryer, and standing there I could look out the window to the expanse of the beach below, and the swelling Pacific as far as the eye could see. Eddie's suitcase was on the floor next to the table, and I hunched down to quickly paw through it, until I found the

airline tickets tucked into a side pocket. There were five, one
for him, one for me, and the rest for Annie and the girls. I
slipped mine in my pocket, and tucked the other four back into
the suitcase. As I reached the door, the maid came out of the
bathroom and stopped in her tracks, looking at me in surprise.
"Amigo," I said, wishing I spoke Spanish. Or was it *amiga*? I
could never remember. I pointed my finger to my chest.
"Amigo of Señora Bertoli." The maid nodded uncertainly. I
had no idea if I had communicated anything at all. All I knew
was that if I said I was Eddie's friend, it would look bad. Of
course it would look bad. It was bad.

Back in my room I realized how hungry I was. I didn't
want to take any chance of running into Eddie and his family
downstairs, so I called room service and ordered a continental
breakfast. I wasn't sure what that would include, but I was too
tense to eat a full American breakfast. While I waited for the
food to arrive I stuffed all my things into my blue suitcase and
my matching tote bag. I couldn't fit the colorful ceramic cat
into my suitcase, so as much as I wanted it, I left it for Eddie.
I paused over our souvenir coffee mugs sitting out on the
dresser. I packed mine and put Eddie's on the dresser next to
the cat and the Mexican money he had left there.

While I waited for the food to arrive I sat by the window,
noticing now that my third-floor view wasn't as spectacular as
the view from the fifth floor. My view of the ocean was
blocked by one wing of the hotel. No endless Pacific from
this window. I looked down at the palm trees and the pool and
thought with satisfaction of Eddie returning here, after leaving
Annie with the girls at the pool, to find the room empty. He
had been going back and forth between me and his family for
months now. A week with me and then a week with them.
What did they think about that? How could Annie not have
known about me? How could I not have known about them?
And where, I wondered, did he think he was going with this?
One day that villa was going to be finished. Who was going
to move into that brand-new house? I realized that Eddie was
probably operating without a plan.

There was the rattle of a cart in the hall just before the knock on the door. *El desayuno* had arrived. The cart was wheeled briskly into the room, and in no time the table was laid out with my breakfast. There was coffee in a little silver pot, a glass of pale-looking juice, glistening rosy-red papaya slices spiraling on a white plate, and two little rolls nestling in a napkin in a basket. I gave the polite boy some of the money Eddie had left on the dresser, not really sure how much I was handing him, but he seemed happy with it as he backed out of the room saying "Enjoy your breakfast, señora" and closed the door behind him.

I bit into a roll and dry crumbs sprayed onto my lap. The juice was tasteless and the coffee was weak. Only the fragrant papaya was appealing. I ate everything though, because I knew I had a long day ahead of me. I emptied the last of the coffee from the pot into Eddie's souvenir mug and picked through the money on the dresser. I took the bills and left most of the coins. Looking around the room, I felt strangely good. The only things left there were Eddie's—his clothes, his toiletries, and the coins on the dresser. And the ceramic cat. I didn't feel the slightest pang of loss. I thought I'd be all torn up, but I wasn't even sad. Instead I felt calm and somehow in charge of things. I snapped out the long suitcase handle, put my tote on my shoulder, and armed with the mug of coffee, I walked out of the room feeling oddly euphoric, my suitcase rolling obediently behind me.

The hallway was empty and I was alone in the elevator, so it was startling when the doors opened and I stepped out into the noisy, crowded lobby. As I crossed the lobby, keeping an eye out for Eddie and his family, I stopped for a moment to peer into the dining room. It was packed, every elegant white-clothed table occupied with happy brunchers starting their day amid a din of silverware, dishes, and voices. In the background there was music—it sounded like a rumba. I scanned the tables and finally, at the far side of the dining room, I glimpsed the back of Eddie's head. He was leaning over one of his little girls at his side. Maybe he was cutting something up into bite-sized pieces for her, like Rose used to do for me. I turned and walked out of the lobby, past the row of taxies in front of the hotel, and headed down the street.

What a beautiful morning it was, brilliantly sunny but not yet hot, and everything looked clean after the night's rain. There weren't many shops open yet, and the street was empty, its bleached pavement already glaring in the sunlight, and I fished my sunglasses out of my bag and slipped them on. As I walked, my suitcase clattering behind me on its little wheels, I sipped at the coffee, and when I finished it I set the cup down on a chipped stone wall that ran along the sidewalk. I was free. I could go anywhere, be anything, I thought, as I walked away from the mug sitting there on the wall. I was heading down that bright street and into my new life. I wasn't thinking about particulars, just that my life was suddenly wide open.

As I walked, one shoe started to chafe, and the tote on my arm grew heavier and heavier, and then I came to a long stretch of rough pavement where the juddering suitcase made a terrible racket, so finally I tried to hail a taxi. They kept passing me without stopping, because they were already taken, and I never seemed to be able to tell from a distance if they were free. I began to feel overwhelmed, and my throat tightened as tears welled up. Plodding down that broken sidewalk, my blue suitcase clattering behind me, I remembered Franny's old advice, and began to recite in my head the towns on Highway 101, from the days when I'd go with her to stay with her dad in Santa Rosa. Santa Rosa, Sebastopol, Rohnert Park, Cotati. Was Cotati before or after Rohnert Park? Then Penngrove, Petaluma, Novato, San Rafael . . .

Finally a taxi stopped for me, and I got a ride to the airport. Once there I was so busy checking my bag, changing my ticket and unsuccessfully trying to argue my way out of the change fee that it wasn't until I sat down to wait the forty-five minutes before boarding that I had time to think about what I was doing. And by then my confidence was restored. I celebrated the start of my new life by ordering a piña colada.

Chapter 16

SOME GUY SAID Life is a Temporary Condition. He said we have to live it to the fullest, because it will soon be over. Life is a temporary condition. I can't think of anything as sad as that. Because if you think of it that way, then what is the point of anything we do? It's all going to be for nothing. Why should anyone try to do the right thing, make the right choice, make any choice at all? Why should you try to live your life without screwing it up when it's all just going to be over soon? What's the point?

For years I've been having a dream that I can barely remember when I wake up, when all that's left is a fragment of an image, a momentary flashback that I can just begin to grasp, and then as I try to fix on it, it moves faster and faster, blurring into a dark and spinning hole. All the memories rush down this hole like water down a drain, and I can't make out any of the details. But as it accelerates I see one thing clearly, just one thing. I see a bottle turning over and over, end over end, flying through the air. Over and over, end over end. I never see where it comes from. I never see it land. It just turns over and over, end over end, in an arc through the air. Sometimes I wonder if it has something to do with the bottle that AJ hurled over the cliff into the sea. But I don't think it does. That was a happy day, and this dream isn't happy. It is dense with anxiety, it crackles with fear.

Rose comes in to fuss around me and complain that the flowers on the twigs are dead and how hard is it for someone to notice and throw them away. She pesters me about eating, but I tell her to stop bringing that up, I really don't want anything. She's grumbling about Honey, too. I can't make out what the problem is. She mutters that Honey is blowing her off.   I ask her what she's talking about, and she never explains. No one explains anything to me. Or they do and I'm just not following it. When they talk, they all talk too fast, with words that tumble by me.   Even Bobbie, who comes in all bright and cheery, with a lot to say, says it with words that don't connect, and I can't make sense of what she's telling me half the time. It's all just words. Dieter doesn't talk much. That makes him easier than the others.

Dieter wants Honey to come home. That's one of the things that he and Rose talk about. They go on and on. I guess that's what Rose meant when she said Honey was blowing her off. Sometimes Rose is too hard on the girl. Honey will come home when she can. Rose better watch out, she'll turn into something like my mom the Nazi. I don't tell her that I've asked Honey a million times to come home. To come home because I miss her.

The bottle flies through the air, in a slow arc, turning end over end over end.   I want that to go away, but it keeps coming up, that image, and then it all moves too fast to see. Spinning into darkness.

Chapter 17

WALKING DOWN that bright and dusty Mexican street I had felt strong and confident and free, as if I could fly away on my own strong wings. It was a heady feeling. Walking out on Eddie put me in control. And walking out was the right thing to do. The right thing for a lot of reasons, reasons that I kept ticking off in my head. Eddie was too old for me. I was too young for him. His wife was too nice for this. And most important of all, with the intimacy of Eddie's family's hotel room fresh in my mind, he was a dad. He had two kids who needed him to be *there*. The whole thing with me and Eddie was nothing but a dead end. So I had set that empty coffee mug on a whitewashed wall in Ixtapa and walked away from it, walking away from Eddie and into a new life.

As I waited to board the plane I looked around at the passengers, mostly tourists headed home from a vacation, tanned and smiling, wearing shorts and flip-flops. Who knew, maybe someone in that very room would be part of my brand-new future. I stepped into the plane all wrapped in a glow, with a little film running in my head of my arrival in L.A., soft-focus images of me somehow getting around town, finding a picturesque little place to live, landing a vague but glamorous job, driving a convertible past rows of tall, slender palm trees, and hanging out with attractive friends.

But as the plane droned on, the seat became hot and uncomfortable, the piña colada wore off, and the peanut bag emptied. All that elation seeped right out of me, leaving me sobered and depressed. Who was I kidding? This wasn't a plan, it was a daydream. It was all too vague. Those were nice pictures, but there just wasn't enough detail. And I was left with an ominous question staring me right in the face. I mean, how on earth was I, Honey Barkin, suddenly going to know how to survive? Eddie owned the apartment, paid all the bills, and gave me my spending money. I had to admit he pretty much took care of me. Now, overnight, I was on my own. On my own with a voice in my head that refused to be still. Finally the voice that Rose had always talked about. Full on and critical: *So where am I going to live? How am I going to pay for it?* And more immediately: *Where will I sleep tonight?* I couldn't stay at the villa. Or could I? Would it be wrong to stay there? After all, my stuff was still there. *I need to go to the villa to get my things.* But how would I get there? A taxi would just suck up all my money. And back to the big question: *Where am I going to sleep tonight?* I looked around at the other people on the plane. All these people knew where they were going. They had an actual place to go. And me? I was on a plane flying to where I had no place to go. What kind of loser does that? *I should call Sandy. She can pick me up and take me to the villa. Should I stay there? Maybe, just for the night.*

And what should I do if Eddie calls again? He called twice while I was waiting to board the plane. Of course I didn't answer, but I was beginning to have some doubts about what I had done. *What if it was a huge mistake to leave? What if he decided to follow me? What if he had hopped onto the next plane after mine? Oh, would he do that? For me?* For a moment I was buoyant with that romantic thought, then swamped by a darker view. *What if he hates me now? What if Eddie called his workmen and told them to change the locks?* Then something even worse occurred to me. *Oh my God, what if he hasn't even noticed I've left?* He could be calling thinking I was still somewhere in the hotel. But I didn't have to think about that for long to know it was unlikely. I thought of Eddie holding hands with Annie and resolved to put all thought of him behind me. *I should just go to the villa and pick up my stuff and get right out of there. Sandy will let me stay with her. That Hollywood Hills house has plenty of room. I'll call her right away. But what if she isn't around? What is my backup plan? No problem. I'll*

*look for a cheap motel.   Really cheap.   But can I even afford
that?   How much money do I have to work with?*   I didn't
know how to turn off my thoughts. I had to listen to this stuff
over and over.

I got out my wallet and counted its contents, and tried to
remember how much I had in my money jar at the villa. Not
much, you could bet on it. By this time I was a wreck. What
kind of loser falls for a guy like Eddie in the first place,
thinking she's got it made when it's all just a hollow shell?
Now I had to start all over, cut loose from everything that I
had counted on to take care of me. I used to have my family,
but then I left them to come to L.A. And then I had Eddie, but
now that was over. With nothing left to hold me I was in free
fall, waiting to see what would happen when I landed.

Should I just forget Los Angeles and move back home?
Part of me was tempted to call home and hear someone say *Oh
baby, come home, we'll take care of you.*   But the new me
didn't want to do that. Sure, go home and admit that they
were right about Eddie.   I could still repeat verbatim their
entire chorus of advice when I left home for L.A. Rose telling
me that moving to L.A. to live with some guy I hardly knew
was harebrained. Vivian telling me that Eddie was too old for
me. Bobbie telling me that I should listen to Rose. Dieter
telling me that L.A. was a long ways away if I needed help.
Franny telling me that I should be aiming higher than a career
as some old guy's trophy kitten. It played like a tape-recorded
loop in my head. And guess what? That was their advice
when they didn't even know he was married. What would the
chorus have sounded like if they knew about that?   Rose
would pull out one of her favorite expressions: *certifiably
stupid.*   She would say that I was certifiably stupid to get
involved with Eddie, that this mess was inevitable, and that I
was up shit creek. Sure, I could always head back to the
Welcome Home Motel, and they'd take me in, but I'd be
coming home a loser. I would never hear the end of it.

So what were my other options?   I could figure out
something in L.A. Stay with Sandy, get a job, show them that
I could survive. Of course that was a much better plan. I

figured I would come clean about this mess eventually, but I'd wait until I was a success and then tell them. I had a strong feeling that if I could just get things going it would all flow together.

I leaned back in the seat and closed my eyes. I could see Eddie so clearly. I could see his face lit by the flickering light of a candle in a chunky red glass candleholder, gazing lovingly at me. I could see his hand pick up mine and lift it to his lips to kiss my pathetically chewed nails. I could see him in my mind's eye walking into the hotel room and finding my luggage gone. *In a panic he looks around the room. Gone, everything of mine gone. He leaves the hotel in a hurry. Does he see Annie first? Tell her that it's over? Does she cry, does he—*

"Would you like some more peanuts?" asked the flight attendant, leaning over my seatmate, a small package and a napkin in one hand, her face expectant. I thanked her and went back to my reverie. *Eddie is getting on a plane, the next flight to leave for L.A. He races to the villa and finds me there and—*

That's not going to happen. I can't be there.

So he comes home to the villa, and my things are gone from there too. He calls me, but I'm on a flight to San Francisco, where Franny picks me up. He follows me there and shows up at our apartment and holds me closely to him and whispers Don't ever leave again *and I—*

"Excuse me." The middle-aged woman in the window seat was motioning that she had to get past and I tucked my knees up to my chin while she clambered by. *Danny and I get back together. Then Eddie shows up and he and I have a huge fight. I tell him he can't do this to Annie and his little girls, it's over, I'm back with Danny now. He storms out—*

The woman squeezed by me again and settled herself back in her window seat. Wide awake now, with a slight headache, I knew that none of this would ever happen.

In Los Angeles all the passengers emptied out of the plane, leaving behind a mess of crumpled blankets, napkins stuffed into plastic cups, and sprawling magazines. We moved like a herd to the baggage carousels. All those people who had looked so interesting before when we were boarding the plane now looked as tired and irritable as I felt. We were all stuck together, waiting for our baggage to show up, passing the time by shuffling around, making phone calls, fiddling with text messages, and staring impatiently at the unmoving luggage track. I slumped down onto the carousel rim. I called Sandy but she didn't answer. Franny called, but I didn't answer. Eddie called me two more times, and it was all I could do not to answer. But I kept picturing him with Annie, the two of them holding hands, their heads tipped together in casual intimacy. I didn't doubt that Eddie loved me, but it was clear to me that he loved her too. I knew him well enough to know that. I don't know how he worked this out in his own mind, but that's his story, and it's my story I'm telling. All I could do was wonder and leave him behind.

Finally the carousel clattered to life and I got to my feet to watch as bags began to appear. When my lovely pale blue suitcase appeared I yanked it off the carousel in a rush of adrenaline and set it on the floor. I hitched the tote bag higher on my shoulder and marched for the door and the start of my new life. And then I had to pull up short. I still didn't know where I was going or how I would get there.

I found a bench and parked myself there while I tried to call Sandy again. Basically Sandy was my plan. Still no answer. If I couldn't reach Sandy I needed a back-up plan. The first order of business was to get back to the villa to get my stuff. I needed my coat, for one thing. Even though it was a bright and sunny day, still it was January, and chilly compared to Mexico. I called Sandy a third time, and yet again she wasn't picking up, so in the end I took a shuttle to the villa. It used up a chunk of my money, but I didn't have any choice. I figured I'd play it by ear from there.

It felt strange to pull up in front of the villa knowing that I no longer belonged to it. The workmen were there and the front door was open. I walked in and they smiled and nodded and said *hola* just like they always did.   As I walked across the patio I noticed that someone had cleaned up the pool. It figured. Now that I was moving out it was cleared of trash and ready to be filled with water. I also saw that the bird feeder was empty. My finches probably figured out another place to find food, which was just as well, because I wouldn't be there to feed them anymore.

My key worked in the apartment lock, so apparently Eddie hadn't asked the workmen to change it. Inside the apartment was like an oven, and it had that dusty, musty smell of a closed room. The blinds were down, and in the dark the answering machine's red light blinked impatiently at me from across the room. I raised the blinds, opened all the windows, and then sat down to play back the messages. There were fourteen, thirteen from Eddie and one from Franny. Eddie's were all the same. "Babe, are you there? C'mon, babe, pick up if you're there. You know I love you, babe." I erased them. Franny's message was "Hi, just checking in—your cell phone didn't pick up." I erased that too. I'd call her later. For now I just needed to gather my things and get out. There wasn't that much to do, since my big suitcase and my tote bag were already packed from Mexico.

I got out my second suitcase and filled it, but there were still some things left over. One of these was the little pink pillow with HONEY embroidered on it. I considered leaving it, but Eddie wouldn't have much use for it so I crammed it into the outside pocket of the suitcase.   I went downstairs where I found some empty cardboard boxes in the patio. I took one, knocked the sawdust out of it, and filled it up with my shoes and my hairdryer. I lined everything up by the door, then sat down in the armchair and called Sandy once more.

To my relief this time she answered on the first ring. She was at work, cleaning somebody's house. "Yeah, my phone died. The battery on this thing really sucks. I just got it charged up again and I saw you called. I was going to call you back soon. So where are you?"

"I just got home."

"I thought you were in Mexico."

"I was. But I split up with Eddie. I need a place to stay."

"Whoa, I didn't see that coming."

"Neither did I. Can I stay with you?"

"If you don't mind sleeping on a sofa. I'm in a different place now."

"What happened to the Hollywood Hills house?" I was aware that I was beginning to whine, but I couldn't help it. It didn't seem fair. I had become used to the plan that I would stay with her at that beautiful house with the view and all the bedrooms.

"The owners were ready to move in. I found something else, right here in Silver Lake. You remember Ashton?" I didn't, but I made a sort of noncommittal noise as if I did. "I'm renting a room in his house. Kind of a dump, but it's fun. It's a real party house. And the rent is cheap. Anyway, there's a sofa in my room. It's yours if you want it. While you get back on your feet."

It wasn't the Hollywood Hills house, but still I almost cried with relief. She said she would come by as soon as she finished the house she was cleaning, so I hauled my stuff down to the steps and sat there to wait for her, both arms around my coat, holding it to my chest. I was exhausted.

Sandy and I pulled up to a stucco bungalow that was distinguished by a Porsche parked in the middle of its dusty yellow lawn. As we walked to the door we could hear music coming out the open windows and someone shouting and laughing inside. On the porch we had to step around boxes and a heap of clothing. Sandy told me that these belonged to some girl who had been living in the house.

"She had to go to the emergency room after she fell off the roof, and her parents came to get her and took her home to Bakersfield. We put all her stuff here so they could come by and get it, but they never did. I don't know what we're going to do with it. Give it away I guess. If you see anything you like, help yourself."

"Off the roof?"

"She was fucked up."

Inside, the house was a mess. We walked into the living room where there were beer bottles and precariously stacked dirty plates, take-out coffee cups, and Styrofoam boxes with their clamshell lids sprung open. These had probably been licked clean by the dog, a golden retriever, who lay on top of a USC sweatshirt chewing on a flip-flop. He stopped chewing and looked up at us, his tail slowly banging the floor. The room was full of people draped over the furniture, but at first only the dog seemed to notice us. Everyone was nodding to the music and watching a young man with long blond hair kneeling on the floor, hovering over the coffee table. I could hear the telltale *tink tink tink* of a credit card on the glass surface.

"Is Ashton here?" Sandy asked. A lanky guy in an armchair with his back to the front door sat up and turned around. He looked at me in an appraising way, then shrugged. "I think he's around," he said.

"This is Honey," Sandy said, "and she's going to stay in my room for a while." The blond guy said, "Hi, I'm Scotty," and a couple of the others said, "Hey," and then all the cokeheads turned back to Scotty's activity on the table.

I followed Sandy upstairs to her room. "This house," she said, "used to belong to Ashton's grandmother. He inherited it when she died. Imagine having a house handed to you. Some people have all the luck."

"What does he do?"

"Not much." Sandy laughed. "He's got a trust fund. He enjoys life. He's fun. Smart. Funny. It must be nice to have a rich family who put money in the bank so their kids don't have to work. But he won't have it for long, the way he's going through it. All these people mooching on him, the blow, the clubs, the restaurants, the gym, the car, the house, the cleaning lady."

"Are you his cleaning lady?" I asked.

"No, thank God," she said, shaking her head. "I'd hate to have to clean up after this lot. Ashton has a nice little grandmotherly Mexican lady who comes in a couple times a week. Something happened to her this week and she hasn't been here. Usually it's not this nasty. When she comes in regularly it looks a lot better."

Sandy's room was small and crowded, with a bed, a small sofa, a large dresser, and a bookcase lined with shoes instead of books. The sofa looked pretty bad. It wouldn't have won any beauty contests when it was new, but now it sagged, and the brown upholstery was mottled with anonymous stains. There was a hole on one arm, and the foam erupting from it looked like big yellow lips. Sandy gave me a sheet to cover it and a couple of blankets, and it turned out to be much more comfortable than it looked. Then she took me down to the kitchen and showed me her shelf in the refrigerator. Leaning against a jar of olives was a piece of paper with "Don't Touch" scrawled on it with a thick black marker. "You can keep your food on my shelf. Everyone knows not to touch it," she said, gesturing to the note, "but I have to keep reminding them." We took a couple of soft drinks from Ashton's side of the refrigerator and went back up to her room. We sat back on her bed, and while Sandy rolled a joint I told her about Eddie and Mexico.

"So all this time he was going back and forth between you and his family. That's so sleazy."

"And it makes me feel like a fool."

"You are not a fool." Sandy looked at me sternly. "You didn't know. It's not your fault. He's the one who lied. Both to you and to his wife. Jeez, what a dickhead."

"And the worst part about it, she is so nice," I said mournfully. "I want to hate her but I can't."

"That's okay. Just hate him," said Sandy confidently, waving a matchbox in a magnanimous gesture. "This is probably for the best." She paused to light the joint. "He was an old fart. You'll be happier with people your own age."

She told me that I would have a lot more fun living in this house.

"If you're a friend of Ashton's, he'll take you along when he goes out. And he gets into the best clubs in L.A. *And* he always has a table for his friends." Sandy leaned forward, wide-eyed. "You wouldn't believe the clubs we go to. Forget the places we used to hang out. These are so stellar. They are ten times better." She leaned back again, handing the joint to me. "A lot of people come around, hoping to be part of Ashton's scene. They start showing up in the late afternoon, early evening, and some people crash here afterward." But Sandy wasn't just crashing at Ashton's house. She paid rent for her room, which gave her a certain status over the crashers. She was part of what she called his inner circle.

"So how did you meet this guy?" I asked.

"Through Marcos." Marcos the boyfriend, the DJ in New York. "Marcos and Ashton were roommates at USC, back when Ashton was in the film school and Marcos was studying music."

If I had known my question was going to bring up Marcos, I wouldn't have asked, because when she gets started talking about him, she goes on and on. I listened for a while and then tuned her out. I can only listen to so much about a person I've never met, and my mind was foggy with the weed. When I tuned back in she was saying she thought he had been in New York for way too long, and she was getting nervous that maybe he was having too good a time there without her. She was seriously thinking about moving to New York if he didn't return anytime soon.

"If Ashton likes you, maybe you can take over this room when I leave," she said. I looked around the room, trying to picture what it would be like to have it to myself. It would save me the hassle of finding a place on my own. Things were beginning to come together. But I seriously needed to get a job.

Later that afternoon I met Ashton when he appeared suddenly in the doorway. Sandy was mistaken when she said I had met him before. I'd remember him if I had. He was very good-looking, like some kind of movie star. Sad to say, though, he seemed to know it. Standing there in Sandy's doorway, one arm up against the doorframe, the other hand in a hip pocket, Ashton looked like he'd been practicing in front of a mirror all his life so that he would always know exactly how to create the best effect.   Mr. Look-at-Me-I'm-Good-Looking.   Then he bent down and picked up a gray-and-white cat that appeared at his feet.

"Did you meet Madonna?" he asked, cradling the cat in his arms.

I was pretty sure he was talking about the cat, but I didn't want to sound dumb.   What if he meant a person, or even the real Madonna?   This guy looked like he could conceivably have met the real Madonna.   I took a chance.   "You mean the cat?"

He did.   I guess she was his icebreaker.   Who would have thought that someone like Ashton would need one?   Madonna purred like an outboard motor, her face tilted up and her eyes closed, while he scratched her chin and soft white belly.   Since then I've seen him use the cat to start conversations with other people, so I'm guessing he was actually shy.   Surprising, but that would explain why he put in so much mirror time.   He was worried about getting it right.   Anyway, he didn't stay long there in Sandy's doorway, but before he sauntered away with the cat he invited me to come along when they all went out later that night.   Sandy silently gave me a thumbs-up.

Then she was all business.   We went through my clothes to decide what I should wear, and she kept saying no, not this, not that.   It had to be the right look.   When you go out with Ashton, she explained, you have to look more than hot—you have to look like something out of a magazine.   I ended up wearing one of her dresses.   When we came downstairs the two of us did look good.   I'm prettier than Sandy, but she has the glamorous hipster look the clubs like.   It's hard to believe she cleans houses for a living.

At first I was disappointed that I wasn't chosen to ride in Ashton's Porsche.   Instead I was told to go with Scotty, who apparently didn't live in Ashton's house, but hung out there a lot.   We walked out to his car and I was surprised to see that it was a beat up old thing with gray primer spots on it.   But he was really proud of it—apparently it was a big deal, a classic old Jaguar that he was renovating. Who knew.

We drove on the freeway for a while, then took one of the downtown exits. I was excited thinking we were heading for an elegant downtown restaurant, but no, we kept driving until we were in the middle of nowhere, surrounded by warehouses. We turned a corner and found ourselves in a line of fancy cars, in front of what Scotty said was a restaurant, though it didn't look like much from the outside. There were valets in matching jackets in front, and men with cameras milling around. Scotty said there must be a celebrity sighting to bring out the paparazzi. When we pulled up, a valet pounced on the car to open the doors. I would have thought he would snub a car that looked this old, but instead he practically drooled with compliments as Scotty handed him the key.

Inside the restaurant the first thing you saw was a huge flower arrangement that was something like six feet wide and had entire tree branches in it. Next to it there was a curvy red sofa that looked like it had just landed from outer space. The maître d' fell all over Scotty, and kept touching his arm as he took us to a table where Ashton and Sandy and some other people were already seated. By this time I was so excited I could hardly focus. After a few minutes I took a good look around, but I never saw the celebrity who had attracted the paparazzi.

After a dinner that I can't even remember eating we got back into the cars and drove to the club. Out in front there were more valets. A lot of people were milling around, hoping to get past the bouncer, but when we walked up to the door he nodded to Ashton and waved us right in. Inside the place was throbbing with music and lights and energy and dancing, and it was as stellar as Sandy had said it would be. Ashton danced a little, but mostly he talked and watched, looking as languid as a cat. I danced, though. I danced until I was exhausted, and it felt wonderful.

The next day I woke up late, groggy and thirsty. Sandy was still sound asleep. I got up quietly and went downstairs. The house was silent. In the kitchen I looked for some coffee but I couldn't find any. I helped myself to some juice in the refrigerator and then looked into the living room. It was dark, the shades still pulled. There was a girl sitting there in the dim light, with the TV on but the sound off. She was listening to her iPod while she watched a daytime talk show. She had been part of our group the night before, but I couldn't remember her name. She looked like she didn't want to be interrupted, and the silent TV didn't look very appealing to me, so I went for a walk. Walking was something I was used to doing when I was bored. And there would be coffee on Sunset Boulevard.

Even in January the weather can be glorious in Los Angeles, and this was a beautiful sunny day. The hodgepodge of houses stacked up the hill were picturesque with their palm trees and orange trees and their lush green gardens. All this color should have made my spirit soar, but it just reminded me that I was in Silver Lake without Eddie. The villa was not that far away, just on another hill, but it might as well have been in Italy.

I kept thinking about Eddie in that Ixtapa hotel. I pictured him walking into our room to find my stuff missing. Was he surprised? Relieved? Angry? It occurred to me that I had never seen the bad temper that he once told me he had. Probably just as well. I don't think I could have stood up to someone who yelled at me. But maybe he wasn't angry when he found out I was gone; maybe he was just sad. Should I have left him a note? I was tempted to walk over to the villa to write one.

I thought of the dinner he and I had at the hotel's fancy restaurant, with the margaritas and the big steaks, when we danced the rumba together. That night he told me that I was his luscious girl. When I thought of that I got a momentary lift in my stomach, like you do when an elevator starts. But then I thought about seeing him holding hands with Annie, the two of them looking completely natural together, and I forgot all about how sweet Eddie had been with me. So you can see the problem I was having. My emotions were swinging wildly all over the place. I missed him, yet I was angry with him for being such a shithead. I was sorry for the kids, I felt badly for Annie, and even worse for me. What a bunch of losers we all were. I resented the hell out of the whole situation. But out of all that mess another side of me emerged, one that was coldly realistic. Because even I could see that there was no future in Eddie for me. That was clear as day. I figured I might as well do something right in my life. Leaving Eddie was the right thing to do. I needed to stick to that thought. Franny would have been proud of me. And not just Franny. Rose would have been proud of me.

Over the course of the next few weeks I fell into the routine of living in Ashton's house. It was fairly simple, with the nights spent on Sandy's sofa and the days spent walking around the neighborhood looking for a job and trying not to think about Eddie. Some days I gave Sandy a hand with her work so I could pick up a few dollars. Eddie called several times, but I never answered. I just listened to his voice messages. He was trying to get through to me by using his low, sexy growl, saying "Hey, babe," and it almost worked. But then I put it out of my mind. I would have been certifiably stupid to go back to a situation like that.

I spent a lot of the afternoons hanging out in the living room, watching TV with some of the zombie moochers who showed up and sat around waiting to see what Ashton had planned for the evening. It all depended on what Ashton felt like doing. Sometimes all he wanted to do was hang out, which I found boring. When he hung out with the moochers, all they talked about was movies, arguing about how good or bad each one was. And then they put the movies on a list on the wall. And by wall, I mean right on the wall, with a Sharpie pen. I kid you not. I wonder what Ashton's grandmother would have thought about what they were doing to her house. I mean, who writes on the wall? I have to wonder how I managed to live in not one but two places with indoor graffiti. At least you could argue that there was some practical value in the phone numbers penciled in on Danny's kitchen wall. But Ashton and the moochers were doing something completely meaningless that they thought was totally significant. They had one list for good movies and one for bad movies, and they had a third category called SRV, Some Redeeming Value. The lists started out looking neat at the top, but as films were added they began to slope downward and the columns slumped to one side, then the other, and it got messier when a movie was crossed out on one list and entered on another. Sometimes they were crossed out again and moved back. I kept wishing Franny were there—she'd have loved all that talk, and she'd think the lists on the wall were cool. But I really couldn't contribute much to these conversations, and they had limited entertainment value, so I much preferred it when Ashton wanted to go clubbing. Nobody else seemed to care one way or another. They went along with whatever he chose. The moochers were like a flock of sheep.

There was a pair of models who rented a room from Ashton, and they were as bored with the sheep as I was. They were Kelly and Claire, and at first I had a hard time keeping them straight, because they looked the same to me. They were both abnormally tall, and anorexic, which is not so surprising because like I said, they were models, and they both had long, dark hair and dark eyes, and dead-white skin. As I got to know them, though, I was surprised that I had ever confused them. They had very different personalities. Claire was sweet and easygoing, while Kelly was sarcastic and abrupt. I must have rubbed her the wrong way. I kept trying to be nice to her, but she was so snippy that I finally stopped trying. I found her too intimidating to be around. And they both were so style-conscious that I felt frumpy next to them.

Sandy liked fashion too, but she wasn't about to let it run her life. She had a lot more going for her. For one thing, she was a lot smarter than Claire and Kelly. Sandy's real name wasn't Sandra, like you'd think. It was actually Alexandra, but she had decided that she liked the sound of Sandy, and when she went away to college she took the opportunity to go with that. She said Sandy was more informal. It suited her style better than Alexandra. She asked me once about my name. You could tell she didn't approve of the name Honey.

"No one is going to take you seriously if you let them call you that."

"It's my name. I can't do anything about it."

"That's crap. Of course you can. Just change it."

"Change it? To what? And how? It's not like I'm going away to college."

"Choose a name and tell everyone that's what you will answer to. New name, new persona."

I told her I'd think about it. I didn't like being bossed around like that. But usually Sandy wasn't bossy. In fact, she was pretty much the only person I could talk with in that house. One of us could start a sentence and the other could finish it. Just like with Franny. But Sandy was gone pretty much all day every day cleaning her houses. On some days she was cleaning as many as four houses, so I was pretty much on my own during the day.

But it's not like I was alone. In Ashton's house people came and went all day long. Scotty was there a lot, though Ashton didn't care for that dog of his, who went everywhere Scotty did. The dog chewed on things and chased Madonna. Ashton also complained that Scotty was a slob. So what else is new? Actually it wasn't just Scotty. Everyone pretty much trashed the place. I felt sorry for Remedios, the housecleaner. She was very patient to put up with that crowd. The night before her cleaning day Ashton would admonish everyone to clean up. "Listen up," he'd announce, "Remedios is coming tomorrow, so clean up your stuff," and when they didn't, he got really angry. When Scotty left his blow on the coffee table on Remedios' day, Ashton went ballistic, yelling, "Dude, I told you to get your junk out of here. Get it fucking out of here when Remedios comes." Scotty put it away, chuckling to himself.

The first time I met Remedios it was when I was in the kitchen trying to figure out why it smelled like something had died in there. She came in, stopped in her tracks and made a face. We poked around together, looking for the source of that disgusting odor. It turned out someone had left a roast beef sandwich in a bag that dropped behind the garbage can. I guess Scotty's dog couldn't reach it there. Remedios shook her head and took the nasty thing out, while I tried not to gag. We got to talking, and she said, "Ashton is a sweet boy, but the others, a bunch of crazy kids." To hear her talk about Ashton, you'd think he could walk on water. All I can say is he must have paid her well.

Ashton took care of the moochers too, so everyone put up with him, even when he got crazy and yelled about the mess. The two models got huffy when he did that, and you could hear the tension in the house, a low hum of offended voices in the next room. Sometimes there was tension and I didn't even know the cause of it, but I could tell it was there from that telltale hum—indistinct, murmuring, rising and lowering, pushing and whining. The voices of the models, or Sandy, or Ethan who had just come from Tel Aviv and slept on the sun porch, or Scotty complaining in the kitchen. Even Madonna felt it. She would snap at your hand when you tried to pet her. For a while the tension was because Ashton had gone to Spain for a week and came back eating dinner every night at midnight and no one else wanted to wait that long to eat. But that blew over, just like everything else did. Eventually everyone was back to normal, mooching off Ashton and talking about movies.

Except me. Sometimes I felt like a little cat that got picked up and petted now and then, but who lived her own cat life in a house full of people. Me and Madonna.

Chapter 18

FOR THE LOVE OF GOD will Dr. Steinberg just pick up the fucking phone? If they page him one more time, I think I'm going to haul my ass out of bed and go find him myself.

Bobbie gave me her iPod to listen to while I'm here. For some reason I keep pressing it in the wrong place and exiting the playlist. My back feels sweaty and I need to have the pillows adjusted. I've picked off most of the nail polish Dieter put on so carefully, so my hands look like shit. And I can't tell what time of day it is. If the Vietnamese nurse shows up, it's daytime. I asked her what she does when she's not here, and she said she takes care of her baby. She has a little baby at home, and she takes care of big babies here.

Dieter loved the babies. Some men are natural parents, and Dieter is one of those men. He would hold Honey and Franny, and talk to them and carry them around. When they started eating real food, he would feed them Cheerios, one by one, and talk to them while they smiled and babbled and ate the Cheerios. One day, out of the blue, he said to me, you need to tell the dad so he can be part of her life. And I just told him she'll be okay, she's got me.

I tell Dieter that I don't know who the dad is, and that makes him crazy. He doesn't believe me. I've stopped arguing with him, because nothing I say erases that little bit of doubt he carries around with him. If he wants to think he might be Honey's dad, well, let him. He's the best thing that happened to our family, but I draw the line at making his dream come true. I've had my reasons. Do you think I want to have someone looking over my shoulder all the time, telling me that I'm doing something wrong, or forgetting something important, or messing things up yet again? And you can bet

that's exactly what I would have on my hands if there were a
dad actively involved.   If it were Dieter, anyway.

Chapter 19

I NEEDED A CAR. Which is another way of saying I needed a job, because in L.A. the two pretty much go hand in hand. There was no way I could afford a car until I got a job, but job-hunting without one was exhausting. Public transportation in this city is a joke. But even with a car it's hard to get around. The city is so big and sprawling that no one thinks twice about driving an hour to get anywhere. So I muddled along, sometimes taking buses but mostly walking to nearby areas of Silver Lake and Echo Park. Sandy let me use her car sometimes, and when she did it was a relief to drive for a change. Sandy claimed that owning a car was a hassle. She was always worrying about checking the oil, and checking the tires, and checking who knows what else. She was all the time saying that it was better to live in New York where you didn't need one.   But she was just taking her car for granted, forgetting what it would be like here in L.A. without it. Even an old car like hers was better than nothing at all. And hers was better than my mom's car, that old Honda that you could hear rattling up the street from a block away.

The job search was a discouraging process. I filled out applications, mostly for counter help at sandwich places and coffee shops, but nothing ever came to anything because they said I didn't have any experience. I was too young to work in a bar. I thought about Bobbie's old job as an exotic dancer. It sounds much more glamorous than it actually was. Franny and I found that out first hand when we were in fifth grade and Bobbie took us with her to her old club because the bartender there owed her some money. Not exactly the best place to bring a couple of kids. I'm sure that if Rose knew about this she would have declared Bobbie certifiably stupid. Sometimes Bobbie didn't think things through. But she knew enough to hurry us past the main part of the club to the back room so we wouldn't have time to take in the three naked gum-chewing girls who were languidly moving about on the stage, barely keeping time to the deafening music. Even as we were being hustled across the back of the room we could see that their eyes were empty with what we thought was boredom. Now, looking back, I know they were probably zoned out on some kind of zombie shit. Then Franny had to use the bathroom, and while we were there, the three dancers came barging in, buck naked, one of them gasping, "I thought I was going to die I had to pee so bad." Up close they didn't look too good. They looked tired, and their bare tits were pale and sweaty. They all needed to shave their armpits, which had too much stubble to be glamorous, in my opinion. I didn't see Bobbie quite the same way for a while, though looking back on it now I can appreciate how much she has changed her life since her dancing days. But meanwhile I was not too eager to go find myself a job in that line of work.

I stopped for coffee one afternoon at a little café on Sunset Boulevard called Evie's Pie Shop. After a couple of weeks of job hunting and endless walking around, I was bored and discouraged. I needed a car, I was bone-tired, my days were full of rejection, my nights were spent tossing and turning, and my life was so empty that I was hanging out in this sorry ass café because I had nothing better to do. Even worse, I was sipping my coffee as slowly as possible, to make it last longer so I wouldn't have to buy another. How lame was that? I could feel my throat constrict like there was a rock in it, and tears filled my eyes. It happened so fast I didn't even have time to start listing the cities along San Pablo Avenue. The next thing I knew, tears were running down my cheeks, off the tip of my nose, and splashing on my hand. I hunched down, hoping that no one was noticing. Fortunately the café was almost empty. I was mopping up the tears with my napkin, trying not to sniffle and sob, when I felt a hand on my shoulder. It was the man from behind the counter.

"Hey, are you okay?" His voice was so kind that I really lost it. Now I was a gushing fountain of tears. "Is there anything I can get you?"

It was embarrassing, but I couldn't stop. The man sat down next to me, patting my arm. Then he waved at someone behind the counter, who brought more napkins so I could blow my nose. So I found myself telling him about Eddie and Mexico, though I left out the part about Eddie being married. It wasn't anyone's business that I was that dumb. I told him that I got dumped and I needed a job and I didn't know what I could do. I couldn't look directly at him, because his sympathetic face just made me cry more. Instead I focused on the table, staring at a crack in the red Formica tabletop. It was the same kind of red Formica as the tables in the Last Stop, so I felt like I was talking to Rose, and when I finished explaining my sorry life I half expected to hear Rose answer me, but instead it was this gentle man asking me could I work evenings. I looked at him, barely comprehending. I looked around at the pie shop and then back to him.

"As a waitress?"

"Sort of," he answered. "Not in here, though. For my wife's catering business."

His name was Frank, and it turns out the pie shop was just a little side thing, while his wife's catering business was the main event. He took me behind the counter and through the doors into a huge kitchen, ushering me past a couple of Mexican boys who stopped chopping carrots and peppers long enough to watch us parade by. Frank opened the door on the far side of the kitchen. The next room was apparently the wife's kingdom.

In some ways it was a normal office, with a desk, several chairs, gray metal file cabinets, and a beat-up bookshelf full of catalogs. But what set it apart from any office I've ever seen were three racks of colorful costumes. There were costume parts and props draped all over the place. And sitting in the middle of all this, pulling hot-pink ostrich-feather headdresses out of a large cardboard box, was a plump, middle-aged woman in tight purple jeans, metallic gold sandals, a voluminously flowing pink-and-orange top, and several layers of gold-chain necklaces. As she pawed through the box, she stopped to pull out one arm, holding it aloft to shift the tinkling stack of gold bangles back toward her elbow, and then she looked up at us, pushing a long curling black-and-gray lock of hair out of her face, from where it had fallen out of the bundle loosely clipped at the top of her head. She greeted us with a beaming smile. She had fire-engine-red lipstick on, kohl-lined eyes, and false eyelashes that were, as Rose would say, big enough to rake leaves. Frank introduced us. This was his wife, Evelyn. But everyone called her Evie.

Just from that first impression I could tell that Evie's catering business was going to be interesting, that nothing about it would be run-of-the-mill. Evie was clearly not the sort of woman who would find satisfaction in putting on a pair of black pants and a white shirt to pass around shrimps on toothpicks. No, as she explained to me, she put on themed parties. All her girls and boys, as she called her servers, were young and pretty, and they all worked in costume.

"We do a Summer of Love party where all the girls and boys are dressed like hippies. And a Saucy Shakespeare party, with the girls dressed as Elizabethan wenches," she explained. "And Pirate Pandemonium, ditto. A lot of cleavage and pushup-bras on the girls, tights, big boots, and codpieces on the boys. There's Arabian Nights. All the girls are dressed like belly dancers, and the boys are bare-chested and wear turbans. Then there's Vegas Lights, with lots of fishnet and sequins and feathers. Stars Over Hollywood with wigs and dresses to do, oh, you name it, Marilyn Monroe, Audrey Hepburn . . ."

"Joan Crawford," suggested Frank.

"Joan Crawford." She nodded. "All those old-time Hollywood stars. The old queens love it. And then there's my Roman Orgy with skimpy togas. I'd love to do a Disney party with Snow White and Aladdin and the Little Mermaid, but the licensing thing is a bitch. Anyway, the list goes on. And these are off the shelf. If a customer wants something custom, and can bankroll it, I can work with him. But it's all on the up and up. Sexy, but not dirty, you understand."

"Nothing you can't write home about," said Frank, laughing. He was looking at Evie adoringly. You could tell he loved being part of this circus. He was so quiet, and plain, and gray, you could walk past him on the street and never see him. The fact that he was married to this woman revealed a whole other side to the man. You could see that every day brought new entertainment.

"We do birthday parties, bar mitzvahs, anniversary parties," she went on. "Lately we've been getting a lot of call for a party we call Sex, Drugs, and Rock and Roll. It's for baby boomer birthdays. We don't supply drugs, of course, but there's plenty of booze. People love us." She beamed at me. "We're hot."

"And the food is good, too," Frank added.

"Of course it is. Frank sees to that." She reached up and cupped her hand on his cheek. I loved these people.

"So," she said, turning briskly to me. "You want a job. Do you think you can do this?"

I was so excited I could hardly breathe, and the words came out in a whisper. "Oh yes!"

"I'm sure you can. You're lovely. How about tonight? We're doing two parties tonight, Vegas Lights and SD double R.

"SD double R?"

"Sex, Drugs, and Rock and Roll. But I don't need you for that. What I could use is another showgirl."

I couldn't believe my luck. This was the perfect job. Evie had me sit right down and fill out the forms. I put Sandy down as my emergency contact. My family was just too far away. So that was how I ended up somewhere in Beverly Hills that night, in fishnet tights, a red satin bustier top, and a huge feather headpiece that took a bit of getting used to, passing around a silver tray of bite-sized morsels made with cucumber and shrimp and something white. Earlier that evening everyone had gathered in Evie's office to change into their costumes. Meanwhile Frank and his kitchen crew had prepared all the food and loaded it into their big white truck. On the side it said HOLLYWOOD CREATIONS in huge letters, with EVIE & FRANK'S in smaller black lettering above that. One of the other servers explained to me that when Evie got her first truck it had the name Hollywood Creations already painted on the side, and she saved money by making that the name of her business. I don't know if that's a true story or not. I asked her about it once, much later, and all she did was laugh.

At the party our job was to keep circulating, answering questions about ingredients and saying reassuring things like yes, everything was organic, or no, this didn't have dairy in it, or yes, there were peanuts in it. And when the tray was down to half full we were to head back to the kitchen, emptying it along the way. In the beginning of the evening the guests made much over us, telling us how adorable we were. As the evening wore on and they got sloshed, we got more than compliments—we got tips stuffed into our bodices and tucked into the legs of our leotards, which was a good thing, because by then we were exhausted, and our feet were killing us, and the only thing that kept us going was the thought of the money we were making.

Evelyn told me I was a good worker and promised me she'd use me regularly. And she did. I worked every night my first two weeks on the job. I even got to be Marilyn Monroe once, with a light-blond wig and a pouty low-cut white dress, but usually Evie gave roles like that to actors, because she said it was as much impersonation as it was serving. There were a surprising number of actors working for her. Surprising to me, anyway, because I had always thought Hollywood actors were rich. But apparently that wasn't true, because all the actors I met were looking for work. They loved doing the Saucy Shakespeare parties, because that meant they could show off by talking like Romeo and Juliet.

We had to provide some things ourselves. False eyelashes were required on the girls, and I was glad that Bobbie had taught me how to trim them and put them on. Evie said I was a pro. The other thing we provided were our shoes. Evie was fairly flexible about what we came up with, as long as it fit with the costume.   She was very fussy about our hands. "Hand check!" she'd announce, and we were all supposed to put our hands out so she could check the nails.   "When someone serves me with broken nails and chipped polish," she said with a dramatic grimace, "it turns my stomach." We were expected to have long shaped nails and polish. On the first night she handed me a package of false nails—to cover mine, which as usual I had chewed up. She told me that in the future I needed to keep my own supply of false nails always at the ready. She looked at the boys' nails too. They were supposed to buff theirs to a gloss and keep them clean as a whistle. On my second night of work, she pounced on Kenny, one of the cute gay boys, and sent him into the bathroom with a scrub brush.

Working every night meant I couldn't go out with Ashton and his moochers, but I didn't mind so much, because I liked the people I worked with. We all had a lot of fun kidding around together.   Besides, many of the parties were like something out of a movie, in huge houses so fancy they could be in a magazine, and sometimes we saw celebrities. At one of the parties I saw Angelina Jolie. I could hardly believe it. I actually served her. Well, okay, not actually. I offered her the tray, but she didn't want the cheese thingy. Evie said not to take it personally, because it was probably about the calories in cheese. She said all movie people were on strict diets. And they all worked out every single day. "It's a full-time job to look that skinny and beautiful," she liked to point out.   Evie said life was too full of good things to eat and drink to go through it trying to be skinny.   You could tell she lived this philosophy.

I saw other celebrities at the parties, because L.A. was full of them, but I never saw anyone else as hugely stellar as Angelina Jolie.   But I actually talked with a young actor named Evan Moss, who had made a movie called *Blue Moon* that he said was scheduled for summer release. For an actor who had just made a movie, he wasn't stuck up at all, though I suppose it makes a difference if no one knows you yet. But I couldn't wait for the movie to come out, because I'd never seen anyone up there on the big screen that I'd actually met and talked to. Sure, some of the kids working for Evie were actors, but they were in dog-food commercials, or acting in plays in a warehouse somewhere. Not in real movies. Evan was seriously handsome, with warm brown eyes and a lock of brown hair that fell forward on his forehead. He also had the most perfect teeth I'd ever seen, and a nice mouth with rosy lips. I would have melted if those lips had touched me. He left the party with a woman who was dressed in a skimpy silk top, satin leggings, and four-inch heels. I guess I couldn't compete with that, and I probably wouldn't have a chance with a guy like that anyway.

Most of the parties were for regular people, not celebrities—regular people with enough money to have a fancy party. There were a lot of bar mitzvahs, which took some getting used to, all those amped-up kids getting lavish parties thrown for them. I never knew anyone who had that kind of bar mitzvah. When Sarah Wiseman had her bat mitzvah, her parents rented a room at a hotel in Berkeley and decorated it themselves with balloons. It was catered with deli platters, and Sarah's older brother was the DJ. We thought it was fun. We had no idea that it was way down near the bottom of the chart as far as parties go.

Working every night meant that I was finally earning some real money. I told Sandy I could help her pay for her room, but she said she felt bad taking my money, since my bed was just a sofa. And she liked sharing the room with me. I bought her a really nice orange bag at a designer consignment store as a thank you gift. And after a time we worked out a small rental agreement.   I was beginning to feel like my life was finally taking shape.

When Bobbie called me she said it was to invite me home for Franny's birthday party. But it didn't take long for her to get to the real reason she called. She wanted me to come home because she was worried about my mom. "Something is seriously wrong with Vivian," she told me. Bobbie was such a pushover. Vivian acted sick to get attention. She'd sit in a corner and cough until someone said *Are you okay?* And then she could talk about herself. And even if she was really sick, what did Bobbie think I could do about that? It was not like my visit would boost her immune system. So I told Bobbie that seeing me wouldn't have any effect on Vivian, but I would come home anyway, because I missed Franny. I was not going to let Vivian make me feel guilty.

And now that I was making real money, I felt confident enough to buy a plane ticket to fly home. Evie was disappointed because she had several parties scheduled, but she said I could go have a few days with my family. "Family is important," she said. "But sweetheart, you'd better get your tushie right back here, because I've got a full schedule coming up."

So here I was, on a plane again, like some kind of jet-setter. I was feeling successful. I had told everyone at home about my new job, and they were all excited for me. Still, there were a few things I hadn't mentioned. I didn't tell them that I was sleeping on Sandy's sofa. I figured it was better they didn't know that. It would just detract from my success. A bigger issue was telling them about Eddie. I didn't actually lie about it, but I had never quite mentioned that things hadn't worked out. I figured it would be better to come clean in person when the moment was right. And I figured the moment might be right in the car driving home. Driving is usually a good time for serious revelations, because people seem to be calmer in cars. They can't slam any doors. And everyone is looking straight ahead, so you don't have crippling eye contact. But when Vivian and Bobbie met me at the airport, they were so overjoyed to see me that I held back. Why remind them how dumb I was? But wouldn't you know it, when we got to the apartment, we barely had time to hug each other when Rose came out with "So your friend Eddie called the bar a bunch of times, asking how to reach you."

You could hear that proverbial pin drop. It had never occurred to me that Eddie would call them, but of course he knew about the Last Stop and all he had to do was look up the phone number. I looked at their expectant faces. Clearly they were dying to know what was going on. So I had to admit to them that things hadn't exactly worked out. To my relief they were surprisingly supportive. Probably they were simply glad that I wasn't with Eddie anymore, since they seemed to suspect him of dark intentions. Though later, when I mentioned that to Bobbie, she said "We didn't suspect him of dark intentions. Hey, you are a pretty nineteen-year-old girl, and he's a horny thirty-nine-year-old man. It was his regular intentions we suspected." Fair enough.

Franny had a lot to say about it too. "So your silverback turned out to be a real jerk."

"Thanks for pointing that out to me."

"Aw, c'mon. I'm saying it sympathetically."

"So you don't think I'm lame?"

"Well, maybe a little. You got what you deserved, letting him take care of you."

"It wasn't even bonobo sex."

"Well, there's your whole problem!" Franny whooped. "You went for the wrong monkey. You went looking for a bonobo and found a silverback gorilla instead."

"Very funny, ha ha, I'm cracking up" was the only answer I could think of.

But there were some good times during the visit. We had a little party for Franny. Bobbie and I sat on the sofa, side by side, blowing up balloons. That was sort of a family tradition. We always had balloons. Dieter picked up a cake at a bakery, and we had lamb chops for dinner, which was one of Franny's favorite foods. It felt like old times.

But overall the visit was a letdown. And not just because I had to tell everyone that Eddie hadn't worked out. And not just because they all spent the whole time lobbying me to move back home. But because Bobbie had been right: Vivian didn't look so good. Her coughing was becoming really noticeable, especially in the morning, but she brushed Rose off every time she brought it up. And what really got Rose ticked off was that Vivian wouldn't quit smoking, and refused to even discuss it. And she was exhausted most of the time. So that pretty much pulled the mood down. On top of that, I was feeling lousy myself. I was barely dragging my butt around the house. So the two of us were not exactly a couple of firecrackers. Franny tried to liven things up, but the tone around the place was gloomy. Rose wanted to take us to see doctors, but we both resisted. She told me she thought I probably picked up a bug in Mexico, an idea that completely creeped me out. But Rose said that happened all the time, and it would probably just work through my system. I hoped she was right. Anyway, I thought, if I did get a bug from Mexico, then all I could say was, it figured. That Mexico trip was bad news all around.

All in all I was relieved when it was time to drive back to the airport. Franny drove me. We pulled up in front of departures, hauled my suitcase out of the trunk, and then stood there looking at each other. Whatever words we said at this point, we both knew what we really meant.

"Well, have an uneventful flight," Franny said. I knew that was her way of saying *I love you, I'll miss you.*

"Okay. Well, say goodbye to everyone again for me." That was my way of saying *I love you too, and I'll miss you terribly.* Franny took the blue cashmere scarf from around her neck. It was soft as a kitten, and she knew I loved it. She wrapped it around my neck, and then, tugging on the scarf, she pulled me to her in a hug.

When I got back to L.A. I found that the bug that I had picked up in Mexico was getting worse and worse, and pretty soon I could count on feeling queasy every morning. Finally I realized that maybe we weren't talking about some Mexican bug. Because you know, it was the old calendar thing. And oh boy, my calendar was trying to tell me something. My period hadn't happened in a long, long time. So I was beginning to suspect there was a pretty life-changing reason for my queasy stomach. I went to Walgreens and got one of those do-it-yourself pregnancy tests, and it was no huge surprise when it went all positive on me. So I entered the next major phase of my life. My pregnant phase.

Chapter 20

I ENDED UP HERE because I didn't take care of myself, but I'm going to turn over a new leaf. No more smoking. Not even one a day. And cut down on the booze. Maybe to one a day. Maybe limit it to beer; beer is nutritious. Because if I don't take care of myself, this thing could kill me. Rose was very explicit about that. She says I have a death wish with my smoking. I tell her to take a hike. To stop being so dramatic. Because no one has a death wish. Life is the one thing we are given. It is everything. That is why we fight so ferociously to keep it. It is our only possession.

It is an astonishing thing, when you think about it. The whole body ticking right along, all systems go, blood and bones and synapses functioning in all their complicated ways, and sometimes not functioning so well, but still keeping on, and our mind at the center of it. That's life. It is a light in our eyes. They say you can look in someone's eyes as they are dying and know when the light goes out. How does that work? How is it we recognize when life slips out of their eyes? One moment these are the eyes of a person. The next moment they are empty marbles and that person is suddenly and mysteriously gone, an inanimate piece of meat staring at nothing. The carcass may resemble the person who used to inhabit that body, but it is as far removed from the live person as a stone-carved likeness.

We can't see into another's life. We have no hold over anyone else. Not lovers, not daughters. We can't slip into their heads and make them do what we want. We can only inhabit ourselves. We have only our own life, inside our own skin. Alone. And one day it will be over, though it is hard to imagine it stopping.

I try to imagine that. Try to imagine being dead, and everyone around me, looking at me, sad and crying, staring at me as I lie there dead. But if I were really dead, I wouldn't be able to see them looking at me, so it's all just too hard to imagine. And besides, I'm going to turn over a new leaf.

Quit your whining, Rose said.

I need to get healthier and get back to work. When I'm working things are better. Bookkeeping is a reassuring line of work. The ledgers and the numbers always add up. To something. They tell a story that is simple and straightforward. There is plus and minus, in and out, and it all lines up. Nothing slipping off the page, spinning out of reach. In real life everything is open to interpretation. In real life the accounting becomes so much more complicated. What do I owe Honey? What do I owe Dieter? Or Suzanne? Or AJ? And when does it come due? And when do you know you've paid enough?

Chapter 21

PREGNANT.   One of life's little jokes. Of course I couldn't
tell the family. Not just because they'd tell me that I was
certifiably stupid, but because as soon as I shared this with
them a huge death ray of energy from four overzealous adults
would be focused right down on me. They would tell me to
get an abortion. Or talk me into keeping it. Or urge me to put
it up for adoption.   Jesus fucking Christ, I had no idea which
of these things I did or didn't want to do. Even without them
to confuse things I was vacillating all over the place, trying to
decide. All I knew was that I didn't want anyone telling me
what to do.   And that's why I didn't want to get Eddie
involved, either. He'd be another person with strong opinions.
I'd probably see that bad temper he said he had. He'd go
ballistic on me, screaming how on earth could you let this
happen. Because I was supposed to be on the pill. But I
forgot to refill the prescription before we went to Mexico, and
I thought since I normally took them faithfully I would have
some kind of protection. Well, apparently not.

Evie caught me barfing in the wastebasket in the hall
behind her office and yelled at me, saying no way could I
work with food if I was sick, and it was irresponsible for me to
show up like that. So I had to tell her. She was the second
person I told. Sandy was the first.

"No way!" Sandy had exclaimed.

"Yes way," I answered glumly. I had to explain to her all
about forgetting the pills in Mexico, and you could tell she
thought I was an idiot, but she tried not to show it.

Both Sandy and Evie kept nagging me to tell my family.
Neither of them understood that I couldn't. Sandy got really
exasperated with me, but Evie got all motherly. She sat me

down in her office one afternoon and asked me what I was going to do. I had no idea how to answer that. All I could think of was to ask it back to her.

"What do you think I should do?"

"Listen, sweetheart, no one can tell you what to do. You need to do some serious thinking."

"Do you think I should get an abortion?"

"I think you should consider it. Yes I do. That thing isn't a baby yet. It's a potential baby, but right now it's still part of your body and you can end it if that's what you decide. You'll be sad, but it may be a necessary choice. But you listen to me, sweetheart, if you decide not to get an abortion, if you decide you're going to have it, then you need to do it right. It will be a real baby, and you will need to take responsibility."

"What do you mean, do it right?"

"I mean you need to eat right, take your vitamins, clean up your act. No drugs, no alcohol."

When I look back on it, I think it was this conversation with Evie that swayed me. Not because she was trying to sell me one way or another but because of the way she explained things. The abortion side of the equation sounded so vague, while on the other side, keeping the baby came with such a clear To Do list. I didn't have a clue how an abortion was accomplished, so I couldn't begin to picture it, though I was pretty sure pain was involved. I just couldn't picture myself in a doctor's office having that procedure. On the other hand, the more I thought about it, the more I could clearly see myself doing all the things Evie said I had to do if I kept the baby. Eat right, take my vitamins, quit drinking, quit smoking weed. I could really picture myself eating salads, and saying no when Sandy offered me a joint. In the end going through with the pregnancy seemed the far more tangible choice.

So I told Evie and Sandy that I was going to have the baby. I figured I'd just wing it, deciding my next step when the thing was born. Things would be clearer then. But I could tell they didn't approve of my decision. Sandy said I would regret it. When I told her I didn't think so, she shrugged and said, "Well, you can forget about the clubs. They don't want to look at a pregnant lady, unless she's Angelina Jolie." Sandy was just trying to be light, because she knew she couldn't change my mind. Evie got all stern with me and first she said I was delusional, and then she said she hoped I had a specific plan for what I was going to do in October when I had the baby. Well, obviously. I hoped so too. What did she think, that I didn't want to have a plan by then? For the next couple of days Evie and Sandy kept showing their disapproval, probably thinking I would come to my senses and get an abortion, but they got over it. And next thing I knew Evie was telling me what to eat and buying me prenatal vitamins. And she got me a stroller.

She explained that she was driving down the street and passed a house holding a garage sale, and there it was, sitting out in the middle of the walkway. She hit the brakes, pulled the car over, and marched back to the house to put her hand possessively on the stroller handle so that no one else would make off with it while she haggled. "It's a real find," she said enthusiastically. "A treasure!"

Well, maybe she considered it a treasure, but I wasn't convinced. It was sitting in the middle of her office so that it was the first thing I saw when I walked in. It was enormous. Privately I thought it would make more sense to move a baby around in one of those little umbrella strollers that don't take up so much room. But Evie insisted that this was superior. According to her this was the Cadillac of strollers. I was willing to take her word for it, but it was hard for me to feel any sort of connection to it. At this point, when I thought about the baby growing inside of me, I pictured something along the lines of a tadpole. If I really thought about it, I knew that one day there would be a real baby, and that I would actually hold it in my arms, but that was like knowing that someday I would be middle-aged and have gray hair. A real possibility but way off my radar, if you know what I mean. But here was Evie, beside herself with excitement, presenting me with this stroller and pointing out how clean it was, explaining how expensive it had been, and demonstrating its most exciting feature, an infant car seat that was built right into it. She lifted the car seat off the stroller, then insisted I follow her to her car, where she strapped it into place, then lifted it back out and snapped it back onto the stroller with a triumphant *tada* gesture that was completely lost on me. I wasn't ungrateful. I mean, I thanked her, but I couldn't picture myself using anything in which having a built-in car seat was a major feature. I was deeply touched though, that she cared enough about me to get me something that elicited so much reverence. Of course now I know just how precious her treasure really was. Now I know that it was one of the things that saved us when my life fell apart. But back then I had no idea just what this tadpole was going to need.

Another thing Evie was doing was figuring out what we would do when I began to show, because of course I couldn't be a sexy serving wench with a bump. She sat me down one day and told me she had a plan. When I was too big to work the parties, I could work in the kitchen with Frank. Even better, she and Frank decided that I could start working in the kitchen right away, and between that and the party work, I would be a full-time employee and they would put me on their health plan.

"I don't think I need a health plan," I said. "I'm pretty healthy."

"Sweetheart, you have no idea what you're getting yourself into, do you." She took both my hands in hers. "Honey, you are going have to go to the doctor every month until that baby comes, and when the time comes you are going to have to go to a hospital to have it. All of that costs money, more money than you can begin to imagine. More money than you are going to make working a couple of parties a week."

I started out chopping and mixing and assembling things under Frank's direction, with the two boys I saw there the first day. They were Alberto and Luis, and they were from El Salvador and spoke mostly Spanish, but we got along all right considering our communication was limited. We were the basic crew, but on party days there were other people who joined us. The kitchen got pretty crowded at times.

I also started working more on the café side of the business, and eventually Frank taught me how to make pies. Every day we made several fruit pies, a couple of custard pies, and five quiches. In addition to that we always had two soups and several sandwiches on the menu. I worked behind the counter too, making the sandwiches, cutting up pies, dishing out soup, and ringing up the orders. It was the sort of place where people got their orders at the counter and then found themselves a table, so all I had to do was bus them when they left. I liked working in the pie shop, because the pace was slower and more relaxed than the kitchen full of party-food preparers. I think Frank felt that way too. Once I asked him why he bothered with the café when the parties were the main business. He told me that when they found the place, the kitchen was what they wanted, and the little shop in front just came along with it. "We figured we might as well put it to work too," he said, smiling. But I think he liked to have a break now and then from the chaos that surrounded Evie.

One good thing about working in the kitchen was that I could wear sweatpants. I was surprised that even without a noticeable bump I was having problems finding something comfortable to wear. That little tadpole was already making itself known.   I could force my pants zipper closed, but I couldn't tolerate anything binding around my waist, so I had to pin my jeans with the top partly open. Even leggings felt too tight. Drawstring sweatpants were so much easier.

But at night I was still squeezing into the party costumes. My waist wasn't the only thing getting bigger; my breasts had become spectacular, and they seemed to be getting bigger every day, which was perfect for the showgirl and the wench costumes. But they were tender, too, uncomfortable when I moved, and painful to sleep on. I remembered back to when I was nine years old, when they began to emerge. They were tender then too, and like now, I had to get used to a whole different thing going on there. I remember I felt strangely grown-up when I looked in the mirror and they stared back at me. Mike McConnell couldn't keep his hands off them. We were in, what, third grade or something, and he was already a sex maniac. He would show up when I was walking home from school with Franny, and he'd walk backwards in front of me, moving closer and closer, slowing us almost to a stop, and then he'd cup his hand over one of my breasts and then run off laughing like a hyena.

Now that I had health insurance, Evie started nagging me to see a doctor. She gave me the name and phone number of a doctor one of her friends recommended, and when I didn't call to make an appointment, she made it for me. And she drove me there.   On the way she pumped me about the baby's father. She was very disapproving of my silence on that subject. Almost as disapproving as she was of my not telling my family. I could see that this was going to be a recurring discussion.

While I was sitting in the examination room, buck naked under a flimsy paper gown, I looked at the posters on the wall that showed a woman's body as if she were cut in half, and it reminded me of Franny's library book with the human anatomy pictures on acetate layers. On the doctor's posters you could see a baby curled upside down inside the mother where her stomach should be. There was a plaster statue with the same cutaway view, and in that one too the baby was upside down. How could a baby sit like that without getting a headache? There was a knock on the door and the doctor came in. Dr. Shastri was a very dark little woman, small-boned and fine-featured, with beautiful black eyes.   I wondered if she wore a sari when she wasn't wearing a white coat. I thought a sari was one of the most beautiful things a woman could wear.   Even fat, dumpy old women look beautiful in a sari.

But I didn't have much time to think about all that. Dr. Shastri was very businesslike, and right off the bat she was asking me questions. At the same time she was kindly, so I felt comfortable with her. She told me I was in good health and gave me a lot of lists. There was a list of things to avoid, like smoking and secondhand smoke, and booze and drugs, toxic household cleaners and cat litter. There was a list of things to include in my diet, like dairy products and leafy greens and fruits and prenatal vitamins. And there was a list of phone numbers for all the various doctors and agencies that had anything remotely to do with the whole baby process. She also gave me a little cup sealed in plastic. I was supposed to pee in that cup first thing in the morning on the day of my next appointment. You don't think of things like that when you're doing the fucking that gets you pregnant.

Dr. Shastri shook my hand and told me to make my next appointment on my way out. The whole thing was much less intimidating than I had thought it would be, though I had a lot of information to digest. Evie drove me home, stopping at Walgreens on the way to buy me more prenatal vitamins. She spent the entire drive asking me questions about the examination, and launched into her usual rant that I needed to confide in my family. And to tell the father. This became our monthly routine. I peed in the cup, and then Evie took me to my checkup, sitting in the waiting room while Dr. Shastri looked at my blood pressure and weight and touched me and told me everything looked good. And then Evie took me home again, asking me the whole way home what Dr. Shastri had said exactly, and reminding me, yet again, that I really had to tell the father and confide in my family. Dr. Shastri's nurse once referred to Evie, sitting patiently in the waiting room, as my mom, and I didn't tell her otherwise. I guess it felt good to have a mom in the waiting room.

Sandy finally decided to move to New York. And Ashton agreed when she asked him if I could take over the room from her when she moved. This was a relief, because I was worried that he would want someone there who was more of a party animal but I guess he was too lazy to deal with it, and I was a bird in the hand. I was definitely not a party animal. I had stopped drinking and felt exhausted all the time, so when I got home from work all I wanted to do was lie down. Once in a while I went out with the others, sometimes to a movie, sometimes out to eat, but I didn't go to the clubs with them anymore.

I had a social life outside the house, though. I went out with some guys during that time. Now, when I look back on it, their faces are mostly a blur. It's funny how when you start dating a person he fills up your life, and then he's gone—poof—and you can hardly remember him a year later. But at the time I was thinking about each of them a lot. For one thing, pregnancy makes you really horny. But when my bump started to show, it was surprising how many guys were creeped out by the whole idea of being with a pregnant woman. Except for Carlos.

Carlos was not one of those people who faded from memory. He was tall and gaunt as a scarecrow, with a fierce face, a hooked nose, and glossy black hair slicked back into a long, thin ponytail. He wasn't old, like Eddie, but he wasn't young either. I thought he looked completely intimidating, but he turned out to be one of the sweetest guys I'd ever known. Almost as sweet as Dieter, which is saying a lot. But you had to get to know him to find that out. When you first met him, all you saw was the dangling silver scorpion earring in one ear and a scorpion tattoo on his shoulder, which made him look dangerous. I liked the idea of a tattoo, but I never got one myself. I seriously thought about it when I turned eighteen, and Madison and I went into a tattoo shop on Telegraph Avenue in Berkeley. She got a star on her ankle, but I chickened out when I found out there was a possibility that pain was involved.

Carlos loved women. Women of all types, all ages. In fact, when you went out with him, for sure you had to know that you were not the only woman in his life. He even mentioned the others from time to time, dropping their names in casual conversation. But when he was with you, he was completely with you—he didn't even answer his cell phone. At that time he lived in a studio apartment that was smaller than Eddie's apartment at the villa. There was just a mattress on the floor, a spotless kitchenette along one wall, an old wooden trunk that looked like it was a hundred years old, and a huge bookcase along another wall, crammed with books. He was a writer, though when I asked him what he wrote he was vague about it. His laptop sat on the floor, and books and magazines were stacked around it, but everything else was neat as a pin.

I met him at work. Carlos bartended for Evie, but he refused to wear a costume, although he did agree to wear a vest that related to the theme or at least the color scheme. That was as close as he ever came to a costume. A vest. I don't know how he got away with that—Evie had an iron fist with everyone else. But she was crazy about Carlos. Because of course he had her wrapped around his little finger, just like every other female in his life, whether he was sleeping with her or not. This was because Carlos knew how to look you right in the eye and convince you that you were beautiful and interesting.

We would hang out after working a party together, usually going to one of the obscure bars that he liked. He scoffed at the trendy spots that Ashton thought were so hot. One place he took me to played only jazz; another one played Italian opera recordings one night and Portuguese Fado the next. We'd talk about the party we had just worked, and whether the guests were cool or boring or pretentious assholes. Once he told me about some guy who was trying to impress his girlfriend by acting like he knew all about wine, like he was a real connoisseur, and then he asked for white zinfandel. "It's the worst wine ever," Carlos said contemptuously, reaching for his glass. I'd slip out of my shoes because my feet were killing me, and we'd both sit back and count our tip money, smoothing out the crumpled bills, lining them up in neat piles. If I did well that night, I'd treat myself to one of the bar's snacks in addition to my usual Sprite. We always paid separately. Carlos insisted on that. The first time we went out I assumed he would pay for the drinks, but he paid for his own and then looked at me expectantly. When I didn't catch on he pointed out that women needed to step up and be equal. Those were his words. "Always pay your own way, Honey," he admonished me. "You'll be happier in the long run." Rose would love Carlos.

He usually ordered a scotch. I had a sip from his glass once, while he went to the men's room, and I thought it tasted like lighter fluid. To each his own. Once in a while I ordered a glass of wine, but Carlos was as disapproving of that as he was of girls who didn't pay their way, so I stopped. He was shocked that I would drink while I was pregnant, and he told me I wasn't taking my pregnancy seriously. He, on the other hand, was extremely interested in it. He was curious about how it felt, and he liked to touch my bump and feel the taut skin over the baby's hard presence. He wanted to know if I could feel the baby moving, and was enchanted when I told him that there were all kinds of movements I could feel, some hard like a kick, some tickling like fingers, and some so soft I felt like I had a butterfly inside. He liked to lay his hand on my belly, his long thin fingers splayed out ready to catch the tiniest movement. When he felt it move, he laughed and he wanted to know how I felt about that, whether I pictured the baby, whether I sent my thoughts in its direction, whether I felt like my body was embracing it. I had to tell him that to be honest, I was having trouble with all these things. For me pregnancy was mostly a hassle. He just laughed when I told him that, and he wrapped his arms around me and held me close to him. This is why I say he was probably one of the sweetest men I've ever known.

He was also one of the most appreciative. Like Eddie, he said I was luscious. These days I wondered if Eddie had been playing me, when he said that, but maybe that's not fair. Maybe Eddie really felt that way. But he never sang to me like Carlos did. Carlos sang "Simply Irresistible" grinning and dancing with me in his tiny apartment, looking like a tall, angular bird, like a black flamingo. He crooned as he danced, "She's so fine there's no telling where the money went." Carlos was a sweet lover, too. No one since Danny knew his way around a clitoris like Carlos did. So while I didn't see all that much of Carlos, when I did it was bonobo sex.

Then he went to Seattle, where some theater group was going to produce a play he had written, and though we talked on the phone now and then, it just wasn't the same.

Soon my bump was really showing. And not just my bump. I was plumper all over, and could barely squeeze into my clothes.   Sandy found a consignment shop for pregnant women, and we got me fitted out. It was a relief to wear clothes that were especially made for an expanding body. Maybe it was those clothes, but around that time I realized I no longer regarded the creature inside me as a strange little tadpole but as an actual baby, and I found myself accepting that this baby was going to be a part of my life.

Then in July Sandy packed up and left for New York. There was a big party for her in the house. She was in tears, but she wasn't going to change her mind about leaving. So now the room was going to be all mine. I wouldn't have to sleep on the sofa anymore. Not only was the sofa not all that comfortable, but I was tired of sharing it with Ashton's cat, who thought it was hers. I had to push her off when I wanted to sit there. Madonna had done a pretty thorough job of shredding one side of it, sitting up on her haunches and tearing into it with savage intensity. She could have it all to herself now. And with Sandy's stuff out of there, I'd have room for the baby things that Evie told me I'd need. As it was, the enormous stroller parked in the corner took up a lot of floor space, so for now I was using it for storage.

It wasn't until after Sandy left and I was all alone in that room that I realized how lonely it would be. I had grown used to the companionship of a roommate. That first week I called Sandy every day. She was so thrilled about being in New York that she didn't really pick up on my loneliness, which I couldn't blame her for, but I would have liked some sympathy.   Evie and Frank were sympathetic, but they couldn't take Sandy's place.

The good news was that I bought Sandy's car when she moved. She was glad to sell it, because she wanted to have a big wad of money for New York, in case it took a while to get a job. The car was just an old Toyota Corolla, with something like 110,000 miles on it and a dent on one fender, and its cheerful red color had long since faded, but it was mine, all mine. I was beginning to feel like a real upstanding citizen. I hoped that Sandy wouldn't be disappointed in New York, since she had burned all her bridges to get there. But I guessed that's what you have to do when you're in love.

I was still working some of Evie's parties, but because I was too big now for the costumes I stayed in the kitchen setting up trays. I missed the fun of the costumes. I constantly needed to pee, my legs hurt, and I was sleepy in the evenings, but I was glad to be there because I was with my friends. Since Sandy had gone to New York, the people working the parties were pretty much my only social life. The best of these friends was Sanjay, a gay Indian boy who had just started working for Evie. At this stage of things, hanging out with Sanjay was better than dating. It was sublimely uncomplicated. He was funny and entertaining, and no matter what he did, he had a good time doing it. He pranced around Evie's parties flourishing his tray, and guests loved him as much as we did. He'd swoop into the kitchen for a refill, announcing in a falsetto, "Tray Wallah coming through!" and the mood in the kitchen would pick right up. He and I would go out after the party, and have a drink together and gossip about all the others before we went our separate ways, me to go home alone and Sanjay to go party all night with the legions of friends that populated his life.

He not only had tons of friends, he had all kinds of social activity with his family. "My alternate Indian universe" he called it, when he went off to a wedding or an engagement party or a huge Indian barbecue. For someone who was not very traditional, sexually speaking, he spent a lot of time with his family.

"Do they know you're gay?" I asked him.

"Oh, girl, we don't talk about my sex life," he said, laughing.

He told me his mother hardly ever called him anymore with names of nice Indian girls that his family had vetted for him. "They think I'm too lazy to get married," he said with a chuckle. I loved hearing about his family. He talked about them with real warmth, and I wished I could feel that way about mine. I had been getting calls from Vivian every time she got really lit, to deliver one of her harangues. Mostly about the fact that I was in L.A. I wondered if I should just stop taking her calls, because they left me so depressed.

It didn't help that I was missing Sandy, missing Franny, missing Eddie, missing Carlos, and I couldn't help worrying about carrying around a baby I couldn't even picture. But Sanjay would sit and listen and offer what he thought were helpful suggestions. He thought I could meet people if I took an aerobics class, but where was I going to find the energy for that? And he thought I should get a job modeling maternity fashions, as if that was going to happen in the couple of months I had left before I wasn't pregnant anymore. So they weren't very good suggestions, but the fact that he was sympathetic enough to try to be helpful made me feel better.

Sanjay and I went to see *Blue Moon* when it came out. This was the movie with Evan Moss, the actor that I had met at one of the parties. Sanjay decided that he was in love with Evan, just like I was. The movie didn't impress us—it was one of those arty movies with too much talking in it—but Evan was just about perfect. I thought about him all the time. I was very horny during this part of my pregnancy. I seriously regretted not having a boyfriend. I found myself thinking a lot about my past lovers, and about how sweet it had been with them. Every night before sleep I was diddling myself.

Sanjay wasn't the only person I could talk to when I was feeling down. There was also Remedios, Ashton's housecleaner. I gave her a ride home a couple of times when her husband couldn't come right away, so she wouldn't have to wait for him. She lived just off Alvarado, in an old Victorian house that had been chopped up into about fifty apartments. When I told her that I was pregnant, she brought me a Lady of Guadalupe card, a little laminated picture of the Virgin in a turquoise robe with rays of light all around her. "*Dios mío*," said Remedios, shaking her head. "You need her now."

I still couldn't think of how I was ever going to mention the pregnancy to the family. I guess what it came down to is that I didn't want to. I didn't want their comments, their censure, their butting in. So I had to let them think I was happy and working and living a normal life. But it got harder and harder to conceal it from them. I felt like I had been pregnant forever. Once I came close to confessing, when I was feeling low and exhausted after a long day in the café, but when Bobbie answered the phone she sounded so happy about my lies, and so concerned about Vivian, that I decided to let it go. She told me that she had started taking a kickboxing class, and that Vivian thought that this was really hilarious. I had to ask Bobbie why she was taking kickboxing and she explained that it was a really good cardio workout. First regular boxing and now kickboxing. Who knows what she would do next? Anyway, she was worried because Vivian had been going frequently to the doctor, and clearly there was something really wrong with her, but she wouldn't share any details. Bobbie wanted me to call her and talk some sense into her. As if my mom would ever listen to me. "Jeez, Bobbie, if she's going to listen to anyone, that would be Rose." Bobbie admitted that I was right. And I managed to get through another conversation without telling anyone I was pregnant.

Meanwhile, Evie was not letting up. She was still on a full-court press to convince me to talk to the baby's father and confide in my family. She even tried to weasel their names and phone numbers out of me, but I was not going let that happen. She had Sandy's number, because I had put it down on the emergency form, and Evie actually called Sandy in New York to pump her for information. Sandy wouldn't tell her anything and just politely brushed Evie off when she tried to enlist her in the grand effort to talk some sense into me. This didn't deter Evie.   In fact it only made her more determined. So finally I just lied to her, telling her that I had told my family. She backed off for a while, but then she came sniffing around again, still suspicious. One day she came right out and said, "They don't know yet, do they!"

"Okay. No, they don't."

"I don't understand why you don't tell them. I really don't understand. Explain it to me so I can understand."

"You don't know my family."

"What's that supposed to mean?"

"I can't tell them."

"Why, would they hurt you?"

How could I explain that I couldn't let them see that I had finally turned into Vivian. This was the one thing they had all tried to prevent.

Chapter 22

QUIT YOUR WHINING, Rose said, and deal with the drinking.

AJ and I knew we drank too much, but it wasn't like it was messing up our lives. We had a good time together. In the beginning anyway. It wasn't until later that I began to wonder how much he was hustling me. But that shouldn't have been a surprise. All along I knew the kind of person he was. Most of the time it didn't really bother me, but once we had a big fight over one of his sleazy car deals.

AJ made a killing on a Mercedes that he had picked up for practically nothing after it was in an accident. He got some bodywork done to make it look good, but he admitted it would never be the same. And the worst thing was he never replaced the air bags. Just sealed up the dashboard again so no one would ever know they weren't there. He thought that was funny, that some poor slob bought that piece of shit thinking it had airbags. That freaked me out, but AJ said I was overreacting. According to him, anyone with half a brain should be suspicious when a car is too cheap. He said he wasn't going to lose any sleep over it.

It made me wonder about him. And we split up for a while over that. But then I missed him so much that I found myself overlooking things. Like I say, I knew he was a hustler when I first started seeing him. He'd always been one. When he was ten, on the school playground, he was selling the records that his dad had confiscated from his older sister because rock and roll was the work of the devil. This was 1964, and her evil collection was just a bunch of Motown 45's. Their father had boxed them up and put them in the trash. And AJ pulled them out and sold them.

I sometimes felt like I was the only person who understood AJ. The two of us a couple of black sheep. And I guess I just missed how good he made me feel. AJ made me feel beautiful, he made me feel desirable. One thing led to another and then we were seeing each other again. And I have to say this was a good time in my life. Sure we fought when we were fucked up. Because when he got too fucked up he had a chip on his shoulder and a hair trigger-temper. But we made up when we were sober.

When we woke up hung-over we had a great cure. We'd go to A-1 Burgers and order their Ranch Burger with caramelized onions, fries as thick as his fingers, and cokes. We'd sit at the counter and eat our burgers and feel better in no time. The woman behind the counter knew us, and she would say the usual? And we'd say yeah and it would feel like the world couldn't be better than that. Sounds dumb, but it was nice to have a usual with someone.

One day AJ came and announced he had something important to tell me. He sat me down and he looked at me and then he said, very deliberately, I'm an alcoholic. Well, I knew that. Who did he think he was kidding? But I guess he didn't know it, and now here he was going to AA meetings and he was doing the twelve-step thing, and he was trying to change his life. And basically I knew this was a good thing. He had never hurt me, but I had heard that he had an ex-girlfriend somewhere with a restraining order to keep him away from her. So I knew I had to support him when he decided to go clean and sober. But frankly he wasn't as much fun when he was sober. I feel badly saying that, but it's the truth. He still wanted to see me, but not with everyone else, not at Rose's, not anyplace where there was booze. He wanted to go to movies and go to the A's game, go to the car show, go get an ice cream cone and walk around and talk. And talk and talk. That was okay, but I could see where it was going. He was going to try to change me. And he did try. And I tried. But it didn't take long before I was letting him down. And he'd stand there saying don't you care about us? Don't you care about yourself? And I could never come up with a good *answer until long after he'd left, and then it didn't do me any good. And they probably weren't good answers anyway.*

But that phase didn't last forever, and pretty soon he was back to drinking again and the pressure was off, though it meant going back to living with his drama when he overdid it and got nasty. But for the most part I guess I was relieved that things had gotten back to normal. Though Dieter says my life has never been normal.

Dieter says I am wrapped up in myself. One night he told me he was hurt because we had talked for an hour and I never once asked him how his day was. I felt terrible that I had hurt his feelings, but didn't he know that if he wanted to tell me about his day, he should just come out and tell me? So I felt bad for two days because I had hurt him, and I hate feeling bad like that. It just wasn't a good thing for us. He didn't mean to be, but Dieter was like a dark cloud that followed me everywhere, reminding me that I was letting him down. I got so I needed to get away from him just to get back into a good mood. I couldn't stand being under that dark cloud for long. Can you blame me? No one wants to be the one who is wrong. No one wants to be the one who is the loser who brings things crashing down. But that's what I was. Because eventually he would come to me to tell me my love is deficient and it would be over.

One day you find yourself lost, without a map to know which way to go. And you think maybe if I go a little bit further, it will become clear. But it never does. It just keeps getting denser with things adding on, the things that happen and the people who become part of us, and it never gets clear.

Chapter 23

BY AUGUST I had stopped doing the parties and just worked in the café. My feet were killing me and I was expanding rapidly. Frank was acting like I was his granddaughter or something, fussing over me and telling me to sit down for a while, but I knew that if I sat down, nothing would get done, so I just toughed it out. By September I was as big as a house and I felt like I could hardly walk. I was grateful to have Sandy's car, so I wouldn't have to walk home after work, and it was a huge relief to pull up to the star jasmine hedge in front of Ashton's and smell the heavy vanilla fragrance and know that I was home and I could lie down and take a nap. The weight of the bump, which now looked like a big beach ball under my clothes, pulled down on me, a constant drag. And it sat right on my bladder, so I was continually running to the bathroom to squeeze out a few drops of pee. I was taking naps every afternoon, falling into a deep sleep that felt drugged, then waking up horny. And I was having strange dreams. The strangest was the one where I gave birth to kittens. Kittens. What the fuck was that about? And dreams being what they are, in this one I was thrilled, and didn't even think that having kittens was weird. Meanwhile the only clothes that fit comfortably were big as tents, and I was sorry for the remarks that Franny and I used to make about Rose and her huge shirts.

Frank and Evie had a baby shower for me, and they invited everyone who worked for them to come and give me baby things. There was a big cake, and champagne, and bubbly apple juice for me. Just about everyone was there. Evie gave me a box full of practical things like baby bottles, binkies, diaper rash ointment, and a mysterious rubber bulb. I asked her what the bulb was for and she told me that if a baby has a cold, you use this thing to suction the snot out of its nose. I thought she was kidding, but it turned out she was dead serious. All I could say was, my baby had better not get a cold. I couldn't help but wonder if I was cut out to be a mother.

Everybody else gave me baby clothes. Later I found out from Sanjay that none of the employees had a clue about what a baby needed, so Evie went to Marshall's and bought a huge bag of baby things—blankets, tiny T-shirts, undershirts, and onesies—and handed them out to everyone who worked for her, informing them that they had to come to the shower and give me "their gift." I laughed my head off when Sanjay told me about this. I love Evie.

It was while I was working in the café one day that I felt a little ping inside, and suddenly there was a *whoosh* of liquid coming out between my legs. It was totally embarrassing but I couldn't do a thing to stop it. Frank knew immediately that my water had broken. I think Evie had briefed him on all the possibilities. He put one of the guys in the kitchen in charge of the counter and hustled me into his car, handing me two dish towels to stuff between my legs. "What about my car?" I wondered and Frank said that was unimportant, that he would drive my car over to Ashton's for me. He had more important things to discuss. On the way to the hospital he made me promise that after the baby was born I would call my family and tell them all about it, and that I would go straight home so they could take care of me.

"Honey, they'll want to help you. You can't do this all by yourself. Promise me you'll call them?"

I didn't know what to say. It wasn't fair, really, for him to extract a promise from me when I was under so much stress. But s*tress* was too mild a word. I was terrified, now that it was all starting to happen. So all I could do was nod numbly.

"Straight home?" he said. I nodded. "As soon as the baby is born? Promise?"

"Okay, okay" I said.   "I promise."   And then the contractions began.

I should have said yes to the damn tattoo when I considered it a few years ago. I can't believe I didn't just because I was worried about a little pain. After this childbirth thing I'll never worry about pain again. Childbirth has everything beat. It was like another state of being, one that took place in a dark tunnel, a black tunnel that lit up with deep-red electric-shock explosions with each wave of contractions. I had no idea what was going on around me. People were in the room, but I hardly knew it. I wasn't aware that Evie had shown up until I found myself holding her hand. Doctors and nurses came and went, and poked and prodded, and there were discussions and directions, and I followed their disembodied orders the best that I could. But I felt miles away from any of them. All I knew was this thing that was going on inside me, as though I were deep inside my own body the whole time. I went in one end of that long, dark tunnel with the baby inside of me, and I came out the other end, gilded with sweat, holding this little creature in my arms.

She was a red little thing, with a squinched-up face and a mewling cry like a kitten. I stared at her and could hardly fathom how she got there. While I was giving birth the world somehow went on without me, but for me time stopped completely while I was in that dark tunnel. I looked out the window of the hospital room to the street, and I could see cars passing by, and it seemed strange to me that everything had continued as usual while she was being born. Elsewhere no one even knew that time had stopped for me, no one knew that this miracle had happened. The nurse told me that the Santa Ana winds were blowing and there were wildfires somewhere, and I could barely make sense of her words. At home Vivian was probably flirting with some loser, and Rose and Bobbie were taking care of the bar, and Franny was in some class taking notes while a teacher droned on and on, and none of them had any idea that my life had just turned itself inside out. That I in fact had just turned inside out. In more ways than one. There I was with my tender inside feelings on my outside now, raw and emotional, and all of me focused on one thing. My baby. I was living in a dream, all soft baby and milky love.

A nurse came in with a birth certificate form and told me I needed to fill in the blanks. One of the blanks was for the father's name. I wondered if Eddie would be angry that I put him down as the father, and later I realized how foolish it was to think that way because after all, there was no getting around it, Eddie was the father. Meanwhile the other important blank on the form was for the baby's name. I had given this some thought, and I already knew what it would be. I had decided that if she were a little girl she would be Angelina. Little angel. After beautiful Angelina Jolie, who I actually saw at one of Evie's parties. And after Los Angeles, which is the City of Angels. And now I had a little angel of my own. Angelina.

That night Sanjay came to visit, appearing suddenly in the doorway with a big bag in his arms. He had gone to Ashton's, where he found my keys, and drove over in my car. I had to laugh out loud when he told me that. Who else would think of doing such a thing? I had forgotten all about Ashton's house and the world out there that was so different from the little cocoon that wrapped me and Angelina together. I showed her to him and he picked her right up. Sanjay was full of surprises. Who would guess that he knew all about holding a baby? "Oh my family is crawling with babies," he said. He put her back in my arms and sat on the edge of the bed.

"I've brought you some goodies," he said in a conspiratorial voice, reaching into the bag. With a flourish he pulled out a box of chocolates. "You need chocolate, girl. You've just been through a lot." Then he pulled out a bottle of lotion. "It's jasmine. You need to pamper yourself." Then he pulled out a stack of celebrity and fashion magazines. "A little entertainment will pick you right up!"

I wanted to hug him, but I was holding Angelina and my lap was covered with his gifts. I looked at him with moist eyes.

"Isn't this the best baby shower you ever had?" he asked.

"Thank you," I said. "I love you." He leaned down and pursed his lips to give me a quick kiss. He promised to pick me up the next morning and drive me home. Then he flirted with the guy who emptied the wastebaskets and schmoozed with the nurses on his way out, and everyone was left in a better mood. I had a feeling that things were going to come together.

The next morning Sanjay swooped into the room, carrying the infant car seat, startling me with his cheerful "Okay, boys and girls, all aboard the Gujarat Express!" On the way back to Ashton's we stopped at the pie shop so I could say goodbye to Evie and Frank. I lied to them. I told them that I was going back to Northern California to my family. Evie was thrilled that I had finally told them, just as I'd promised. In fact she was so moved she actually cried. "We'll miss you, Honey," she said, "but you're doing the right thing." They both hugged me and made a big deal about how beautiful Angelina was, even though that was stretching things a bit. She was still red and wrinkled, and *beautiful* really wasn't the word I'd use to describe her. But I had made them both so happy by lying to them that I felt pretty good about it myself. Then Sanjay drove me to Ashton's.

I brought Angelina up to my room and put her in the stroller. That would be her bed for a while, and for the first time I began to appreciate just how useful it was. At night I could move it next to my bed, so that I could reach down and touch her. During the day I could take her out for walks in it, her comfy nest on wheels.

She was starting to fuss, so I lay down on the bed, holding her to me, and began to nurse her. The next thing I knew, the door pushed open and Ashton was in the doorway. I felt a little uncomfortable nursing Angelina while he watched. He stared for a moment, and then he said, "I don't know about having a baby in the house." I had a few reservations about that myself, because this house wasn't exactly the environment I would choose for a baby. But what was I supposed to do? I didn't have anywhere else to go. Scotty came up behind Ashton.

"You won't even know it's here," he said. "You allow dogs, and they're a whole lot more trouble than a baby." Ashton rolled his eyes, then turned and left.

"Thanks, Scotty," I said.

"No problem," he answered and then he was gone too.

For three weeks I lived in the myopic haze of my love affair with Angelina, in my baby love cocoon, oblivious to the rest of the world. Every waking hour revolved around Angelina. She woke early, stirring and fussing when the air was still blue with the dawn light, and I lifted her out of her stroller and into my bed with me to nurse. She lay alongside me, suckling, while I fell back asleep with my arm around her. When she finished one side I turned over, lifting her to the second side, and went back to sleep as she nursed. She woke again around seven, and we went downstairs so I could make coffee and have some cereal while I carried her in a sling that Evie gave me. I loved the feel of this little pink animal against me. I wondered if Vivian had felt that about me. Maybe she had. This was a new way to think of her.

After breakfast I usually packed Angelina into the stroller and headed out. I didn't want to stay in the house, where we were sure to wake everyone if she cried. We walked all over Silver Lake, just as I did when I lived in the villa with Eddie. We walked up and down Sunset Boulevard and up the hill to the reservoir, and we had our regular places to sit and watch people. I was self-conscious about how I looked, so I usually tried to blend in with the background. It was a shock to me that my bump stayed for a while. I had assumed that after I had the baby I'd go home and put on my old clothes, but it doesn't work that way. For all too long after Angelina was born I looked dumpy and fat, wearing my maternity clothes until they flapped around me as my body gradually went back to its original shape.

Sometimes I stopped at the grocery store to get my staples: cereal, bread, cheese, milk, and bananas. I tried to keep my food simple and inexpensive, because I was worried about running out of money. Taking care of Angelina was consuming all my time, and it was beginning to sink in that there was no way I could hold a job as well. I couldn't imagine what kind of work I could do that would pay well enough to cover a babysitter or daycare. I missed working for Evie and Frank, but I knew I couldn't go back there. They thought I was in Northern California, safe in the arms of a loving family.

At noon I would head back to the house to make my lunch and get upstairs to my room just as Ashton and the others began to wake up. In the afternoons the noise of the house picked up. And by evening, with all the moochers dropping in, it was a zoo. I found that if I could start nursing Angelina before the house got noisy, I could get her to fall asleep before the music came on.

I was beginning to notice that everyone in the house referred to Angelina as "the baby", as if she didn't have a name. And they were calling her an "it." Before I had Angelina I wasn't so different. I had never given babies any notice. They had no role in my life and only appeared now and then in the background, blocking the sidewalk in a bulky stroller, sitting and staring at me from a grocery cart, or peering over a parent's shoulder in line at the bank. I was put off by the way people would go on and on about how cute they were. What was all the fuss? They were little larvae that ate and pooped and cried, and I was pretty sure that a dog communicated better than a baby did. They became marginally interesting to me at about three or four years old, when in my opinion they started to become intelligent. So I was bowled over to find out that even a tiny infant is aware of everything going on around her. I looked at Angelina's bright eyes taking everything in, watching every move I made, showing me how she felt, and I had to hug her, she was so perfect.

Cupping her head in my hands, I would stroke her dark wispy hair with my thumbs and stare into her almond-shaped brown eyes. When I undressed her I melted at the sight of her tiny shoulders and vulnerable bare back, strangely covered with fine dark hair. "This hair will go away eventually," said the nurse at the hospital, "but meanwhile she'll be your little monkey." She didn't mean it in a bad way. So Angelina was my tiny monkey, so small that my outspread hand spanned her scrawny back. She was not one of those plump babies you see in ads. She was a thin little thing. But so was I, when I was a baby. Vivian told me once that her mom, Victoria the Nazi, nagged her all the time saying that I wasn't being properly fed. But I grew up to be normal, and I guessed Angelina would too.

She loved it when I talked to her, and we completely understood each other. I knew when she was saying she wanted me to pick her up, or give her the binky, or open up my shirt to feed her. Her skin was soft when I kissed her, and her tiny hands reached up to touch either side of my face as I nuzzled her. We spent time just staring at each other, and my heart would feel like it was going to burst. I had never loved anyone like I loved her. And this made me think of my mom. If this was how mothers felt, mine must have felt this way about me. I don't know why I had never thought of it that way before. It made me miss my mom, but when I called her the conversation was strange and unsatisfying. Vivian seemed to sense something, because she asked me several times what was up, but I couldn't really tell her anything. I knew I had to tell her one of these days, but I didn't know how to begin.

One evening another girl in the house said she'd watch Angelina if I wanted to go out for dinner with Ashton and the moochers. All of a sudden the thought of going out sounded really good. But I went back and forth trying to decide if it was okay to leave Angelina with Whitney, until finally she told me she was the oldest in a family with five kids, so she knew all about babies, and that I should go and have a good time. She said she didn't feel so hot, she had cramps, so all she wanted to do was stay home and watch TV.

This was the first time since she was born that I had gone anywhere without Angelina. It was an odd feeling. I was so accustomed to lugging her around or pushing her in her stroller that without her I felt physically lighter, as if I had suddenly sprouted wings that were lifting me off the ground. It felt so good that I was suddenly overwhelmed with guilt— what kind of mother feels relief for ditching her baby? But then I thought some more about it and came to the conclusion that everyone needs a break now and then. I had two, maybe three hours before Angelina needed to nurse again and I figured I could just make it back in time. So I relaxed and began to enjoy the evening. But after we got to the restaurant I started thinking about Angelina, and found myself worrying, wondering if she was okay. I figured she was probably fine, but I knew I'd feel better if I called Whitney. I pawed through my bag looking for my phone, but I had left it behind in my room. I was beginning to freak out when finally Ashton let me use his phone. I had to step out to the sidewalk in front of the restaurant to make the call because it was too noisy inside. The phone rang and rang and then went to voice mail, so I began to panic. I tried again and this time Whitney picked up. She said everything was fine, but she sounded sleepy, so I had something new to worry about. I went back to the table, and had some of the calamari salad that the waiter had said we just had to have, but all I could think about was Whitney taking handfuls of pills while Angelina choked on something in the next room.

The pasta came, strange looking ravioli with a pink sauce, but I was too worried to eat, and finally Ashton got exasperated and said do you want to go back, I'll call you a goddamn taxi if that's what you want, so I did. He gave me cash to pay for it, which was really nice of him, but I didn't get invited out again. When I got home Angelina was sound asleep with Whitney on the living room sofa, so all that panic was for nothing. But you never knew. By then my breasts were becoming taut and achy, full with milk. I had barely made it back in time to feed her. When I saw myself in the mirror later there were two wet circles on the front of my blue silk shirt.

By this time I was late paying Ashton for my room. It was hard to live in a house full of people who were only there to have a good time, while I had to take care of a baby, but I didn't plan to stay long. As soon as I had a job I would find a better place to live. But without a job I couldn't do anything, because I was fast running out of money. I had received a late notice for my cell phone bill, and I was carefully rationing my food money. What I needed was a job I could do with a baby. Which, I was beginning to realize, severely limited my options.

Actually, what I needed was a miracle.

Chapter 24

THE BOTTLE DREAM keeps coming back. I don't have to be asleep to see it. Now it appears when I'm awake. A bottle is flying in a slow arc through the air, turning end over end over end. But everything is spinning and the bottle disappears in the center of that spinning vortex. Then it starts flying all over again. It's an endless loop and it's driving me crazy. I don't know how to turn it off.

Some things won't leave your head, no matter how hard you try to rinse them away. Like all those ancient fights. After all this time I don't remember what we fought about, I don't remember the words, but the sound and shape of them is still in my head. AJ and I fought as much as we loved. Especially late at night. The later the hour the more things blew out of proportion. There was the time when, angry with me, who knows why, he called me a bitch, and I would have jumped out of his truck except he was driving too fast, and I had no idea where we were. We swung around a corner, and there was a little gas station, all bright lights and waiting pumps, empty of cars, and a sign that read MIN ARKET *looming over the road as we raced by, while AJ shouted you fucking bitch.*

The strange thing is that after all that passion I don't feel much for him anymore. Except for the sound of the fights left ringing in the air, all that emotion is gone. There's something sour lingering over the memories, a reminder that there was something toxic at the core of it all. AJ and Suzanne, that's the sour memory. AJ and his itch for her. And I didn't know a thing. Of course, that makes it even more difficult, when you find out you're the stooge. So who could blame me for having such a crazy response to it all?

AJ was supposed to meet me after work, but he called at the last minute and said he had to go to the airport to pick up his boss, Wayne. I bought this, until I drove by the Box Club and there was his truck parked out in front. Did he think I wouldn't notice? It took me fifteen minutes to find a parking spot, two and a half blocks away, and as I walked (I can still hear my high heels clicking, each step a stab at the dirty pocked cement), I grew angrier and angrier. Then I was half a block away and I could see him walk out of the Box Club with a blonde hanging on to him like she was some kind of vine wrapped around him, and she was laughing with her head back, her hair hanging down her back and her mouth wide open, her red mouth in the middle of a doll-pink face, that red mouth open with ha ha ha ha coming out. And they walked over to his truck, got in, and drove away, while I stood there with my own mouth open and my life stuck in my throat.

Chapter 25

I NEEDED A MIRACLE, and then like an angel Remedios gave me one. She appeared in my doorway one morning to say she thought she could help me. Her husband worked for a janitorial company, cleaning the big offices downtown. He said two women working on the janitorial crew were sneaking their little babies onto the job site. A sympathetic foreman told them that as long as they worked hard and kept the babies out of sight, as long as they quickly nursed them before they cried, the bosses needn't ever find out about them.   For Remedios he would get me onto the crew.

"No one is around to know," said Remedios. "It's at night and the office workers, you know, they're all at home. The other cleaners and the bosses don't have to know. If the baby is a good sleeper, then things are okay. If baby has a bad night, the mom gives him Benadryl. That keeps him quiet." So Remedios brought me my miracle. Maybe it was that Lady of Guadalupe card she gave me. I promised myself I'd never get rid of that card.

I drove Remedios home that day when she finished cleaning, and her husband brought me with him to the company's office, to sign me up. We left Angelina in the truck while I filled out the paperwork. Leaving her there alone made me nervous, but I couldn't think of anything else to do. Then we drove to where we met the foreman's van, and he took us downtown. As we rode along the busy freeway, the sky was darkening with twilight and a chain of red tail lights like a ruby necklace stretched out before us. The cluster of downtown high-rises loomed in front of us, their windows beginning to light up in the dusk, and it was as beautiful and magical as thousands of stars in the sky.

Then we were off the freeway and down on the streets among the tall buildings. The van dropped us off, and the three of us moms carried our babies in front slings covered by big sweatshirts while we walked into the building with all the other workers and separated into work teams. This became our routine, every night. We went from office to office, emptying wastebaskets full of paper and coffee cups and half-eaten sandwiches and dripping takeout-food containers. We vacuumed and dusted, mopped the lobbies and cleaned the glass. We wiped the grimy fingerprints from the doors and swept up the fallen leaves from potted plants. And we cleaned the bathrooms.   You'd think all those people who worked in fancy offices would be civilized, but you'd change your opinion in a hot minute if you saw how they trashed the bathrooms. Everyone knows that some men aren't all that concerned with their aim, but not everyone knows about women who are so freaked out about germs that they won't sit on the toilet seat. Instead they hover over it, and their pee hits the side and bounces out, so there's pee everywhere, on the seat, down the sides, on the floor. We had to clean it up, bag up the nasty trash around the toilet, clean the sinks and counters and floors, and polish the mirrors.

And all the while we had our babies sleeping on blankets nearby. We stopped to nurse them, using the time to drink water and eat our lunches, so that we wouldn't need to stop for the lunch break with all the other workers.   The other two women spoke together in Spanish, while I just sat nearby, for the comfort of their company, listening to them and wishing they spoke English. But they were friendly and included me when one of them found a box of donuts in the trash, which we polished off while we nursed the babies. Then at three in the morning, or as late as six if we worked extra hours, we would leave the building, our babies concealed in our sweatshirts, pressed against us in their slings, to stand on the corner to wait for the van.

One morning, when we had worked overtime and the sky was already turning light as we waited for the van, we saw a chilling sight. Walking with halting, unsteady steps right down the middle of the street was a tall, slender young man in a dark grey suit wearing only one shoe. He had no socks and his bare foot and ankles were a startling sight beneath that suit. Even stranger, he wore no shirt, his smooth-polished bare chest showing under the open jacket. As he drew nearer we could see that his hair was wild and his eyes were vacant and puzzled, as though he was trying to figure out where he was and how he got there. It was a chilly morning, and he clutched his jacket around himself, wavering on the center line as a car drove past, rudely honking. We drew together, horrified, and looked away from him to avoid his gaze. You wonder how a person could get so lost. He probably had gone to work nicely dressed in his business suit the day before, and God only knew what he did over the course of the evening after work to end up in the flotsam of the city by morning. He saw us and began to drift in our direction, and we all stiffened. Even with our babies slung hidden under our sweatshirts we were still part of the normal everyday world. What could we do for this person who had stepped outside of that? We were relieved when the van pulled up just in time to rescue us.

After two weeks I had enough money to pay my phone bill and to give Ashton part of his rent. I held some back because I needed cash for food and diapers. And I wanted to start saving money so I could move out of Ashton's house and find a room where I wouldn't be treated like some kind of freak just because I had a baby. I told Ashton that I would pay him the rest in a week or so and that I planned to move out soon. After that whenever he saw me he'd look at me with one eyebrow raised, and I knew he was silently asking about it. I could tell he thought I was a loser. Ashton had no idea what other people go through.

But I wasn't going to let him get to me. Things were working out. In fact, I was proud of myself for managing so well. It was hard to adjust to working at night and sleeping during the day, and it was a hassle to bring Angelina to work, to get my cleaning done and keep her quiet at the same time, but I was pulling it off. All I needed was a little time and I'd be out of Ashton's house.

And wouldn't you know it, just as I started feeling good about myself, it all fell apart. Some guy named Edwin showed up and walked in on me while I was nursing Angelina. Edwin was a supervisor but normally we never saw him. So maybe someone had tipped him off. I didn't know who would do that, or why, but Remedios said it was probably someone who had a friend who needed the job. Anyway, Edwin said didn't I know they had a no-kids policy. What a jerk. Of course I knew they had a no-kids policy. Did he think I was an idiot? No one wanted to bring their kid to work. Still, as much as I longed to, I didn't give him a smart-ass answer, and I just mumbled something, trying not to be confrontational. But being conciliatory didn't do me any good. Of course he said I was fired, that I could finish out the night's work, and pick up my last check on Monday. And don't let the door smack my ass on the way out.

The rest of the night I worked in a daze, my mind reeling with the enormity of this disaster. How many jobs could you find where you could bring your baby to work? When the van came to pick us up, I asked the driver if there was any chance I could come back to work the next day, and he just stared at me in disbelief. "Not if he fired you," he told me.

Overwhelmed, I spent the next three days just hanging out in my room, taking care of Angelina and reading magazines. Sometimes I came downstairs to watch TV, mostly at night when the others were out partying. I found myself avoiding them because they made me feel uncomfortable. It was clear they thought I was pretty dumb to have a baby. In their world babies were like something from Mars. Meanwhile, Angelina was going through a really fussy time. Just my luck.

It was two in the morning on the third day after I lost my job, when Ashton showed up in my doorway. I was holding Angelina and shushing her while she whined and fussed, and I was thinking about giving her some Benadryl to keep her quiet. He was sober but surly, so things must not have

worked out for him that night. "This isn't a day-care center,"
he said. Then he turned and walked away.

Chapter 26

I WAKE TO DIM LIGHT, and I see Honey sitting next to the bed. Finally, my baby is here with me. I wish I could hold her in my arms. I reach out my hand to her. I try to speak but she doesn't respond. Then Bobbie walks briskly into the room with a cheery greeting. She is carrying a coffee cup in one hand and strides over to the window and opens the blinds. Sunshine pours into the room, changing everything. Honey becomes Bobbie's coat draped over the chair.

When I think of Honey as a tiny baby, what I mostly remember is being completely overwhelmed. Bobbie and I were both exhausted by what our babies did to our lives. I don't know how we would have done it without Rose. They were such a physical presence, with their crying and their shit, their needs at all hours, the constant feeding and the constant laundry. I guess I liked Honey best when she was asleep, because then she wasn't demanding something that I hardly understood how to give. When she snuggled against me, sound asleep, breathing noisily and pursing her little lips, I felt true tranquil love. I guess that's what motherhood is. You feel love even when the creature seems like something that dropped into your life from outer space.

I had just lived through a crazy soap opera, and my souvenir was this fatherless child. The doctor was dispassionate when she confirmed that I was pregnant. You could tell she knew better than to act like it was good news or bad. She told me when she thought the baby was conceived, and it was up to me to figure out who I'd been seeing at that particular time. I knew it had to be AJ, but I put that thought right out of my mind. It's hard to think how much he had meant to me once, but by the time I could feel the heavy load of that life inside me, I was ready to turn my back on men in general, and Rose said I could come stay in her little motel. So all the time Honey was growing inside me I lived in a woman's world, a world without the nuisance of men and their pride and their peckers.

But after some time I got interested in men again. I could leave Honey with Rose and go out when I wanted, and I wanted to go out with guys who didn't make me feel guilty for things that had gone on in the past. Gradually Dieter, with his hangdog face, got used to it, and finally he met a girl who caught his attention one night in Rose's bar, and in no time she had him wrapped around her little finger. I think he just wanted to be in love with someone. But while he could let go of me, he couldn't let go of the idea that he was Honey's dad. I kept telling him I didn't know who her dad was, and finally I flat-out told him that for sure it wasn't him, and he backed off after that, though you could see it was with reluctance. I don't think he ever believed me. Deep down I think he truly felt he was Honey's dad. Or at any rate he wanted to be.

Chapter 27

ASHTON'S WORDS—*this isn't a day care center*—kept me awake all night and cast a gloomy shadow over the next day as I went downtown to pick up my last check. When I got back to the house I saw with a sinking feeling in my stomach that there was a pile of someone's belongings dumped on the porch. And sure enough, it was all my things, left in a cluttered heap. Ashton wasn't around, but already there was a girl in my room. I walked in and startled her as she sat on my sofa, stroking Madonna. She was a strange-looking girl, with hair bleached almost white, severely cut in a bob, and eyes ringed with black liner. She looked like a raccoon. She said Ashton had told her she could have this room, and as for the stuff on the porch, she didn't know a thing about it. I couldn't get angry with her, because it was clear she didn't know what really happened.

I never saw this coming. I was too shocked to even know how to react. It's tough to lose your job. Or to lose your home. It's terrible when both happen at the same time. Add a baby to that and it's a catastrophe. I knew that Ashton was unhappy about Angelina, and I was still behind in the rent, but I somehow thought that because I lost my job he'd cut me some slack while I figured out what to do. How could I have been so dense? He wasn't going to do that. I sat down on the porch next to my heap of stuff to try to figure out what I could do. Angelina was still cranky, so I jiggled the stroller to keep her quiet. I couldn't go to the family with this. I had become the certifiably stupid loser that Rose always predicted when she was getting on my case. Next to me, Vivian was looking pretty good. I had turned into an even bigger loser than she was. Now I would just have to get my sorry ass out of this mess, and do it on my own.

Thanks to the check I'd just picked up, I did have some money, but not much. I emptied my purse and the box where I kept my money and counted it all up. I had a grand total of $468.76. No way was I going to waste it paying Ashton what I still owed him on that shabby little room. But the sickening truth was rent anywhere would wipe it all out in no time, so another room somewhere else was out of the question.

But it wasn't a complete disaster. I still had some assets. If I was really careful about spending, I could get along for a while. I had two big bags of diapers. I had the stroller, which was, thank you Evie, like a bedroom on wheels for Angelina. I had my phone. And the biggest asset of all, I had the car. We could actually sleep in the car that night. In the morning I would find out about soup kitchens and line up a homeless shelter to take care of us until I had a job to pay for a room somewhere.

Thinking this out made me feel better. In fact, I felt all charged up, ready to take action. Meanwhile, Angelina fell asleep, which was a godsend, because I needed to focus on getting the hell out of there. I figured that the place to start was to load my things into the car. I looked at everything loosely piled up against the two bags of diapers, my laptop and the big suitcase. That's when I noticed that some things were missing. My smaller blue suitcase wasn't there. And there was no sign of the little iPod speaker that Dieter had given me as a graduation gift. I quickly looked through my clothes and discovered that my peach-colored cashmere sweater from Eddie was also missing. I walked through the house to see if I could figure out who took them, and I found the suitcase in the hall closet but I couldn't find the sweater and the speaker. My cosmetics and toiletries were in the bathroom. Whoever had collected my stuff had forgotten all about that. I threw them into a paper bag, and then I added some other supplies while I was at it. Fair is fair. I was going to need them, and I had no intention of spending the precious little money I had on things like toothpaste, hand lotion, and tissues.   If I was going to get thrown out unceremoniously like this, I didn't feel too bad pilfering from Ashton and the rest of them.

We wouldn't be in soup kitchens and shelters during the day, so I needed to think about food supplies. I went into the kitchen and filled up another paper bag with my personal stash of food from the refrigerator and the cupboard. I would have to get an ice chest for the cheese, yogurt and milk. Meanwhile I supplemented my food supplies with a couple of plastic bowls, some spoons and forks, a steak knife, a roll of paper towels, a box of crackers and a box of Oreos. I found my Ixtapa coffee mug there, and seeing it reminded me of that last day in Mexico when I left Eddie's mug sitting on the wall down the street from the hotel. That seemed long ago, though it had not even been a year. I went back out to the porch where Angelina lay quietly snoring in her stroller. It occurred to me that I needed bedding if I was going to sleep in the car that night. I went back to my former room and told Miss Raccoon Eyes that the blanket and pillow were mine, and she just said oh, and watched me bundle them up and take them. Well, they were mine now.

I walked through the house one last time, looking for my missing things, and finally saw my iPod speaker in the back bedroom that the models shared, but Kelly was there asleep. She was the snippy one, so I chickened out and just left it. I never did find my pretty sweater. Whoever is wearing it now, I hope she gets a skin disease.

I started loading the car while Angelina slept in her stroller. The bags of things from the kitchen and bathroom all fit in the front seat, the suitcases fit in the back with just enough room for Angelina's car seat, and everything else I dumped loose into the trunk. It's funny, but here I was in the worst predicament of my life, and what was really bothering me was that my stuff was a big jumbled mess in that trunk. The first thing I wanted to do was to sort it all into some kind of containers. For that I needed boxes. I seem to have spent a lot of my life moving my stuff around in cardboard boxes.

I carefully unsnapped the car seat from the stroller without waking Angelina, and strapped her into the backseat, silently thanking Evie as I remembered her enthusiastic demonstration of this feature. I packed the stroller into the trunk, on top of my things, and then drove to a nearby grocery store. There was a boy in the back breaking down cardboard boxes and he let me help myself to some. Right there in the parking lot I sorted things out, refolding and neatly repacking everything into those boxes.

Then I entered the store, startled to find it crowded with what looked like half of Los Angeles piling food into overloaded carts. I had forgotten all about Thanksgiving, now only three days away. The aisles were nearly impassible, crowded with irritable shoppers, gridlocked around the huge display of frozen turkeys and the bakery's delicious-looking pumpkin pies. Well, there wouldn't be any big feast for me this year. But I didn't have time to feel sorry for myself because I had to get right to the important business of survival. First on the survival list was food that I could keep in my car for the next day or so. Right away I thought of peanut butter, a perfect food because one, it didn't need to be refrigerated, and two, it was one of my favorite foods. Next I got bread, cereal, a gallon of water, and a cheap Styrofoam ice chest and some ice. I was feeling extremely resourceful.

Now that I had my food supplies worked out, my next big problem was where to go to the bathroom. That's something you take for granted until you don't have your own place to do it. That first day I went to Starbucks a couple of times, and that night I went to McDonald's, where I ordered some chicken nuggets and used their restroom. I figured that if I bought something each time, and made a point of leaving a coin or two in the tip jar at the counter, I could keep the people on my side if they started noticing that I was spending a lot of time there.

Next was where to sleep. You can't just park your car on Sunset Boulevard and pull a blanket over your head. Until I found myself a homeless shelter, I had to figure out a place to park and sleep, a place off the beaten track where no one would walk by and see me. I finally settled on the far corner of a parking lot near a Starbucks. It was cold, so I dressed Angelina in several layers of clothing. For myself I kept adding layers until I had piled on two T-shirts, two sweaters, and my jacket. I wrapped Franny's blue cashmere scarf around and around my neck until it covered my face up to my nose. I felt stuffed as tight as a sausage, but I went one step further and wrapped myself and Angelina together in the blanket, grateful that I had thought to go back and get it, and finally I began to warm up. Still, it was difficult to sleep. If you've ever tried to spend the night in the backseat of a car, you know that it slopes in an uncomfortable way. I tried to prop myself up with a folded-up pair of sweatpants and the pretty embroidered boudoir pillow from Eddie, but they didn't help all that much. Even worse than the tilt was the fact that I couldn't stretch out my legs.

I spent that wakeful night worrying that someone was going to come peek into my car and see us, and then hassle me, or assault us, or it would be a cop who would arrest me. I didn't know if it was illegal to sleep in a car, but I had the feeling it was frowned upon. Then I needed to pee and I could see on my cell phone that it was only four-thirty. I figured I'd just have to pee in the gutter next to the car. I untangled myself from Angelina and the blanket and opened the car door. The interior light went on like a floodlight there in that dark parking lot, putting me in a spotlight for everyone to see. So I quickly stepped out, closed the door, and wrestled my pants down in the dark. All the time I peed I was worrying about getting urine on my cuffs. I didn't, but that small relief was eclipsed by all my other worries. I was awake the entire night.

Finally at dawn I figured it was time to give up on sleep and get up. I was dying for a coffee, but I knew Angelina would have a hissy fit if I went into Starbucks before she was fed, so first I nursed her, trying not to think about coffee. Finally she pulled back, looking around all bright-eyed, milk running out of the corner of her mouth. Little did she know what a mess I'd made of our lives.

I hauled the stroller out and strapped her in, keeping my eye on some scruffy-looking people sitting on the pavement alongside the parking lot. They definitely looked homeless. I wondered how long it would take me to look homeless. Two days? Three? Maybe I already did. That was an awful thought. I tried to ignore them as I tucked Angelina in, but to my horror one of them was walking right over to me. She was a tall gaunt woman with stringy gray hair and mismatched clothing. She looked like she was wearing everything she owned.

"Got any spare change?" she asked. Why was she hitting on me? Couldn't she tell I'd been sleeping in my car? She was probably just nosy. But I decided I needed all the friends I could get, so I gave her a dollar.

"God bless you," she said, and smiled. She was missing a front tooth. "And God bless your beautiful baby."

I thanked her and beamed at my sweet girl. Angelina was lovely all snuggled up in her little pink pajamas. But I didn't really want to get into a conversation with a toothless homeless person, so I started to edge away.

"You watch out, CPS will take her away from you."

I stopped in my tracks. "CPS?"

"Child Protective Services. They don't like no babies living on the street. They'll take that little girl away from you so fast you won't know what hit you, and they'll put her right into foster care."

I stared at her in horror. "They can do that?"

The woman grimaced and said angrily, "You watch out. They do whatever they please. They don't give a shit."

I had no idea this could happen. But then, how would I know such things? I'd never been homeless before. Now I had a whole new level of worry. I needed to sit down and figure out what my options were. "Thank you," I managed to stammer, as I turned the stroller towards Starbucks. I ordered a cappuccino and dashed for the bathroom, where I cleaned up as best I could. Then I picked up my coffee and sat down, taking Angelina on my lap, and slowly savored the strong hot coffee in that bright clean shop full of people on their way to work, people who had safely spent the night in regular beds, in actual bedrooms, in houses they could call their own.

With some coffee in me I could start to think clearly. I was in much deeper shit than I originally thought. If I was going to avoid Child Protective Services, I had to stay away from soup kitchens and homeless shelters. I had to keep a low profile or I might lose Angelina. When I thought of that possibility I felt the crying stone fill my throat as tears welled up in my eyes. We couldn't be separated. I realized now that mothers and babies have an invisible bond that is like a connection of the flesh. Me and Angelina, we were one unit. If she were taken from me it would be as if part of my body had been removed. No, worse. It would be as if I had been parted from my soul.

I wondered if Vivian had felt this way with me. Like me and Angelina, I was all that Vivian had. And we both had had babies without a dad in the picture. When I thought of it that way I felt guilty that I wasn't telling Eddie, because maybe one day Angelina would wonder about her dad like I did about mine. Once when I was thirteen I got up the nerve to ask Rose about my mystery dad, and I told her how angry I was about that, how bitter I felt toward Vivian for not letting me have a dad, and Rose said she thought that maybe Vivian didn't know who it was. As simple as that. So that gave me more to think about.

But this wasn't the time to be thinking about Vivian. I had to take care of the two of us. And do it on my own. If we were going to survive I had to be sure to park at night where we could sleep in the car without being discovered. I had to find a way to eat and bathe and take care of the two of us without looking homeless. I had to ration my meager funds. No more cappuccino; it would be regular coffee from now on. And more urgent than ever, I had to get a job. A job was the only thing that was going to save us. It was time to stop floating through life. Now I had a full-time project.

I called home on Thanksgiving, and heard all about the mashed potatoes that were lumpy because Rose had put Vivian in charge of making them and somehow she had screwed it up.   They all thought that was hilarious.   I pretended to think so too.   I told them I was having dinner with all my friends, and then I told them the cell connection was breaking up and ended the call.   As long as I could keep up this pretense they would never find out what a disaster I had made of things.   What would they say if they could see me like this?   Even worse, what would they say if they could smell me?

Cleanliness was a constant hassle.   I washed my face every morning in the Starbucks restroom, but my skin was getting irritated by the restroom soap, even with the Jasmine lotion from Sanjay.   Somehow I had neglected to pack my nice face wash, so I had to go out and buy some so that my face wouldn't turn into lizard skin.   My hair was looking lank and greasy, and my scalp was beginning to itch.   I seriously considered renting a cheap motel room for one night to take a bath and wash my hair.   But I couldn't risk running out of money.

It didn't take long to get into a daily routine.   Each morning began at Starbucks with a quick cleanup in the bathroom.   Then I'd order my coffee and a muffin and find a spot with an electrical outlet where I could slowly savor my coffee while I charged my iPod, laptop, and cell phone.   After I'd been at Starbucks for as long as I could stretch it, I'd pack up my things in the stroller and we'd move on.   I usually spent the day walking all over Silver Lake.   I pushed Angelina up and down Sunset Boulevard, taking care to avoid the vicinity of Evie's Pie Shop.   Then I'd head up the hill to the reservoir, to hang out there for a while.

I was sitting on a low cement wall by the reservoir, reading an *LA Weekly* that I had picked out of the trash and slowly rolling the stroller back and forth while Angelina slept, when to my horror I saw Frank approaching, jogging along in his little red running shorts.   Lucky for me he had white wires running to his ears, which meant he was probably listening to

NPR on his radio and wouldn't be paying attention to his surroundings. I quickly held the *Weekly* up in front of my face until he was well past me. Of course I felt ridiculous hiding behind the paper. That was the kind of corny stuff that would make you roll your eyes if you saw it on a sitcom. I should have remembered that Frank jogged there a couple of times a week. I couldn't hang out at the reservoir. And not just because of Frank. Who knew who else might turn up and see me there?

So I reluctantly switched to the park that wrapped around Echo Lake. I guess I liked having a body of water to look at. There were ducks and geese to watch, and benches where I could sit and hold Angelina or watch her sleep in the stroller. As I pushed her around in her fancy bed on wheels, I'd think of Evie, and how she knew this stroller was a treasure, back when Angelina was a tadpole. Someday I would visit Evie and show her how well I was taking care of my tadpole.

Throughout the day I would return to the car from time to time, to move it to a new parking place and to nurse Angelina there in privacy. When I got hungry I usually made myself a peanut butter sandwich. The ice chest was not such a great idea after all, because the ice quickly melted and I didn't want to keep buying more, so after I finished the milk, cheese and yogurt from the first day I mostly lived on peanut butter and bread. I found a little bakery on Sunset that sold its day-old bread at a fraction of the price. Vivian threw away what was left of a loaf of bread when she bought a fresh one—I'll probably never be able to throw food away now. Another cheap food was oranges from the Mexican man on the street corner. He had bags of damaged and overripe oranges at half price. I could cut off the rotting part and the rest was fine. So I was protected from scurvy. I kept the fruit and the peanut butter in the Styrofoam chest—even without ice it kept them from getting too hot in the car.

Then weather complicated my life. I woke during the night to the sound of rain on the roof of the car. The next morning I lingered in Starbucks as long as I could, ordering a second coffee, drinking it slowly, watching the rain out the window and reading the papers I picked up from the other tables. Then I moved to sit in my car listening to my iPod while the rain pounded the windshield. Finally I drove to a huge indoor mall called the Beverly Center. I didn't want to pay for parking, so I found street parking a couple of blocks away and waited for a break in the rain to hustle the stroller over to the mall as fast as I could. Once inside I slowly rolled Angelina along, savoring all the beautiful things set out in tempting displays. There were pyramids of brightly colored dishes, rows of butter-soft leather bags, racks of silky blouses, gorgeous things as out of reach as a Beverly Hills mansion to me, but I never got tired of looking at them. And the atmosphere was cheerful. The place was decorated for Christmas, and jazzy versions of Christmas songs sounded over the shopping din.

Christmas was less than a month away. This would be my first Christmas spent away from the family. It would just be the two of us for the holidays. How festive is that? One day I was pushing the stroller down a shady street and I found a box of six ornaments on top of a carton of men's shoes sitting on the curb. They were shiny red balls, each with SOFTWIRE printed in gold on the side. I guess someone didn't want Christmas decorations with business logos on them, and put them out with the shoes for charity collection, but I didn't care and they were mine now. I hooked them onto a clothes hanger and hung it from the back of the front-seat headrests, so that Angelina and I could see them when we went to sleep at night. She was fascinated by them. This would be her first Christmas.

Part of me was still hoping that I'd find a job really soon and think of a way to break the news of Angelina to my family so that I could go home. But another part of me was saying *hey doofus, what kind of job are you going to find with a baby*? I was beginning to realize that this would take a miracle, and I'd probably run out of miracles. I had to face the fact that I was homeless, and that this was going to last a while.

At the end of each day I went to McDonald's for chicken nuggets, fries and milk, and used the restroom to clean up. They had a changing table in the bathroom, something I had never appreciated before.   I'd give Angelina a sponge bath and brush my teeth and wash my face.   Then we'd go out to find a place to park for the night.   I moved the car around a lot, trying different locations, because I was constantly worrying about being discovered.   I couldn't sleep very well in the car. I ached to stretch out.   When I had to pee really badly I used a Starbucks cup and emptied it out in the gutter.   I was hungry most of the time; just my luck, nursing makes you ravenous. On top of all this, it was cold.   Seasonally speaking my timing was terrible.   Even in Los Angeles, December is cold.

Each morning I felt as though I hadn't slept at all.   I couldn't make up for it by taking a nap during the day.   You can't exactly stretch out on a park bench and not look homeless.   I counted my money every morning, portioning out what I thought I could use for the day.   I filled out a few job applications, for waitress jobs and a counter job at a deli, even though I had no idea what I would do with Angelina while I worked.   I used Eddie's villa for an address.   I walked by there and saw that it was empty, with a For Sale sign in the front yard.   That was sad, and I wondered what happened, but it made it safer for me to use it as my address.   As long as I checked the mailbox there every day I could probably get away with it.   I used it for my phone bill too.   So I was covered.   No one knows you're homeless if you have an address and a phone.   And the phone and my laptop made my life so much easier to bear.

Sanjay called frequently to give me all the gossip about the catering crew.   Of course he thought I was in Northern California.   He'd ask me what I was doing, and I'd casually answer I'm hanging with the baby.   I couldn't put a picture of Angelina on Facebook because Franny would see it, so I told Sanjay I didn't believe in showing her face on the internet.   He bought that. Wouldn't he be amazed if he knew that I was still in L.A. but homeless now?

Evie called too, and told me how relieved she was that I was home with my family. It was so good to hear her voice. Carlos called a couple of times, giving me a scare once when he said he was thinking about stopping by to see me on his drive down from Seattle to Los Angeles. I had to do some fast thinking. I told him that I was going to Tahoe for a week and wouldn't be around when he was in the area. That was a close call.

And of course, Sandy called me. She mostly complained that New York was freezing cold. "I can't wear any of my cute L.A. clothes," she told me. "I've had to buy all new stuff, and I don't know how to put it together yet." I felt like making a crack about what a tough time she was having, braving December in New York with fashion difficulties while I was here in beautiful L.A. Oh, except by the way, Sandy, I'm living in my car and it's fucking cold here too. But instead I commiserated with her, saying the right things, umm hmm, oh I hate it when that happens, oh too bad, and then I got off the phone and cried, I felt so sorry for myself.

After that call from Sandy I was so depressed I called home, thinking that just hearing their voices would pick me up. Bobbie was the only one there, and she was really glad to hear from me. Part of me wanted to confide in her, to tell her what a complete mess I had made of things. Instead I just told her that I had quit my job and was looking for a new one.

"Oh, well, good luck with that," she chirped.

"I've been feeling that I should be thinking things out a little better," I told her.

"That's just who you are," she answered. "You live in the moment."

That sounded really nice, but I wasn't sure she would say that if she knew what my moment looked like.

So that was my daily routine. And a routine felt good. For one thing, I was beginning to realize that Angelina needed to live by a regular schedule. I had never thought about this before, but kids need routine. Angelina needed to nap at her normal times, and when I didn't recognize that, like when I didn't put her down for her morning nap right at eleven, she fell apart. When I went along with her routine, she was happy. So I planned my day around her schedule. And it felt good to give her that, because it made her happy and secure. I tried to picture Vivian accommodating a baby's schedule, and I realized something about my mom. I don't think that a schedule was something she was capable of. But lucky for me, Rose stepped into Vivian's chaos, and when Vivian couldn't provide routine, Rose could.

Chapter 28

THE BOTTLE TURNS over and over in the air. I want it to go away, but the image keeps coming back, and then it all moves too fast to see. I try to think of something else, to change the subject, but that doesn't work. It just keeps coming back to the bottle. The bottle turning over and over flying through the air, in a constant loop. And suddenly there's something new in the loop. Now I see Suzanne too, Suzanne with her eyes so wide the whites are all I can remember. White all around the cold blue centers. I see that bottle, and I see Suzanne. Over and over. I can't sleep with this thing repeating over and over on a crazy loop. I can't sleep and I can't breathe. I take a breath and it does nothing. Nothing. I can't breathe. I panic and buzz for the nurse and she gives me something, and now I'm trying not to think about the flying bottle.

I called him after I saw them, after I saw the two of them coming out of the Box Club. Of course I did. And called and called and finally he answered and he was smooth, smooth, smooth. He was all, Wayne wanted to go to the Box Club, and there was this woman there who had too much to drink, and I was just going to drive her home because she shouldn't be driving, and who did he think he was kidding? But I accepted it because I wanted to. So I guess it was me he was kidding.

Until I found a lip-gloss in his truck. AJ didn't wear pink-tinted cherry-flavored lip-gloss. I held it up in the air so he could see it, and made a question mark with my eyebrows. Isn't that yours? he asked, looking as innocent as a baby. Nice try, I answered. I don't wear candy on my lips like a teenager. I wear grown-up lipstick for God's sake. He tried to say it belonged to someone he worked with, Patty or Patsy or Pam or something, and he didn't have a quick answer for how this lip-gloss found its way to his truck.   He wasn't as slick as he had been before.   Now he looked like someone who'd been found out.

And then it really unraveled for him when I came over to his place and I heard him on the phone, his back to me and so intensely involved in the conversation that he didn't hear me enter. Don't be such a bitch, he shouted as he turned around, his face red and distorted, surprised to see me standing there. He wasn't so smooth then.   He didn't have any good answers at all when I asked him point-blank so what bitch would that be. His ex-wife, he finally said. Suzanne. So now she had a name. Suzanne. And a title. Ex-wife.   But I couldn't help but notice that while his mouth formed the word ex, *his voice didn't sound like the voice of an ex.   It sounded currently involved.   And there was that picture in my head of the two of them coming out of the Box Club, with Suzanne entwined around him like poison ivy and her head thrown back laughing, laughing, laughing. She may have been an ex, but he was still sniffing around following her scent. Following both of us at the same time. So I told him what he could do with her for all I cared, and I left.*

Chapter 29

ORIGINALLY I had thought that sleeping in my car would be something we'd have to endure for only a couple of days, but it was clear now there was no end in sight. I had been crazy to think I could save us by getting a job right away—with a baby to care for my job prospects were dim.   And without a job I couldn't see any way out of this. I had to face the fact that we were homeless and would be for a while.   That was a lot to take in.   But I had a lot of time on my hands to take it in. With all the walking and hanging out I did, I had a lot of time to think.

Sitting in the car as I nursed Angelina I thought about that sunny morning when I left that brightly colored coffee cup behind on a whitewashed wall in Ixtapa.   What a wasted gesture that was.   I was sure then that I was embarking on a brand new life, that I had the world by the tail.   I must have been delusional.   How did I think I was going to support myself?   I didn't have a clue.   Let alone realize that I was going back to L.A. with a tiny souvenir of the trip, a little fertilized egg blossoming inside me.   That was a bombshell that would seriously complicate my life.   But even when I found out I was pregnant I still hadn't realized what it meant. How could I have been so blissfully ignorant?   Now I knew, as I looked down at Angelina sucking vigorously with a drop of milk running down her cheek, that while I wouldn't trade her for anything in the world, my life would be a hundred times easier without her.   It seemed wrong to think something like that, but the new me was going to be honest.   No more delusional thinking, because look where that got me.

I wondered how I looked to other people.   Did I look homeless?   Did I look pathetic?   Or worse?   I remembered with a shudder the young man I saw on the early morning street when I waited with the cleaning crew for our van. We were horrified to see him shirtless, sockless, with one shoe missing, staggering down the middle of the street. The day before I'm sure he was perfectly normal. He shot out of orbit in one short night. My slide had been more gradual. I wondered how extreme things would get for me before they got better. I thought about Sanjay and Carlos and Frank and Evie—all of them just blocks away. What would they say if they found out I never went back to my family? If they found out that I was homeless and sleeping in my car right here in Silver Lake? They would all shit in their pants.

My family would be even worse. First they would be stunned and then they'd go berserk. I couldn't go back to them, no matter how much I wanted to. It's funny, but when we are young we spend all our time straining to get away from home, and we put all our energy into pushing our relatives away. We never want to think of them as people to lean on. But when we have broken away and they're no longer around, then leaning on them sounds wonderful.

Nursing really makes you hungry, so I was spending a lot of time thinking about food. And I was spending a lot of time thinking about money, constantly calculating and recalculating how much I was spending and how much was left. I worried about spending too much on food but there was no way around it, I had to eat. I also worried a lot about my phone bill, and the car. They were both critical because they made it possible for me to pass as a normal person. So far the car had just needed gas, though that was no small thing. I was terrified that one day I'd get a flat tire, or need some expensive repair. I kept the Lady of Guadalupe card on the dashboard, hoping that somehow her magic would protect the car. I counted on her to protect Angelina too. What if she got sick? How would I ever pay for a doctor?

I worried about diapers. Honest to God, diapers were one of my big worries. They were such a huge expense. I began to recycle the ones that were not too wet, letting them dry out and then putting them back on Angelina. I tried to make it up to her by giving her a sponge bath every time we were in a bathroom.

Bathrooms were another thing I thought a lot about. I had never given them much thought before, but now a whole lot of my time was given over to thinking about them. I was sick to death of public restrooms. Starbucks was my bathroom of choice because it was limited to one person at a time, and it was clean and safe and had a changing table, but even then it was a pain to try to do the kind of sponge bathing that I needed to do. Still, it was better than some of the park restrooms, with their muddy, wet floors gummed with toilet paper, the dank urine stink, the yellow dribble on the toilet seat, the clogged toilets marked with black lines on their porcelain throats from all the times they've been snaked out.

Around this time I lost my laptop charger, leaving it behind by mistake when I was gathering my things to leave Starbucks. When I came back it was gone. I knew I couldn't spare $80.00 of my savings to buy another, so less than a day later my laptop battery ran out and it shut down. From then on I just left it in the trunk of my car, blind and mute. Everything on it was out of my reach now, all those pictures and messages that continued to accumulate from the colorful universe beyond my pale little homeless world.

If I told everyone I couldn't afford to buy a new charger they would wonder what was up, so I told them my laptop died and I couldn't afford a new one. They were sympathetic, and said hey, I could still text and call them. But I was strangely disconnected from everyone, though I thought about them all the time. I missed seeing Franny's pictures. And seeing what Danny was doing. I thought about Madison and Sanjay and Carlos. And Sandy. I really missed Sandy. I pictured her sitting on her bed, smoking a joint and passing it to me, warm companionship wrapping around us with the smoke. Now when she called me she was back to loving New

York again. I guess she finally got used to the cold. She said she might not ever come back to Los Angeles. They might even move to London, even further away from me. They had gone over there for a couple of weeks to stay with some musician in Shoreditch who wanted to work with Marcos. I had enough trouble remembering that there was a three-hour time difference between New York and California. London was something like a whole day ahead. If Sandy went to London, it would be as if she had stepped through a time tunnel into another universe. Already I felt like I had lost her completely.

Another thing I missed was how sweet it was to sleep with someone else. Danny and I slept with my leg draped over his. Eddie usually turned away, needing his own space to sleep, but he let me sleep with my back up against his. Carlos liked to spoon. One of the great things about sleeping with them, and about sex, is the feeling of skin on skin. I missed that, though I had something close to that when Angelina nursed, and I held her against me, with my sweatshirt over her so that she stayed warm. While she nursed her hand wandered up and down along my side, stroking me. Carlos would probably like that she did that. He was so interested in her movements inside me.

Danny would be amazed if he saw me now. I am sure he never thought about having a kid. I pictured him standing on the sidewalk looking heartbroken as he watched me drive away in Dieter's truck. Now I knew that he and I wouldn't have made it in the long run. He was fun to go dancing with, and we had bonobo sex, but we didn't have much to talk about outside of sex and dancing, not to mention I think he was developing a serious booze problem. Not that things with Eddie were much better, though at least Eddie and I talked. But I think now that with Eddie it was mostly about playing at being a grown-up, and I was flattered by his attention. I promised myself that when I got my shit together and started to have a normal social life, I was going to have a lot more sense about what I got myself into. No more married men.

No more half-assed arrangements.   No more sweet-talkers working without a plan.

Still, we had some nice times, and when I thought of Eddie I saw him smiling in the flickering light of the candle in the chunky red glass in Mexico. I saw his expressive brown eyes, brimming with warmth.   I wished I had one of those candleholders to remember that night by. Because memories are embedded in things. Like the Ixtapa mug and the pink boudoir pillow, both dense with memories of Eddie.

I don't understand people who say they want to be free of possessions. Each of my things spoke of how it came about, who had touched it, who had touched me. The set of suitcases from Rose and Bobbie, the CD with Bobbie's playlist, and Franny's blue cashmere scarf—they were rich with memories, and I treasured them for that. Every time I rubbed Sanjay's Jasmine lotion into my skin I thought of him with a smile. The car and the stroller stood in for Sandy and Evie. And the things that got lost over the years? The things that disappeared, things that were left behind? The iPod speaker from Dieter, the Tastee display basket, Danny's tape measure, and Frank's pie? All gone, but like ghosts their outlines remained, still carrying memories.

I wondered what I had from Vivian. I couldn't think of anything. I could only think of what I didn't have from her.

How different would my life have been if I had not grown up in such a completely female world—Vivian and Rose and Bobbie and me and Franny?   God knows we probably even had synced menstrual cycles. If there had been some brothers, a father, a boy cousin perhaps, maybe then I would have understood guys a little better, and maybe then there wouldn't have been so many disappointments.

When all this thinking got me really depressed, I would try to find something to do to put it out of my head. Usually I would reorganize and refold my clothes. For some reason that made me feel better. In an alley one day I found a cardboard file box, with a nice tight-fitting lid. It was clean and white, with a small label where someone had neatly printed *Statements*. I emptied its contents into a trash can, transferred my food into that box, and felt much better. Sometimes it was better to do something, anything, rather than just spend all my time thinking.

Echo Lake was a dependable place for me to hang out during the day, but some of the other people congregating there made me uncomfortable. There were a couple of homeless people who looked crazy, dressed in rags, their faces raw and sunburned, with shopping baskets piled with what looked like trash. There were other people there who looked suspicious to me; I wondered if they were dealing drugs. And at one end of the lake there were day laborers, compact, brown-skinned men with cowboy hats, loitering together, hoping for work. While none of these people actually bothered me, it wasn't a family feeling, if you know what I mean.

One day I was sitting on a bench holding Angelina when a police car drove by very slowly, and the two cops in the car looked right at me. I tried to act nonchalant, but I was worried sick that they were wondering if I was homeless, and would report me to CPS, who would take Angelina away and put her into foster care. So I quickly put her down in the stroller, even though she began to cry, and started to walk along the lake. The cop car went by again, and by this time I was a wreck and Angelina was screaming because she wanted to be held and she didn't understand why I was ignoring her. The cops stopped at the corner and began to talk to the day workers there. So maybe they weren't interested in hassling me at all. I wished I knew for certain whether or not CPS could actually take my baby away from me. I began to avoid Echo Lake and spent more time hanging out in Starbucks, sandwich shops, and malls.

I wanted to call Franny. I needed someone to confide in. I'd tell her about the mess I was in, and maybe she'd have some answers. The hard part would be to break the news about Angelina. I should have told everyone about her right from the beginning. I could see that now. I should have told them when I was pregnant. Or at the very least when

Angelina was born. If I told Franny now she would be appalled, and so hurt that I hadn't told her sooner that we wouldn't be able to get past that. Still, I was tempted to try.

As I clicked on her number I decided I would wing it. When she answered she was bubbling over about the exciting internship she had landed for next semester. It was at a big Sacramento public relations firm that worked with politicians. And the FOBs had all gotten together to give her an early Christmas gift, a gift certificate so she could buy a professional-looking wardrobe. She was so full of chatter about jackets, and pumps, and skirts that weren't too short that I couldn't even open my mouth. Here my biggest problem was where to go to the bathroom and how to keep clean. How could I tell her that? She was thrilled with her new black cardigan sweater, and I was saving up for deodorant. She felt really smart because she figured she'd be meeting the governor, and I felt really smart because I figured out that I could use mouthwash as a body wash. Seriously. I had a brainstorm one day as I looked at the bottle's label, remembering Franny's science experiment when we were in high school. Mouthwash was antibacterial, and what caused body odor? Bacteria. Bingo! So I wiped my armpits and crotch with it. It was a bath without water. Who knew how useful that would be? But I couldn't tell Franny about that. So in the end I didn't tell her anything at all.

Dieter called me around this time and actually asked me point-blank if everything was okay. I could tell he didn't believe me when I said it was. Maybe he knew from the sound of my voice.

"Have you found a job?" he asked. I guess Bobbie had told everyone that I wasn't working.

"Yes," I said as brazenly as I could muster.

"Where?"

There was a silence while I thought as fast as I could. "Okay. Well, not exactly. Not at the moment." There was another silence. "Actually I'm looking for one right now."

"What happened to the last one?"

"It fizzled out. They laid people off."

"Being a night janitor fizzled out?" He wasn't going to back off, was he? There was a long silence. "Why don't you let us help you?"

"I don't need your help, Dieter."

"Honey, sometimes I have to wonder if you *want* to fail."

"Jeez, what would be the point of that?"

"Well, that's a good question. What would be the point of that?"

"No kidding. You're asking me?"

"I am. What would be the point?"

"There is no point here."

"I think you're trying to prove to your mom that she messed you up. That she deprived you of a dad. That she damaged you."

"I think you're trying to be a fucking psychiatrist. Maybe you should just back off."

And he did. But I was in tears when I got off the phone, and I didn't take any of his calls for a while after that. Maybe he was right. And maybe that simply proved that I was just like my mom. Like mother, like daughter. And my mother was a fuckup.

What's it like to have a mom who is straight up crazy? You want to somehow wave a magic wand and make it all normal, and at the same time you want to escape all that drama. When I was in high school all I could think of was I had to get the fuck out of there. And wouldn't you know it, that's when she resolved to turn over a brand-new leaf. She actually told me that she felt terrible that she had been an immature mom when I was little, so she was going to make it up to me. I wasn't too sure how I felt about that. It's gratifying to have your mom apologize to you, but making it up to me had its problems.

For one thing, she started coming to school functions. She baked brownies and lemon bars for the Sweet on Art bake sales to raise money for the art department, although Franny pointed out that she was doing this because the art teacher was a fox. Vivian bristled at that suggestion, but we noticed that when she marched into the multipurpose room in her strappy sandals with four-inch heels, her plastic-wrap-covered plate clutched in front of her, she was dressed in her cute orange sundress that made her waist look tiny. But to give her credit, those days she was also showing up for the parent-teacher conferences. She even came to the parents' college-planning meeting, although I think we all knew by then that I wasn't going to apply to any of the state universities, at least not in this lifetime.

Unfortunately her timing was bad. Because when you're a little kid, having your mom come to school is the best thing ever, but when you're in high school, you don't want to see your parent anywhere near the place. So here she was, making all this effort, and it was just a total pain.

But even when Vivian was making an effort, it seemed like it just brought her up to the slacker side of normal. And high school is way too late to try to fix that. When I was young other kids had moms who came on field trips, brought cookies and cupcakes for special occasions, and came to the classroom to give the teacher a hand when we did art. My mom kept dodging the requests. She went on one field trip when I was in kindergarten, and afterward she complained long and loudly that the other mothers were Nazis because they didn't approve when she stepped out for a smoke. But smoking wasn't the real story. Vivian just couldn't picture herself doing any of these things, and if you can't picture yourself doing them, why would you try? She thought she was hitting a home run when she remembered to sign a permission slip.

But don't get me wrong. It's not like she didn't love me. It was her own life she was screwing up—she never intended it to be mine too. She just didn't think. But she did care. When I think of those years when I was little, I don't think about Vivian's absence at school. I think about how she held me when she got home late at night, and I could feel her warmth and smell her, which sounds strange but it was comforting to smell her. I could probably pick her smell out of a lineup. It was a combination of Shalimar, toast, and cigarette smoke, and when you leaned in close to her and smelled her warmth, there was something underneath the Shalimar and toast and smoke, a faint warm funk that years later I recognized was the smell of sex.

Chapter 30

IT'S ONE THING to walk out, to make a statement like that, but it's an entirely different thing to walk away forever.   I guess I wasn't ready to do that.   AJ started right in with his sweet talk, telling me that it was just some unfinished business he had with Suzanne, but that was the extent of it.   When he said it was all over between them, I wanted to believe him. And I thought I did believe him.   Still, there was a nagging voice inside of me that kept raising questions.   That was the voice that I heard one night at Rose's bar when I came out of the ladies' room in time to see AJ slide off his bar stool to leave.   He said he had to get up early so he was heading home.   I guess part of me wanted to believe him, and another part of me didn't.   And the part that didn't won out, because on an impulse I picked up my coat and bag and slipped out the door after him.   I stood in the bar's entrance watching as he got into his truck, and as he drove away I got into my car and followed him.

And where did he end up?   At Suzanne's house.   I knew this because I stopped on the other side of the street, parked in the shadows, and watched him get out of the truck and go up to the door.   And there she was, Suzanne, opening the door to let him in.   My anger surged inside of me as I felt the blood rush all over, to my fingers, to my knees, to my head.   I saw red behind my eyes.   I felt sick inside.   But I just went home and waited for him to make the next move.

He came over the next night, and I told him I knew about Suzanne.   That I had followed him to her house and seen him go in.   And this time he didn't argue with me.   He said he didn't like being followed.   He said it was a deal breaker.   And he said maybe he would work things out with Suzanne.   Give it a shot, anyway. He and I were finished. And I got that sick feeling that you get when you know he means it and it's not what you want to hear and there's nothing you can do about it. Nothing at all. So I just stood there as he walked away, walked to his truck and got in, drove down the street and turned the corner. He never looked back.

Chapter 31

ONE DAY the park bathroom had a lock on it, so that was one more reason not to hang out at Echo Lake. But with this new problem came a brilliant idea. If I wanted to have a pleasant place to hang out every day, a place with clean, law-abiding people, a water fountain that worked, and a bathroom without a lock, what I needed was a rich people's park. Rich people have clean, safe parks, with nice bathrooms and lots of grass and trees. They don't put up with junkies and day laborers and homeless people. I realized that I should be looking for a park in a really nice neighborhood. I got into my car and headed west on Sunset Boulevard and into Beverly Hills.

You know you are in Beverly Hills the moment you get there. Suddenly it's all huge houses hidden behind fancy fences, with lushly green and manicured landscaping. This is what money looks like. You know they would have nice parks in a place like this. Rich people's parks with nice benches, soft grass and bathrooms. And sure enough, after driving around for a while, I found it. Coldwater Canyon Park. It was perfect, with a nice little creek for kids to play in, and a playground filled with children and their moms and nannies. There were no junkies. No homeless people. No day laborers. Angelina and I would be able to fit right in. And we did. But I didn't plan to stay there at night. Beverly Hills was too fancy a neighborhood to take a chance on sleeping unnoticed in a car. So even though it used more of my precious gas, every evening I drove back to Silver Lake where I felt more secure. It was kind of like I was commuting.

I was still starting the day at Starbucks, to charge my phone and iPod, and take advantage of their nice single occupant bathroom. I didn't want other people seeing me brush my teeth and giving myself a sponge bath. As a matter of fact, I didn't even want to see myself. I hated to look in the mirror because I looked like shit. My hair was dirty and stringy, and I had lost weight so that my face looked strangely gaunt. Not a chance now that anyone would call me luscious. All I could hope for was to look clean. But there was only so much you could do in a public bathroom before someone pounded on the door saying hurry up. Still, one thing I made sure to do was to spend some time on my nails. I figured my life might be a mess, but at least there was one thing I could do that was positive. Stop biting my nails. So I bought a scrub brush and scrubbed them every morning and when I was hanging out in the car, I'd file them and touch up the polish. I couldn't take a bath, my hair was dirty, and my legs and armpits were hairy, but my nails looked great. Probably they were the only thing that kept me from looking like a wild woman. The hairy legs were annoying though. They gave me the creeps. All I can say is, it was a good thing it was winter and I was wearing jeans all the time. If it were summer, I guess I'd just have to crawl up onto the counter in the Starbucks bathroom and stick my feet into the sink to shave my legs.

What I really needed was a shower. In fifth grade my teacher told us that a pearl was created when an oyster got irritated by a grain of sand. My poor body was so irritated that I was going to be one pearl of a girl. All I could say was, thank God I wasn't having my periods. That would be unbearably gross. Evie had told me that as long as I nursed I wouldn't have periods, so every time I nursed Angelina I thought gratefully of that.

At Coldwater Canyon Park I eventually got up the courage to sit with the nannies on the benches by the playground. They were mostly young, though there were a couple of older Philippino ladies. Finally I had someone to talk to. Of course I didn't tell any of them about my real situation. I made up a story to explain why I was spending all day every day at the park. I told them that I lived with my mom nearby and she drove me nuts so I preferred to stay away from the house. The old Philippino nannies couldn't understand why I didn't get along with my mother, but the girls my age sympathized, saying they couldn't imagine having to live with their moms now that they were in their twenties.   We all sat around on those benches with our strollers in front of us and talked about manicures, movies, boyfriends, and bosses.

One day all the talk was about something called the Pretty Baby Contest.   One of the nannies, an Asian girl named Melody, knew all about it, and she explained that this was a contest at a downtown hotel, and the winning baby's picture would be used on a baby-food label.   And there was a cash prize.   Melody was going to enter her boss's baby into it, and if he won, she was going to keep the cash and just tell her employer the part about the picture on the label.   The rest of us looked at each other with our eyebrows raised.   Sounded like she was headed for trouble.   I didn't have an employer I'd have to lie to, so to me this contest sounded like a really good idea.   After all, I had a pretty baby.   And I sure could use the cash prize.   So when a nanny named Carmella said she wanted to go and give it a try, I volunteered to go with her and give her a hand because she had two kids to take care of, a baby and a six-year-old.   She appreciated the offer, and on the day of the contest we piled into her employer's station wagon.   I figured if I couldn't get a job, maybe Angelina could.

We parked in the parking garage under the hotel and took the elevator up to the lobby, where we stepped out into an immense elegant space, immediately feeling overwhelmed by the oversized light fixtures, huge planters with full-sized trees, and busy-looking people in business suits hurrying around like they were late for something.   The cavernous lobby echoed with a general humming din, overlaid with the splashing of water in a huge fountain and some generic music playing in the background.   We wandered around for a while, pushing our strollers, until we saw a sign advertising the Pretty Baby Contest.   We followed the directions to go up in another elevator and then stepped out into a wide hallway.   It was lined with banquet rooms, each with its own name and holding a different event.   The Pretty Baby Contest was supposed to be in the Sierra Room. We could see the sign for it at the end of the hall. On the way we passed the Mojave Room, where another sign caught my eye:

JEANNE LA BELLE
COSMETICS
NOT JUST A JOB
A FUTURE!

That stopped me in my tracks. Right away I knew that this could very well be my future. Imagine having a job that involved cosmetics. How perfect would that be? I told Carmella to go on down to the contest, and I would catch up with her.

Inside the Mojave Room there were a lot of chairs set up to face a podium, and a lady at the door handing out bright pink folders. A woman ahead of me told her she was there about the Jeanne La Belle job. She pronounced it "Jahne," and the lady at the door laughed and corrected her. "It's pronounced *Jeanie*," she said, and told her she was in the right place and just in time. They were about to start. She must have figured we were together because she handed us each a folder and directed us to some empty chairs in the back of the room. Then another lady, all dressed in pink, came out and introduced herself as Beth Ann Margolis, Jeanne La Belle sales manager for the Los Angeles Region. For the next forty-five minutes Beth Ann gave a pep talk about how she got rich being a sales representative for Jeanne La Belle Cosmetics, a line that didn't use toxic chemicals, was not tested on animals, and that with a regular regimen of use would keep anyone's skin fresh and youthful. She used all the products herself, and her skin was like a nineteen-year-old's. Whatever that meant. But the big point was that she was making cash hand over fist, enough to buy a BMW. And the best thing was that all we needed to do to land a job as sales representative was to attend the first training seminar and buy the sample kit. That was it.

I couldn't believe it. Here was something I could do. It was like a gift. For starters, I knew all about cosmetics.

Finally, all that makeup experimentation with Franny would pay off. And while I was selling door to door I could have Angelina with me in her stroller. This was the miracle job I was waiting for, almost too good to be true. And then I found out that in a way it was. Because the next thing that Beth Ann told us was the price of the sample kit. This wasn't a measly ten-dollar kit. It cost a hundred and fifty bucks. Which would pretty much wipe out most of my savings. I slumped back in my seat, feeling sick with disappointment. But only momentarily. I knew that I just had to figure out a way around this hurdle. I raised my hand and Beth Ann looked brightly in my direction.

"Yes?" she said briskly. "Question?"

"Do we have to buy the kit?"

"Oh yes," she said with a laugh. "You're not going to make any sales without it."

I raised my hand again, and she nodded toward me, her eyebrows raised. "Can we buy it in installments?"

"No," she said firmly. "That's against company policy. But you can charge it on your credit card."

Terrific. I briefly wondered if there was a way to fake a credit card. But only briefly, because I knew that was just crazy desperate thinking. But without a credit card I had to dip into my precious savings. It was a huge chance to be taking. If I paid a hundred and fifty bucks for the kit, all I would have left would be about seventy-five lousy dollars and a handful of change. With gas, diapers, food and who knows what else, that would be gone in no time. But I didn't have any other job options. This was pretty much the bird in the hand. If there ever was a time to make a bold move, this was it. I took a deep breath and signed up. Beth Ann shook my hand and told me I'd made the best decision of my life and that the training seminar would be held that evening right in the same location. I told her I'd be back for that, and I took out my wallet and fished out my savings. I counted out $150, and she gave me the sample kit, a bright pink case with a fake alligator texture, and JEANNE LA BELLE COSMETICS written in gold on the side. My very own sample kit.

Then I realized I had forgotten all about the Pretty Baby Contest. I stuffed the sample kit into the back of the stroller and pushed it as fast as I could to the end of the hall, where the contest was still going on. That room was hot and noisy with all those mothers and nannies talking and all those babies crying, babies who had no ambition at all to win the Pretty Baby contest. I found Carmella in the long line of contestants waiting for their baby's picture to be taken on a brightly lit table. She was only halfway up the line, and pretty grumpy. "They're taking forever," she grumbled, "and I've got to get the kids back home." So we decided to ditch the contest and drive back to the park. As soon as I got there I loaded Angelina into my car and we headed right back downtown so I could go to the training seminar. I didn't want to waste any time, because no way could I park in the expensive hotel garage and I needed time to find street parking. It took about thirty-five minutes, but it was worth it, and the parking place was only six blocks away. Then Angelina was hungry, and I had to nurse her before I walked to the hotel. I barely made it in time.

The training seminar began with Beth Ann describing each product and how to use it, plus tips on how to increase the amount of a sale. Here's how that worked. If a lady was interested in getting rid of her wrinkles, you sold her the wrinkle cream and you sold her the stuff you smooth on before the wrinkle cream, and you sold her the wrinkle cream that is specially formulated for the eye area, and you explained to her that the night cream was made to complement the wrinkle cream. And then you told her the hand lotion prevented hand wrinkles, and so on and so on. I figured I could do that.

Then we were told how to place orders. We had to pay for the merchandise before we collected it at a warehouse on West Slauson Avenue, before we delivered it to our customers. So Beth Ann suggested that we get our payments up front so that we were using our customer's money and not our own. The good news was that the customers paid full retail price, and we got the stuff for the wholesale price, and as Beth Ann said, "the difference, ladies, goes right into your pocket." She handed out fat order pads. I could hardly wait to get started. I didn't have any illusions about buying a BMW, but I sure was looking forward to getting a room somewhere. A room with my very own bathroom.

Then Beth Ann talked about a Professional Appearance, and I realized I had a wardrobe problem. I didn't really have the right clothes for this. I had jeans, a couple of cotton skirts, and a lot of T-shirts and sweaters. And I had some fancy clothes for going out. But I needed to look Professional. And clean and well groomed, not like I was sleeping in my car. I would have to see what I could find at a thrift shop. That was the best I could do.

When it was time to fill out all the paperwork, I did something new. I put my name down as Torie. I thought maybe I would try that on. No one batted an eye. Why would they? They had no idea that this name was new for me. For my address I put the villa address, but I told her I was moving and I'd let her know my new address when I had it. I didn't want her sending anything to the villa if I could help it. She said, "You be sure to do that, girlfriend, because we need to know where to send your bonus checks!"

After the training seminar I drove back to Silver Lake to park my car for the night, making my usual stop at the villa to see if there was mail for me in the mailbox. Sometimes there were catalogs that I took with me to thumb through later, but not this time. There was a flier from Steam Machine Carpet Cleaning offering me a special deal. There was a letter selling car insurance. There was a coupon for half off a small-sized pizza, which I put in my wallet. And a letter from Chase Bank offering me a Visa card. I stared at the letter, tempted to go for it and use the card for a while and then, well, then what? And then I saw that it was addressed to Eddie. There was no way anyone was going to give me a Visa card.

And there was my phone bill, so now I had to add that to my expenses. Who knew when I'd be able to pay it. After the hundred and fifty bucks for the sample kit I didn't have much left to work with. I needed to hold back money for food and gas. I needed to get some professional-looking clothes. I was almost out of mouthwash. And Angelina needed diapers. I realized that I couldn't keep buying disposables. I would have to get some cloth diapers, yet another expense but cheaper in the long run. Of course, that would mean I would have to find a way to wash them. Maybe I'd wash them by hand in the Starbucks bathroom and hang them up in the car to dry. Or go to a Laundromat every few days to wash the damn things, which would be yet another cost. I wondered if I should give up the morning cup of coffee at Starbucks and just sneak into the bathroom. But that shot of caffeine was the best part of the day. And it was the only place I knew where I could charge my phone. When the money was gone, I had no idea what I was going to do. It gave me a headache just to think about it.

I drove around looking for a place to park for the night and came upon the street where Mrs. Hansen lived, the lady with the walker that I used to see when I lived at the villa and went for walks. Beside her house there was a driveway with low-hanging trees that was overgrown with weeds, so you could tell it wasn't being used. The windows on that side of the house were all covered with drawn shades. The trees screened it from the street. I turned off the car lights and slipped my car into the driveway, and that's where I spent that night. It was the safest place I had found so far.

The next morning I had one of my most brilliant ideas yet. I needed an address? I could use Mrs. Hansen's. All I had to do was pick up her mail every day, pull out anything addressed to me, and deliver hers to her front door, like I used to do with her newspaper. She'd be thrilled, and I would have an address. I couldn't believe how smart I was becoming. I was so proud of myself that I was dying to tell someone. I wished I could call Franny and tell her. But she would have crapped in her pants.

I drove out of the driveway at dawn and went down to Starbucks for coffee and cleaning up. I felt guilty spending the money for the coffee, but I wasn't ready to give it up. I did skip the muffin. Those free-spending days were over. Next I went looking for cloth diapers. Which sounds easy, but it turned out that I was the only person in all of fucking Los Angeles who wanted to buy cloth diapers. Everyone else uses disposables or a diaper service. I went to three places looking for them, getting more and more discouraged, until I finally found some at Target. This not only sucked up twenty bucks, but it sucked up half the morning, and on the way back I had to stop to get gas. There went another twenty bucks. I barely had time to get back to Mrs. Hansen's street in time for the mail. At the villa, just a few blocks away, we got our mail at about ten in the morning. I figured Mrs. Hansen's mail would be delivered around the same time. When I got to her street I parked a few houses away and took Angelina for a walk in the stroller. Sure enough, at ten-thirty I saw the mail carrier coming up the street. I slowed the stroller down so I could time it right. This would be my big move. I'd bring Mrs. Hansen her mail that morning, offer to do it every morning, and I'd be all set.

It worked like a charm. She was deafer than ever, and I had to repeat myself several times before she understood what I was trying to tell her. But fortunately she remembered me, and she was so grateful for my offer that she invited me in for coffee, and this time I accepted. I told her my name was Torie. She oohed and ahhed over Angelina, and offered me cookies and a glass of milk, and showed me pictures of her two kids, a son in San Bernardino and a daughter in Baltimore, and her grandchildren, and her husband who died in 1974, and pictures of her at work at Warner Brothers, and of her trip to Spain, and finally pictures of her garden, back when she could still keep it up. Now it was overgrown, but it was still beautiful, and she wanted to give me a tour. We left Angelina, who had fallen asleep because it was eleven in the morning and she was like clockwork with her naps, and stepped out the back door into a jungle of green. There were rosebushes arching over the path, and even though it was November some still had flowers on them.

Thickets of weeds and shrubs covered every inch of the yard. In the back of the garden there was a miniature house. "My daughter's old playhouse," Mrs. Hansen explained. "It's a shame that no one enjoys it anymore. Go on, take a look. You have to see how cute it is." I pushed my way through the brush to the front door. I had to pull hard to open it, because it was jammed shut, and I had to stoop to enter the five-foot door, but once inside it was surprisingly roomy. There were two child-sized chairs with a table, and a wooden box painted a soft spring green with stove burners drawn on the top with black paint. There was a dusty shelf full of grimy plastic dishes, a moldy braided rug on the floor, and musty curtains on a little window, complete with little glass panes. I came back outside. "It's adorable!" I exclaimed. But inside my brain was going full tilt. I was having one of my most brilliant days ever. This little playhouse was going to be my new home.

But I would deal with that later, when it was getting dark. My first order of the day was to get some working clothes. I went to an Echo Park thrift shop on Sunset where I found black jeans and a black wool blazer. The blazer was a little big for me, and the jeans had a bleach spot on them, but it was near the hem and not very noticeable, and I figured I could fill that in with black ink. With a T-shirt, the black jeans and the jacket, I would look stylish enough to sell cosmetics. For shoes I would just wear my black ballerina flats. When the weather got warm in the spring I would figure out another outfit. I saw a cute baby sweater too, but it was three dollars. It was hard to pass on it, because it was soft and well made, but I had no choice. As it was, my total cost was $5.75. Next I had to go to the dollar store for a box of candles and some matches, and that was yet another expense that chipped away at my meager savings. I wouldn't have much to live on until I made some cosmetic sales.

I sorted my things and put some into a box that I would move into my new home—the candles, my bedding, some diapers and wipes, my water bottle, and a couple of oranges. I figured I'd keep most of my food in the car, because I would need to feed myself during the day when I was at the park. That night I drove to Mrs. Hansen's house, timing it so it was almost dark when I got there. I switched off the headlights and turned into her driveway. Then I got out and quietly made my way to the end of the driveway, carrying Angelina in one arm and the stroller in the other. When I got alongside the house, a security light went on suddenly, scaring the daylights out of me. I froze, expecting to hear someone challenge me, but then the light went off, and I realized it was on a motion detector. I waited a bit longer and there didn't seem to be any reaction to the light from the house, so I carefully stepped through the shrubs across the back of the garden to the little playhouse. Inside I could barely see a thing. I wanted to set Angelina down while I went back to the car to get the other things, but I realized she would start to cry if I left her, so I had to schlep her back to the car with me. Then, with her in one arm, it was too awkward to carry the box. I hadn't thought of that. I put one candle, the matches, a diaper, and an orange into my purse and went back through the shrubbery to the little house. I would come back when she was asleep for the box and my bedding.

I lit a candle and looked around at the mess. Thank God Angelina couldn't crawl yet. I could clearly picture her putting a spider in her mouth. Who would have ever thought that one day I'd give anything for a lousy broom? I stepped outside and broke a branch off a shrub and used it to sweep the place. It wasn't very effective, but better than nothing. There was an old newspaper folded up in the corner, and when I lifted it, a silverfish scuttled out and ran across the floor while I tried frantically to stamp on it. What a creepy insect, so fluid and so fast. The beautiful name silverfish is wasted on a creature that everyone instinctively wants to crush. I took the musty curtains off the windows. The fabric was rotten and fell apart as I took them down and put them outside. I would use the curtain rods to hang diapers to dry. I had already planned to wash the days' diapers each evening when I cleaned up. I rolled up the dirty braided rug and set it against one wall. I thought of that carpet-cleaning coupon in the villa's mail. It would be hilarious to call them to come out to clean this filthy mildewed rug. Just to see the look on the guy's face when he saw he was called to a homeless person's makeshift shelter. I didn't want to sleep on that rug, because who knew what was living in it, but on the other hand the thought of sleeping right on the floor made me ache all over. I'd have to compromise. I would wrap myself in my blanket before I lay on the rug, so that there was a layer of blanket between me and whatever creatures were living in the rug. I envied Angelina and her lovely stroller.

I ate the orange, and Angelina nursed, and I rocked her for a while. Thank God she was so easy to feed. One day she would need to be eating solid foods. The nannies were talking about this. One of them ground up regular food in a blender to feed the baby she was taking care of. What a colossal hassle that would be.

As soon as she dropped off to sleep I laid her carefully in her stroller and got right to work. It was very dark now, and I could barely see a thing when I went out to get the box I had prepared in the car. The security light went on again, and I froze, but like before nothing happened, so I quickly went over to the car. I fumbled through the rest of my stuff and pulled out my framed photographs to add to the box. I would come back to get the bedding and my suitcase in a second load. I had to carry everything up that overgrown path, groping my way along through the overhanging shrubs in the pitch black, trying to stay far enough from the house to evade the motion detector, but no matter how careful I tried to be, I set off the light each time. Thank God Mrs. Hansen was not only deaf as a post, but she seemed to be completely unaware of her security light. Or maybe she thought it was raccoons.

I set up my bed and arranged my things. The chairs were too little for me to sit in, so I sat on the floor and used the chairs as little tables. I wiped off the wooden box with its painted stovetop, and placed my framed photos in a row there, leaning against the wall, where I could look at them when I sat on the rolled-up rug. I could barely see them in the dim light of the candle, but I liked knowing they were there. I looked around the shed. It was dark and dirty, but I felt protected and safe. Home sweet home.

Chapter 32

WHEN I LOOK BACK to that time, it's hard to understand how I could have become so crazy. But when AJ said it was over, that was when it all began to come loose, when my life began to slide off center. And all because I couldn't let go of the fact that he turned me down for Suzanne. Now that I knew where she lived I'd drive by several times a day, and not just to see if his truck was there. Who was I kidding? I was stalking her. I wanted to know what she was. What did she have that made him want her more than he wanted me? What did she have that I couldn't compete with? I couldn't get her out of my mind. I would drive by slowly, looking for his truck, looking for signs of her. I knew this was acting crazy, but something compelled me to do it. Once I saw her through her window, standing in her brightly-lit kitchen. Another time I saw her lifting a bag of groceries out of her car trunk. One night I saw Christmas-tree lights glowing through the blinds. I was watching her, watching her, watching her, trying to understand. All this drama seems pointless now, but it was everything then.

Chapter 33

I WAS ALL PUMPED up for my first day as a Jeanne La Belle sales representative.   That morning at Starbucks I brushed my hair back, tucking it tightly into a sleek bun. I had found that my greasy hair looked better when it was slicked back like that, the way the Mexican girls wear their hair. I was wearing the new jeans and blazer, and I had dressed Angelina in her cute pink sweatshirt. Everything was in place for a brilliant start. As soon as I delivered Mrs. Hansen's mail, my new life was ready to begin.

My original plan was to go to Beverly Hills, but the closer I came to actually settling on a target neighborhood the more I realized that the huge estates there, with their locked gates and mansions hidden from the street, all of it practically dripping with money and prestige, were just way too intimidating. There was no way I was going to go try to sell to those people. So I wimped out and drove instead to West Hollywood, where the streets were lined with normal houses that looked like they had normal people living in them.   I mean, they were really nice houses, and they were probably filled with rich people, but on the scale of things, compared with Beverly Hills, these people were normal.   But even there I found to my disappointment that selling door to door was daunting.   Most of the time no one was home. I guess they were off working a nine to five to pay for the nice house. Of the folks who were home, I swear half were gay men. And the rest? God knows. Just getting someone to open the door was a humongous challenge.   Who knew how difficult it would be to sell cosmetics? It seemed like it should be easy. Even though I didn't wear a lot of makeup, it wasn't because I didn't love the stuff. I was just too lazy to bother with anything more than eyeliner, mascara, and lip-gloss, and I wasn't old enough to need anything for wrinkles. But I love the idea of makeup, and you'd think that if you loved something, you would be able to sell it. So there I was with my eye cream, wrinkle treatments, masks, emollients, under-foundation cream, color tint, foundation, gloss, cheek color, and lip liner, and most of the time I didn't even get the chance to tell anyone about it. Most people took one look at me, glanced over my shoulder to Angelina staring at them from the stroller behind me, and shut the door. They didn't even bother to say anything. A few were polite enough to say, "I'm sorry, I'm not interested." Rarest of all were the ones who invited me in. Once in, mostly I ended up hearing about their problems. My first actual sale was to a lady who whined about wanting to go back to school. I had to hear all about how she wanted to get her credential because she was bored now that her kids had grown up. She was ready for a change. She bought a lipstick.

Over the next few days I made only one more sale, to a lady who was hoping her grandchildren would come to visit her, though their mother never wanted to make the trip from Chicago. She bought night eye cream. Four days walking around West Hollywood trying to sell this shit, and two lousy sales were all I could manage.

If I didn't start making some real money, things were going to get seriously dire. When I remembered back to my first homeless days, it seemed incredible to me now that I had thought it would just be for a day or so. And that I actually thought it made sense to spend some of my precious money on face wash. How could I have been such a moron? Now with most of my money gone, and the prospect of making a sale so difficult, I was trying to spend as little as possible. And that meant one thing: I was trying to eat as little as possible. I was finding out what it was like to be really hungry. I was constantly thinking about food. I was daydreaming about past meals and drooling at the thought of future meals. I thought of eating an entire bag of salty potato chips and licking my greasy fingers afterward. Of hot little tacos with tender roast pork piled on them and rich meat juices running through my fingers. Of thick, buttery mashed potatoes the way Rose made them, with crushed garlic. Of hummus, rich and creamy, tangy with lemon juice. Of a cold, crunchy dill pickle. All things I once took for granted but were now sadly out of reach. At this point I probably had better odds of becoming mayor of Los Angeles than sitting down to a juicy steak. It was time to get creative about finding food.

I had already found ways to get free food. Early on I had figured out a way to get free milk. Every morning at Starbucks, when I had finished my cup of coffee, I'd slip quietly over to the side counter and fill the cup back up to the top with milk. I worried that I'd get caught doing this, but it was worth the risk, and so far no one had paid any attention to me.

Then there was found food. My first found food was a pomegranate on the ground by the dumpster behind a grocery store. There was nothing wrong with it, but still, it felt strange to pick it up off the ground, as if it were contaminated by its proximity to the garbage. I cut it open and picked out the little jewels inside, remembering when Franny and I were young and Rose would give us a pomegranate and make us swear we would eat it outside and not bring the mess inside. And a mess it was. I had to go to Starbucks to clean myself up afterward. But it was delicious, and beautiful, with its chambers like a heart, filled with what looked like drops of blood. It reminded me of the cutaway picture of a heart in the anatomy book that Franny liked so much. It's funny that a heart, a chambered piece of muscle, means so much, represents so much. What if we were to find out that the center of love is located in an entirely different part of the body? Like the lungs, or the stomach? Maybe tourist shops would have T-shirts that say I STOMACH LA instead of I heart L.A.

The pomegranate was a nice treat, but it didn't do much for my hunger. My next found food was more substantial. I was rolling the stroller along Mrs. Hansen's street one Sunday morning when I noticed that the newspapers, delivered in plastic bags to protect them from the morning's drizzle, contained little sample boxes of cereal.   Free cereal.   Cereal samples that meant a lot more to me than they would ever mean to the residents sleeping late on this drizzly Sunday morning.   I rolled up and down the street, summoning the nerve to take them.   On the one hand it would be pure embarrassment if someone saw me, and called out to challenge me.   On the other hand, they tantalized me, these little boxes full of delicious food lying there within reach. Finally I got up the nerve, stopping only at the houses where the tossed newspaper had landed within feet of the sidewalk, so that I didn't have to walk up to the house to get it.   I snatched the newspaper, peeled off the plastic bag with its treasure, and tossed the paper back into the yard.   Then I briskly walked down the street to the next house.   I did this until I couldn't stuff any more boxes into the stroller, hidden under the blanket around Angelina.

That took some nerve, but not as much as I needed the next day at Echo Lake.   I was sitting on one end of a bench, just hanging out while I waited for Mrs. Hansen's mail delivery, when a girl came and sat on the other end.   She opened a small bag and unwrapped something that smelled wonderful.   It was a breakfast sandwich.   I could smell the bacon and my mouth literally watered.   I'd always heard that expression, but until this breakfast sandwich I never knew it was something that actually happened.   Then while I was practically drooling all over myself, she stopped eating, carefully wrapped the half that remained, put it back into its bag and stood up.   When I saw she was headed for the nearby trash bin I had a fraction of a second to make a decision.   Maybe if I'd had any more time I wouldn't have done it, but I said, "Don't throw that away. Please can I have it?"   I had to stand there and try not to look too pathetic as she stared at me and then, unsmiling, handed me the sandwich.   It was worth the humiliation.   That sandwich was delicious, every mouthful as heavenly as its fragrance promised it would be.

Asking for that sandwich was no small thing.   It was a serious turning point for me.   It meant I was no longer in the normal civilized world of people who get their food legitimately. I had crossed over to free food scrounging. And pathetic as that was, once I crossed I was liberated.   I no longer had any qualms about scoring other people's leftovers. I was ready to go into food scrounging big time.

One of the places that I hung out in was a donut shop that served breakfast and sandwiches. I noticed that a lot of people got up and walked out leaving some of their food, and that the old Chinese man behind the counter was slow to clear the tables. So there it would sit. A half of a sandwich, an order of toast, a bite of a donut. Skinny people were the ones most likely to leave food. Fat people usually cleaned their plates. So I'd buy a cup of coffee and sit and keep an eye on the skinny people, and when they were finished and got up to leave, I walked casually past their table and picked up any leftovers before the old guy had a chance to bus the table.   I couldn't tell if he noticed or not, but if he did, he let me get away with it, probably because I was discreet and I still looked fairly respectable, a young mom with my baby in a fancy stroller.

I almost blew it, though, when a group of slutty-looking Latina girls came in, with their skimpy shirts and big hair, all blinged out in cheap jewelry. They talked loudly and smacked their gum while they waited for their milkshakes and fries, and then piled around a table across the room from me. Finally they got up to go, leaving a plate of fries behind. I walked over to their table as they were leaving, my eyes on those fries.   I should have been paying more attention to them, because they had stopped in a bunch at the door, comparing text messages. As I reached for the handful of fries one of the girls turned and caught me red-handed.

"Oooo, white girl!" she challenged me.   "Whachoo you doing?"

"You gonna to eat that?" shrieked another.

"We spit on it!" the first one exclaimed, "That shit's garbage now," and they all laughed.

"Fucking stupid bitches," I muttered. And just my luck the crazy chongas heard me, and next thing I knew all four girls were coming at me like animals. Terrified, I ran to the back of the shop just as the old man came out from the back, shouting for the girls to get out before he called the police. Strutting and taunting, they filed out and he turned to me with a stern face and told me I'd better leave. I did, but the fries were mine. And they were delicious.

My pathetic sales were discouraging. Actually that's an understatement. At this rate Angelina and I were going to starve. I called Beth Ann to ask her for some selling advice. She told me I probably needed to slather more of the makeup on myself. She said people didn't buy makeup from someone who doesn't wear a lot of it. "You've got the samples—wear them!" And she told me to promote the skin-care products. "A lipstick is nice, that's a good way to get in the door, but the real money is in the skin care. You need to sell them on the Jeanne La Belle regimen. They have to go for the full product line to get the benefit." Then she added cheerfully, "You can do it!"

The next morning I slapped the stuff on like clown makeup. I don't know if it helped any. I did manage to get in the door with an older woman who was depressed because her dog had just died, and we talked about dogs and I told her about Muppet, and I helped her decide that she would feel better if she did something for herself. She ordered a bottle of the Age-Reversing Miracle Emollient Cream. That was a forty-dollar order, my biggest yet. But she was reluctant to pay me in advance, so I had to compromise and ask her to pay half in advance. Then I had to make sure I didn't spend it on myself, because I'd be screwed if I did. I needed that money to pay Beth Ann so I could pick up the order and deliver it to collect the rest of the payment. But it was all I could do not to spend it. The car needed gas and my cash was almost gone.

That night all I could think about was food.

Before heading out to West Hollywood the next morning I stopped by the donut shop to see what I could find for breakfast. I snagged an order of whole wheat toast left behind by an old lady, but as I was walking back to my seat where I had left the stroller, a man took my arm and held me lightly by the wrist as I turned to him in surprise.

"Having a tough time?" he asked, smiling sympathetically. I was mortified. He must have seen me take the toast. "I've seen you here before," he added.   Now I was really embarrassed, and worried too. Was he telling me he had seen me score leftover food? Would he make a big fucking deal about this so that the Chinese man would have to ask me to leave and never come back?

"Why don't you join me for breakfast?" he asked, and then he chuckled when I shrugged. I wasn't sure if he meant it. "C'mon, sit down," he said as he looked up at the menu on the wall. "How about some pancakes?" I just stared at him.   At that moment I wanted pancakes more than anything in the world. My mouth watered. I could taste them.

"That would be wonderful," I said softly.

He ordered pancakes, juice, a side of sausages, and a glass of milk too because, as he said, nursing mothers need milk. I ate everything in sight. I even finished the toast that came with his eggs. His name was Larry, and he said he owned the video store down the street. Larry was probably in his fifties, and not all that good-looking, and under normal circumstances I wouldn't have given him the time of day, but he seemed kind enough, and I was so grateful for the food that when he said, "Hey, come on, I'll show you my shop," I went along with him, pushing Angelina asleep in her stroller.

There was no one in the video store except a fat, greasy-looking man with heavy black glasses behind the counter. "Hey, Wally," Larry said to him. "I'm going to be in the blue room," and Wally just nodded, pushing his glasses up his nose as he stared at me. Larry led me through the rows of shelved DVDs to the back of the store, where there was a door painted blue with a sign on it that read ADULTS ONLY. He held it open while he gestured me in with a courtly sweep of his hand. I pushed Angelina ahead of me into the room.

One look around and I had a bad feeling about this. On the walls over the DVD shelves there were posters of barely dressed women with unnaturally enormous breasts, their legs spread, mouths slackly open and eyes half closed, advertising X-rated movies. I should have seen this coming. Of course I was going to have to pay for that breakfast one way or another.   I turned, thinking I might have just enough time to dart out of the room and escape, but the stroller was unwieldy and by the time I began to turn it around Larry was leaning on the door, blocking my way.   He took my arm while he unzipped his pants with his other hand. Jesus fucking Christ, a blow job in exchange for breakfast. How disgusting was that? It was straight out of one of the movies on the wall. I briefly wondered if I should scream or something, but I had the feeling that I could scream all I wanted—Fat Wally wasn't going to do anything about it. I figured I'd better give Larry what he wanted and get out the door. Or better yet, maybe I'd try to get more out of it than a breakfast.

"I need some money, too," I said as he started to press down on my shoulder.

"Hmmm," was all he answered. He pulled himself out, his penis like a soft pale mushroom, damp, grayish pink, and beginning to lift. Then I was distracted for a moment because I heard Angelina making little noises like she was waking up. Larry pushed down on my shoulder so that I lost my balance and almost fell. Wrapping his hand around the back of my head, he pulled me to him. It smelled like cheese. *What's wrong with this guy, doesn't he shower?*   By this time I figured I wasn't going to get anything more out of him. The best I could do was to get it over with and get out.

I had fucking turned into Coyote Girl. What a depressing thought. But you know what? While this was a lousy turn of events, it wasn't the end of the world. It was stupid of me to have come back here with this douchebag, but I would just have to be more careful in the future so I wouldn't be that stupid again. Angelina began to cry. At least the stroller was facing away from us. I would have hated to think she could see what I was doing, though I guess she wouldn't have known what was going on. And as long as I didn't make a big scene, she wasn't likely to remember this.

Afterward Larry pulled five dollars out of his wallet and stuffed it into my jacket pocket as I brushed past him to get out the door, hungry Angelina wailing in the stroller.

That afternoon I called in my order to Beth Ann and then with Larry's five bucks I put some gas into the car so I could drive to the warehouse to pick up the merchandise. I wanted to make my deliveries the next day, because the sooner I did that, the sooner I'd get paid. It took me forever to find the warehouse. I drove down busy Vermont, in a part of town dense with taquerías, discount *mercados*, liquor stores, and beauty salons, past the Liberia Christian, the Numero Uno Market, and the Manual Arts High School which in my opinion looked like a prison, until finally I found West Slauson Avenue, a busy potholed street that ran along rusty railroad tracks lined with weeds and plastic bags, bottles and anonymous trash. Along the tracks were the backs of warehouses, every inch covered with colorful graffiti. The Jeanne La Belle warehouse was tiny compared with the others, its roll-up door half closed. A little man, dark and stooped, with a tiny mustache and very white teeth, emerged from the shadows in the back of the warehouse. I gave him my order and paid for it, and he brought me my merchandise in a cardboard box. Finally, I was in business. I was going to make some money. A total of $30. It wouldn't cover the phone bill yet, but I was on my way.

Chapter 34

THE DREAM is back with the bottle flying end over end, and suddenly Suzanne's face is there, her blue eyes startled, popping wide. But when I try to fix on her it all swirls into that spinning blur, and then out of that I see the bottle again in its graceful arc. End over end.

I was there that night. Yes, I was at Suzanne's house before that bottle was launched into the air. I had been sitting at Rose's bar for too long, thinking about AJ and his itch for Suzanne, when I came to the conclusion that it was time for my daily drive past her house to see if AJ's truck was there. Rose told me I was in no shape to drive, and she took hold of my purse and fished my car keys right out of it, giving me a pointed look, her eyebrows raised. She thought she was so smart. But I gave her the slip. When she was at the other end of the bar I reached over and snatched the keys, and walked right out before she even noticed. When I got to Suzanne's there was no sign of AJ, but I rang her doorbell and I talked with her. Yes, I talked with Suzanne.

That much I remember, but I never told anyone. Oh, I might have said something to Rose and Bobbie long afterward, but I don't think they had any idea what I was talking about. No one knew. AJ sure didn't. But he must have been there later, because they say he killed her. Did she look as surprised when she opened the door to him as she did for me? No, no, when she opened the door, that's not when she was surprised. The surprised look was later, her startled face frozen in time, her bright blue eyes so wide. When she opened the door she wasn't surprised; she didn't even know who I was.

And what was I doing there? It's too hard now to peer back into the confusion to try to figure it out. Something terrible did happen at Suzanne's that night, and AJ was arrested and at the time it seemed fitting that he would be. But this dream has plagued me ever since. For more than twenty years I've been seeing this bottle on its relentless loop.

Chapter 35

BY MY FIFTH night in Mrs. Hansen's playhouse I was completely over my worry about the dirty rug and what might be living in it; after sleeping in the car it was such a relief to be able to stretch out. While I nursed Angelina I lay on the rug and looked at my photographs.

I was glad that I had brought them into the shed, all lined up along the wall in their neat black frames. One was a small picture taken when I was four, sitting with Vivian with the big flamingo mural behind us. Vivian looks beautiful in this picture. We look happy, both of us smiling at the camera. Maybe I was making a wish on the moon.

Another picture was of our family from when Franny and I were babies. It was taken in the Last Stop. It figures. Where else? Babies have no business in a bar, but that place was so central to our moms' lives, I guess they felt like it was their living room. Another picture was from the big party that Rose threw in the bar for our high school graduation. There was Rose and Bobbie and Franny, and of course me and my mom. There was Dieter and his girlfriend, Bobbie's mom, the FOB's and the Troll, plus some bald guy with a mustache. Rose usually knew of one or two regulars who didn't have anywhere else to go, so there have been a couple of those losers standing around in the background of every one of our family parties. Danny was the person taking the picture, so even though he's not in it, when I looked at that photograph I remembered looking at him, so it was just like he was in the picture too.

Finally there was a picture of me and Eddie at a Mexican restaurant in Los Angeles, taken just before we went to Ixtapa. Standing behind us in the picture was a man in a sombrero, holding a guitar. There were no pictures of anything after that. None of Evie and Frank, or Sandy, or Carlos or Sanjay. And none of Angelina. Those were all in my dead laptop.

Looking at my pictures made me lonely, so I called home just to hear everyone's voices. They were all there. I told them I had a new job selling cosmetics. When I explained that I had to pay for the start-up sample kit, Rose pelted me with questions, her voice crackling with suspicion and disapproval. Imagine what she'd have said if she knew how much I had to pay for it. I managed to duck that question. Then my mom and Bobbie got on the line, and they were much more supportive. Bobbie told me she thought I would be good at cosmetics sales, and Vivian wanted to know if I did people's makeup. She sounded disappointed when I said that I didn't. Dieter got on and said he thought I should go sell the stuff in Beverly Hills, and I said maybe I would. I didn't tell him how intimidating those Beverly Hills mansions were; it wasn't worth trying to explain. They all meant well. They didn't know I was walking around in thrift shop clothes, trying to sell this stuff while I pushed a baby in a stroller. And that in six days I only made $30. If they knew all that, they would have flipped out.

But from my point of view things weren't all bad. Now that I had my little home set up, I was a lot more comfortable. In fact I was rolling in the lap of luxury compared to lying awake at nights in my car, cramped and worried about being found. I still took a lot of precautions. I came and went only when it was dusk or dawn, never in broad daylight. I found plastic leaf bags in Mrs. Hansen's garage and hung them over the windows, so that when I lit a candle it would be less visible from the outside. The plastic covering made the room even darker at night, but I couldn't take any chances. Sometimes the motion light outside would come on, and that made me nervous, thinking someone was out there, but it was probably just a raccoon or a possum. There were a lot of them around. The possums looked like white rats, only huge and slow-moving. I didn't mind them, because they didn't want anything to do with me. The raccoons were scarier.

The third night in the shed I came home to find my food box had been ransacked, and there were orange peels all over the floor. There was a family of five raccoons outside, humping along with their backs arched and their heads down in the funny way that they walked, as they headed down the driveway to melt into the dark under the hedge. Three were youngsters, but the adults were huge, much bigger than a large cat. I realized I needed to keep all my food in the car.

At night in the shed I usually wore my sweatpants and sweatshirt over my clothes, not just for warmth but also to keep my clothes from getting dirty from the filthy floor. And then I sat there nursing Angelina as everything grew darker and darker, and the photos lined up along the wall became dimmer and dimmer, until I realized it had grown quite dark and I couldn't see them at all, and I didn't know at what point it crossed from gray dusk to black night.

Then I would light a candle, and change Angelina. Laundering diapers was a huge hassle. I still had a few of the disposable diapers, but I kept them in the stroller for emergencies. I cleaned her with wipes, yet another thing I had to ration. Then I put out the candle, because I had to ration those as well, and ate my dinner in the dark. Dinner was a peanut butter sandwich—the same thing I had for lunch every single day— and a pint of milk that I got at a little Mexican grocery store on my way home. Peanut butter practically made me gag now, but it didn't need refrigeration and I figured it was a lot of nutrition for the money.

When I finished eating, I'd sit in the dark holding Angelina and listening to my iPod. I could barely see Angelina in the dark, her face just a pale oval, her big dark eyes staring back at me, her mouth a round bud. Looking at her filled me with love. I was so bursting with love of her that I was dying to share it, longing to tell someone, anyone, everyone, about her. I guess my mom must have felt the same way about me. And probably my grandmother Victoria felt the same way about her. So why did it get so complicated later? Was it because we were a family without dads? There were now three generations of us without a dad around. My mom grew up without a dad too, after her father was killed in an airplane crash when she was just a little girl, so she grew up with no one to fight with but her mom. Now that I had Angelina looking up at me in the dark, filling my heart with love, I had to wonder how it had gone so wrong with Vivian and her mother. Once when I called home I asked her if Grandma Victoria had been sad that she never came around, and my mom snorted and said, "That Nazi. What made you think of her?"

It was hard for me to picture my mom as a little girl. But she had been a child once. And she must have felt hurt that she didn't have a dad. Then she kept me from having one. And now I was doing the same to Angelina. Eventually I was going to have to contact Eddie to let him be a part of her life. Not now, though. I couldn't let him see me like this. He never called anymore. I guess because I never returned his calls.

Each day now was monotonously the same—waking up at first light to nurse Angelina, slipping out to pee in the bushes behind the shed, charging my phone at Starbucks, stopping by the donut shop, checking Mrs. Hansen's mailbox, and heading to West Hollywood where I'd push the stroller through those manicured neighborhoods, trying to wheedle my way into someone's house so I could transform some woman's life with Jeanne La Belle creams and emollients.

I was proud that I had everything so well thought out. I had found us a place to sleep. I was finding food. I had a job, if you could call it that. And I was taking good care of Angelina. Wouldn't you know it, I finally found something I could do well, and it just sucked that what I was good at was being homeless. It was sad that no one could see what I was doing, to be impressed. I kept thinking, if only Rose could see me now. Of course on one hand she probably would have gone crazy over the idea of me being homeless, but on the other hand, I think she would have eventually recognized that I was resourceful. That was one of her favorite words, *resourceful*. She liked resourceful people. And I figured that someday I'd be able to tell her just how resourceful I'd been. The word finally applied to me. I planned to keep on being resourceful to get myself out of my predicament. To move us into a little apartment, with a bathroom and a kitchen. I'd have a bathtub and lavender bubble bath. A mattress and sheets and a thick poufy comforter. A table with a tablecloth. And I figured one day I'd have a social life again, and meet a guy who didn't mind that I had a baby. In my daydreams he looked like Evan Moss—the actor in *Blue Moon* that I met when I was working one of Evie's parties—and in these daydreams he was crazy about me and Angelina.

One day I'd tell Eddie about Angelina so he could be a dad to her. I really didn't want her to grow up without a dad the way I did. One time I actually got up the nerve to ask Dieter if he was my dad. It took a while. That was something I had considered for a long time, and by a long time I mean like most of my life, and I had put off asking him because I wasn't sure I wanted to know the answer. He didn't say anything right away, and then finally he said, "I like to think I might be," and he hugged me to his side, which didn't really answer my question but felt good anyway.

I didn't know why my mom was so squirrelly about this issue. When I was younger I just had to accept it, and I didn't let myself dwell on it. Now that I had Angelina I was seeing everything in a new way. My guess was that Vivian had no clue who my dad was. She was queen of the one-night stands when she was on a bender, so that probably explained it. But that was just one theory. I had others. Like maybe she knew who my dad was but she didn't like the guy, so she didn't want him to be part of her life. I could definitely see Vivian doing that. Or, on the other hand, maybe it was Dieter, and she knew he was so sweet and upright that he'd be a constant nag, so she wasn't going to let him have a foot in the door. I could see Vivian thinking that way too. And maybe I'd never know. Dieter said Vivian was someone who always held her secrets close.

Sitting in the dark in the shed, I held Angelina to me, and she clung to me like a little monkey. Sometimes I felt as though I could stand up and let go and she'd still be clinging to me, hanging on all by herself. I was proud that she was so strong, and I liked to feel her grip. As we sat there I could smell her head. She had her own smell. My mom used to smell my head, and it drove me nuts. We'd be standing side by side someplace, someplace in public, say at a birthday party, and she'd hug me to her and I'd feel her head dip down to mine and I'd know exactly what she was doing. I'd pull away, ducking my head and saying, "Jeez, Mom, I know what you're doing," and she'd laugh. Now I understood why she was doing it. The smell of my baby was the greatest smell in the world. Franny told me once that fawns have no scent. They lie quietly without moving, without sound, without scent, so that predators can't find them. But I'll bet the mother deer knows exactly how that fawn smells.

Now that I'm a mother myself I'm remembering my childhood in new ways. Franny says no one has memories from when they're really little, but that can't be true because I do have one. I was maybe three years old, lying on Rose's bed with Franny, both of us fingering the white chenille balls on the bedspread, admiring their order. We thought they looked like cabbages, planted by a tiny farmer in perfectly straight rows, perfectly spaced. We were probably supposed to be taking a nap, but instead the two of us were entertaining ourselves, murmuring and fingering the chenille balls in our own little bedspread world. I think that is my earliest memory.

And I remember when I was maybe five years old and I woke up alarmed by the strange sound of Vivian shrieking and laughing in the kitchen. I slipped out of bed and peered out the bedroom door. The hall was dim, lit from the kitchen at the end, where all the noise was coming from. I padded quietly to the kitchen door and peeked in. My mom was sitting on a stool in the center of the kitchen, her skirt all bunched up above her knees. Her feet were bare and her face looked wild. Her lipstick was smudged on one side, and her hair was sticking out in short spikes on each side of her head. Marvin, her boyfriend of the moment, was standing with his back to me, a pair of scissors in his hand. My mom's beautiful long auburn hair was scattered all over the floor in dark, wispy piles. She saw me and she shrieked again, and as she pointed to me, her laugh turned into a pig snort and she leaned over and fell off the stool. Marvin turned around and saw me. For a moment he just stood there, staring at me, the scissors slack in his hand, his face all pink and his mouth making an *O*. Then he looked down and said, "Vivian, Vivian, hey, are you okay? You'd better get up," and all I could do was cry. I stood there wailing while Vivian got up off the floor. She must have finally pulled herself together because the next thing I remember is her sitting with me on the bed, quietly rocking me on her lap. We sat there rocking for a long time.

Those are some of the things I'd think about when I sat in the dark in the shed. I tried not to think about food, because that just made me hungrier. I had lost something like fifteen pounds, and my jeans were really loose. So loose that I needed to find myself a belt pretty soon. Thinking about hamburgers and spaghetti and Caesar salads wouldn't do me any good. All I could hope for was a tiny dip of my finger in the peanut butter for a snack. Once when we were kids Franny and I saw a homeless man with a crude sign that he had made with a red marker on a piece of cardboard box. The sign read "NO HOME NO FOOD". Later I asked Rose what do homeless people eat, and Franny interrupted, "Boogers!" Rose told her to knock it off, but Franny thought that was hilarious. Now I thought she was not too far from the truth. Peanut butter might as well be boogers as far as I was concerned. Personally I couldn't think of anything edible that wasn't better than peanut butter. And it was hard not to be constantly thinking about all the food that was better than boogers and peanut butter.

The other thing I still thought a lot about was sleep. It never occurred to me that this would be one of the hardest things about being homeless. Early on, when I was still spending nights in the car, I had considered splurging on a bottle of cheap wine to help me sleep, but I feared I'd turn into Vivian. Self-medicating, as Rose liked to call it, and I didn't want to go down that road. Drinking messed you up too much. But Vivian never really thought of drinking as a problem. It was her solution. I think she always saw it as a way to smooth things out in her life. Or maybe she used it to help her slow things down. The universe spun too fast for Vivian. Over the years she kept making an effort to catch up to it, to adapt to it, to do what everyone else did to stay on track. To check the oil in the car, get me to school on time, show up for the job interview. But she wasn't very good at managing those everyday things. And she always knew it. She had to live with the fact that she was a continual screwup.

Rose once called her a train wreck, though later she felt terrible for saying that, and she apologized for it. But you can apologize all you want, once you say something the words are loose, they're out there. It doesn't matter how bad you feel, it's been said. And that probably made everything all the worse. Knowing she was a screw-up colored everything Vivian did, so that no matter what, it was sure to go badly. She was forever trying to hang on to that spinning universe, but she would sort of slide off to the outer edge of things. And I guess I knew that one day she would finally let go and then she'd be gone. But I felt as though I'd already lost her. Somewhere along the way we had stopped connecting, and I thought maybe it was time to light a candle to Saint Anthony, to see if he could find my mother.

And now I was sliding too. I was a train wreck. This was exactly what Rose would say about me if she saw me sitting in the shed. She wouldn't say that I was resourceful. Who was I kidding? She would say that I was a train wreck. All these years I had been feeling superior to Vivian the train wreck, but now I realized that I had fallen farther than she ever had. Did she ever give a guy a blow job in exchange for breakfast? Probably not. Was she homeless? Living in a car? Living in someone's backyard shed? No. Though, when I thought about it, in a way maybe she almost was. Who knew what she would have done if Rose hadn't been there to help her? More than once over the years. What would she have done if Rose had not taken us in? Maybe then she would have been homeless after all. Homeless with me, just a baby.

On the other hand, maybe she would have gone back to her mother, my grandmother, and they might have finally figured out how to treat each other. Rose said there's a period of time when a person becomes a grown-up, and the parent has to get used to a new way to treat this adult who used to be her child, and the grown child has to learn how to treat this parent now that they are both adults. And she said if they didn't make the effort, then they could lose each other. I think that's what happened to my mom and my grandmother. They hadn't worked out the adult-to-adult thing, and my mom took off and never gave it another chance.

Dieter said Vivian wasn't a train wreck, he said she was just sensitive, more sensitive than most people. Rose said he cut her too much slack. But I don't think so. I think that he loves her, and cutting slack is exactly what you should be doing for someone you love. I was pretty sure he would do the same for me. And that Vivian too would do the same for me, but still I felt I should get on my feet before I let her know how far I had slipped.

And then I would tell her everything. And let her know that I knew that she was good at love even though she wasn't good at life.

Chapter 36

THERE WAS a Christmas wreath on Suzanne's door. It was covered with fake snow that looked like Spackle. I can see that wreath, see my gloved finger pressing the doorbell, hear the two tones of the bell, see Suzanne opening the door and looking at me expectantly. And then it all begins to spin.

Dieter asked me about it later, and I couldn't tell him any more than that. The spinning made it impossible. He found me asleep in my car in front of my apartment, and he shook me and said Vivian wake up, wake up, are you okay? And I told him of course I'm okay, I was just taking a nap. And he brought me in and helped me to bed, and then because I was shivering with the cold, he got into bed with me and held me.

The next day he kept asking where were you, where were you, we were going to meet for a drink, but I still couldn't talk to him about it—the spinning made it impossible. And after we heard the awful news about AJ and Suzanne, Dieter asked me if I had been there that night, and I couldn't talk about it so I just looked away. And he reached out and took my cold face in his hand, cupping my cheek, a gesture so kind that I began to melt, and with his thumb he wiped away the tears that escaped. A car alarm went off in the street outside, while we sat in the silence inside. We just sat there together in the dusk as the room gradually became dark, and neither of us said a word. I think he knew everything.

When I am gone is this gone? No, not until all the players are gone. When AJ, and Dieter too, are gone.

Chapter 37

I SET OUT to make my product deliveries so I could finally collect the rest of the money. That morning had been unusually cold. The sun was out, but it was a pale, cold, white sun, and it didn't do much to warm me up. Still, I was excited to make my deliveries, so I set out feeling really good about things. But nothing is ever as easy as it sounds. The lady who had ordered the lipstick was home, but the other two were not. I went back twice to their houses and there was no sign of either one. I hadn't thought about that possibility. The night-cream lady had paid me, but the dead-dog lady hadn't. On top of that I had to carry their stuff around.   It was clear that selling door to door was a lot harder than it sounded. It didn't help that I was so hungry that I felt faint.

I was seriously thinking about visiting the video store again. I wasn't proud of what I did with Larry, but on the other hand I wasn't going to lose any sleep over it. And if the only way I could eat meant going back there to give him another blow job, show him my breasts, drop my panties, or whatever that pervert wanted, I wasn't going to make a big deal about it. Because I was fucking hungry, and I was getting really concerned about how long it was taking to earn some money. Not to mention I had that phone bill coming due. I wondered how long I had before my phone would be cut off. Still the thought of Larry's nasty gray penis was too depressing, so I pushed it to the back of my mind.

Then I was forced to take a break from selling that afternoon because Angelina made such a huge poop that it exploded out into her jammies. Sometimes this happened.

The stuff oozed out mustard yellow from the diaper and down her legs, and when I went to change her, wouldn't you know, I found I had only one outfit left for her that was reasonably clean. It was time to go to the Laundromat. So there I was, sitting and watching diapers and baby clothes and T-shirts and my sweatpants sloshing around in a washing machine when what I really needed to be doing was some serious selling.

Someone had decorated the windows of the place with red paper bells and gold tinsel garlands. It would have looked nicer if the windows had been clean. They were grimy and the plastic chairs lined up in front of them were faded and cracked. Still, it was nice to see that someone was making an effort to show some holiday spirit. Rose always put a wreath on the front door of the Last Stop, and above the mirror on the back of the bar she'd hang a fir garland with red bows. It looked like real fir branches, but it was fake, and she rolled it up and put it back into a box every January.

It was clear to me that there was no way that I was going to earn enough money to go home to El Cerrito to spend Christmas with my family. How was I going to break this to them? For sure I couldn't tell them why. And what could I send them for Christmas gifts? Forget gifts—I didn't have enough money to feed myself. It was a shame I couldn't even afford to give them Jeanne La Belle products. That stuff would be perfect for gifts.

And then it hit me: *holiday shopping* should be my sales pitch. Why hadn't I thought of this before? All I needed in order to sell this stuff was to have a good hook, and now I had one. This was brilliant thinking, practically money in the bank. And after I paid off my phone bill and got some groceries, I was sure I'd have enough left over to give Jeanne La Belle cosmetic gifts to everyone in my family. Not anything expensive like the creams, but maybe lipsticks. Except Dieter, of course. I'd have to think of something else for him.

By the time I finished the laundry it was late afternoon and too late for sales. The next morning I got an early start, and all pumped up to try the Christmas-gift angle in my sales pitch, I drove over to a lovely street in West Hollywood. It was lined with big trees arching overhead, the winter-pale morning light slanting through their bare gray branches. A tree-lined street like this wasn't what you usually thought of when you thought of Los Angeles. Usually you thought of the big boulevards with all their hustle and bustle. The rest of the city was humming with activity, but this street was quiet and peaceful. The houses were not large, but they were picture-perfect, like something on the cover of a magazine, mostly white stucco with red tile roofs, Spanish style, with lawns so green they look fake.

I tried out the gift angle on the first house I went to. "Take care of all the women on your list!" I said cheerfully, "in one simple order." That lady wasn't interested, but she told me to try her neighbor, because she was a shut-in, and it might appeal to her. So I went next door, and maybe now I was getting the hang of this sales thing, because while the neighbor didn't go whole hog, she did buy about sixty-five dollars worth of cosmetics. Larry could just go jerk himself off.

Now I was feeling more cheerful. I walked up to the next house, and as I approached the front door it swung open and there was a blond woman in a gray pencil skirt, a crisp, white sleeveless shirt, and heels standing in the doorway with her phone to her ear. "Take it easy, I'll be there. In fact she's here now." She waved me into the house, the phone still clamped to her ear. I hesitated and she waved again, impatiently this time. I wheeled the stroller over the bump of the threshold, and into the center of a high-ceilinged foyer, as she rattled on. "I'm on my way. Just keep him busy, and show him the financials. Give him snacks. Send the new intern, what's-his-name, Todd, for some sushi. He loves that stuff." She held up one finger to me. "You'll manage," she said into the phone. She paused, listening, and looked at me, rolling her eyes. "No, don't show him that. In fact don't mention it at all. Just feed him and show him the numbers. I'm leaving now."

The woman ended the call and turned to me with a bright smile. "Thanks for coming on such short notice. The agency said it was iffy, but I knew something would come through.

I'm Astrid." She held out her hand. I shook it. Her handshake was firm, her arm toned and beautifully tanned. What kind of agency? I wondered. Somewhere deep inside of me a new and smarter voice told me to keep my mouth shut. I wasn't going to say a word until I knew who she was taking me for.

She wheeled around and strode out of the room. I scooped Angelina out of her stroller and trotted after Astrid, who was firing over her shoulder, "I have to dash, I'm late for a very important meeting. What a day for Isabel to crap out." She stopped and whirled around so suddenly that I almost ran into her. "You're legal I hope."

"Legal?"

"American citizen?"

"Of course," I said.

"Good," she said, turning and marching through a gleaming white kitchen, never missing a beat. "Isabel had some kind of problem with the INS, and she's left me in the lurch. Wouldn't you know it, just when school goes on Christmas break." She turned just as she reached the door to the backyard. "The kids are outside. Be sure you put sunscreen on them every time they go in the sun. It's here by the door. There's lunch stuff in the fridge. I'm out of milk, so there's cash on the counter. You can take them to get frozen yogurt when you go to the grocery store. You do have a driver's license, don't you? Good, you'll take the Volvo. Be sure they stay in the car seats. Siena tends to squirm out of hers."

We stepped out the back door onto a sunny patio next to a lush green lawn. Two little girls were playing with toy pots and pans on the lawn. I thought of the toy cooking set I helped Eddie pick out for his four-year-old daughter. The two girls looked up and stared at me. "Jordan is six and Siena is four. They need quiet time from three to four o'clock, when they can read or play quietly in their rooms. The only TV they are allowed is public television. I'll be home at five-thirty, six at the latest." She looked brightly at me. "They didn't tell me they might send someone with a baby, but I'm okay with that. As long as you can handle everything. What did you say your name was?"

All this took about two minutes. It wasn't a lot of time for making a major life decision.   Would I tell her the agency didn't send me?   The new and smarter voice in my head prompted me. "Torie," I answered. This was a gift from God and I figured I should seize it. I could work out the details later. Astrid wheeled around, grabbed a large glossy handbag and a gray jacket, bent down to kiss each of the girls, and then she was gone.

It took a while to win over those little girls. They were shy at first, and apparently they liked illegal Isabel because they kept whining about her and asking me where she was. But when they found out they could play with Angelina, I guess they decided I was okay. It was about this time that the agency phoned.   I told them that the position was filled. I figured I could come clean with Astrid when she got home. All I had to do was be a stellar nanny. I could do that.

The two little girls watched, fascinated, as I nursed Angelina, then gently placed her in her stroller for a nap. I settled the girls at the family room table with paper and markers ("Why don't you draw a picture of the baby?") and set out to explore the house. After living in Mrs. Hansen's grungy little shed, sitting on the dirty floor and sleeping on a moldy braided rug, Astrid's house was stunning. In the living room my feet sank into the thick pile of the softly cushioned champagne-colored carpet. I bent down on one knee to touch it. It would be heaven just to lie down right there on the floor in the middle of the living room. The sofas and armchairs were richly upholstered in glossy silks and thick velvets, tufted and pillowed and inviting. The dining table was as dark and polished as Rose's bar, and on a side table there was a collection of glass candlesticks in front of a huge mirror framed with the same dark polished wood. Everywhere there were glass bowls and brass lamps and mirrors and crystal vases, all winking and twinkling and sparkling with reflected sunlight and glowing from loving care and premium household products.

I walked into a hall. The floor was a rich glossy wood. I realize I'm talking a lot about floors here, but you have to understand that after the constant grit of the shed and the interior of my car, these smooth, gleaming floors were a wonder. The hall led me back to the family room, all blond wood and bright colors, with a huge flat-screened TV and two enormous woven baskets full of toys. The girls were still bent over their drawings. This room was cheery and attractive, but it was eclipsed by the kitchen, gleaming white, with expanses of clean empty counters and immaculate stainless appliances. It had everything—a dishwasher, a microwave, a trash compactor, a commercial stove, and two ovens. And an enormous refrigerator.

When I opened the refrigerator I gasped out loud. It was stocked with everything you could possibly want to eat. Not just the eggs, cottage cheese, and apples that populated our refrigerator when I was growing up. Astrid had grapes, sliced turkey breast, sliced prosciutto, fresh-squeezed orange juice, little containers of organic yogurt, a jar of large green olives sprinkled with herbs, another of little black olives, two kinds of pickles, two kinds of lettuce, four kinds of cheese, and a jar of Seville orange marmalade. Then there were the leftovers. There was potato salad, lasagna, and a takeout container of lentil soup. I helped myself to the green olives while I stared at this abundance until Jordan called out to me, "Mommy says not to leave the refrigerator door open." I closed it quickly and continued my tour of the house.

Each girl had her own bedroom. Jordan's was mostly blue and Siena's was bright with yellows and pinks. There was a guestroom, with an old-fashioned multicolored quilt on an antique-looking black bed. And then there was Astrid's bedroom, all plush white carpet, silky white comforter and bright orange and pink pillows. She had a huge exercise machine set up facing the window, and an upholstered armchair and ottoman in a corner with magazines on the table beside it.

But the bathrooms were what stopped me in my tracks. After the dank public restrooms at Echo Lake, with soggy toilet tissue clumping on the wet concrete floor, after the muddy footprints and mysterious spills of the Quik Stop bathroom, after the Starbucks restrooms with their glaring lights, wet counters, and drifts of damp paper towels on the floor by the wastebasket, Astrid's bathrooms left me weak in the knees. It wasn't just that they were so bright and pretty but that they were so dry and clean. And there were so many of them. There was a fancy little half bath off the front foyer with a green marble floor, gold faucets, and a gleaming black sink. There was a bathroom for the guest bedroom, with sparkling white tile and bright yellow towels. And the kids had their own bathroom between their bedrooms. But the showstopper was the master bathroom. Glossy blue-and-white Mexican tiles covered everything. A spotless mirror spanned the wall over the counter with its two gleaming white sinks. There was a little upholstered bench in front of a dressing table. There was a Jacuzzi tub. And there was a glass-enclosed shower that was big enough for four people to shower at the same time.

A shower. The last time I had showered was the morning I found my belongings piled on Ashton's front porch. My hair was so greasy it stuck to my head. I could smell myself all the time, even when I tried to clean up with Listerine. I didn't need to think twice when the new smart voice in my head said this was my big opportunity. Angelina was still sound asleep, and I could count on her to sleep another half hour. The two girls had abandoned their drawing and were now deeply engaged in dressing their Barbies. The coast was clear.

I used the guest bathroom so that Astrid would be less likely to notice anything. I sniffed all the products there before I chose a pungent rosemary-scented shampoo. In the shower there was a bottle of conditioner and a bar of lavender soap. In a drawer I found a scrub brush, a pumice stone, and a bag of disposable razors. I stripped off my clothes, turned on the water, and reached my hand in. The water was hot, streaming out of the showerhead in a generous spray. I stepped in and turned my back to the water, letting it run over my head. I almost groaned aloud with pleasure as the hot water washed over me and down my back, over my bottom, and around my calves. For a long, luxurious time I just stood there, every pore feeling that water run hot and fresh. Finally I came to and got to work. I shampooed my hair, rinsed it, shampooed it again, and rinsed it squeaky clean. I soaped myself up, rubbing the rich lather over every inch of me, soaping my crotch not once but several times. I lathered up my legs again and shaved them smooth while the hot water ran over my back, then shaved under my arms. I put a generous dollop of conditioner on my head and rubbed it in, feeling the tangled mass turn silky and smooth. I squatted and rubbed my feet with the pumice stone, the stream of water pounding my back. Then I stood up under the hot water, and soaped and scrubbed myself all over yet again. Rinsing off, I turned so that the water splashed on my face, my eyes tightly shut, and then turned my back to let the heat penetrate my shoulders before I finally, reluctantly, turned the water off.

The room was hot and steamy, the mirrors frosted. The shower was filthy with gray scum, dirty dead skin finally sloughed off like old rags, leaving me pink and glowing and new. I never thought I'd be so happy about cleaning a shower. I laughed as I wiped it down and then dried myself with the thick yellow towels. I found a hair dryer in a drawer, and dried my hair. Finally, I smoothed lotion all over my body, on my face and neck, on my back and shoulders, my belly, my legs, on my feet and even between my toes.

I hated to put on my dirty underwear after that, so I put my clothes on without underwear. That felt odd at first, but the feeling was immediately forgotten—it was nothing compared to the sheer joy I felt, scrubbed and radiantly clean at last. I felt lighter on my feet, like I could just float away. My hair was springy and soft and my skin was smooth and fragrant. I almost wept with happiness.

I let the girls help me with our lunch. We made sandwiches with thick slices of fresh bread slathered with butter and mayonnaise and stacked with sliced turkey breast and crisp lettuce leaves. We had grapes, pickles, and orange juice. The girls pulled their lettuce out of their sandwiches, and left half their grapes, but I finished all of mine and cleaned their plates too. Except for the breakfast Larry bought me, and some found food here and there, this was my first real meal in almost a month that wasn't peanut butter.

Then we piled into the Volvo and drove to Gelson's. That was a fancy grocery store that I knew about because I had been there with Sandy. We bought some organic low-fat milk, which Jordan selected, informing me that it was what her mother bought, and then we went to a little shop nearby for frozen yogurt topped with berries. After I polished mine off, I finished what the girls had left in their bowls, then ordered a second one for myself.

Then we returned to the house so the girls could have their quiet time in their rooms. My plan was to launder the towels I had used in the morning so that Astrid would never know I had showered. Even the laundry room in Astrid's house was beautiful, all white tile and clean counters. The enormous turquoise-colored washer and dryer had big round windows in front, side by side like two eyes. As I looked around for the detergent I opened a cabinet and found Astrid's dirty-clothes hampers. And this was when I had another one of my brilliant ideas. I was becoming a genius. Not only did I launder the towels, but I did all of Astrid's laundry too. How was that for resourceful thinking? Doing laundry would make me a stellar nanny. And I learned a few things too. I learned that apparently there was no Mr. Astrid. No sign of men's underwear. I learned that Astrid worked out a lot because there were lots of acrid, sweaty workout clothes. I learned that those little girls liked to do art, because there was red, yellow, and purple tempera paint on some of their clothes. And I learned that Astrid probably didn't like to do laundry, because there was so much of it. When I finished I brought it all into the family room where I let the kids watch TV while I folded it. By the time Astrid rolled in at 5:47 I had all the laundry folded, the towels put away, and the girls seated at the table having a snack of carrot sticks and olives.

Astrid loved me. She was thrilled when she saw the girls eating a healthy snack. She was bowled over when she saw the folded laundry. And she was satisfied when she surreptitiously checked the counter and saw the pile of change there where I left it when we got back from buying the milk and frozen yogurt. She did take a second look at me for a moment, her eyes narrowing just slightly. "Did you do something with your hair?" she asked, and I answered as casually as I could, "Oh, it was up before." She didn't say anything more about it. But using her shower was nothing compared to the news I was going to have to break to her. Sooner or later she would find out that I was freelancing. And hard as it was to tell her, better from me than the agency. I knew that much.

"I'll tell the agency that you're working out just fine," Astrid said warmly.

"Well, actually . . . " I started. Then I paused. There was no easy way to do this. "I'm not from the agency. I came here to sell cosmetics. But—"

She freaked out. Of course she did. What did I expect? I had to let it run its course. It took a while, but I finally got her calmed down and after about half an hour I was able to convince her that I went along with her misconception not because I had dark intentions but because this was the perfect job for me, and that I was the best thing for Jordan and Siena. She wanted references, but by this time it wasn't because she didn't trust me. She was already sold. She just needed to assure herself that she was doing everything correctly, even though she was hiring a complete stranger who came in off the street and lied to her in order to take care of her children. Go figure. I'd never have trusted Angelina with someone like me.

For references I gave her Sandy and Madison's phone numbers, and for my address I gave Mrs. Hansen's. "Oh, I love Silver Lake," she said as she wrote that down. Then she straightened up and looked sharply at me. "I'm going to take a chance on you. I just hope this isn't crazy." She squinted a little. "You're not anorexic, are you?"

"No, just naturally thin." *Naturally thin*. Ha. That's a good one. I was gaunt from all the walking and nursing, not to mention my scanty diet. Nothing was natural about my current lifestyle. But I needed to say whatever it took to make her happy.

"Lucky you," she said. "Well, help yourself to anything you want when you're here."

I couldn't believe how well this was working out. The minute I walked out the door I texted Sandy and Madison to say don't take any calls from Astrid's number until I had a chance to explain. I talked with each of them later that night, filling them in on my posh new nanny position, and they each promised to vouch for my stability, my responsibility, and my marvelous way with children.

"I didn't know you even liked kids," said Madison. I told her life is full of surprises.

Chapter 38

BOBBIE COMES BY with her cheerful smile and some lotion that she rubs into my hands, massaging each finger as she chatters on and on about Franny and her internship.   It doesn't make a lot of sense, but I like to hear her voice.   Then she brushes my hair, and the brush feels good on my scalp. The back of my neck feels prickly and sticky, so she brushes my hair up into a twist.   But that makes a bump where my head lies on the pillow, so she raises my hair to a bun on top of my head.   There, she says, that should be more comfortable. She leans over and kisses me on the cheek when it's time for her to leave, and I smell her fruity fragrance.   Probably her makeup.   Or shampoo.   And then she's gone.   In her absence the room goes quiet.   And I am left with myself.

I can see it so clearly now.   Suzanne's front door.   The cold evening, my white breath, the wreath covered in crusty fake snow, and my gloved finger pressing the doorbell.   When Suzanne opened the door she didn't know who I was, and she looked alarmed when I pushed in past her and turned and started in on her.   What did I say?   Did I sound unhinged?   I could see her face change as she realized who I was; she no longer looked alarmed, just annoyed.   Arms crossed on her chest, head cocked to one side.   So you're the bimbo, she said quietly.   So you're the bimbo.

The bimbo.   The bimbo.   The bimbo.   I felt my rage reach down to my fingertips.   Why are you here she asked.   I couldn't give her a good reason, and she said I'm not the one you should be yelling at, you're angry at AJ, you should be yelling at him.   Let me guess.   He said we're going to get back together.   And you believed him?   Oh please.   She rolled her eyes.   He just wants the money from the house.   He may be charming, but he's an asshole. If you had any sense you'd forget about him. He isn't interested in you.

Suddenly I thought she's jealous, and I told her so, and then she was laughing. Laughing at me. Jealous she said laughing. No, you can have him for all I care. But don't kid yourself, he calls you a loser. Just another loser bimbo. You should get your act together. Jeez. Find some self-respect.

And she turned away.   I was left standing there in the doorway, where everything was spinning.   Outside it was freezing cold. My fingers felt numb even with gloves on. I pulled my coat around myself as I watched her return to her kitchen. There was a loud ringing sound, an awful sound that spun around me while the room turned, and I tried to center myself by pulling the coat closer. I followed her into the warm kitchen, where an oven timer was ringing like an alarm clock, and she bent down and opened the oven.

I had a fleeting thought that I probably shouldn't have come here when I was this fucked up. My head was still spinning as I watched her lift a casserole dish, crusty brown, bubbling, fragrant, using a towel to protect her hands from the heat, and set it on the counter. She turned back to me. You need to leave now. She was calm, she was secure, she was watching me on my trajectory out of orbit.

You're drunk, she said. She said it with disdain. I could see the pity and the disdain on her face. The helpless rage had reached my eyes and now everything was colored red. It had taken hold of my heart and I could hardly breathe. You need to leave, she said, but you know, you really shouldn't be driving. Do you want me to call you a taxi? The room was spinning, spinning, spinning, red with rage, and Suzanne just stood there. I'll call you a taxi, or I'll call the police, but you need to leave. She turned away and reached for the phone. I could see that phone sitting there on the counter. I stared at it while the room spun around me with the phone at the center. It's up to you, she said. And her voice sounded far away. And there it is again. The bottle in the air, end over end.

Chapter 39

I HAD TURNED into Cinderella. I would start each day in my dirty hovel, and then go to Astrid's castle, where I would be transformed into a princess rolling in luxury, and then, before my coach turned into a pumpkin, I would return to the hovel for the night. The only thing missing was a prince. There was not much chance of finding one of those anytime soon. Still, at this point I wasn't thinking much about that. Because I was finally earning some money. Astrid was going to pay me every Friday, and the morning after my first payday I celebrated by going out for breakfast at Denny's, buying a huge bag of disposable diapers, and paying my phone bill. Next I would get a charger for my laptop. But after that I promised myself I'd do nothing but save. Every cent I could spare would go into the pink plastic baby-wipes box that held my savings. That box was my entire financial future. My plan was to sock it away there until I had enough savings for a studio apartment.

I put in a change-of-address form at the post office and started using Astrid's address. I was taking a chance that something could show up in her mail when I wasn't there on a Saturday, but I rarely got mail anyway, so I figured it would work out, and if it didn't, I'd come up with some kind of explanation. But this way I no longer had to wait for Mrs. Hansen's mail delivery, and I could go straight to Astrid's first thing in the morning. I explained to Mrs. Hansen that I had a new job, and that I'd pick up her mail at night for her. I apologized, but she shushed me and said she was grateful for all that I had done, and that she would manage. She was so effusive with her thanks that I felt badly that I had been doing this for her just for my own purposes, so I promised I would visit her on weekends, even though I wasn't picking up her mail anymore. She was such a sweet old lady, and she was grateful to have someone to talk with, even if it was just me.

"The curse of old age," she said, "is not the arthritis, the pains, the inability to keep up. It's the loss of all the people who loved you when you were young, people you grew up with, people who shared memories with you. To be the last one standing, with no one left to say 'remember the time when.' No one left who remembers where you lived and why you loved living there. No one left who remembers that you were once slim and lovely. That is the saddest thing about old age." It made me feel sad that I never knew her when she was slim and lovely. And I thought about my mom, and about Franny, Rose, and Bobbie, and about Dieter too, and how they all knew me before I was homeless.

I quickly became indispensible to Astrid. She was rarely ready to leave when I arrived in the morning. I had to get her organized and out the door, out of my way so I could have that house all to myself. I had begun to feel like this was my house, and that Astrid was one of my charges, no different, really, than her daughters. Because Astrid needed a lot of coddling. I had to spend at least fifteen minutes every morning in the wake of her whirlwind as she strode around the house, coffee cup in hand, rattling off what needed to be done that day. Some mornings when I got there she was still working out on her elliptical machine, her cell phone planted against one ear, a line of dark sweat down the back of her T-shirt, and a cup of cold coffee on the nearby table. I'd make a fresh pot of coffee in her fancy coffeemaker while she showered and got ready for work. Then I'd find her briefcase, her car keys, her cell phone, and her jacket, and retrieve her travel mug from her car, rinse it out, and fill it with coffee. I'd hand these things to her and get her going.

As soon as Astrid left, the house was mine. I turned on the TV, set the girls down in front of it, and put Angelina in her car seat next to them. They loved to play with her. She was like a big doll that they never tired of.   And she seemed to love their attention. Somehow she knew that these were kids just like she was, not adults, and that kids had a special relationship with each other.   She responded to them the minute she saw them. I think she loved our new job as much as I did.

Once I got the girls settled I was free to shower. I had begun to feel that the guest bathroom was mine now, and the lavender soap and the expensive rosemary shampoo were mine too.   After my shower I enjoyed a leisurely cup of coffee, sitting in the sunny family room, reading a magazine. Then I prepared snacks and drove the girls to Coldwater Canyon Park. While they played I joined the nannies on the benches, with Angelina in her stroller lined up with the other babies in their strollers. Now I really was one of them, doling out snacks to our charges and comparing stories about our employers. But I was so grateful for Astrid's house that I never said anything bad about her.

It's strange how well I felt I knew Astrid, considering that I hardly had any contact with her. I saw her only coming and going, and that was blurred by the flurry of activity that always surrounded her. I really only knew her by the imprint she left. By her things—her shoes, her food, her floors, her magazines, her laundry. And by the things her daughters said about her. That she didn't like camping. That she didn't want a dog because it would be too messy. That she loved to swim. That she and Daddy argued over the car. And that shrimp made her throw up. All these things combined to create a shape, and in that shape was Astrid.

In the afternoons we would do errands. Astrid loved me for that, too, because she hated doing errands. We went grocery shopping nearly every day. We went to the shoe repair, the cleaners, the special pharmacy that had environmentally-friendly products and organic toiletries, and to a little boutique called Kinder Earth for beautiful German toys to bring to a birthday party. And sometimes we went to the Jeanne La Belle warehouse to pick up my orders. I can't imagine what Astrid would have said if she knew that her little girls accompanied me to a dingy warehouse in a scary part of L.A., but they were okay strapped into their snug car seats in the solid navy blue Volvo.

After errands we went home for quiet time, the girls in their rooms, and Angelina and I to sleep together on the guest room bed. Sometimes I did Astrid's laundry after my nap, so in her opinion I was some kind of angel. Every day I put my towels into the dryer so Astrid wouldn't guess that I was showering there, and then once a week I laundered them, along with my own personal laundry, when I did Astrid's. While the washing machine was running, I'd get the house cleaned up so that it would look nice when Astrid got home. Yes, Astrid loved me.

Christmas was less than a week away. I ordered some Jeanne La Belle products for everyone at home. And now that I was earning some money, I could do better than a lousy little lipstick for each of them. I ordered Anti-Aging Miracle Emollient for Rose. Cocoa Tanning Spray for Bobbie. Earth Goddess Clay Masque for my mom. And four different lipsticks for Franny. For Dieter, a bottle of Aloe Mint Care & Repair Hand Lotion. Astrid had asked me to wrap her gifts during the girls' quiet time, so I used her gift wrap for my gifts as well. And I boxed them up and mailed them when I took Astrid's boxes to the post office.

I called home and to my surprise Dieter answered. Dieter was there at the apartment during the day? That was odd. He told me Vivian couldn't come to the phone. "She's sleeping, Honey." I asked him what he was doing there, and he hemmed and hawed for a bit, and then he said he was there a lot those days, taking care of her. That alarmed me. She needed Dieter there to take care of her? Then Rose got on the line. Naturally she wanted to know why I wasn't coming home.

"Your mom is pretty sick," she said. "She's got an oxygen tank now."

An oxygen tank. It took me a moment to take that in. All this time I had been thinking that Vivian was just trying to get attention. But this made me realize that she must be truly sick. I tried to picture Vivian hooked up to an oxygen tank, but I couldn't.

"She's got COPD, that's something pulmonary. Chronic obstructive pulmonary disease. It means her lungs are all screwed up. This is serious, Honey."

But what could I do? I told Rose I would come home and visit in the spring, that I couldn't get any time off from work now. Even though I finally had a job, I still wasn't quite ready to face them. Not with my accidental baby and my homelessness. And I didn't want to spend all my savings on a plane ticket. I figured by spring I'd have enough money saved to get my studio apartment. It wouldn't be long before I was no longer homeless. That's when I would come clean with the family. But just about Angelina. I'd never tell them I had been homeless.

Rose told me she had sent me a box, and of course she mailed it to Mrs. Hansen's address. I had to go over to Mrs. Hansen's every morning to see if it came so I could intercept it. Finally on the third day it arrived, full of Christmas gifts. There were three sweaters from Bobbie and Rose, a pair of earrings from Franny, a white knock-off Chanel handbag from my mom, and from Dieter, an immersion blender. Taped to the blender box there was an envelope with some smoothie recipes inside from Bobbie. Well, someday I'd upgrade to a place with actual electrical outlets and be able to use that thing.

For a few hours on Christmas Eve I babysat the girls for Astrid while she went to a party. I braided their hair with curly red ribbons, made them hot chocolate, and read them *The Night Before Christmas* and *Rudolf the Red-Nosed Reindeer*. Then Angelina and I went home to the shed. What a colossal letdown that was. Christmas day was as depressing as I thought it would be. No festivities for me and Angelina. We hung out at the park and watched kids show off their new scooters and bikes, and I called home and told everyone I'd been to a party the night before. I made it sound like it had been a blast, and they believed me.

In January the girls started school again. Each morning I dropped Jordan at her elementary school and Siena at preschool, and later I picked them up again. I found I missed the girls while they were at school. I really liked taking care of kids. Who knew? I loved to read to them. After Christmas Eve I started reading to them all the time. Astrid wasn't much of a reader herself. You could tell this because there were hardly any grown-up books in her house. But she had all kinds of kids' books, so many it was like a library. There was a fairy-tale book that was full of horrifying stories. But maybe they were only horrifying if you're a grown-up and you could clearly see all the implications. I read "Hansel and Gretel" to the girls, and while they were okay about it, I was freaking out. It gave me the creeps. I couldn't see how the girls could be calm hearing about parents who sent their children into the forest to get rid of them, and the trail of crumbs being eaten up by birds so that they couldn't go home again. But they just leaned their little blond heads over the page and pointed out the birds in the illustration as if the story were about a picnic. I suspected then that little kids aren't very empathetic.

So I read to the girls every day, and we went to the library too, and we watched TV together, and I let them think they were helping me in the kitchen. I knew I was an important part of their lives. Of Astrid's life. I was holding their household together, and this made me feel wonderful. And my plastic money box was getting full.

Weekends were a letdown because I didn't go to Astrid's. I left the shed early in the morning and started the day at Starbucks, just like old times. I hung out at the park, and tried to sell cosmetics. Sometimes on Saturdays I'd go to the West Slauson warehouse to pick up my meager orders. I realize now that I was not a very good Jeanne La Belle sales representative, but I still made a sale now and then, and every dollar earned went into that little pink plastic box. At dusk I'd slip back into Mrs. Hansen's shed for the night.

On the weekends I not only missed the girls, but I missed Astrid's house. Her house made me see a home in an entirely new way. I think too I began to see work in an entirely new way. Astrid really worked hard for her house, her bathroom, her towels, her refrigerator full of food. Like Evie and her catering. Like Beth Ann and her cosmetics empire. Like Franny too. Franny the overachiever. And like Rose and Bobbie and the bar and motel. I used to look at all of them and think that they were working far too hard. I thought Evie was crazy, I thought they were all crazy, but now I see that each was determined to keep her world afloat. And I was too, as I found myself working harder than any of them. Being homeless is hard work. No one ever thinks of it that way, but it is.

Meanwhile my job was expanding. One day Astrid asked me to make a dessert for a monthly potluck at Siena's preschool. It was a good thing Frank had taught me how to make pie. Astrid's mixer wasn't as nice as Frank's big Hobart, but I made a lemon meringue pie that was such a hit with everyone that Astrid took credit for it, according to Jordan. I wasn't offended. This was just one more thing that made her dependent on me. And it opened the door to cooking dinner for them, and for this she said I would be paid extra. At first I panicked because I didn't think I knew that much about cooking, but then I calmed down and went through Astrid's cookbooks, and I realized that there were a lot of things there that looked familiar, from the days when Franny and I were in our cooking phase during middle school, or from helping Frank in the pie shop. So I roasted chicken, and made chili, and I branched out into tacos and enchiladas because Astrid had a Mexican cookbook for children that spelled everything out really clearly. Then she began to ask me to make things like tuna salad and potato salad for her to have on hand for lunches on the weekend. And she asked me to make her daily snack packages, because she had decided that the bagels she bought each afternoon were making her fat. Each day I assembled a set of little plastic containers that she could fit into her bag, with crackers, toasted almonds, fresh grapes, and dried apricots. Then on the side I assembled my own little package of snacks that I brought home to my hovel each night.

Jordan and Siena loved my cooking. I made smoothies from Bobbie's recipes every day for lunch, with yogurt and orange juice and bananas. And I made quesadillas or grilled cheese sandwiches, and fruit salads that I let them eat with their fingers, pulling out the pieces of orange, the grapes, and the apple slices, dripping with yogurt and sprinkled with brown sugar. For snacks we had cream cheese on crackers and olives and pickles. I don't need to mention that we never had peanut butter. I'd had enough peanut butter to last several lifetimes.

It was Franny's twenty-first birthday in February. That's a big deal, turning twenty-one. My twenty-first birthday was coming up too, in a few months, but it wasn't real to me yet. Besides, at this point it wasn't going to make much of a difference in my life. So what if I could go to a bar and order a drink without having to use my fake ID? Who would take care of Angelina? And who would I go with, anyway? But Franny was pretty pumped up about it, and she wanted me to come home to celebrate with her. I could tell that she was getting annoyed with me because I'd been evasive.

I was lying to everyone. To my family, to my friends. Evie had been calling periodically to see how I was doing. So had Carlos and Sanjay and Sandy, and I just kept elaborating on my fictional life. Dieter sent me a box full of little surprises—cookies, freshly ground coffee, and a T-shirt. I lied and told him I loved the coffee. It was reasonable for him to think I had a coffeemaker and the electricity to use it. The cookies were good and the T-shirt was nice, but it was too big for me. It said SWEET across the front in big pink letters. It was just like Dieter to send something like that. It made me miss him terribly. I missed them all. When I called Dieter to thank him, he sounded distant and distracted. Then he explained that he was at the hospital with Vivian. It took me a moment to absorb what he was telling me. This was more serious than I had thought. An oxygen tank was bad, but at least she had been at home. When did Vivian get so sick that she needed to be in the hospital?

"How long will she be there?" I asked anxiously.

"We don't know. We're hoping it's only for a few days. Why don't you come home?" he urged. "Forget that job, quit it. Come here and be with your mom. You can get a job here."

My mom had been spiraling down and down, even more than I realized. But I had too, and the family had no idea how much I had turned into her. They didn't know that while I had been so busy trying not to be the Troll or Coyote Girl I had forgotten to try not to be Vivian, and I had actually turned into the train wreck that was my mother. Now they wanted me to come home as if nothing were the matter. I couldn't explain to Dieter that if I came home before I was a success, I was going to turn into her completely.

Still, other times when I thought about it, I realized that maybe that was the lesson here. That turning into Vivian was inevitable and I just had to deal with it. That even if I had walked away from Eddie that day in front of the Tastee booth, I still would have met someone else, and gone somewhere else, and still messed it up there, and still turned into Vivian, just in another city instead of Los Angeles.

Dieter said that he thought Vivian was dying, and then he hung up, to leave me with his voice and those words in my ears for days. I knew I had to go home and hold her in my arms. As soon as I figured out how to go home from this, from here.

Chapter 40

IT MUST BE NIGHT now because the redheaded boy nurse is here, and he asks me something.   I think he wants me to eat and I tell him to leave it, maybe later.   I can always give it to Bobbie. Bobbie is always hungry. I don't want to eat. I don't want to sleep either and see that goddamn bottle again, turning through the air.   But I see it every time I try not to think about it. And the phone.   I see Suzanne turn to the phone.   It's up to you, she says, and this is where I see the bottle soaring through the air and into the spinning void. I see it turn end over end, dark green, a big wine bottle, and just as it reaches her Suzanne turns to me with the phone in her hand and freezes with her eyes so wide the whites are all I can remember. White all around their cold blue centers. And now in the silence, the endless silence that follows, I hear it land with a crack, a crack like a melon hitting the pavement.   It lands with a crack on her head.

The room was still spinning, still red, and Suzanne lay there without moving, and nothing was clear, nothing made sense, the taste in my mouth was vomit, and I left her there so she could sleep it off. Later Dieter found me in my car, in the freezing cold, and asked me where I had been and I couldn't tell him, I simply couldn't remember a thing. Just this awful dream.

Chapter 41

THEN ONE MORNING Franny called. "Hey, guess what?"

It's never good when someone starts out with *guess what*. You know you're not going to like it. "What?" I answered guardedly.

"I'm right here."

"Here?"

"Yes, here, in Los Angeles." I couldn't think of what to say about this catastrophe, so there was silence for a beat or two. "I went to your address and some old lady there had never heard of you," said Franny. "What's with that?"

Mrs. Hansen didn't know me as Honey, that was what. To Mrs. Hansen I was Torie. "She's senile," I said.

"Well, I want to see you. Where are you?"

"I'm at work now," I told her.

"Can I come by?"

"No."

"Well, how about after work?"

My mind raced. "I'm tied up then."

Franny was silent. Then she sighed and said, "Honey, don't you want to see me?"

"I'm a nanny. I take care of kids. My hands are kind of full."

"Well, I can appreciate that. I'm not asking you to leave them alone. Can't I come by for half an hour? I can give you a hand with whatever you're doing."

"No."

"Honey, is something wrong?"

I thought for a moment. "Okay, we can meet in the park this afternoon." I figured that would be manageable. I gave her the directions, and she seemed satisfied.

I dreaded this meeting until the moment I saw her standing at the park entrance. She looked beautiful, and to feel her arms around me in a big hug brought tears to my eyes. She wiped them away and kissed my eyes and hugged me some more.

"Honey, you're so thin!" she exclaimed. She thought this was thin. She would have shit in her pants if she'd seen me in December. I changed the subject by introducing her to Jordan and Siena, who were anxious to start playing on the climbing structure. I let Franny assume that Angelina was one of my charges too. I introduced her around to the other nannies, and then we sat down on a bench apart from the others, where we could watch the girls as they played.

"A nanny. It's amazing to see you doing this," Franny chirped.

"I like it."

"I was getting a little worried when we talked. I was beginning to think you were a sex slave or something."

"A *what*?"

"Well, you sounded like you were trying to put me off, like you had something to hide." Jeez. Thanks for the vote of confidence. "But I can't believe how skinny you are. What are you, anorexic or something?"

Time to change the subject again. I asked her about her classes, her friends, her internship, and about Bobbie and Rose. Anything but Vivian. While we talked Angelina started to fuss, so I picked her up, praying that she wasn't hungry. Then the girls came over to ask for their Barbies, so I had to stop and pull the dolls out of the stroller. And wouldn't you know it, Siena had wet her pants. It figured. It was time to get out of there. But just as I was going to tell Franny that I had to go, she came to the real point of the visit. Which I guess I already knew. The point was Vivian.

"Honey, I don't know how to tell you this, but you have to know. She's still in the hospital. She's dying, Honey. You wouldn't recognize her, she's changed so much."

First Dieter, now Franny. Until now I hadn't accepted this as a dying thing, but there it was. It was real. I couldn't think of what to say.

"My pants are wet," Siena whined.

"We'll go home in a minute," I told her. Meanwhile, to my horror Angelina began to whimper and root around, grabbing at my chest and pushing her face into my breast.

"Why haven't you come home?" Franny finally asked. I shrugged. "What's going on?   Dieter and I decided someone had to come and find out what's up."

"Nothing's up. I didn't know it was so serious. I told Dieter I'd come home. In, I don't know, maybe two months."

"Won't these people let you have time off?"

"No."

"Honey, they are lucky to have you. I'm sure you are a terrific nanny. They should show their appreciation." I could hardly hear her because I was struggling to push Angelina away without being obvious about it. She began to cry in earnest. "They should understand that you need to visit—" Franny stopped midsentence and looked at me sharply. "That baby wants to nurse."

"Yeah, isn't that funny," I said, wishing it were actually funny.

"No, it's weird."

Angelina began to wind up into a full-blown hysteria.

"That's a hungry baby.   Don't you have a bottle or something?"

"No. In fact, I really have to get these kids home," I said as I peeled myself free of Angelina, who was screaming in rage at being ignored. I strapped her into her stroller, told Siena to stop whining about her pants, gathered our things, and began to herd the girls over to the Volvo, with Franny trailing behind. It seemed to take a lifetime to get them all into the car, but finally I was ready to make my exit, and I turned to give Franny a quick hug. "I'll talk to you soon," I said brightly, trying to ignore Angelina's racket. She was hysterical now.   Franny looked hurt, but I couldn't do anything about it. I jumped into the Volvo, backed out quickly, and then roared down the street. In the rearview mirror I could see Franny getting into her car. I felt guilty for leaving her like this.

The moment I got to Astrid's house I practically ripped off my shirt so Angelina could nurse. She was so distraught by this time that she could hardly calm herself down, her body still convulsing with sobs and shudders and gasps as she tried to suck. What a disaster. Who knew what Franny was thinking?

It was growing dark as we headed home to Silver Lake. Angelina was so exhausted by all the crying that she fell asleep as soon as I got her into her car seat and didn't even wake up when I eased the seat out of the car and walked past Mrs. Hansen's house, setting off the motion-detector light, and then through the shrubbery to my little shed.

I thought about waking Angelina, because if she slept now, she was more likely to wake up during the night. But after that afternoon's hysteria I didn't have the heart. She needed to sleep. And I needed time to think about what Franny had told me about my mom. It was clear that I had to go home right away, and that I should never have waited this long. Why had I been so determined to wait until I had a home before I went back to the family? After all, I was on my way. I had a job, I was doing well, I was a good nanny. I had options. It was time to talk with Astrid about some time off. I'd just have to use the money in the pink plastic box for a plane ticket. And finally introduce Angelina to her family.

I lit a candle and began to put on my hovel clothes, the ratty sweatpants and sweatshirt. Outside the motion light flashed on; I could see the light through the plastic over the window. I knew it was probably a raccoon, but it always made me nervous when I saw the light turn on. Then as I stepped into my sweatpants and fumbled for the drawstring tie, I heard what sounded like stealthy steps through the garden, coming closer and closer. I froze, standing there, tightening the drawstring. Just as it occurred to me that I should blow out the candle, the plastic over the window moved aside, and a pair of eyes, squinting and cupped by hands, peered in.

Franny's eyes. Horrified, I reached for the door just as she shrieked, "Oh my God! Oh my God!" I opened the door, grabbed her wrist with one hand, and frantically waved my finger in front of her lips, trying to shush her, but she wouldn't stop.

"Oh my God, Honey, you sleep here?" Then she dropped her voice to a fierce whisper. "You do! Oh my God, you're homeless! Oh. My. God." As I pulled her inside and closed the door behind her, she saw Angelina. "Oh my God, that baby, it's yours, isn't it! Oh. My. God."

"You're going to rouse the whole fucking neighborhood," I hissed. Then there was a silence that seemed to go on forever. I couldn't think of what to say next. How did Franny know I was here? She must have been watching Mrs. Hansen's house, waiting for me to come home. What kind of explanation would she buy?

"For God's sake, Honey," she finally whispered, trying not to raise her voice. "You have a baby and you're fucking homeless."

If I needed a reminder of why I was keeping this from the family, this was a pretty good one. I realized I was still holding her hand, and I let it drop. My mind raced in overdrive as I tried to think of a way to explain everything.

"Oh, Honey." Franny put her arms around me. "We have to talk.

Chapter 42

HONEY is finally here. My sweet kitten. My baby. She smells so good as she lies beside me with her arms around me. Dieter and Franny brought her home, but there was a baby with her. They said Honey brought it home but when did she get a baby? I don't know where she found it. It's all very confusing.

Honey asks again about her father, pressing me to tell her. Does she think I'm going to croak and leave her all alone?

When she was a little girl she was sweet and warm and supple as a little cat. She curled up on my lap and played with my jewelry and brought me drawings that she made at Rose's kitchen table. I would hold her and put my nose on her head so I could smell her hair. The time that we lived in the motel, in the flamingo room, was the best time of my life. Just me and Honey, in that room glowing with pink and green and gold, sharing that big bed facing Bobbie's giant mural. When I rocked Honey to sleep I'd tell her we could step into the picture with the flamingo, into the moonlight, just the two of us, and we could ask the moon for whatever our heart desired. It was corny, but it sounded nice, like one of the children's books that Rose read to the girls.

Chapter 43

THEY HAD ALL put their heads together, Rose and Bobbie, Dieter and Franny, even the Troll and the FOBs, to try to figure out what to do about me and Vivian. Finally they had decided to send Franny to get me. They figured she was the one I'd most likely listen to. Dieter paid for two plane tickets, one round-trip ticket for Franny and a one-way for me. The Troll contributed her frequent flier miles to help out, and with her miles one leg of the trip was free. Dieter drove Franny to the airport, and on the way he asked her if she wanted him to go in her place. But she knew she was the person who could penetrate whatever it was I had constructed around myself. And I guess she was. And I'm glad she did. Because when I finally lay beside Vivian, holding her close against me, I could hardly remember what I had been feeling before.

Even though Franny had warned me, it was a shock to see my mom so thin, haggard, and old. So very fragile. But I quickly got used to it and then somehow when I looked at her, all I saw was the old Vivian, the real Vivian. We watched her slip away from us, growing less and less interested in the day-to-day things that the rest of us talked about—the weather, the laundry, the groceries, the dog, even dinner. But her face lit up whenever I came to her. As for Angelina, Vivian smiled at her, but it was clear she wasn't as interested in this baby as she was in me. We got here too late for that. We got here after she started to withdraw from life, and that's too late to introduce another character. Angelina won't even remember her, except in my stories. But Vivian wouldn't have been the grandma type, anyway. That's okay. Angelina will have Grandma Rose and Grandma Bobbie, who have been falling all over themselves to do things for her. I think they're competing to win Best Grandma award. Meanwhile, when I got home, Rose did tell me I was certifiably stupid. I called that one correctly. But I didn't let it bother me because she said it while she was crushing me into her enormous soft bosom in a huge bear hug.

I guess there won't be any deathbed revelations. Maybe there would have been if my mom had ever accepted that she was dying. Clearly she considered this final hospital stay a temporary setback. She even asked us to bring her the March issue of *InStyle* magazine so she could see the spring and summer fashions. No one said anything, but I know we were all thinking the same thing. She wasn't going to see spring, let alone summer. Rose spoke to the doctor about it. "She's in denial," she said, deeply concerned. Rose would have faced it head on. The doctor said gently, "It's her survival mechanism. It keeps her happy. Don't worry about it." So like I said, no deathbed revelations. All those years she refused to come clean about my father's identity, and she wasn't going to start now. Assuming she knew it. I asked her once, point-blank, if Dieter was my father, and she pretended not to hear me, closing her eyes like she was falling asleep.

Chapter 44

THE ROOM is making breathing sounds. Or is that the sound of someone by my bedside?   I hear murmuring and a light is turned on. It's too difficult to make sense of any of these things, so I surrender to the sleep. When I wake it's quiet and dark. I sleep again and when I wake it's bright, and Rose is beside me.

I keep having the dream, I try to tell Rose. She makes sympathetic noises, and she holds my hand. Was it a dream, I ask, or did it really happen that way? Rose pats my hand. I don't think I am getting through. Then Rose is gone and Honey is sitting beside me, looking at a magazine. She seems so content. It's peaceful here with her by my side. She is talking about someone named Angelina, and I am floating away, tethered only by the sounds of Honey's voice.

It wasn't a dream. No, dear God, it wasn't a dream. I guess I always knew. Always knew but I pushed it away because it was more than I could carry.

Honey is gone now. I must have fallen asleep.   I was going to tell her what I did all those years ago, but she's left. And what's the point of telling her? I can't save Suzanne. I can't give AJ back his years. That's all caught in time, like a fly in amber. It can't be changed. There is no redemption.

Once Rose sat us down, me and Bobbie, and said we had to make out our wills, to take care of our girls if something happened to us. Our wills. What a sobering thought. We each listed the others as guardians. In the event. And Rose said we should also make note of anything we wanted to bequeath. What do you mean bequeath? we asked. Rose said anything special you might want to give to someone. Let's say, she said to Bobbie, you wanted Vivian to have your sapphire ring. You should bequeath it to her. Otherwise it will automatically go to Franny. What do I have, I began, and Rose said you could bequeath Honey a father.

Honey is back now, and she's got that baby with her. I don't care about the baby, I just want my Honey here where I can feel her touch me. Dieter is here as well. I can hear their voices, high and low, back and forth. The only thing I have in me that is good, the only thing I can do that is good, is to give Honey and Dieter what they want most. I could never bring myself to take fatherhood away from him completely, and give it to someone else. That's why I always let him think that the possibility existed. Now I'll tell him that it's true.

My gift to them both.

Acknowledgements

I am so grateful to Alice Rosengard, my extraordinary editor, for her skilled and thoughtful guidance. I also want to thank Gordon B. Scott, Barbara Levy, Meg Stockwell and Lena Kouyoumdjian, all readers of early drafts, for their valuable criticism and encouragement. And finally, I am deeply grateful to my husband, Hratch, for all his support.

About the Author

Carolyn Holm lives in the San Francisco Bay Area. In addition to writing fiction she teaches children's art classes, and wrote and illustrated *Everyday Art for Kids*, a book for parents and teachers. For more about her, and for a Flamingo Moon Reader's Guide, go to **www.carolynholm.com**.